Leah Fleming was born in Lancashire and is married with three sons and a daughter. She writes from an old farmhouse in the Yorkshire Dales and an olive grove in Crete.

Also by Leah Fleming

Dancing at the Victory Café
The Girl from World's End
The War Widows
Orphans of War
Mothers and Daughters
Remembrance Day
Winter's Children
The Captain's Daughter
The Girl Under the Olive Tree
The Postcard
The Last Pearl
The Glovemaker's Daughter

The Railway Girls

LEAH FLEMING

**SIMON &
SCHUSTER**

London · New York · Sydney · Toronto · New Delhi

A CBS COMPANY

First published in Great Britain by Hodder and Stoughton, 1997
This edition published by Simon & Schuster UK Ltd, 2017
A CBS COMPANY

1 3 5 7 9 10 8 6 4 2

Simon & Schuster UK Ltd
1st Floor
222 Gray's Inn Road
London WC1X 8HB

Simon & Schuster Australia, Sydney
Simon & Schuster India, New Delhi

www.simonandschuster.co.uk
www.simonandschuster.com.au
www.simonandschuster.co.in

A CIP catalogue record for this book is available from the British Library

B Format Paperback ISBN: 978-1-4711-7679-1
Trade Paperback ISBN: 978-1-4711-6010-3
eBook ISBN: 978-1-4711-5962-6

Typeset in the UK by M Rules
Printed and bound by CPI Group (UK) Ltd, Croydon, CR0 4YY

MIX
Paper from
responsible sources
FSC® C020471

Simon & Schuster UK Ltd are committed to sourcing paper that is made from wood grown in
sustainable forests and support the Forest Stewardship

Author's Note

The Railway Girls is a reissue of my second novel, originally published in 1997 under my original name, Helene Wiggin as *Trouble on the Wind*. Now that I am better known as Leah Fleming, I'm keeping life simple by sticking to that name.

The novel has its origins in the fight to save the Settle to Carlisle Railway from closure. It was written to celebrate its reprieve.

Leah Fleming

Travel northwards via the Settle to Carlisle route and you will cross the Ribblehead Viaduct over Batty Green Moss to Blea Moor, Arten Gill, Dent Head and beyond. Nature has erased the brief presence of 'navvy time'. Nothing remains of our shantytowns but tracks etched into the turf, spoilheaps overgrown; in lonely village kirkyards rest the bones of us rough men and women who battled against the ferocious climate to build this iron road of blood.

Our spirits roam over the fells like sheep and lament like curlews in the wind. Hear our voices, marvel at our deeds and pray for our salvation.

Glossary

bogtrotter	a tramp
boggart	a ghost, often mischievous
bowdykite	a mischief-maker
to blether	to talk
to bray	to fight
clacking	gossiping
dock	a navvy's lodgings
to mash	make a brew of tea
flayed	frightened
flummoxed	confused
to jack	give up
kelpie	water sprite
ragabash	ne'er-do-well
scuddies	naked
shippon	cowshed
to slope	to leave without notice
taws	marbles
wick	quick and lively
wishin' dance	kiss and cushion dance

The Gathering

April 1871

Rattle his bones over the stones,
Only an old navvy, nobody owns . . .

Chapter One

'Tat! Come back here, yer daft hound! Tat! I'll give yer what for when I catch you! Tatty Widdup ...' yelled a small girl into the wind as she raced across the open fells towards a distant streak of brown whippet leaping over the grey stone walls, sniffing out the scent of rabbit warrens and the flash of white bobtails scurrying for cover underground.

Tizzy Widdup wrapped her shawl tightly across her chest against the stiffening April breeze, picking up her sackcloth skirt which was sticking between her knees, hindering her struggle uphill, cursing to herself. Trust Tat to dive off as soon as she untied him from the handcart.

The family had only just arrived at the makeshift navvy camp high on the West Riding fells. Granda Fettle made a beeline for the ale hut to wet his whistle, while her sister, Mally, leapt off to see if there was news of their father, Ironfist, and his tunnel gang in the camp. Tizzy was just unloading the tent when the tripehound darted off leaving muggins to follow suit.

3

Now he was just a speck on the horizon and the sky was banking up storm clouds. There were sheep dotted on the rough grass like boulders with cottonfluff lambs cowering under their udders for cover as she approached. Tizzy scanned the open spaces fenced by sturdy stone walls which crisscrossed the fellsides, mysteriously disappearing over the brow of each hill. She had never been so far north before. It was a fearsome spot.

When I get hold of him, he'll get such a wallop, panted Tizzy, closing in wearily as the dog stopped in his tracks with one paw raised, ears pricked, catching her call for a second. Tat turned round, his tail curved under his hind legs, sensing trouble from his mistress.

Suddenly from a gap in the stone wall boundary a young man in shirtsleeves and thick breeches dashed forward ranting and cursing, throwing a rock at Tat, stunning the animal. The dog staggered for a second, then keeled over and yelped. Just enough time for his assailant to close in to knock him down, hammering at his skinny body with a stick.

'Stop! Stop it!' screamed Tizzy, frantic to prevent the brutal onslaught. 'He's only a pup . . . He won't do no harm. Please, sir, please . . .' The man was venting his fury, oblivious to her pleas, hitting the dog into the ground. Tizzy pulled at his shirt, beating him. 'Oh please, sir, give over. He won't harm yer sheep!'

'That's what they all say so I'm seeing this one off for good. Are you blind? Can't you see there's lambs in this field and we've lost enough already?' He wiped his brow, vengeance satisfied; a lad in his twenties with thick thighs and a pudgy face dotted with fiery pustules, gathered in red clumps across his cheeks, still weeping from a recent shave.

Tizzy bent over Tat, horrified. The dog was panting, prostrate, but still tried to wag its tail at the sight of her. Tears were rolling down her face, tears of rage at being too small to attack the man, tears of fear that he might start on her next.

'Gerroff this field and take that scrap of bones with you. If I see you anywhere near these fells again, I'll take me belt to you as well.' Tizzy stood stock-still, staring at the young man whose greasy black hair fell over his face like rat's tails.

'Are you deaf or summat?' said the lad, unnerved by her fierce stare. 'That'll teach you navvy scumbags to keep out of Scarsdale and off our land. Go on ... get back to yer sod huts where you belong, scarper.'

Tizzy was rooted to the spot. Instinctively she pulled out the magic dagger which Dad had once found in a drained lake. It was tied with rope around her waist like a belt, looped together with her bag of marbles and a bunch of tail feathers: all her precious collection of treasures. She fixed her eyes, dark as wet slate, sternly on his face. 'I'm telling of you, telling my dad and his gang. My dad's a tunnel tiger with fists like hammers and he'll come and get you for what you done to Tat. So there!'

Then Tizzy spat on the knife and slowly made wild zigzag patterns in the air with trembling hands, trying to remember Owd Granny Reilly's spellings; the pedlar woman had shown her secret runes and signs to ward off warts and the evil eye. Now a strange power was coming over her, lifting her high off the ground.

'Eeny, meeny, miney, mo. As God is the witness, a curse on you shall go. As you did so shall be done to you and worse. So there!' Tizzy spat out, hoping her made-up words sounded solemn, powered by the sound of the hammering stick on Tat's poor back. She stood her ground.

For a second the farmer was transfixed and stepped back at the sight of the wild-eyed child sprouting braids the colour of dried leaves, circling round him with a knife, cursing him to heaven. She was nobbut a skinny lass in a flour-bag skirt and filthy shirt. She looked as if she had not had a wash for weeks and her face was grimy but there was something in the way her eyes flashed. He stepped forward to cuff her but she was too wick.

'Don't you touch me. Don't you dare! You're dead.' Tizzy took her shawl and tenderly covered the bleeding dog, wrapping him tightly, cradling him across her back like the camp women carried their bairns.

As she trundled back down the fellside on the mossy turf, she was deaf to the curlew's bubbling call and skylark's soaring, blind to the beauty of the majestic Yorkshire peaks, emerald and golden against the clearing skies. One thought only possessed her as she bent forward to give Tat a softer ride.

It's all my fault. If I could have run faster, caught up with Tat, but these stupid skirts held me back. Why are girls so weak and useless? If only I'd been a lad ... our Billy would have rescued Tat. But Billy was dead and she had no other brothers to call on. Mally was useless. She had breasts and they wobbled when she ran. Mally liked being a girl and skivvying, curling her hair and eyeing up the navvy lads. Mally was stupid like that.

It's not fair blaming Tat for what he never done. How was he to know the farmer hated navvy dogs? She was fed up of being cursed and spat at just because they tramped the streets to earn a living. Tizzy knew the daggery looks they got when they arrived in a village, pushing their cart. 'Here come the rogues and vagabonds. Shut yer door and hide yer childer, navvies'll steal them like the gypsies.' Mally would hide her head under her shawl with shame but Tizzy put her tongue out and pretended she did not care.

At least they had strong boots on their feet, which was more than could be said for some of the name-callers, and her belly was always full of mutton, for navvy men got good wages and huts to live in. They were not beggars living on the poor box. Oh no! The Widdups tramped from site to site following the railways and Dad said that was important work.

Ironfist told her that the railways would spread all over the country one day, taking goods and passengers from one place to another. He said when a station came to a town then money soon followed and towns were queuing up to buy one. So why was it when they came to build the track or dig embankments no one wanted to have any builders there?

Now they were stuck in the wildest moorland while the gangs were blasting out tunnels and building bridges through the mountains and over the villages to make the fastest line from London to Scotland. Rumour was that it would take years to build the Settle to Carlisle line, so that meant plenty of work for all.

Tizzy did not blame Ironfist for losing his family somewhere along the way. Families always trailed behind. His gang would want to find the Midland Railway contractor's hut and get themselves on site. If only he would send word which part of the seventy-mile track he was on, though. Dad was hopeless with his lettering so they must rely on hearsay and the odd message.

He didn't know about Billy and Granny Widdup. He didn't know how much they needed his money. That was why they had traipsed from Leeds, over Ilkley Moor to Skipton and Settle and up into this godforsaken wilderness to seek him out. She was sick of rumours and false sightings. There must be plenty of work for tunnel miners blasting holes underground with dynamite but no record of Ironfist at Batty Green, the main shantytown. So on they had trudged over drover's tracks, the cartwheels sticking in the ruts, sleeping in barns, climbing upwards and onwards. Living rough was hard with treacle and porridge, oatcakes, bread and scrape, poaching out of the River Ribble and endless rabbit stew. Sometimes they took turns with fellow travellers to fill the pot and no one went hungry but this journey had been made alone.

Tizzy was looking forward to settling for the summer even in these wild open spaces. Now she was not so sure. The sound of the stick kept ringing in her ears but she kept on down the track. Anger made her burden light. Once she got Tat back to the tent then she could nurse him better.

She paused to catch her breath, looking down over the makeshift camp. Already there were muddy tracks carving up the grass fields, spirals of blue smoke curling around the huts on wheels where the contractor had set up offices, buildings dotted higgledy-piggledy on the terraced slopes. She could hear the banging of wooden huts being erected in lines ready for the workmen and their families. The field was on a terraced slope above the valley. Someone had made a bonfire and the smell of woodsmoke wafted upwards.

In the distance a silver stream snaked through trees in the valley bottom; already the tips were tinged with the first green shoots of spring and the beck shimmered onwards to a village of grey houses, snuggled up together, sleeping in the cold misty morning. The camp would be spreadeagled up the hillside, catching the winds as they whirled off the fellsides, but at least the huts would be on a south-facing slope to glean the best of any warmth going free.

Once the shanty huts were up, there would be a dry bed and a fire to cook on with perhaps a canteen to cadge from. Mally would sew and mend, turn rabbit skins into waistcoats and fancy muffs and barter them for eggs and old clothing. She was nifty with her fingers. Granda Fettle would join the night soil men clearing out the earth closets, disposing of the middens. It was all he was fit for since he got the stiffness in his joints. His eyesight was feeble but he was still a wizard with metal, fettling up broken kettles, tools, handles and staying up all night to solve a tricky job. 'Fettler Widdup never gives up on the job' was his motto but he was as worn as a rubbed rag.

Tizzy knew he was tired of tramping, of stinking to high heaven with other people's filth, but someone had to keep the camps clean. It had cost them dear enough last summer when he brought the fever from the reservoir shantytown back to their wagon. They said it came on his clothes and carried off Granny and Billy within a week.

Then everyone fled and the bodies were buried in a pit and burned. Ironfist stayed away. Granda shrunk two sizes and said little but he must have hollow legs the amount he swallowed in the ale huts after that. He would stagger back, fall asleep and wet himself. That got Mally all steamed up and shouting.

Everything was going wrong again, Tizzy snivelled, as she reached the tent: just two arched branches and a canvas cover.

Mally was standing po-faced with her arms folded across her chest, looking stern, with her dark hair scraped back severely making her ears stick out like jug handles. 'Where've you been? I had to do it all myself as usual ... What on earth!' Tizzy off-loaded her dog from her back and laid him on the ground.

'Give us a hand, he's right badly.' Mally bent down to examine Tat, unwrapping the shawl gently. His eyes were open to the sky, his body warm but breath had long departed from his crushed bones.

10

'Who did this?' Mally shook her head sadly and covered him up again.

'No, no, he can't be dead. Get us some help, quick!' pleaded Tizzy, desperately trying to find signs of life. 'We were only up on the tops, doing no harm, and this bloke hits and hits him. He can't be gone. Oh, let's get shut of this place, quick, pack up and move on. Dad's not here, is he?' Tizzy darted into the tent to collect the pots and blankets.

'Calm down, we're going nowhere. I'm tired of traipsing on and on. We're stopping here for a while. Scarsbeck'll be a good dock for Granda and me. Plenty of huts going up, lots of washing and skivvying and a school perhaps for you. They're building one of them bridges right over yon village, to keep the line on course; a fancy bridge with brick arches and masonry so there'll be some decent workmen for a change, ones with tidy ways and clean shirts, well paid to come out to this bleak spot. We could do far worse than settle here for the summer. We'll find out where Dad is at . . .' Mally softened her voice to mother her sister. It always worked to calm her down.

Tizzy backed away in a daze, her tearless eyes transfixed on Tat, her head throbbing. 'I'll get that tyke for what he done.'

'What tyke?' asked Mally, watching her sister pulling at her skirt.

'Farmer in the field what killed our Tat.' Tizzy darted into the tent, rummaging in the basket where Granda kept his fettling tools. She yanked out a small hacksaw blade and sawed off her two long plaits impatiently. Mally, who had crawled into the tent, gasped with horror as she watched the burnished golden braids drop onto the grass. Tizzy looked down with satisfaction. 'That's got rid of them. Fetch me Granda's shaving tackle.'

'Stop this at once, Matilda Widdup. Have you got moon-fever? What on earth are you cutting off yer lovely hair for? No one will buy it here,' pleaded Mally as she tried to prise the saw from her hands.

'Shut up! Martha Widdup, can't you see it's all my fault? If I were a lad not a stupid girl . . . I'm fed up with being a lass so I'm not going to be one any more. I'll bury Tat, get mesen a job and find that tyke.'

'You can't get a job, you dozy brush. You're only ten.'

'Ten and a half bit, so there. Fats boys carrying grease for the wheels, tea-mashers and nippers running errands. They all have misters who pay them. Who's to know I'm any different?'

'Well I do, and Granda will soon enough. You can't just pretend to be a lad . . .' Mally shook her sister roughly.

'Who says I can't? If I put on Billy's clothes. The stuff you never burnt. I know they're still in the flour sack. No one knows us here.' Tizzy had all her answers pat and looked so fierce, Mally knew better than to argue the toss.

'You're loony, you are. How will you get away with it . . . goin' to the bog in front of lads. I bet you haven't thought about that?' Mally's blue eyes flashed, her lips pursed in triumph.

'I have so. I shall use the bushes like I've allus done. And

I'll never take me shirt off. Granda's eyes are bad. He's always callin' me Billy Boy, so don't let on or I'll tell on you.'

'There's nowt to tell, our Tizzy,' sniffed Mally as she stuffed the hair into the sack. It was far too good to be wasted.

'There will be after I've finished spinning a tale. Come on, finish me off proper with the shaving blade or I'll do it mesen and make a right pig's ear of it.' Tizzy knelt on the ground and looked so woebegone that Mally felt sorry for her little sister. She clipped the wavy hair as close to the scalp as she dared, leaving some tufts on top. They stuck upright in defiance.

'We'll have to borrow some Macassar oil to plaster it down. Put this cap on and you'll get by, I suppose. Oh, Tizzy, what've you done to yerself!'

Tizzy rose in defiance, peeling off her skirt and thick stockings and clogs, putting on Billy's breeches which smelled damp and musty, stiff and cold. She thought of poor Billy in that burning hole and shuddered. He would understand it was all in a good cause. This way she was free to roam the camp and village unrecognised. Tizzy was going to find Tat's killer, if only to find out if Owd Granny Reilly's curses really worked.

Chapter Two

At last a grand day for washing and a chance to crisp up the starched linen, smiled Ellen Birkett as she stood back to admire the line of whites billowing like flags in the breeze. Living high on Scarsdale tops had one advantage; washing dried quicker and cleaner far from the sooty smuts and chimneys of Scarsbeck village. Down in the valley she could see the smoke blow like bonfires across the rooftops and towards the slopes of Whernside and the farms at Paradise. Someone else would be getting the coal dust and gubbins on their smalls. Paradise fields might get a south view and afternoon sunshine but Middle Butts Farm boasted the soft rays of the setting sun, all the orange-pink tinges on rocks and boulders plus a stiff drying nor'westerly straight from Morecambe Bay.

As the petticoats and pinafores danced on the line, the girl sighed at the absence of any shirt-tails and nightshirts along-side the female stuff. Since Father died and went to glory there were no thick woollen stockings, corduroy breeches or combinations to scrub and no brothers to ease her load.

Ellen tested the cottons to see if they were ready to fold up and noticed the northern sky was thickening into a plump cushion of slate-grey clouds, full o' feathers, Dad would have said. Surely not more snow at the end of April when the new crop of lambs was so far out on the fells?

She turned back towards the farmhouse with pleasure at the sight of its soft grey stone peeping over the little walled herb garden which nestled under the window. She noted with relief that the small green shoots of spring were poking gingerly out of the loamy soil: clumps of lovage, thyme, sage and southernwood, gillyflowers and lemony primroses, ready to tuck themselves back down if the frosts returned, as they often did right to the end of May.

Middle Butts farmhouse seemed moulded into the fellside, sheltered by a line of coppery trees and cushioned at the back by bracken banks rising to the hummocky fells, bordered by stone walls. It was hard to think that fierce Norsemen still left their mark on features of face and landscape here. It showed in the very shape of the house with long rooms linked one to another by stone passageways, attached sideways to the barns and animal quarters; this was once a Viking longhouse, snuggled into the hillside. On winter nights it was grand to know family and stock were all packed in tight within fire-warmed walls, over four feet thick, peering out through mullion-paned windows at the lanterns in the snow blinking across the valley, signalling all was well.

Close to the farm ran the ancient stone track, winding over the moorland, straight and direct, built by the Roman armies on their way north to the borderlands. Wild storm winds roared over limestone pavements there and the gnarled trees rooted in the clefts of the rocks bowed in submission to the greater force.

The stone lintel over the door was carved with intertwining initials, J, M, B, 1601, some of her own Birkett forebears who were tending these pastures when Good Queen Bessie was on the throne. That took you back a bit to think that perhaps they too kept the weathered oak farmhouse door open on all but the stormiest of days and they first wore smooth the stone-flagged hall passageway as they walked from the same panelled dining chamber, the oak polished to the colour of warm earth but still smelling damp and musty, to a sitting parlour used only when visitors came and for funeral sidings. How many of her ancestors had lain like Father, solemn in their Sunday suits before the final rest in St Oswy's kirkyard? One minute he was stacking straw stooks on that hot August morning and in his burial box by teatime.

Ellie scurried through to the houseplace, hearth of the home. Here Mother cooked on the fiery furnace of a cast-iron range – the range which Dad had burst his guts to give Annie Birkett so she could hold her head well above the other farmers' wives in the district and be on nodding terms with the cook at Scarsbeck Hall to compare recipes. Their range had a hot-air oven and a boiler for hot water, all the latest features, even a separate bakestone to bake oaty bread and a crane contraption from which hung the kail pot over the fire. This contraption filled the whole of the old inglenook fireplace but Mother insisted it was black-leaded and brass-polished to the standard of a locomotive engine.

For Ellen it held no delight, only the promise of more servitude and humiliation. That very morning she had been berated by Mother in front of the hired hands who were waiting nervously for their eight o'clock breakfast at the long oak table which straddled the large room, waiting for their chizzocks, curd and currant pastries, their warming tea, waiting in vain for the meal to be served. The grandmother clock ticked patiently in the corner of the kitchen and the men sitting on narrow benches, fingering their pewter bowls as they glinted in the firelight, watched Ellen struggle to roll out the pastry cases and stir the porridge.

Mother stormed in just as the pan of milk bubbled and boiled over onto the hot plate. 'Glory be, Ellie! I leave you five minutes and you ruin that pastry. You've warmed it into shreds. Look at it, like a patchwork quilt. How many times have I told you? Warm hands won't roll it. Cold hands will. You manhandle it to death. I don't know. Yer sister, Mercy, is nobbut a threepenny bit and she can do better than you. What's got into you? These lads are starving.'

Annie Birkett grabbed hold of the dough with arms as plump as a goose and doused it in flour. 'Give it here and move over.'

Ellie's cheeks were burning like rosy apples shining with heat and embarrassment, watching the farm boys smirking and Sunter, her cousin, trying to look sympathetic, the wens on his spotty chin looking fit to burst. 'You know I'm not cut out for housework . . .' she whispered, hoping to redeem her failure, but Mother was on the warpath.

'Not cut out! Whatever will yer cousin, here, think of a girl who can't bake an apple pie without turning it into a cow pat,' laughed Widow Birkett as she slapped the pastry onto a plate, sloshed on the curd tart mix and whizzed it into the oven, giving the door a satisfying slam.

Ellie cleared away the baking stuff in a huff and a puff. She could not care less what Sunter Lund and his father, Uncle Warwick, thought about her culinary prowess. Let him bake his own pies. He turned her stomach with that stupid lovesick look on his face. He was always stalking her in the farmyard, peering from the stables, offering to carry her buckets but she couldn't abide him within a kick's distance. Dad was hardly cold in his grave before the Lunds came calling, as humble as that Uriah Heep in the penny reading magazine. They meant well enough but she knew that Middle Butts Farm was a much better proposition than their own at High Butts. The pastures were lusher by the beck and the farmhouse grander and the dairy herd a credit to Father's canny eye for a good beast.

Uncle Warwick having the only son and Ellie being of a marriageable age, what seemed more natural than to keep it all in the family! Ellie would have none of it.

Mother followed her into the scullery to deliver the hard word. 'You be nice to yer cousin. We need all the help we can get. It makes sense that my brother's son should want to take over our tenancy one day.'

'Over my dead body! Father worked hard to build up this farm and I'm not having that halfwit giving me orders,' snapped Ellie, clanging the pots.

'He's not a halfwit. He nearly went to the grammar school. Mr Bulstrode coached him good and proper in the schoolhouse.'

'And look where it got him. Nowhere. He's as thick and lumpy as our Mercy's porridge and bone idle. He is rough with the cows and careless with the sheep, I can shift just as much as he can any day. Let me go full-time on the farm and forget about this stuff,' pleaded Ellie with her bright blue eyes blinking earnestly. Mother turned away to check the cheeses, stacked on shelves over the slate slabs in the dairy.

'Don't start that again. It's indecent. If only yer father and I had managed a son! All that bulling and no blessings . . . just a wayward daughter and an afterthought: two ewes and no tups! God must have had His reasons to take yer father afore his time.' Annie Birkett shook her head sadly, the wisps of grey straggles poking out of her mobcap, feeling every one of her forty-five years. The harsh winter had taken its toll on her cheeks, rough and chapped by the weather; her body had shrunk and sagged and now she was cursed by that awful time of change whispered about at the sewing circle as a time of madness and heat.

There had always been Birketts at Middle Butts, tall fair strapping men just like Jim. She had eyed him up for years knowing that he was just the man for her. They had struggled together to build up a decent dairy herd but their own breeding had been a disaster and no mistake. 'If only poor William, Jimmy and Kester had lived we'd have a future here; three bairns born not the size of rabbits all buried in the kirkyard and what's left? Two strapping lasses who can eat me out of house and home, one who can't fry an egg without burning it and the other with her head stuck in books. Why were you born so awkward?'

'Because I'd rather be out lambing, cowing, walling. That's why!'

'No man'll wed you unless you shape up, lass. Who wants a woman as can't cook?' spat her mother, mopping her brow. There was silence between mother and daughter, a frosty silence chilling the air.

'Is everything all right, Auntie Annie?' Sunter simpered, cap in hand, peering round the door. 'I'm going to wall up that gap on the far side. We've lost a few lambs up there and what with them navvy camps going up fast, you can't be too careful. I'll be back s'afternoon if you need me.'

'Thank you, Sunter, yer a good lad to yer old aunt. Think on, Ellie, what I've been saying. You can't afford to be picky at your age. Girls years younger than you are being snapped up like hot cakes at the village socials. The last thing we need is an old maid to feed and clothe.'

All day Mother's threats had rankled inside her head. She was only eighteen and there was no shortage of admirers when she sauntered down to Scarsbeck. Was it her fault if she towered over the village stockmen like a Viking princess in the story books? She was tall with sunbleached golden hair curling softly around her plump face, bonny and round with a strong frame and firm large breasts which seemed to end up pressed against the noses of the chapel swains when she swung them round in the dancing. Her boots were cobbled on a man's last and all her skirts shrunk indecently above her ankles and needed lengthening each summer.

Ellie stood just under six feet tall and sometimes tried to curl her shoulders to reduce her height. It never worked, though, and she ended up with a sore neck and backache from stooping. What she needed was a lad she could stare up to, whose arms would go round her waist when they danced, not clasp themselves around her thighs!

When she looked over the other lumpen farmers' sons, Ellie was not impressed by any of them. She'd biffed and bashed most of them at the dame school, fought over conkers with them on Scarsbeck playing green and had no desire to kiss any of them at the kiss and cushion dancing. She was fussy so she'd do without like Miss Cora Bulstrode, single for twenty years, a shadow behind her brother Mr Ezra Bulstrode, the headmaster. It was just like that poet in her *Palgrave's Golden Treasury* said:

> *Full many a flower is born to blush unseen,*
> *And waste its sweetness on the desert air.*

Not that Miss Cora was all sweetness. She could cut you down to size with one of her haughty stares down her metal-rimmed spectacles as if you were a stolen fart. She hovered over the schoolhouse like a dog guarding the gates of hell. Only the scholarship boys, one by one, were admitted for extra lessons, poor sods! For twenty years Mr Bulstrode had striven to get Scarsbeck lads to jump through the scholarship hoop. He had managed only six. Six hopefuls who bettered themselves and never darkened the doors of church, school or chapel again.

Uncle Warwick and Aunt Blaize had been right suited when Sunter got his chance but he fluffed it somehow. Now they were looking in her direction for a lift up the social ladder. She felt sorry that the other lads scoffed at him and gave him a wide berth. They thought him stupid, no doubt, to bother with book-learning when there were trees to climb, becks to dam up, lassies to chase or fish to be poached.

As she folded up the day's washing she had to admit that perhaps she and Sunter were two of a kind, for different reasons. He was a lone worker and so was she. Ellie had too many chores to perform on the farm, cows to milk, butter to churn, cheese to press, sheep to tend, lambs to gather in and wool to spin, to mess about with the village girls. It was church on Sunday, of course, Miss Bulstrode's needlecraft evening class in the summer and a trip to the sheep fair, if she was lucky. In winter they were sealed off on the tops by blizzards and snowdrifts, cocooned in Middle Butts, carding wool, spinning yarn, knitting a crop of stockings and gloves for the market, watching Mother knit gossamer-soft shawls which could pass through a wedding ring they were that fine.

Ellie carried the wicker basket through the house, her metal boot tips clacking on the milk-polished stone slabs. Mother was mending as usual, sitting on the high-backed settle, darning stockings while keeping her eye on a bubbling pan of vegetables and stock for the evening broth. She inspected the washing basket, sniffing up the windblown garments. 'Smells fresh enough but is that soot I see on yon blouse?'

'Must be the camp fire smoke across the valley,' replied her daughter.

'We never wanted that camp near us. It's a good job there's a meeting tonight in the village room. Trouble's on the move and we've got to have our say. I heard there'll be thousands and thousands camped around us. We'll be besieged like the Israelites, besieged by hostile Philistines. Goliath and his hordes waiting to conquer, not safe in our beds of a night. They've been parading in the village, bold as brass. Cheek of them!'

'Oh Mother, they're only doing their job. The camp's a mile away from Scarsbeck,' argued Ellie.

'Not three fields away from us!' came the reply.

'As the crow flies, Mother, come on, as the crow flies.'

'Them navvy devils is more like swallows on a barn roof, sporting blue jackets, fancy white moleskins and red neckerchiefs. I've seen them bogtrotting past our bottom gate, all dolled up, fair-weather birds, that's all. Here for the summer work and once the cold comes off they'll flit, leaving all their mess behind. Why does Scarsbeck need a station halt?

Trouble on the move, I reckon we'll pay for it one way or the other. AND if I catch you as much as tweaking your curls in front of any one of them ragabashes ... We all know where there's men and maidens, mischief is soon afoot! By heck, just you start smiling in that direction and you'll be up them stairs in yer room with not so much as a crumb for yer supper. I'm warning you, my lady.'

'Oh Mother, honestly, I'm sure they're not as bad as they're made out. You know what Parson Hardy said last Sunday about being charitable to these poor wandering souls, "We must show forbearance and fortitude in our hour of trial ... true Christian forbearance." ' Ellie mimicked the vicar's plummy tones, making her mother smile and sink back onto the cushion.

'Lass, I don't know where you get it from, yer a caution. You can twist yer tongue to anything but think on, I mean every word I've said.'

Chapter Three

There was a steady stream of traffic on the turnpike road following the rough bleak track over Ribblehead Moor towards Dent and Hawes; a queue of draycarts and wagons loaded with wooden planks, coal carts and delivery traps with Dales ponies shining like black glass. On foot were a straggle of men and women pushing handcarts with babies and toddlers wedged between iron bedsteads, straw mattresses, birdcages, chickens poking out of baskets bobbing up and down, squawking in protest at the bumpy ride, tormented by the array of scruffy tethered dogs which snapped and snarled at strangers. Children gambolled and darted round covered in dust and dung, waving pots and pans in noisy chattering groups, with bundles on sticks over their shoulders, teasing and bantering with each other on the long journey northwards.

One young navvy staggered into the brightness from the Gearstones Inn with barn-straw dust still on his shoulders, his mahogany eyes staring forward as if in a trance; a gigantic navvy in a huge moleskin monkey jacket, a loose bundle slung over his shoulder. He looked the worse for his Saturday night's spree, having drunk away his wages, his favourite waistcoat with pearl buttons, six flannel shirts, his best boots, three pairs of extra-thick knitted stockings and a silver watch with gilt chain. Now his head was throbbing and there was no choice but to tramp on to the next camp to earn a few more bob and top up his hangover with a hair of the dog.

At the sight of this flame-haired giant, men parted in front of him like the Red Sea before Moses. His reputation walked before him, a reputation for having knocked several men to kingdom come at the fisticuff contests held after midnight, behind the pub, out of reach of the constables.

'Nah then, Fancy, how do?' one little workman said as he doffed his cap, smiling. 'Coming to try yer luck in Paradise camp? I hear it's a bit on the small side for a cock of a dock like you . . .'

The tall traveller strode past groups of men, waving his hand in a grand gesture. 'That's Fancy, the Highland tiger, they say he's just out of the correction house for braying three men to pulp . . . a one-man army when fired up wi' whisky, snappy dresser but mind the missus when the wind's in his direction,' rumoured the men to each other down the line.

Fancy strode on past the hawkers lugging bundles of wares on their backs, past packmen with mules laden with panniers, catching up with huge carthorses whose tails were gaily decorated with ribbons and tail plaits, their muscles glistening as they steamed and plodded uphill. In his nostrils was the warm tang of freshly dropped manure to clear his headache.

The gaggles of women nodded approvingly as he sauntered past, admiring the jaunty angle of his forage cap, his gypsy-length copper curls, caught up in a pirate's tail down his back, the way his broad shoulders tapered neatly into a firm round bum which emphasised his thick thighs and sturdy long limbs. Even from the back he stirred the senses with sinful possibilities.

Behind them to the left, the hillside echoed with a fearsome clamour, a cacophany of clankings, blastings and the noise of wagons rolling down embankments like the thunder of a thousand hammers ringing in the ear. In the distance were tunnel shafts sunk deep into the bedrock and men drawing up rocks from cranes, spoil heaps, brown bankings of soil, mud-encrusted men and boys pushing barrows of earth like busy ants. A world of rock and stone, mud and dust; an all-too-familiar prospect, this shovelling muck for a living.

Fancy smiled as he sang the old ditty:

> *'Rattle my bones, over the stones,*
> *Here's a poor navvy who nobody owns.'*

He was in a poeticky mood and the sight of the bare green hillside, the limestone scree and the dramatic sky stirred the muse in his head. He could feel the words cascading over him and he needed to stop and catch the phrases before they got lost amongst the noise or sank into the earth for ever. He sat down on a damp tussocky clump and felt the spongy moss soaking into his breeks and picked the scratchy straw bits from his neck. A doss down in a fleabitten byre was no prize for a champion fighter but the money had long been swallowed up and he had no idea how he landed from Batty Green shanty to the Gearstones Inn. He was sobering up fast enough, fishing out a crumpled leather-backed notebook, the only thing he had not pawned for a bottle. He rummaged for a stump of pencil in his coat pocket and began to scribble down the lines in his head. Shaking his head furiously, he shook out more straw which landed on his paper to distract his concentration. He crossed out words and tried again to compose a rhyming couplet worthy of his bardic ancestry. His head was still woozy and phrases dripped slowly instead of the usual gushing waterfall. His brain was hungry and dried out and he was gasping for a drink.

Fancy had tramped for a day on an empty stomach, spent his last penny in Batty Green and the rest was a blur. His pockets were bare and there was nothing else to pawn but his best tartan waistcoat with silver-tipped horn buttons if he was to eat that night.

He cursed at himself. What was this son of the clan MacLachlan doing in this godforsaken bit of Yorkshire, far from the homelands of Argyll and his bardic forefathers? Why was he reduced to tramping out a living on foreign soil, dispossessed of his heritage and lands by those callous English lords who had cleared Father from his croft to graze their stupid sheep? How he hated sheep and now he was surrounded by them. Fancy cleared his throat and proclaimed in Gaelic the famous lament of his clansman, John MacLachlan of Rahoy.

> *'On an April morning I no longer hear*
> *Birdsong or the lowing of cattle on the moor.*
> *I hear the unpleasant noise of sheep.*
> *And the English language, dogs barking . . .'*

The family had been driven off the land and forced into the city, His father, Lachie, had soured and ranted, old before his time. He saw his sons born in exile and died young, leaving Fancy's mother, Eilean, to raise children in a Glasgow hovel close to the Broomielaw docks. This poor woman watched bairn after bairn die of enteric fever from the muck of the Clyde which washed through their basement and eventually it carried her tired spirit away. Fancy was the only survivor, taken into a dour orphanage, given a little schooling, enough to pick up the rudiments of English letters. In his head was always the flowing of Gaelic sounds like beautiful music but the dominie would beat him if he spoke the mother tongue in class.

No one could ban memories of Mother's stories of the glens and fighting men or their marvellous deeds in battle; of clan chief Lachlan MacLachlan, Prince Charlie's henchman.

Fancy was proud to bear his name. Sometimes his anger burned so fiercely in his head at the injustice of their treatment that even now only whisky would cool down the rage. Yet *uisge beatha*, that very water of life, raised its own fighting fire and he lost menial job after menial job because of it. Nor would he stoop to take the Queen's shilling to fight in foreign lands for the Crown, nor would he police the streets as a peeler, the other fate of tall strapping Highlanders. So he left the streets of Glasgow far behind, tramping not northwards but reluctantly southwards to Carlisle, selling his brute strength digging roads and reservoirs, embankments and tunnel heads to slake his thirst.

Lately his boots wearied of bogtrotting from one camp to another but a restless spirit drove Fancy forward, just in case. Some day he would stop roaming but he had found no reason to stay in one place so he kept on looking. It was always the sameness of camp and task which drove him off again.

First he would join the queue at the contractor's hut; shuffling forward he would sign on the dot, receive his chits, bargain for lodgings in some hut, put his bags in his locker, seize the bottom bunk of one of the truckle beds lined up against the walls like in a barracks, inspect the bedding for fleas and the face of the hutkeeper's wife. If she was plain so much the better; the temptation of a pretty lassie, slattern though she be, was more than he could resist. He always chose the sourpuss. The more she grumbled, the more he charmed and often ended up with the best bit of the boiled mutton, the largest slice of the pie.

He had fled too many docks through the window at midnight with a jealous husband lunging at him with a knife with barely time to put on his trousers and grab his sack. What a life for a man of twenty-five summers.

A restless dissatisfaction at his given lot burned within him but he never stayed long enough to learn a skilled trade. He fancied the open-air life, the hillsides and green landscapes beckoned him. He spurned city jobs, preferring to rough it in the cold. He liked a big stretch of sky over his head with stars to count at night when he slept rough in a ditch. He hated being cooped up in the huts with only the snores and farts of smelly men for company. Men whose idea of a good wash was to dunk themselves occasionally in the water butt.

That was how he had got his nickname, Fancy. He might only be a navvy digger, lowest of the low, but no one could accuse him of smelling like a sewer even if he dug them. Fancy was fastidious about his appearance. He liked nothing better after knock-off than to find the nearest burn, strip off and bathe away the muck of the day. Then he would put on a cleanly laundered shirt and breeks, finished off with one of his collection of waistcoats and shiny boots, comb out his drying locks which frizzled into coils and splash a little oil on his whiskers, framing them into cones over his full lips and straight set of teeth. The thought of selling his clan tartan waistcoat with its rich blue, scarlet and green plaid pattern to some dirty workman, to sick over it, was unbearable. He would rather go hungry.

They called him Fancy, for his fancy waistcoats, and he liked this handle, so it stuck. Woe betide anyone who mistook his handle for that of a fop, thinking him a pushover!

Not that any self-respecting navvy used his given name, not if he was fleeing from some woman or the constabulary. Your real name was incriminating evidence and only yielded to a priest at the last rites. They were not all criminals, thieves and drunkards. Fancy was proud to have the acquaintance of many good workmen and their families who happened to like the travelling life.

Nicknames were their secret code, just like their own rhyming slang. It showed you were one of them and knew the ropes. It got you respect as did your fighting spirit and strength and Fancy had plenty of that. Lanes Tommy, Devon Whiskers, Gripper York, Whistler, Bones and Billy Two Hats, he had passed them all on the road up and if they made up a gang together they would set the tone of the dig by their speed and strength. If they made him their ganger, gaffer of the team, that would suit him fine and he might stay the whole summer or even see the job through.

Sometimes Fancy dreamt the same dream: he was on a tramp and he felt there was someone waiting just around the corner but always the face, the place was fuzzy. He would drop his tommy sack and run, hopeful and expectant, only to find the vision vanished just out of reach perhaps around the next corner and he would chase into the mist. He woke then with a sadness which hung over him until he reached for the barrel of ale hidden in their digs for just such a comfort.

If only he could see what it was, waiting there out of reach, but he would keep on tramping until it appeared.

Fancy searched through the muddy main camp at Batty Green, the wildest, windiest, coldest, dreariest of shantytowns. It was filling up fast with tramways and tracks, a mission, post office, limeworks, brick factory; already crammed with people, too much a city and too public a place for a poet, for that was what he was; a bard with stories in his head to share around camp fires and taprooms. There were ancient lays ringing in his head and he needed space to coax them onto paper so he was tramping on up Ribblehead to the next camp, just in case.

Now he was turning left off the Hawes road towards Dent down another rough track, the wind beating furiously into his face from the north-west. Fancy was glad he had not wagered his jacket and bent his head in defiance. At last they were going downhill and in the distance a grey-misted valley opened up before him and he felt a strange lurch in his stomach at the sight of this hidden glen. For one giddy second he felt like some chieftain surveying his domain.

For that moment he forgot he was cold and hungry, with thin soles on his second-best boots and straw itching its way down his back, forgot his anger and stood stock-still. His heart was thumping and he didn't know why but it terrified him more than six navvies with hammers cornering him in a dark alley. He took a deep breath and turned to the entrance of Paradise camp where the contractor's wagon on wheels was waiting patiently to lure him in.

There was the usual queue and he stood in line, admiring

the view across the dale to the patchwork of stone walls marking out the moorland, the clumps of trees in the hollow and the lush green pastures either side where the shorthorn cattle were grazing contentedly on the fresh grass. Now cows were a far bonnier prospect in view. You knew where you were with kine.

His vision was distracted by the sight of a small boy by a stone wall, struggling to swing a pickaxe over his head, nearly turning a backwards somersault in the effort to control the heavy handle. The boy was trying to make a hole by the wall but the ground was hard and stony and he was making little headway. Visions of blood gushing from the bairn's shins stirred Fancy from the queue, catching the axe mid-air. 'Hang on, laddie, yer too wee to be swinging yon like a sword. Let me gie ye a hand.' He took the pickaxe and crashed it down, splitting the earth. 'What are we hiding ... a bit of stolen treasure have we here?' laughed Fancy, seeing the bundle covered with dirty sacking. Tizzy stood in awe at the sight of this man as tall as a tree bending to examine the bundle.

'It's me dog, Tat. I'm burying him under the wall so he can sniff out rabbits.' She pulled back the rag to show the man the sad stiff corpse.

'Worn out with tramping, was he?' said the giant as he hacked out a hole skilfully. 'There, that'll make him a comfy bed to lie in. It's a sad day when yer friend comes to the end of his years,' he said gently to humour the child.

''Snot fair, he were only a pup. He were brayed on by a farmer up there,' she said as she pointed across the beck to the rising fields high up, dotted with sheep. 'He were brayed to death with a rock for going in a field full of lambs. He weren't doing nothing but laiking about . . .'

The man stood up, his warm brown eyes hardening. Sheep again, always trouble around sheep. He stared across to see if he could see anyone still working in the field. There was always trouble with farmers on the line, grousing, griping on about stock going missing and fences broken or daughters up the spout. Miserable beggars. 'Were you after getting his name?'

'Nah, I were scared in case he'd set on me. But I'd know him when I see him, poxy-faced with a fat belly and black hair, about yourn age. If you meet him tell him he's dead meat,' said Tizzy, trying to sound tough.

'Dinna fash yersel. If I see him, I'll be giving him a real Fancy's welcome, one he won't forget in a hurry. I promise you.'

'Thanks, mister.' Tizzy doffed her cap, revealing the worst of Mally's scalping. 'Here, do you need a tea masher for yer gang? I can run errands and sprog wheels too.' Tizzy seized the moment and stood squarely, giving him one of her piercing stares.

'I've only just arrived myself. Give me time to draw my breath. If we do need a nipper, I'll be for givin' you yer chance. You look awful small to me for sprogging wheels.' Fancy smiled at this lad's brass neck in sticking himself forward. He liked to see that in his crew.

'What I lacks in size, I make up for in speed.' The boy

leapt over the wall. 'Now you see me, now you don't, Jack in a Flash!' Fancy smiled at the scruffy boy in his overlong breeks and skinny legs.

'Well, Mr Flash, I'll be looking out for ye. Where's yer dock?' asked Fancy.

'I ain't got one yet but me sister, Mally, is a good cooker and skivvy and she'll get us summat. Ask for Billy Boy Widdup but you can call me Flash if you like and thanks for the job.'

'I'm not promising, mind. You should be at school. Get an education, laddie, or you'll end up like me!' Fancy tried to look stern but there was something unnerving about those grey eyes and the freckles across the bridge of his nose, the tufts of amber hair which reminded him of himself at that age.

'Nah, I've been there, nowt to it but squiggling and sing-ing. I could do sums in me head quicker than the teacher. Don't reckon much to it. I could allus read letters and I can show how them numbers add up sideways, upwards and downwards. I worked it out mesen. Easy as pie.' Tizzy picked up a flint of slate and drew on it with a stone. 'See, if you take a three and double it and treble it and add another . . .'

'You've lost me there, laddie, but I'm sure you're right. You should stick with yer numbering and it might earn you a living.' Fancy waved and drifted back to the queue bemused by the razor sharpness of the child. Billy Flash still had that wide-eyed innocence which believed everything was possible, that justice would be done for his dog. Well, Tat would get his revenge. Fancy would sign on, wash down in the burn and sort out that young farmer before the night was out.

Chapter Four

'Put yer clothes on, parson, we don't want to be late for the meeting. Don't worry, that'll fettle yer back up for a few more weeks,' laughed a white-haired woman as she lifted the flat iron off the brown paper covering his torso.

The priest in charge of St Oswy's, Scarsbeck, in the West Riding of Yorkshire, moaned with relief as he unpeeled himself from the dog-haired rag rug in front of the glowing open fire. On his face was a look of satisfaction usually reserved for market day afternoons when the blessed Liddy Braithwaite sent him to heaven locked in the juicy wetness of her cavernous thighs while Farmer Braithwaite patted the rumps of his best shorthorns at Hawes market.

'Ooh, that's much better,' sighed the naked man as he reached for his woollen combinations warming on the brass fender rail.

'Trouble with you is weak foundations and not enough strong through stones to hold up a wall the size of your back.

Walls need bedding in firm rock and get yerself covered up before I get blushing at the size of you – like a stallion and twice as eager, no doubt.' The woman smirked, unable to avert her eyes from his swollen member. 'Time you got yerself a wife, she'll soon cure yer aches 'n' pains. I'm too old to be stooping over you and that's a fact.'

'Bethany Wildman, you're an angel sent from heaven to minister to the afflicted. What would I do without your sheep-grease rubbings and flat-iron presses? And as for being too old, why, you're still in the prime of life,' replied the vicar in his soft southern accent as he dressed himself.

'Stop all that flannel, Ralph Hardy, it don't wash on me, save it for them silly ewes who run when you whistle. Hurry up, get them breeches on before someone sees you here again. Gossip walks on four legs in these parts, sheep tell tales and drovers pass my gate. If they keep seeing yon dappled grey horse and trap of yours hitched to my post then it'll be clacked all round the village that parson's getting his comforts again from the owd Nag On the Moor and I'll be for it with all them jealous hussies.'

Beth Wildman stood squarely with her hands on her ample hips, her pinny scooped up either side of her ragged skirt, in the old-fashioned way, pointing her finger in mock annoyance. Then her eyes softened at the sight of his winsome expression, the way his glossy mane of hair cascaded down from a centre parting, the slight tilt of his upper lip, the symmetry of his features and the childlike sparkle of his beautiful eyes.

'You always shame me,' smiled her patient as he stretched himself, banging his head on the low ceiling beams, sending bunches of dried crinkled herbs scattering like rice confetti over the table, cluttered with lavender-scented sheep salve and greasy paper.

'Well, someone has to. I'll name no names and you can tell me no lies but there's nowt hid in Scarsbeck that shan't be known. I'm not one to put legs on a snake but one of these days you'll be caught with yer breeks flapping to the wind and you'll be horsewhipped out of Scarsdale. Is that why you were put here with this far-flung flock, to cool yer ardour and mend yer ways? Yer a mite younger than the usual relics put out to grass in this pulpit.' Bethany laughed as he averted his gaze. 'So I hit nail right on the head then. Come on, you can do yer Christian duty and take me down the fell to this gathering tonight. I'll not be missing all the baahing and bleating that'll rise to the chapel rafters. I've got me own piece to say while we're all in the same pen. But first you can help me shift them ewes down from the top fields. I can smell snow on the wind.'

'Surely not? It's the end of April.'

'Makes no difference, you should know by now. Weather is its own master in this dale. Nine months winter and three months fair to middling, if we're lucky, and every now and then it blows a fit just to let us see who's gaffer. Anyroad, April snow makes good manure but it's the very divil for young lambs.' Beth flung open the wooden door and untethered her sheepdog, which strained eagerly at the sight of her. 'See yon sky, swollen fit to burst o'er us heads before the night's gone. So stir yourself, fasten up that fancy tweed jacket. You've had enough coddling for one day, naughty lad. I mean it. Get yersen a wife and stop yer capers in yer own sheep pen. Shame on you, a man of the cloth! Get yerself on yer knees and pray to the Good Lord to deliver you from yer sloth and sinning ways or I'll cast a spell and dip that big wick of yours in the bog and you'll never shift it again.'

'There you go again at my conscience but what else is there to do in these hills?' pleaded the young vicar as he tried to keep pace with her up the steep fellside.

'I smell trouble on the wind, vicar, and if you don't guide the flock you were given, there'll be such a scattering. Don't be a milksop. Don't let yer true friend down.' Beth bent forward, her weathered face serious, stern, the sound of her ragged garments flapping like the beating of wings.

'But I never wanted this parish or to be a blessed parson in the first place. It was dumped on me by the family. My mama wanted me to follow in her father's footsteps to a bishop's palace. She is so disappointed,' came the hesitant reply.

'Well, just stop bleating and mooching about like a lazy loon. Get off yer backside and stiffen yer sinews, stand up to the squire, resign if you must. You can start by finding out about this railway line. I hear he wants it shifting half a mile off his land so it won't spoil his terraces and disturb his slumbers. That'll mean trouble for Middle Butts pastures and Widow Birkett has enough on her plate at the moment. Make yerself useful for a change. For God's sake wake up before it's too late and this dale is ruined forever. Get cracking or you'll wake up one morning and find yerself an old man before you catch on to what it's all about. There, you've got me preaching sermons again! I'll shut up.'

'Be blowed if I'll ever know what this life is all about. You have more answers than I've ever found in textbook or sermons,' answered the young man with dove-grey eyes.

'Then search for answers. You'll never catch me across your church portals until you've something to say worth hearing. You may speak proper, spout poetry from yer pump, look like the Angel Gabriel in the stained-glass altar window but from where I'm standing, you should have had yer bottom leathered long ago.'

'Oh, I did, I did and I still love a good spanking,' quipped Ralph Hardy with a smirk.

'Stop that smut! You shame yer calling and I'd rather manage on my own if yer going to take that tone with me. Go home, I'll put the lambs to bed mesen.' Beth leant on her crook and limped off ahead of him in disgust.

Ralph chased after her. 'I'm sorry . . . please forgive me. I forget myself. Miss Wildman, you are the one person I can be honest with and I've gone too far again. You must see I am a hopeless cause.' He pleaded with his grey eyes, fringed with thick black lashes, blinking nervously for her reply.

'This is yer last chance, sonny. We all have to choose our path at the crossroads or stand there forever going nowhere. Yer time's coming, vicar, and there's no going backwards so think on.'

Ralph sighed with relief. He needed Bethany Wildman's approval and her skill. She was a wizard with her fingers. She would soothe the devil himself in his torment as she stroked and massaged away his backache.

He looked back at her small hut, little more than a ling-roofed hovel to some eyes with its small window, earthen floor and simple fire hole. Inside it was plainly furnished with a boxed bed by the fireside. The iron and tin were polished into brass and silver and the plain deal table stained and deepened to an oaken hue. There was more wisdom and peace within these rough stone walls than ever he found in the empty vicarage where he rattled around on polished floors.

How did she guess he was on his last chance, sent out into the sticks to contemplate his calling, sent far away from the temptations of a busy city parish with its rounds of social visits and eager churchwardens' daughters who mistook his interest in them as offers of marriage? At nearly thirty, he had narrowly escaped two breach of promise suits only through some fine feather-smoothing by the bishop. Now some dis-creet rope-pulling on the bells of St Oswy's by Father, who had met Sir Edward Dacre by chance in the club in Leeds, petitioning him as a distant relative, had secured the position for his wayward son.

Still, he had to admit this hidden dale turned up many treasures; the beautiful landscape which he attempted to convey in his watercolour paintings, an amazing supply of trout which he could tickle out of the beck with his fingers, some decent horsemen to ride alongside at the local hunt and a bevy of beauties who gazed up at him from their boxed pews each Sunday. What more could a country parson wish for?

Everything was under threat. The peaceful idyll would be disturbed by incomers, strangers already demanding extensions to the church school to accommodate scores of navvy brats and a new schoolteacher from the Pastoral Aid's Educational Mission to the Deserving Poor. Even now, the teacher was en route to the post, no doubt with more expectations of his vicar's role.

No wonder the Reverend Ralph Dalesford Hardy needed to seek solace for his jangled nerves. There was no harm in Beth pleading him to take a wife to service his needs but he loved all women too much to settle with just one. How could a woman of his class, some mealy-mouthed prissy missy, satisfy his hungry appetite for comforts?

Ralph Hardy worshipped at the throne of plump pink flesh, tender as suckling pig, savouring the floury juices of sex. He found the idea of making love to an overbearing woman quite off-putting; women like Miss Bulstrode, the headmaster's sister, terrified him into a shambling cowardly retreat. She had eyed him up briefly on his arrival, when there was still some bloom to her bony cheeks, smiled weakly in his direction and scuttled back to her brother in the schoolhouse with scarcely a backward glance.

Loud voices and earnest opinions also made him back off towards the exit door when the squire's aged sister, Miss

Augusta, tried her hand at fixing him up with some of the county 'gels' during their coming-out season in the shire. All in all he was a social failure and preferred to prop up his favoured bench in the Fleece Inn to sup ale, listening to village men talking sheep, shop and fodder prices.

He tried not to let religion bother him too much. He had no time for ranters and radicals, baptist dippers and evangelicals. It was enough to say the Offices dutifully each day when it was convenient, fill in the parish registry, perform whatever service was required with half an eye on the gallery clock and keep out of the vicarage as much as possible, to discourage casual callers.

As he strode behind Beth up the grey fellside, over poor tussocky grass and rocky limestone pavements which were slippery after rain, he watched the shepherd woman limp. The cobbler in Scarsbeck had done his best to rectify the shortfall in her right leg by designing a clumpen boot which seemed to drag back her stride. It must be hard to be crippled but never once had he heard her complain. Her father, Simeon Wildman, was the Hall's shepherd, tending the estate flocks over the fells, gathering them at each point in the season for lambing, clipping the fleece, spaning the lambs from the ewes, salving and tupping. When he died, Bethany picked up his crook and carried on and no one gainsaid it. She was too valuable an asset to the village to be turned out of the cottage which stood back from the crossroads of drover's tracks, high up overlooking the hidden dale.

If truth were told, Ralph was a little afraid of her witchy

eyes: one green, flecked with amber, and the other palest icy blue and duller. He wondered if her eyesight was really as clear as she claimed. What she might lack physically was made up for by intuition, sensitivity and cunning.

Sometimes he thought she was reading his very thoughts before he did. She pierced his soul with her harsh words. Had she been young and pretty he knew he would have steered clear of her path. She was a holy woman, untouchable, and he envied her certainty, her rootedness and farsight. Beth was a weather breeder; she scanned the skies accurately and knew things others could only guess at.

The first time he had passed her cottage on horseback. She came out quietly, observing the horse and rider; standing with a lamb shoved down her sheepskin jerkin. 'Watch his fetlock!' she said, and pointed to the lower limb of the horse. 'It's weakening.' Ralph dismounted, examined the joint and sure enough there was a swelling and heat. He thanked her and introduced himself but she knew all about him and invited him in for a brew.

It was strange-smelling herbal tea, soothing on his palate and oddly relaxing. He found her presence disarming, relaxing his usual prejudice towards stern wild women with windburned cheeks and map lines of broken veins, hair straggling under a man's flat cap. She looked as old as the hills, dressed as if from a bag of rags, yet dignified and regal at the same time, utterly confusing to his senses.

When she smiled the stern mask vanished as if someone had wiped a cloth over it. He found himself confessing his sorry life story and all his woes. How unsuited he was to the life of a clergyman. How misunderstood he was. Beth sat in a ladder-backed chair rocking gently, saying nothing, hands resting on the lap as the lamb squirmed and settled down her bosom. They were strangely beautiful hands for a peasant woman: long fingers, square palms, unlined and he knew then that this was the wild one, Beth ont' Moor, 'Crow Woman', spoken of warily in the village out of earshot of the apothecary who did not hold with hedgerow medicine.

Ralph laughed at such notions as gatherers of green herbs dispensing wisdom and potions from their firesides; women who could mend a sick calf, heal a wound, stop or start a baby as the need arose, forecast the weather: surely witches by another name. The Church would have him steer clear of these dubious powers but her healing was stronger than his puny sermons would ever be and she talked common sense for all her fairy ways. She commented on his stance and diagnosed his aching back, promising to relieve his pain if he would visit her again.

Soon he preferred her quiet company to anyone else's in the dale. He responded to her teasing honesty and fiery challenges to his behaviour but conveniently forgot her warnings when his loins were stirred by his entourage of adoring housewives. He kept clear of single girls since the unfortunate misunderstandings in Leeds.

What would she ever know of the lure of a full bosom, heaving out of a lace fichu, the tantalising glimpse of a deep hollow as he leant over the third tier of the pulpit? How could he help it if the good housewife then knelt before him to receive Communion, staring boldly into his eyes, willing him to remember their naked romp over her counterpane while he stared down her dress to watch her nipples hardening in response and the skin flush with a suffusion of sunset glow. Was it any wonder it took him all his time to keep his hands from wobbling the chalice and spilling the Blood of Christ down his surplice? How could he ever think of settling down when there was such a tempting array of tender morsels, begging to be nibbled, bitten and sucked by his eager lips?

The biting wind cooled his mounting ardour and he watched Beth and her dog prepare to round up the sheep. The dog slithered and snaked over the ground, ears pricked, waiting for instructions. Beth whistled and the dog raced forward rounding on the sheep in the time-honoured fashion, nipping and rounding any stragglers. The shaggy ewes called in their lambs, which dived for cover close into the safety of the centre of the flock. Recognising the familiar smell of the shepherd, the gathering made its way down the fellside and Ralph opened up the gates and closed them again, the fresh air clearing away his fantasies, sobering him up for the coming meeting.

The squire, Sir Edward, was hoping that the visit of the railway subcontractor and his team of resident engineers would reassure the village worthies and families against needless rumourmongering in the dale. It was hoped that perhaps some villagers might offer lodgings to the more respectable operatives and trading arrangements and deliveries might sweeten the bitter pill of their invasion.

The arrival of the surveying team, back in 1869, had caused enough division, rancour and suspicion. No one wanted this hidden dale bitten through chunk by chunk. Farmer had fought farmer to keep the track off their land. Most were tenants of Scarsbeck Hall and would have little say in the route. The squire had been their ally for a while but then the lure of wayleave fees, telegraph poles and modern communications, a chance to speed up estate produce to market and the promise of a passenger halt swung the balance in favour of the Midland Railway's plans.

By this time it was rumoured that the railway company was blowing cold on the whole ambitious scheme but groups of landowners were now screaming for action and the first sods were cut down at Settle Junction. Their coming would mean more work for everyone including himself.

He would have to bury the dead, take sides in disputes, uphold the Christian values of family life and the sacredness of wedlock, refuse to christen bastard offspring. He blushed when he remembered his own effort in the pulpit last week; his throat had been as dry as his sermon to prepare the faithful for the onslaught with platitudes and false reassurances, like a padre on a battlefield.

It was no use; Bethany Wildman was stirring his heart with her warnings. It was unnerving to know that Scarsbeck was looking to him for leadership as their spiritual shepherd but he was no lionheart, just a feeble misfit. He hoped to God it was true that the Lord tempered the wind to the shorn lamb. There was a sick fear in his stomach that this idle shepherd would abandon his flock to the mercy of wolves. Perhaps the Wesleyan minister was more up to the job. Not that they mixed much.

There had been several defections down Church Brow up to the main street, to the packed chapel and the arm-waving energetic Revivalist shindigs. It warmed bodies up on frosty Sunday mornings, no doubt, singing so lustily. He noticed the dismay of his saintly churchwarden, Ezra Bulstrode, who was his unpaid curate, choirmaster and organist, as he watched from his pipe organ loft over the dwindling con-gregation with theatrical anxiety. Nothing like this bit of a threat to put farmers' bums back on their family pews, Ralph mused to himself as he returned to the cottage with Beth, cheeks aglow.

Beth grabbed a dusty overcloak from the hook on the door, threw her cap on the table and fished under the lamb basket for her battered straw bonnet; a weird concoction with black and blue feathers tucked into the hatband like a cockerel's tail, tied under her jutting chin in a crumpled bow. This fearsome decoration was Beth's token extra dressing-up for the gathering and gave her the nickname of 'Crow Woman' among the village wastrels and wags who loitered on the bench outside the ale house, clacking and gawping at all who passed by.

As they joggled down the track, Beth Wildman stared

ahead grimly, chuntering softly to herself, as if preparing herself for some solemn speech. In her hands she sifted lambs-wool through her fingers like a rosary.

'What's bothering you now?' asked the vicar.

'I dunno . . . I got one of me feelings, summat's got stirred up and I can't shake it off. Trouble's on the wind. I can smell it coming with the snow.'

Chapter Five

As daylight slid behind Whernside, as twilight shadows crept over the bony ridge of stone walls, darkening the valley, a steady trickle of bobbing carts and wagons dribbled down towards Scarsbeck. Across the fields in farmhouse kitchens there was a last-minute flurry of scrubbing off dung, flinging muddy clothing into the inner porches alongside caked boots and smelly jackets and a quick dunk in the water bowl to freshen up while the farm women, to save time, shoved sandwiches into a basket to eat on the road.

At High Butts, Blaize Lund rushed Sunter through his stew and dumplings, forced him into a clean stud collar and dragged him reluctantly to the front porch where Warwick sat on the cart impatiently, his Sunday hard hat pressing on his forehead making him want to scratch. Blaize hung back, posing in the hall mirror to titivate her own bonnet to the right angle, pulling down the net veil over her face to save what was left of her ravaged complexion.

After forty years of farm food, stout as a barrel, her figure, like her principles, was as firm as her whalebone stays, worn only on the most dignified of occasions of which this meeting was one. She jabbed a hat pin into her bonnet, buttoned up her thick jacket, for there was a bite to the wind, and out of habit tapped the weather glass noting with surprise that the mercury was rising ominously.

Sunter Lund sat stiffly beside his father, his head still aching with the screams of that silly brat cursing him. As they passed Middle Butts Farm, he looked out hopefully for signs of life; dogs shut in the byre barked a welcome and the geese hissed and fussed but the Birkett women had left earlier to pick up neighbours further down.

In Paradise camp, the resident engineer, Mr Henry Paisley, gathered his papers together nervously. He was not looking forward to tonight's affray. When the poor buggers heard that the line was now altered slightly to accommodate Sir Edward's requirements and that meant placing the viaduct right over their main street, they would be braying for his blood! The subcontractor had promised to do the explaining but he would have to show the plans and alterations and take the brunt of their ire.

What he would not be sharing with them was that it would all take much longer than expected. The ground was unreliable, tough to bore, workmen were still scarce and numbers at the camp were well under their estimation. It was just too remote a spot and Contract one would have to up the daily pay to seven shillings for skilled labourers to lure them up from Batty Green or down from Contracts two or three or even four; Appleby and the Carlisle end.

Not enough shovel and spade men meant delays and there had been too much of that already. The contractors were well over budget and Mr Hirst was sweating now in case delays cost him his profit. It was a hell of a difficult stretch to build with arches over ravines and a track to be carved around the contours of the mountainside. He did not blame navvies for preferring the bright lights of 'Sin City' at Ribblehead.

It was not much fun for him either, stranded in one of the smarter huts with Ben Robson, the other engineer, and his wife and baby, who squealed like a stuck pig all night long.

After tonight's little show, no one in Scarsbeck would offer him more comfortable lodgings in the village and he'd be lodged with the Robsons all summer. He walked through the dismal camp, watching youngsters racing around the buildings like a pack of wild dogs. The company would have to sort them out before there was a serious accident on site. They must erect a reading room for night classes, with one of the missioners teaching Sunday school even. The camp was too sparse; too few services to attract decent families.

Lanterns twinkled in the dusk through hut windows as the men settled down to a serious night's drinking. Henry Paisley strolled over to the temporary stables to collect his mount: a fine bay gelding saddled and waiting to transport him down the hill. He slung his shoulder bag across his chest, leapt onto the saddle and trotted forth with a sinking heart.

As far from Paradise as was possible, snugly set in a wooded ghyll, was the country seat of Sir Edward Dacre and his widowed sister, Augusta Hartley, who both saw it expedient not to be present in Scarsdale that month. Their land agent, Reginald Ingomells, commissioned to accompany the subcontractor, Mr Joseph Hirst, to the village assembly, was giving him a privileged tour of the terraces of Scarsbeck Hall, after a splendid tea of gammon and eggs in the estate office which occupied a corner of the cobbled yard, tucked out of sight to the rear of the grey stone building.

The subcontractor was disappointed that Sir Edward would not be gracing the meeting himself, thus leaving the agent and the railway company to convey the change of plans. This squire was obviously far above involving himself with such minor details.

Joseph Hirst stared at the mansion, lifting his stovepipe hat in awe. Scarsbeck Hall was faced with smooth rectangular blocks of stone, graced with an imposing façade overlooking the terraced lawn in which a fountain jetted from a circular pool. Four Doric pillars supported a semicircular pediment before the front door. Inside the door he could see a circular staircase of fine Dent marble, a green–grey limestone, polished to bring out the pattern of ingrained fossils in the stonework at Scarsbeck. No wonder the old squire did not want his peace or his view disturbed by noisy engines or coal dust on his flowerbeds.

As the subcontractor climbed into the sprung carriage and peered out onto the gravelled exit and an avenue of copper beech trees, burnished by fresh young growth, he groaned at the losses he must sustain, the margins of profit whittled away now in granting the wily old devil his viaduct, redirected high over the ravine to avoid disturbing the squire's land. The curving track cut from the rock face would have to be blasted and faced and the alterations mapped out onto job sheets for the engineers to follow and the navvies to build.

As they rattled down the darkening narrow lanes etched with spring growth, the land agent stared stony-faced at open fields and the small dairy farms encircling the village. He tapped to the coachman to hurry up for they were running late and he wanted to have a word with the vicar about the batting order before battle commenced.

The main street was sliced into two halves by the beck; on the right were the residences of the respectable, to the left were the rest, depending on which way the village was entered. Perched on a hilltop sat St Oswy's parish church like a little fortress overlooking the village rooftops. At the opposite end, but on the same side, standing foursquare, was the newly extended Wesleyan chapel and schoolroom, with a parquet floor and classrooms partitioned off. Its generous kitchen was ideal for social events. The national school and neat Georgian houses with walled gardens and coaching stables lined up on this side too and then, standing sentinel like a toothless dog further down the narrowing stringy lane, was the lonely Ebenezer of the Primitive Methodists: a one-room building which was only used on Sundays.

On the other side of the beck, however, stood the forces of

Mammon, a line of shop windows – butcher, baker, cobbler, apothecary and high-class grocer, a pie shop and confectioner: all that was necessary to service a remote village. Then came that scourge of the temperance movement, the Fleece, a low-slung sprawling ale house with lodging rooms upstairs and a courtyard full of barrels, horses and stabling. Cheek by jowl leant the meaner cottages, packed around the pub and down the side streets, snickets and folds with steps up to attic rooms. Hidden in the back streets were the artisan workshops, the tanner, the blacksmith, wheelwright, joiner and undertaker, living above their premises, like support troops holding up the rear.

Tonight the street was littered with vehicles and the coach had to deposit the two men where there was space, opposite the school; a no-nonsense brick building with tall Gothic windows etched with flourishes high up the walls, out of view of dreaming pupils, red brickwork clashing with the soft grey stonework of other buildings in the street. Next door, with barely an arm's width between the walls, was the matching schoolhouse, set back from the street almost with its back turned on the village. Its windows were narrower, set at an angle to exclude the light, giving it a gloomier prospect. The curtains were already drawn in the front parlour.

In the schoolhouse kitchen Cora Bulstrode was giving her live-in 'maid of all things', Susan Hindle, instructions as to coal fires, mending, and a list of jobs to keep her out of mischief until their return. Cora believed in the age-old cap and pinny principle that the eye of the mistress was worth two of her hands. It was attention to standards which set the Bulstrodes apart from the rest of the village. How else could she flaunt her status as sister to the village headmaster but by maintaining strict procedures with her staff of one and presenting her person on every occasion as an example of up-to-date modest gentility?

Tonight she was wearing a grey two-piece woollen suit edged with maroon fringing which was flattened at the front and gathered up into the latest bustle effect at the rear by a hooped panelled underskirt. Her brown hair was draped across her ears like curtains, looping up into a matching bonnet and veil in a soft burgundy. Around her neck, which was no longer one of her better features, she placed a fox tail fur wrap to keep out the draughts. Cora carried an umbrella to balance the elegant effect.

How else could she survive in this dreadful dale without her dressmaking catalogues; the gown styles she slavishly copied on her sewing machine? Being carefully turned out on every public occasion, knowing she was scrutinised by the village ladies, gave her some purpose. She felt so deprived of decent company and poor Ezra was so overburdened with duties as scarcely to be able to give her the time of day. For twenty years her fulfilment had lain in easing his path as he devoted his talents to pupils, classroom and the spiritual life of the parish.

Even now he was huddled in his study with one of his hopefuls for this year's Fawcett, a scholarship granted from the trust of one Eliza Fawcett in 1649 for the further education of a village child at the ancient grammar school, the other side of Dent.

She would have to knock on the door discreetly. He would never allow intrusions on concentration, even for a minute, but she had warned him that they must not be late. It would not be seemly for the headmaster not to be in the front row as befitted his rank. He got so carried away with his endeavours to raise up bright boys above their lowly station that the pale-faced students would stagger out with relief and dart off into the street without a backward glance or a word of thanks. Parents had great confidence in his abilities, leaving pheasants in season or the odd tray of eggs or bottles of primrose wine as humble tokens of their esteem. Ezra would sigh modestly, 'They shouldn't . . . my dear, they needn't.'

It was hard to keep up appearances on forty pounds a year and Cora would gather up all offerings to eke out their modest housekeeping. Every year they built up their hopes for the examination but the scholarship boys often dropped out and gave up their studies when harvest came and they were needed on the farm. It was bitterly disappointing for him and she watched her brother's shoulders stoop. For twenty years he had laboured in this remote vineyard, unrewarded, unrecognised, and she as his helpmeet soothed away his darkest broodings, kept delicious meals on the table and their schedule running like a clockwork automaton.

The school must be seen to support Sir Edward and the appalling Ralph Hardy who had the effrontery to call himself a priest! There would be questions about the mixing of navvy children, all born out of wedlock, if one was to believe rumour. The school must assure the village that these unfortunates would be the sole responsibility of the new teacher, Miss Herbert, in a separate classroom to keep any contamination away.

Cora Bulstrode had made few preparations for the arrival of the said teacher that night; a cold collation of Sunday's left-over joint and some tired fruit cake. The teacher was late and there was no time now to pamper her arrival. Miss Bulstrode did not want another female in the household challenging her authority, disrupting Ezra's routine with requests. With Susan in the attic bedroom, the third bedroom was used as Cora's sitting-cum-sewing room with tapestry frame and sewing machine ready for her use. This gave Ezra the front parlour as his library and study and no one went in there without his permission. Susan was allowed to clean only under supervision.

This was no place for a teacher to bring her camp dirt back into the schoolhouse every day. The less they had to do with her the better. She must find lodgings elsewhere, nearer the camp perhaps.

Miss Herbert had been imposed on them as part of the new curriculum which enforced school attendance for all under the Education Act of 1870. Even navvy brats had to be taught the basics. It was getting too much for her brother, who did not enjoy the best of health despite his portly body and robust complexion.

Sitting in a stuffy chapel hall with menials and workmen

was not how she would choose to spend her evening but they must put in an appearance, however brief, answer any relevant questions and then slide away back to their fireside for cocoa and toasted muffins. Cora could feel one of her headaches creeping round behind her right eye, aching and throbbing at the side of her temple. There was no time now to make a cup of camomile tea or a sup of something soothing from the apothecary's bottle. She knocked firmly on the study door and shouted the time through the keyhole. 'We're going to be late!'

Across the beck in the line of higgledy-piggledy stone cottages, leaning heavily in the direction of the Fleece, village men stirred from their plates of bread and scrape, cold meat and pickle, tapped out their clay pipes and rummaged for a muffler to wrap round thick necks, opened the tilting front door onto a cobbled street. Some took one look at the crowd of horses and carts lining the beck and the bobbing heads of tradesmen crossing the blue slate stone slabs which some wag called a bridge and headed straight in the opposite direction for a stool in the taproom. It were nowt to do with them, this railway job. It warn't putting gravy on their Yorkshire puddings. It was squire and his cronies milking this cow all right so why bother going to hear some blatherhead clatterfarting about nowt as would bother them?

In the chapel back kitchen the copper boiler, lit hours ago, had water on the boil already and the tea urns were stewing and mashing into a thick brew to be eked out by kettles for the refreshments. The coal-fired stove was red-hot in the corner of the assembly hall and the fug made rivulets of condensation stream down the windows. The Methodist ladies, bedecked with embroidered lace-edged pinnies over their woollen two-pieced dresses, darted and flitted anxiously, bonnets tipping jauntily with each exertion. Teacups were checked for dust, starched linen cloths stretched over trestle tables inspected for any creases. It was an honour for the chapel to host this gathering. Just the ticket to give some of the Mothers' Union lot at St Oswy's summat to chew on as they eyed the spread of cakes and fancies, the huge variety of home-made biscuits, featherlight and crisp, waiting for the interval.

The minister's wife smiled and nodded benignly, her hands clasped as if in prayerful thanksgiving as row after row filled up until there were just a few seats at the back. The air was stifling, full of noisy chatter and expectancy. The minister, Reverend Pringle, was busy showing the dignitaries to the podium, trying not to knock off the pot plants and aspidistras which members of the Women's Bright Hour who met mid-weekly for devotions and gossip had filched from windowsills all over Scarsdale to decorate this occasion.

The village was crawling out of the woodwork and no mistake, but the vicar was late as usual and as he was chairing the proceedings they would have to delay the Midland manager, who was mopping his brow and fiddling with the blackboard, anxious to get his lecture underway.

At last the 'late' Ralph Hardy, as he was often nicknamed, dashed red-faced and flustered down the gangway, apologising that he had had to go back to the vicarage to put on his dog collar; a none-too-clean stock, the minister's wife could not help noticing. What a difference a wife would make in that rambling old vicarage!

Then she noted with dismay that the wild-haired Crow Woman was standing at the back in that ridiculous hat. Whatever had she ventured off the moor for? Mrs Pringle hoped there would not be a scene.

Chapter Six

'Ladies and gentlemen, thank you for being so patient with me. There is a lot to digest in these plans,' said the sub-contractor, mopping his brow with relief.

'And thee's given us bellyache, right enough!' shouted the landlord of the Fleece, Wally Stackhouse, standing to his feet. 'You've preached nigh on over an hour just to tell us that we've got to stomach a girt bridge over us heads, shaking the very foundations and giving us headaches every time one of them wagons rolls over the job. How shall we get us sleep of a night, with steam engines roaring past our windows, spewing out their gubbins? I come here tonight like most of these good folk to hear how you intended to keep them savages out of our hair! And now you break this piss 'n' wind over us . . .'

'Mr Stackhouse, please, remember we are mixed company,' interrupted Reverend Pringle, blushing.

'Oh aye? Very mixed up we are. Them who'll have to put

up with navvies building tracks over their privy wall and them, three mile up the dale, who've made sure that no soot falls on their roses.' His reply produced a chorus of ayes, nays and, 'You tell 'em, Wally.'

'What about our washing?'

'Our cows won't let down their milk and our daughters'll not be safe in their beds, once you let them navvies out the camp!' yelled a red-faced farmer's wife whose farm would now be fifty yards closer to the track. 'It's a disgrace! The squire can't just trample over us as if we were horse muck.'

The vicar stared down from the platform at all his parish-ioners, trying to avoid Liddy Braithwaite's cow corner where the dairy farmers sat en masse. In the middle were the sheep contingent and the worthies mainly took up the front rows; candles were flickering and cups were rattled and clinked, fury raising a bigger head of steam in the hall than would ever run on wheels. He saw Widow Birkett steeling herself to rise up, her black bonnet sombrely edged with purple ribbon, while the fair Ellen, clean-scrubbed and shining, nudged her sleeping sister Mercy off her lap to hold her mother in support.

'Shame on you, Reg Ingomells, to be a party to this rob-bery in daylight. My Jim'll be turning in his grave to see you take sides against a poor widow, letting her lose twenty acres of best pasture to feed the vanity of owd Squire Dacre. You know what a struggle we've been having this past year ...' Annie Birkett burst into wails, comforted by her daughters, but her sobbings stunned the room into an uneasy silence.

'I'm sorry, Mistress Birkett, but the meeting will be closed now. If any of you have queries ...' Ralph raised his head to see Beth Wildman hobbling swiftly down the gangway in her black cloak and feathers like one of the Furies. Ezra Bulstrode, nonplussed by this dramatic entrance, shook his head at his sister who flapped her agenda paper like a fan, wishing she could dispose of the animal round her neck.

'Hang on, vicar, I've not said my piece yet,' shouted Beth up to the platform, wagging a long finger at each one of the speakers in turn. 'I'm giving you a warning. Carve up these fells at your peril. It ain't natural, like it ain't natural for us to go faster than a horse. It disturbs things that should be left well alone ... the spirits in these hills won't like it and they'll fight back at us, mark my words. Don't wake'm, leave'm be or else ...'

'Stop that superstitious nonsense, Miss Wildman, don't embarrass us with your ignorant rantings,' snapped John Pringle, waving her away. 'This is a grand scientific scheme to bring prosperity to our dale once more. The company has assured us that they will be as quick as they can and will deliver the land back to us unharmed. No one will know they were ever there. Have you not been listening to a word that's been said?'

'Perhaps if the viaduct was at your end of the street with the walls of the manse rattling your china every night, you would not be so eager to welcome such progress, minister. Let me tell you, they'll fill our graveyard for us afore they go; fill it so full we'll have to push back the walls to get ours and theirs sided away, side by side with offcumdens. Put that in yer pipe and smoke it.'

'Stop this at once! You overreach our patience with this devilment. Shut up, woman, or you'll be removed,' came the reply.

'Tell 'em, vicar, I see what I see. Trouble on the wind. It's coming with the snow . . .' Beth marched to the back of the hall and flounced out of the door. Ralph kept his head down but banged the gavel onto the desk.

'I think we've heard all there is on this matter for the moment and the gentlemen will see that we are very moved on the subject. I'm sure we can rub along nicely once we get to know each other.'

There were scornful titters and booings but the Crow Woman's diatribe was not to be taken lightly. She could put the fear of God in the stoutest heart and wither a man's tackle with scarcely a blink if she was thwarted. Someone would make sure she got a lift back safely just to make sure they were not one of the doomed, destined to be mown down in the coming storm.

Some of the ladies suggested another brew-up before their trek back up the dale but the men had other ideas and sidled out across the beck to warm their stiff backsides in front of the fire in the Fleece.

'You did well there, Wally, to stand up and tell 'em even if it won't change owt. If the squire's sealed it all up there's little we can do but stomach it. Happen we'll soon get used to the racket but I didn't reckon on building works down the street,' said the baker, wondering if he did an extra tray of bread loaves whether he could sell them on to the workmen for their snap.

'Aye, and digging is thirsty work,' smiled the landlord to himself, wondering if he ought to order some extra barrels for knock-off time and keep spares in the cellar for discreet carry-outs after dark.

'Birketts and Lunds must be pig-sick,' whispered Dicky Braithwaite as he watched them sidle over to the bar for a jug of best ale. Sunter sipped his tankard slowly, savouring the warm nutty flavour of the brew. The vicar had come in for his usual warm-up, looking red-faced and uneasy with his neighbours, hoping he had not offended too many in the village with his conciliatory remarks. He wondered if the camp could raise a cricket team and give the village some practice on the green.

Suddenly the taproom door opened and a group of strangers seemed to fill the room, workmen in donkey jackets and red mufflers with flat caps and throaty accents. The room fell silent as the locals stepped back at their entrance; the size of their brawny backs, bully beef necks and leathery fists shrank any commenting to a few raised eyebrows and winks around the smoky room.

Wally Stackhouse pretended to ignore them, busying himself with filling up the ale jug from under the bar. He was in no mood to humour navvies after tonight's revelations.

The tallest man by a head, standing six foot five in his hobnailed boots, banged on the bar in a jocular fashion and glanced over the assembly casually, lingering on each of the features of the local men, eyeing them one by one as if he was looking for somebody. He smiled a beery smile at his mates; his eyes had a foxy glint in the firelight and his bare head almost touched the ceiling. 'They dinna want to take our money,' he said as he glanced over to Sunter Lund and returned to examine the spotty face and the way his hair flopped to his eyebrows. He nudged his mate. 'That's the one, I'm thinking. It's braw bricht nicht, the nicht ...' He winked and nodded in Sunter's direction. The lad, looking puzzled at being singled out by the dark-eyed stranger, turned to his dad.

'He must be one of them furriners, speaking Dutch.' Sunter swallowed the dregs of his pint and made for the door with a 'see thee' to his mates who were rooted to the fireside.

'Not so fast, sonny, not so fast. Would I be right in thinking you're the best stonewaller in the district?' asked Fancy MacLachlan. Sunter stopped in his tracks at the compliment.

'Who's asking?' He looked to his father for support.

'It's just that I'm needing an opinion on something and you will ken just what I have in mind. Come away outside and prove me right.' Fancy bent under the low lintel of the door, putting his arm around the lad's shoulders as if they were old mates, which caused enough curiosity among the taproom to have everyone else troop into the darkness after them. Even Ralph was intrigued to know why the giant should single out the unremarkable Lund boy for such attention.

Outside, the Lund and Birkett women were still chewing the cud of the railway meeting with others loitering on the street and they drifted towards the crowd outside the Fleece. The navvy dipped into a corner by the wall and produced a sack which he dumped straight into Sunter's hands. 'This is for you. I am right in thinking you were up in yon fields opposite Paradise, the forenoon? Go on, open it up. It won't bite ye!'

Sunter shook out the sack and jumped back. 'What the!' he exclaimed as the stiff corpse of the little whippet fell onto the ground, its gashed swollen body for all to view. There was a gasp from Mercy Birkett, who buried her head in Mrs Birkett's lap, but Ellen stepped forward for a closer inspection.

The red-haired navvy caught a glimpse of pity in her sparkling eyes, a flash of golden tendrils framing this noble face, two plaits entwined across the top of a head on which perched an apology for a hat, tied under her chin with blue ribbon. For a second he stood distracted by the sight of such wholesome beauty and wished himself a hundred miles away from this confrontation.

'Is this yer handiwork, sonny, murdering a wee bairn's doggie?'

'It were worrying sheep. They'd no right to be on our land.' He looked again to his father who stood behind him, nodding.

'Aye, he's right. We shoot owt as steps in a field full of lambs. We've a living to make. That's the rules and yer in the country now, mister, so mind who you accuse,' said Warwick, pointing his finger angrily.

'It wasna' doing any harm, man, and he kens that fine. Just a chit of a kid and a wee dog and he killed it afore the bairn. You should be ashamed of yerself.' Fancy towered over the two men. 'Any fool can see it's a wee pup, no a wolf!'

'It was on my land . . . so bugger off!'

'It was our land not yours, Sunter Lund, and you should have told us,' cried Ellie as she stepped out of the crowd.

'Shut yer face, Ellie, it's nowt to do with you,' snapped her cousin.

'That's no way to talk to a lady!' Fancy's leathery fist went whacking into Sunter's jaw with a crack, sending the young farmer flying backwards onto the laps of two old men cowering on the pub bench, sending hats, dogs, people scattering in all directions and the vicar scuttling forward to see if he could calm the affray.

'Gentlemen, please! This is no way to settle an argument.' He was pushed sideways into Dicky Braithwaite's wife who clasped him eagerly and tried to whisper in his ear the time of their next assignation while Blaize Lund knelt over her boy wiping his bloody face with a lace handkerchief, crying, 'Fetch the constable! My boy's being murdered! Don't just stand there gawping at the peepshow! Bray 'em, Warwick! You see . . . not here five minutes and look what's happening, See what we're in for with jailbirds and savages on our doorstep. Someone fetch Constable Firth.'

Ellen Birkett stared up at the handsome face of the navvy, at the deep dark eyes and grinning mouth. 'What my cousin did was wrong but belting him won't make things better.'

She tried to sound cross but then softened as she saw him tenderly put the dog back in the sack. 'You'd better go quickly before they arrest you.' The navvy men were already pulling their mate by his jacket but he was reluctant to break the spell between them.

Widow Birkett, sensing danger, dragged her daughter from the scene. 'Come away, Ellen, this minute! We must get Mercy to bed. 'Tis too late for her as it is!' Fancy smiled a long lingering smile at the two women then raced across the beck into the darkness, with a banshee roar of satisfaction which echoed all the way down the street. As Ellie stared in his direction an anxious mother tugged her sleeve. 'I told you afore. Don't you even look in that direction again, missy. You're not too old to feel the back of my hand.'

As Ralph Hardy shook his head at the kerfuffle around him he felt the first thick flakes of snow on his cheek and watched the feathers settling on the grass verges and sandstone rooftops, blanching the village into a scene from a Christmas card.

He pulled up his collar and turned up the footpath to St Oswy's cold vicarage, Beth Wildman's warning whispering in his ear. Trouble was coming with the snow.

Chapter Seven

The snow swirled and wrapped itself around the hills in great swathes, beating savagely against the struggling bands of carts, lashing the ponies with icy whipcords causing them to stumble and falter, blowing the drifts into huge pillars which closed off the dale track behind, encircling the wagon train, entombing them in a sinister world of whiteness.

'This is as far as we go, ma'am,' ordered the irate driver of the horse and cart to his charge who sat bolt upright like a snow-woman. 'We should have stopped at the Gearstones Inn, like I said. Now we are doomed if we don't take shelter in that barn across there.' He swung the lantern in the direction of the wall where a shippon encrusted in snow stood cocooned in a snowdrift.

'I was not going to spend the night in a public house, Mr Cleghorn. My principles would not allow such a thing,' came a firm reply from the snow-woman.

'Principles won't keep us warm in a blizzard or save my

poor Nippa from a broken leg, beg pardon. It's lucky I knows these lanes like the back of me hand or we would be found stiff as boards tomorrow, frozen to the spot,' argued Isaac Cleghorn.

Would foolhardy offcumdens never learn to respect these hills? You could be hale and hearty one minute and dead of cold a few hours later if you took the wrong track into a bog or got caught ill-clad in a storm.

The woman sitting beside him might be one of these educated schoolmarms dressed up like a nun; a brave little filly, no doubt, but he was not risking the life and limb of his pony just so she didn't have to smell an ale jug. Anyroad where she were going she'd have to bath in beer if she wanted to stay fresh! There were others to think of, following behind in makeshift wagons, frozen, frightened and lost in the snow.

The convoy of sorry travellers slithered into each other with relief and made for their shovels to dig out the entrance to the side door, stamping their feet, gathering belongings, unharnessing the beasts to give them cover for the night. The door, once opened, led into a line of cow stalls where cattle mooed in alarm at the unexpected invasion and the travellers squelched up to the ankles into steamy dung and straw.

The walls were encrusted with dried cow muck which one Irishman quickly started to pick off into thick lumps to put on a makeshift fire as coal. They found the main hall of the barn empty of winter fodder, just a few bits of straw and hay left. The roof was sound enough and the walls thick, the warmth of the cattle and a small fire would keep them safe for the night. A blizzard in late April. How could such a thing be?

Mr Cleghorn thought it his duty to put them straight on a few matters. 'You'll have to expect owt in these parts: frost, hail, thunder, lightning. Whatever the Good Lord in His Wisdom throws at you. This isn't the Garden of Eden even if it is called Paradise camp. That's just the contractor's little joke to get you up here, I reckon.'

Miss Herbert, newly appointed teacher to Scarsbeck school, funded by the Pastoral Aid's Educational Mission to the Deserving Poor, descended slowly from the cart unaided, her hooped skirt sagging with an apron of snow. She tried to feel confident but the cold had seeped through her four petticoats, right into her bones. As soon as her smooth-soled bootees touched the icy pathway she found herself face down, licking the snow while the hooped skirt rose up in an ark behind her. Thankfully there was no one behind her to witness this shaming. Perhaps she would have to reconsider trailing skirts and feminine accessories in such hostile terrain.

Wiping the snow from her half-cloak, straightening her poky bonnet to a less rakish angle, she staggered into the barn and felt the hot foetid mess pouring into her boots. The stench hit her sensitive nostrils; that fruity *mélange* of beasts, sweaty men, unclean clothes, the smoke of a struggling fire stung her eyes into tears. This was not the adventure she was expecting when she left Ingleton Station and took tea with the vicar and his wife at Chapel le Dale. She knew now they had lingered too long over the tiered cake-stand and refills in bone china teacups. The delay cost them the remaining daylight and now a storm had overtaken the wagon train to Scarsdale, stranding her in a smelly barn instead of a warm bed in the schoolhouse at Scarsbeck.

Think positively, praise the Lord in adversity, she scolded herself. She was safe, dry and there would be warm milk from a cow if all else failed. There was one other young woman resting by the wall so she had a chaperone of sorts. The poor Bulstrodes would be worried sick. Perhaps they had sent out a search party for her and she would be rescued, ere long, from this uncomfortable lodging. Perhaps she was being over-optimistic.

The Lord always provides what you need but not always what you want. That was obviously today's lesson.

She found herself a corner alone to shake out her wet outer garments, hanging them over the stalls, and rummaged in her overnight valise for her Paisley shawl to keep her chest snug. She rooted out her unsigned letter and sat down to read it again.

My dear Aunt Jane,

It is with heavy heart that I recall our sad parting yesterday. I would have wished my parents had made the effort to accompany me to the station but the events of the past few weeks have obviously made their feelings plain.

How could they imagine that I would ever consider Frank Warbuoys to be my life's companion? He was always such a weak cup of tea from a pair of plain teapots. I found him neither hot nor cold in his courtship, mostly lukewarm in his opinions, tasteless in his appearance and wishy-washy in his theology.

Thankfully I have other options and the timing of the Mission visit was godsent for this purpose, giving me a chance to escape from the gloomy atmosphere. I know that my parents feel I have ruined any chance of marriage, having refused the one firm offer and not having the physical graces needed to attract other attention.

I grew accustomed early to the fact that I was a plain child of small squat stature and dark appearance. I have few appealing features; a mouth too wide and eyes set far apart with thick brows on a pale face. Added to this intensity of eye and gruff voice is my questioning spirit and argumentative nature. I know these are not qualities suited to a sensitive suitor like Frank. Now everyone is embarrassed by my refusal. I must do what I feel is right and leave the arena of conflict. So here I am stuck out on a bleak moorside in a blizzard.

I had hoped they would give their last-minute blessing to the tremendous task I have undertaken on behalf of the Pastoral Aid. I'm not playing at being a missionary, honestly. I'm not deserting my class by choosing to teach in a remote navvy town with families who do not enjoy the benefits of wedlock. I know it seems the height of foolishness to you all, to sacrifice all the advantages of my elevated position in following 'some fanciful whim', as Papa said.

This is the Lord's doing and I must obey His call. I will

*not succumb to disease, debauchery or worse for I am safe in
the everlasting arms of the Lord who at all times will be my
Guardian.*

*How can they say I will be unchaperoned and untutored
when I shall be with Sister Bulstrode and her brother in the
schoolhouse and the vicar of the parish will be my chaplain
and his family will no doubt take me under their wing? All
my needs will be supplied.*

*And I have my manual of instruction from the Mission
itself which is a fulsome document, alongside the prayer book,
Bible and Commentary, and my journal to record mission
work. Do not be ashamed to let it be known that I have a
vocation for missionary service not marriage. I am twenty-four
and surely old enough to pursue my own decisions on these
matters.*

*If they choose, as they threaten, to dispossess me of any
worldly inheritance, then so be it. I am thrown then on the
tender mercies of the Lord Who shall not be found wanting in
that department.*

*Mama will worry that I do not have the necessities for
survival in such a rough climate but I packed my parasol and
will wear a veil at all times to protect my complexion from
sun stains. I managed to obtain rubberised overshoes and will
wear red flannel undergarments at all times. I have packed a
watercolour painting box, a writing compendium and a box
of Nanny Brewer's herbals, lozenges, tonics and remedies
to add to my toiletries, some camphor candles against moths
in my trunk and enough edifying literature to keep me from*

temptation on warmer days when I might wish to wander out unchaperoned to explore the beauty of God's creation.

I am sorry that you all find the idea of my mission simplistic and very unsophisticated, my aim is to give poor children access to the written Word of God. I realise they will never take kindly to the idea that their only child has chosen to abandon her genteel existence for plain habit and a life of hardship and poverty.

I have not taken legal vows but in my heart I am pledging my life to His Higher Service. Why does everyone call this a waste of upbringing?

Please do not disregard my epistles, but look upon my efforts as journals of a soul who is searching out her salvation in fear and trembling with hopes as tall as spears. I beg you do not let them contact Sir Edward Dacre or Miss Augusta. I want no contact with county life but a simple, unadorned, anonymous existence as Christ's obedient servant.

I have always enjoyed being a Sunday school teacher and the extra training given to me by the Mission will be valuable. I was weary of a social life devoid of purpose.

Yours in continuing disobedience,

Always your loving niece,

Miss Herbert put aside her letter to survey the groups who chattered and shivered in separate corners. Someone lit an oil lamp and another began to play a mouth organ. She heard the clink of pots and did not dare to look to see if any of the navvy men were imbibing spirits. Her eyelids drooped as the wearisome travel took its toll. It was going to be a long uncomfortable night.

Suddenly there came a strange wailing from the young woman who had hidden herself in the darkest corner of the barn, like an animal in pain, shattering the comfortable low chatter with a loud moaning cry.

Miss Herbert shot up out of her dozing, jolted and disorientated for a second. Where was she? What was she doing in this smoky byre? The driver, a little man with wide shoulders built on a slope, seemed to lurch to one side, doffing his cap as he crossed the room to summon her aid. 'I think you should come, miss, women's trouble, I reckons . . . It's on its way with all that joggling.' Isaac Cleghorn was fumbling for the words as they stepped over the men sitting on the floor smoking baccy in long clay pipes, reclining around the little fire.

The girl lay on some sacking, sweating, her belly swollen into a dome under her grubby skirt. 'Me time's come. I can feel it down there ready to drop. Help me, please! I've never done it afore.'

'Where's your husband? How can he let you travel alone in such a condition?' answered the teacher, aware that she now was expected to deal with the situation.

'My fella's tramped ahead to get a hut and sign on. You'll have to give us a hand. Aah! I can't stop the pains.'

'No, I don't suppose you can, but why did you not get out at Batty Green? There's a doctor there, I'm sure,' replied the schoolmistress tartly.

'What do I want a doctor for? I'm only having a babby.'

Miss Herbert prayed for a miracle. There was nothing in her manual of instructions about delivering babies. In fact she had no idea how human offspring actually made their way into the world. She had seen kittens suckling and a lamb slithering out of a sheep's backside but surely the Creator had designed womankind some more dignified exit hole. Surely the belly button must be the place but she did not relish having to open up the girl's stomach. That was definitely a doctor's job. She turned to give her orders to the driver to fetch a knife and some clean linen, rushing to her own bag to find some lace-edged hand towels to prepare the bed for the coming baby. She watched in horror as Mr Cleghorn dipped a sharp knife in a bottle of spirits but now was not the time to protest. She was going to need all the support she could get if she was to perform major surgery.

Her first task was to demand some screening to keep these delicate proceedings private. Someone produced a moth-eaten patchwork quilt which they strung across as a curtain. An oil lamp was lit by the makeshift straw bedding.

'That's just the ticket!' She prayed heavenward for some guidance and the navvies fell silent at the sight of the little woman in a Bible-black hooped skirt and poky bonnet standing with her head bowed over the girl who moaned, 'Hurry, I can't hold it in much longer . . .'

Isaac Cleghorn smiled to himself for as a father of seven he had seen enough rough-and-ready birthings to do it blindfold. This poor soul hadn't a clue but wouldn't take kindly to being told, so he popped his head around the screen and whispered, 'My wife likes to sit up a bit near the end, get herself into a good dropping position, ma'am, to get the best purchase, if you don't mind me saying so . . .' He smiled and the women were treated to a waft of dreadful breath and the sight of two broken teeth glinting in the soft light.

'Thank you, Mr Cleghorn, I'm sure the girl will find that useful. This is my first confinement, as you've guessed.'

'But not your last, Miss Herbert, perhaps one day you'll be blessed, you being nobbut a lass yourself,' came the cautious response.

'No, no, I'm married to the Lord's service. I had no idea she was . . .' Miss Herbert could not say the words 'with child' in front of a man.

'Having a bairn? Why should you? Ladies do not talk of such things and now you will bring a new soul into this dreary world. A baby born in a shippon just like it says in the Bible.' They all smiled.

'Oh yes! How good of you to remind us. What a strange coincidence. Where do I put the knife?' She decided perhaps she might show her ignorance a bit.

'Only to the birthing cord, miss, after it's born, to separate them. She could bite it off herself if she had to though, like any animal.'

The teacher looked at the driver with new respect and then realised with horror he was telling her that humans were animals after all and the nether regions were where she would have to concentrate her efforts. For the first time in her life she questioned her Maker's modus operandi. Out of the bottom indeed! How humiliating, and how vulnerable was this girl, lying prostrate in pain at the mercy of gravity to deliver her child.

'What's your name?' She smiled encouragingly, softening her crackly voice.

'Mary Ann, miss, just Mary will do,' gasped the girl. She looked no more than twenty, with tired eyes and damp sandy hair, and smelt of stale sweaty armpits and boiled onions on her clothing. The girl lifted up her skirt with her eyes closed, embarrassed to show that she wore no dividing drawers with a slit in the gusset. There was only a chemise, more holy than godly and horror of horrors two holes appeared, the front one swollen red, oozing water and blood with a dark dome of wet hair pulsating with each contraction.

Miss Herbert gulped, winged a silent prayer to the ceiling, removed her kid gloves, carefully rolled up her sleeves and got to work. 'I think the baby's head is coming down! Is that right, Mr Cleghorn?' she whispered through the curtain to her instructor. Mary struggled up, trying to lean over her bump to see for herself, but then fell back as the next contraction swept over her.

The silent audience behind the quilt strained to catch any progress; then the girl started to push hard with grunts and the head moved.

'Yes! Yes. That's the stuff to give the troops! It moved, it really did!' shouted Miss Herbert, beginning to enjoy her task.

The audience cheered them on. 'Come on, Mary, give a push for Brummagem Bill and Salty Sam.' The girl took another deep breath and almost burst her eyeballs to shift the football out of her groin. The head was sticking tight.

'Turn it a bit if you can . . .' came the next set of instructions from the quilt and the pupil did as she was told with her eyes shut.

'Keep going, Mary. One more big push and . . .'

The girl yelled out, 'Maammy!' The baby shot out with a slither into a pool of liquid, purple with rage, screwing up its wrinkled face to give a roar of indignation at this undignified entrance into the world. At the sound of the baby the navvies cheered and banged their tin plates, Mary cried and Miss Herbert found tears rolling down her cheeks. Tears of relief and thanksgiving that she had not made an utter fool of herself, tears of amazement as she watched the purple baby flesh turn to a warm pink. She raised the baby for the mother to see.

'Is it all right? Let's see. What is it? Boy or girl?' As Miss Herbert had never seen bare flesh before, she wasn't too sure.

'Give it here. It's a girl, a little cunt. What the hell, she's a bonny, bonny babe. Thank you, miss!'

'Praise the Lord for Mr Isaac Cleghorn and his nous!' came the weary reply as she wondered what a cunt was.

'Nowt to it, miss, and do call me Cleggy. You must clear up the rest of the gubbins when it comes away and we'll bury it later.' She cut the cord, amazed that the baby was untroubled, swaddled the child tightly in one of her own linen towels and passed it to the mother.

'Here, miss, what's yer name? I'd like to name her after you, what's yer Christian name?' asked Mary, opening her shirt and pushing the baby to her breast.

'Miss Zillah Herbert,' answered the missionary. 'From the Bible. It means a shady place.' There was a pause and the girl asked, 'Just the one then?'

'Zillah Jane, actually.' There was a sigh of relief.

'That's better, that'll do. Jane ... I can call her Janey. Ta very much. Here, Janey, meet yer auntie Zillah.'

'We must get her baptised when we reach Scarsbeck village. Nothing like getting them off to a good start,' said Zillah Herbert, not one to miss an opportunity.

'We ain't churchy folk. Us navvies have our own ways.' Mary was unimpressed at such a fancy notion.

'But Janey is my responsibility too. If I brought her into the world, I want to see things done properly. I'm sure the vicar will love to dip her in holy water and welcome her into his flock. Aren't you?'

'I suppose so,' sighed tired Mary as she suckled the baby. Watching the creature nuzzle into the breast and forage for the nipple with hungry lips like a starving animal was strangely disturbing for Zillah. It was as if her own breasts felt tweaked in response and her body flooded with a yearning. For a second she was transfixed, wishing the baby hers and that she could have her own child someday.

'Get thee behind me, Satan,' she prayed. Her life was now dedicated to one thing only: saving souls for Christ. There was no place for distractions. The decision was made. Zillah rose and went over to the fireside where someone handed her a warm cup. She sniffed it suspiciously. Was it the cup that cheers but does not inebriate? A welcome mash of tea or Satan's brew? She was almost too exhausted to care. What a start to her Mission work, and Janey would be her first convert.

Chapter Eight

In the days before the storm blew over Scarsdale, the ewes guzzled greedily on the meagre pasture of the top moor, cotton grass, heather, bilberry shoots and grass. Later they trooped down the fells sensing change in the weather, instinct making them beat a familiar path down towards the lower slopes. The flock was caught by the blinding ferocity of gale and ice, taking shelter where it could in hidden clefts or bunched together behind a wall, frozen, climbing on each other's backs; lambs numb and weak, bleating in vain for succour.

The storm lashed over their heads, gathering up the dale in a blanket of suffocating whiteness, bending the branches of the trees under the weight of leaves and snow.

From the vicarage window, frosted with icy ferns, Ralph Hardy peered down at his parish which floated like a misty island in a sea of snow. Far out on the crossroads, Beth Wildman was fast in, knitting bump-wool stockings with her knitting stick sheathed into her belt, scarcely bothering to leave the fireside, with Lad the sheepdog, allowed into the warmth, wrapping himself over her feet like a rug. The navvies would pay for warmth in their boots and she needed some silver in her purse.

At Paradise camp a relief kitchen was hastily organised, with copper boilers heating vats of mutton stew and dumplings. Mally Widdup found herself peeling potatoes and Tizzy carried bowls of broth to Granda Fettle and his cronies holed up in a living wagon, with a stove burning anything which was not tied down.

Up the lane, the newest resident of Scarsdale nestled warm as toast at her mother's breast, unaware of the wilderness trapping them firmly in the byre with only snow water to boil and loaves and fishes sort of sharing; oatmeal porridge, treacle and stale bread which Miss Herbert cooked over the fire like a demon possessed, spurred on by reading 'Feed my lambs': the text for the day she had plucked at random from her Bible.

Across the valley at Middle Butts, the Birkett women had so much spare milk it was only sensible to make butter. The work camps would no doubt place orders for local produce and their butter was renowned for its flavour. Ellie churned and churned all day but the blessed butter tub had gone to sleep. Not a lump! Then Mother in exasperation popped in some warm milk and at last she could feel progress. Ellie leant dreamily on the handle, smiling at a vision of that red-haired Scotsman, hoping Mother would not guess the secret burning inside her bosom. It was her fault the butter wouldn't come.

A mile above them at High Butts Farm, the Lunds stared gloomily out onto the fell with sinking hearts. It was all they could manage to dig out their porch to see to the stock in the by-land and byres, dragging out precious fodder on a wooden sled to the stricken beasts. For two days and nights the blizzard raged on, relentlessly, unforgiving like a plague trapping everything fast in.

On the third day came the thaw, shrinking the snowline, making rooftops steam, flooding the cellars of Scarsbeck with the overflowing torrent of a quick meltdown. For days afterwards, the sun blazed in an ink-blue sky as if to apologise for the fickleness of climate which made fools and bankrupts of many a small farmer up the dale.

The Lund men were out at break of day. Lawson, the grandfather, plagued with his 'skiatics', could only manage light work; Warwick, the son, went out prodding with poles into the remaining drifts to find their flock.

Sunter, the heir, took their best sheepdog, an instinctive 'setter' which could search out his flock even on top of the snowdrifts while Sunter beat a rescue path through the snow with a sled of fodder to save the lambs. The dog sat on a drift patiently and the lad dug furiously, only to find a pile of bodies and a weak old ewe which could not even stand. The stupid animals had piled up on top of each other and there were no survivors.

Sunter stood grim-faced, his mouth in a tight thin line of

rage, his heart sickened at the loss of their harvest of spring lambs. Everything was going wrong in his life. He felt as trapped as the bloody sheep. The hills were his prison. There was no beauty in this barren country for him, only loathing and fear. His plan to escape was floundering because of old Bulstrode and never taking that stupid exam all those years ago. How he hated the man for setting him up to fail just to satisfy his own need for glory. He felt sick at the thought of him. Now he would be fit only for farm work.

His second plan, to woo Ellie Birkett and take over Middle Butts, was hindered by her obvious dislike of him and his appearance. Not that he really wanted her. All human flesh made him creep and he despised her love of animals. They were all stupid. Was it any wonder he needed to beat them into submission?

Now they were ruined by a freak storm and it was all the fault of that navvy brat from the camp. Had she put the evil eye on him as she promised? His heart was thumping with fear, indignation and humiliation that a slip of a child had power over his plans. As for that navvy Jock who had shamed him before the village, he would be getting even with him as well. There must be a way to destroy all of them. 'Bide yer time, revenge is best eaten cold. I'll get even with them if it's the last thing I do!'

Clipping

Summer 1871

Every valley shall be exalted,
and every mountain and hill shall be made low:
and the crooked shall be made straight,
and the rough places plain.

Isaiah, chapter 40, v. 4

Chapter Nine

'You will go to school, Tizzy Widdup, or I'll tell Fancy yer a lass, not a tea masher! I'm cheesed off with you tagging on to my shirt when work's slack. I've got a round of huts to do for up the posh end. If they take one look at your scruffy clothes they'll not think my laundry up to much, so buzz off. School'll pull yer down a peg or two. Yer getting too big for yer boots since you got yerself fixed up with Fancy's gang. If I hear you say Fancy says this . . . Fancy did that . . . He's only a shovel man, not God Almighty, and he's too big for his boots as well, swaggering across this camp as if he's cock of the dock. Our dad would soon sort him out,' sighed Mally as she pounded the dolly tub with the stick, twisting it from side to side. 'Here, be useful and put these through the mangle. Not a word in the camps. I reckon Ironfist's sloped off with another woman or changed his name.'

'Never. We don't know where all the tunnel tigers is

working yet, wait on a while and we'll find him. He wouldn't just dump us. He still thinks we're in Leeds, remember?'

'Who're you kidding? He ain't bothered with us for months. Since our mam did a bunk with his best mate, he's never looked the road we're on. It's just us three and Granda is going doolally. He don't know the day of the week, he's that betwaddled and pickled in ale. If I want to get a fella and my own hut I want you set up, not round my neck, so jolly well get yerself down to Miss Herbert's new class. They've put on a cart to take you all down to Scarsbeck school.

'I hear she did a good job with birthing Mary Ann's babby and calls on her regular. No one can understand a word she says, mind, but the poor woman can't help her lah-de-da ways. She's even promised to set up a sewing class. Go on, get yerself cleaned up for this afternoon and give her the benefit of all your number work. Bore her to death with it but get out of my hair!'

'Only if I can go as Billy Widdup,' came the reply.

'Oh Tizzy, this is getting out of hand. Didn't your Fancy man biff yon farmer for you? It's never going to bring back Tatty, is it, and now you've got that three-legged monstrosity ...'

'Stumper? I'm just minding him for Teaspoons, he's not really mine. Tat was my dog.'

'I know he was, love, but life goes on and you only get the one turn so take the chance of learning. I never did, we never stayed long enough for me to learn letters or owt. Please? Go as Billy if you must but yer tempting providence, lass, pretending to be what yer not. Go on before you miss the cart,' pleaded Mally in that soft special voice which seemed to get through to her peculiar sister.

As she turned the handle of the mangle Mally smiled to herself. God must have thrown away the mould when he made up Tizzy Widdup. She had too many brains in her head, her forehead bulged with veins and her eyes were rock-hard when she got a notion in her head. There was no stopping this game now. Like a wheelbarrow rolling down the slope of an embankment planking, weighed down, out of control, dangerous, that was what she was fearing for Tizzy. How could a washergirl stop this runaway wagon from going off the rails?

As she carried her baskets Mally surveyed the camp with a nod of satisfaction. It was filling up with workmen and the whitewashed huts were now surrounded by ditch soakaways from out of which poked an array of hens and ducks. Some of the engineers had potted up tubs of marigolds and decorated their porchways with buckets of vegetable plants. Steps were scrubbed with sandstone edges and there were lace curtains draped neatly at the windows. She was thinking that Upper Paradise smelt fresher, more of homes and families, while Lower Paradise was rougher, cluttered with bits of machines, rusting metal, manky dogs and the smell of strong beer wafting out of the mud-splattered doorways, the uninviting, unappetising part of Paradise.

The Widdups had a wagon on wheels stuck at the back of the camp, just a place to doss down, but it would be bitterly cold in winter if they didn't find solid walls and warmth in a hut. The wagon would have to do for now. It stood off the ground, dry enough, but mould was already staining their box of clothes and they had to cook outdoors on an open fire.

The view was grand and Mally loved to peg out washing, watching the cloud shadows creep across the fellsides. Thank God for the canteen on wet days and the tommy shop, where she could haggle for meat and vegetables or exchange her fur-trimmed waistcoats and caps for pots and lamp oil. The supply of rabbit skins was drying up with the demand and she would need to cadge round the camp for pelts or go poaching herself if they were to provide pennies for Tizzy to attend school.

Cora Bulstrode put down her basket in the hall and sniffed a pungent odour wafting from the scullery where Susan, the live-in, stood over Miss Herbert as she dunked her head of hair in a bowl of green smelly water. Susan looked up warily at her mistress as she tried to pour the mixture over the young teacher's tresses, splashing liquid in all directions. 'What on earth are you doing, Miss Herbert? Look at the mess, Susan, get a mop quickly!'

'Yes, ma'am,' replied the maid as she scurried to clear the mess but in her haste she tipped the jug of sassafras oil onto the floor, sending poor Cora into a paroxysm of splutterings and mutterings under her breath.

The arrival of this woman had turned their quiet regime

upside-down; poor Ezra was a virtual recluse in his study and she had had to yield up her precious sitting room to make way for this whirling dervish of noise and activity. It could not go on – her nerves would not tolerate another week of incessant requests and clutter of books, papers, hare-brained schemes and washing. Had she never heard of a weekly wash? The madam flung her garments down and expected Susan to wait on her like a lady's maid.

Zillah Herbert was like no other teacher she had ever met. Oh, she was refined, with a loud plummy accent which commanded respect and a wardrobe of the most unserviceable clothes: trailing skirts and delicate underwear, a hatbox full of frivolous concoctions with full-face veils. Silly girl thought if she toned down her colours she would look less like the wealthy missionary she certainly was. From her silver-topped toiletry bottles, silk parasols and calfskin boots she was as conspicuous as a glasshouse blossom on a compost heap.

Only the voice belied her station. It was more suited to a porter on a station platform. Cora could hear her bawling out to the children in her classroom even through the brick walls of the schoolhouse. She screeched at the piano in a high-pitched voice, slightly off-key, which had poor Ezra gritting his teeth in horror at the awful hymns she would have them shout: Sankey and Moody Revivalist choruses more suited to an Evangelical crusade than a schoolroom, clapping hands and jingles. Never had Scarsbeck national school had to endure such caterwauling. Being high church the Bulstrodes were unused to such cheerful renditions of Christian hymns but the children seemed to like the action songs and jerky tunes, singing out of key with gusto.

Cora and Ezra were positively besieged in this citadel of Evangelical zeal, like two outcasts exiled from their routines by this woman's boisterous enthusiasm. Now she was taking over Cora's domestic domain in some strange baptismal ritual. It was all too much.

'Miss Herbert, explain yourself.' Cora could not bring herself to pronounce her first name. It was too familiar. It might invite intimacy and a reason to stay longer in this house.

'I think I've got visitors,' said Zillah from the bowl.

'Visitors?' cried Cora in disbelief.

'Yes, in my hair, I've been itching for days and then something dropped on the page of my book and hopped.'

Cora jumped back three paces and clutched her chest in anguish at such indelicacy. 'Spare me the details. God preserve us! Now you've brought an abomination into my house. How could you? That is it, it really is. We've had enough, Miss Herbert. It's time you found yourself lodgings elsewhere in the village. It was only a temporary arrangement to see you settled in. I can't have you contaminating our haven of tranquillity with ... with this filthy infection. This is what comes of mixing dirty children in a clean school. What will village parents think?' Cora conveniently forgot the number of times the village children had been infested. 'How can dear Mr Ezra maintain discipline if you undermine it at every turn with your fancy notions? Now you sour our home with some foul lotion stinking to high heaven. How can we concentrate? It turns my stomach just to think of food. Really, Miss Herbert, I'm sure your parents would be appalled to think of you in this condition. If you will wear a flimsy little lace cap on your head then you are a walking invitation for such, such ... things to take up residence.'

'I'm sorry, but once I treat my hair they will disappear, I promise you. If Susan would be so kind as to comb through it with this instrument of torture, that will dispose of the wretched beasts. I promise I will wear a plain mobcap from now on to remind myself of the vanity which caused this little accident. Dear Miss Bulstrode, bear with me, please,' pleaded Zillah but Cora now had just the excuse she needed to rid them of this nuisance.

'I will enquire in the village immediately and find you other accommodation, personally. We will not, of course, mention this little hiccup. Doubtless there are other houses who'll be used to this sort of occurrence and I think you would be far happier knowing that you were not upsetting Mr Bulstrode. This is a church school, not a Revivalist tent meeting. What happens in your classroom is your own affair and that of the Mission. We do think it noble of them to bother educating such unfortunates but thank goodness we insisted that they do not mix with ours. We would now have an infestation on our hands. Poor Ezra has enough on his plate with his search for a Fawcett scholar to coach. I don't want him bothered with this now. Please clear up this mess yourself. I don't want Susan to catch anything either. I feel my scalp itching just at the very thought of it all.' Cora fled to the living room, shutting the door in disgust.

Zillah sniffed up the noxious fumes with dismay. Poor Cora got so overheated. Her first impression of her hostess was of a worrier who somehow got only the leftovers in life; the scrapings which got lumped together but never quite fitted. Cora was so thin, honed too finely at the edges; her home-made clothes hung badly on her flat breasts. Her face was severe, her chin jutted and her neck looked scraggy and dimpled. She waited on her brother like a slave and he sat there calmly never lifting a finger to aid her or say thank you. Zillah watched her darting anxious glances at herself, envying her jaunty air, suspicious that perhaps she might be going to flirt with her precious brother and steal him away.

Heaven forbid. Ezra Bulstrode had a fat face like a toad, with bulbous stary eyes which never even glanced in her direction unless it was to deliver some instructions. He seemed to live cocooned in his own little world.

They were a strange pair, wrapped up in their own joyless concerns, and any comment Zillah offered at mealtimes seemed to disturb them deeply. She would not be sorry to leave this stifling suffocating atmosphere. The rooms were cluttered with dark heavy furniture and Cora fussed over details and ornaments. Everything was crocheted, tatted, edged, covered over with dark greens, maroons, and sombre furnishings at the windows. Even the fireplace was unwelcoming with a mean little fire which was always short on coal heat. The food was frugal and plain with two sittings; one for themselves and then

Ezra sat alone undisturbed with plates full to the brim while Cora hovered silently as he tasted the food to see if it was hot enough, salty enough. Everything seemed to exist for his satisfaction alone. The rest of them had to live on scraps.

Now Zillah's scalp was stinging badly and the dark ripples of her chestnut mane hung lank and stiff with the treatment. Praise the Lord for the manual of instruction and Nanny Brewer's little bottle. Lice hopped from head to head and loved to forage in clean hair so she was a sitting target. For one moment Zillah was tempted to take a pair of scissors to the lot of it, rid herself of this shaming in the twinkling of an eye, but somehow she could not chop her waist-length silky tresses. She loved the way they cascaded down her back like gleaming waves.

Vanity, vanity, Zillah Herbert. Haven't you learnt your lesson yet? How are the mighty fallen, humbled and brought down low, shame on you! She admonished herself as she braided the hair into tight plaits which she roped across her head severely and then sought out a starched linen Quaker cap, tied it under her chin and peered in dismay at the hall mirror. She looked such a plain Jane Eyre, her spirits sank to her boots. No winged squatters would dare trespass on this domain again!

Today she was going to pin down the elusive Reverend Hardy into organising Janey's baptism as she had promised. Four times she had called at the vicarage and left her calling card and four times it had been ignored. The wretched man was never at home. For four Sundays she had endured his dirge-like services at St Oswy's, sitting with Cora Bulstrode peeking out of a high boxed pew while Ezra droned on the little pipe organ and the choirboys whinnied from their stalls and the parson muttered sweet nothings from the pulpit, hardly looking up from his manuscript to address the congregation.

He was one of those preachers who paused overlong on each phrase of his text for dramatic effect. Occasionally she caught sound of a rich deep voice with a southern accent but most of his renderings seemed to seep through the wood-work or evaporate like candlesmoke through the vaulted ceiling.

St Oswy's was a lovely old church with Norman arches in the chancel and little windows, arrow slits, in the stone walls. It was simply decorated, the whitewashed walls ingrained with the prayers of generations long past. It smelt damp and musty in a churchy sort of way and the view from the ancient porch was breathtaking in its beauty and majesty. If only the people were more alive with the spirit of Christian joy and enthusiasm. It was what St John the Divine, or was it St Paul, called 'lukewarm' in its worship and welcome but she could change all that if only they adopted some of the newer, livelier hymns.

As she sat in her tiny boxroom she surveyed her bed of rock, the dark chest of drawers, wooden floor and simple rug. How different from her large bedroom at home with its four-poster bed, soft downy mattress, feather counterpane and draped damask curtains, her own washroom and dressing room, large fireplace and bay window overlooking lawns where peacocks screeched her awake each morning. This room was more like a plain cell for contemplation. She must not complain, for that was the life she had chosen for herself now. This was how ordinary people lived, without cooks and maids to wait on them. It was a novelty to be looking after herself.

How her life changed forever on the night that the Mission preacher came to St Maximilian's and assailed her with the consequences of a doomed condition! There she was all unawares, on the wide road to Hell, living in sloth and idleness, a life of luxury mapped ahead but doomed for eternity! Just the timely jolt she needed to get herself away from Nottingham. Now she was taking a narrower way, a harder road, trying to live independently of her wealthy parents, making a new life in strange hostile territory and loving every minute of it, or was, until she caught nits. That was something she would not be adding to her letter to Aunt Jane, the only relative who was bothering to reply to her regularly.

Poor misguided parents, they still could not stomach all her recent decisions to take up paid work for herself. How could she live off twenty-five pounds a year? It would scarcely cover her millinery bill at Madame Modista's but she would try. Zillah gathered up the long screed she had penned to her aunt, knowing it would be shown to Mama, hoping they might warm to her exploits if she told them about her teaching experience so far.

Dearest Aunt Jane,

I am writing to inform you I am still alive despite being caught up in a snowstorm in April. Would you believe I delivered a girl child to a mother stranded in the snow and now we both have a namesake! Janey is thriving despite her humble condition in the navvy camp. It was all very exciting and not a little frightening at the time but I am fully settled in a charming schoolhouse and have taken up my first teaching post but it is very much like being a teacher in Sunday school so do not worry.

On my first morning I was so nervous I scarce could lace up my stays. I dressed very carefully in my plain grey woollen skirt and striped blouse. I have had to remove the hoop from my skirts as I would not be able to walk up and down the extension room between the benches where the children sit with their slates. I see my classroom as an oasis of light and learning in this dark desert.

I was full of expectation as I prepared my lessons but it was to turn out a little differently. Suddenly I was aware of being inspected by bobbing heads outside the window. I think they thought I would be an easy victim for their pranks. My children are transported on a large cart from the camp, some in the morning and some in the afternoon. Some stay all day. They have to assemble away from the village children and are not encouraged to mix for fear of disease.

I heard the school bell ring and opened the door to the yard. A stampede of twenty-five pupils nearly knocked me over in the rush to find a bench, all shouting and behaving

*in a rough manner. Needless to say this was not allowed to
go unnoticed. I drew in a deep breath to descend like forked
lightning blasting forth like a cannonball over their heads,
making them walk outside again. 'Walk, don't run,' says I!
For a second they stood to see who was capable of deafening
them so they shuffled out meekly, still shocked by my surprise
attack. I picked up the bell and walked out to the yard and
stood as tall as I could on my tiptoes to tower over them.
Many are of stunted growth and look ill-clad and puny.*

*'In future when this bell is rung you stand in two lines,
boys to the right, girls to the left, no talking and no fidgeting
and don't move a muscle until I say so. No slouching and
caps off. Forward march.' They were as meek as lambs after
that especially when I got one of the tallest boys, called Billy
Widdup (I will tell you all about him later), to inspect them as
they went through the door. He grew three inches with pride at
being chosen out of the ranks to do the honours. We did this
exercise four times until I was satisfied with their standard.*

*Then I said a prayer and handed them out some hymn
books but few could read and we endured a dismal hymn
which all too soon became my solo. I decided then to teach
them some action songs and this seemed to cheer up the
service to everyone's satisfaction except Mr Bulstrode who
came rushing in to see what the noise was about.*

*The poor man has worn a perpetual look of worried
bemusement since my arrival.*

*Then I had to make a register of sorts which became
difficult because half my pupils did not seem to know their*

*real names or when they were born. So I put things like:
'Sam (son of Whisky Mac) thinks he is nine.' Each gave me
their weekly penny contribution towards funds except Billy
Widdup who tells me he is now ten and three-quarters which
sounds promising. Sorting them out by size is misleading for
many have old faces and little bodies and bandy legs which
does not help.*

*Mr Bulstrode gave me old reading primers, dog-eared and
ancient, and I tried to test them on their reading which was a
sobering education in itself, Aunt. Only Billy Widdup and a
girl called Poll could read fluently. Then I gave them a slate
to write their name on and this produced nothing but scribbles
from all but Billy and Poll. I decided to write on the blackboard
and easel and let them copy my letters. 'God is Good.' That
was a revelation too. So you see the task is immense, I fear.*

*I plan to divide them into groups and let Poll and Billy
help with hearing the children read the alphabet. The
afternoon flew by but before the cart came to collect them I
gave them each pencils and paper to draw something from
the world outside which interested them. The children looked
puzzled so I told them that I had noticed strange machines
and cranes, steam engines and hoists, roller carts and
locomotive engines pulling wagons in Paradise camp. 'What
do you see?' says I.*

*'Muck and rubble,' said one boy. 'Only hills, nowt but
hills,' said another in disgust. So I asked them to think about
something they liked drawing and waited for them to begin.
One child started to cry because she did not know how to use*

a lead pencil. Another folded his paper into a dart and tried to whizz it across to the Widdup boy but he was engrossed in a complicated drawing of a steam engine, all cogs and wheels and lots of intricate detail. I asked him how he knew such detail and he told me he was a tea boy, running from gang to gang with hot water and tea cans. Sometimes he was allowed to clean spades and instruments or grease wheels at close quarters.

This class will be wasted on Billy Widdup. He is far brighter than the others and I fear will become bored and disruptive if left to his own devices. He should be with the older children in Mr Bulstrode's class but I doubt if that will be permitted. At the end of the session I asked for helpers to hand out books and hands shot up across the room.

'Helpers have to wear clean pinafores and shiny boots, have tidy hair and clean fingernails.' The hands went down. Then Mr Bulstrode came to inspect the children and they were dismissed.

After they left the room he took one look at our efforts and tossed the papers off my desk in disgust, saying I was wasting paper on such drivel. 'You are paid by the Mission to drum the essentials into these children, Bible texts and basics, not waste time on these folderols. I hope you aren't one of these newfangled teachers who want children to enjoy learning!' He thumped on the table. It was the first time I have seen Mr Bulstrode bestir himself. I told him that the children were paying for teaching and the Mission would provide suitable materials for them to grow as healthy Christian citizens. Some bats and balls for them to exercise might be a step in that direction. Games would run off some of their spare energy and teach them discipline too. I suggested a sewing class might be useful for older girls. Teaching economy and thrift would not be a waste of resources either.

Mr Bulstrode went very red in the face and I don't think it was the heat! I showed him Billy's excellent drawing but he was not interested. I shall have to tread softly with the headmaster if we are to remain colleagues.

So you see I am filling my days with useful work and look forward to the challenge ahead. Do not worry about me. Any deficiency in my pupils is more than compensated by the beauty of the village and dale, the hills and grandeur of this district are like a pearl hidden in an oyster. Sometimes I find myself climbing up onto the high road just to breathe the air, upwind of the camp of course. I never expected such landscape to exist in Yorkshire!

Please write to me soon.

Your loving niece,

Zillah Jane

Outside the house the June sun shone across the meadows which swayed with buttercups, daisies, mayflowers and cow parsley; the stone wall banks were fringed with sweet cicely and its lovely aniseed aroma scented the air. It was good to be out of the gloomy house and Zillah strode briskly across the beck bridge to post her letter, turning off up the lane towards the church where Cleggy, the sexton and erstwhile midwife, was scything the grass around the headstones. Since their adventure in the barn he was fast becoming her only true ally in the village. There were few visitors to the schoolhouse for Cora discouraged casual callers and everyone assumed they would be bosom friends by now.

'Is his lordship at home?' laughed Zillah hopefully, pointing in the direction of the picket gate which led to the vicarage.

'Not a bit of it, 'tis far too good an afternoon to be wasted on church work, he tells me as he takes his bait out of the font. Would you believe it? No wonder there's no time for christenings with a font full of maggots . . . He'll be upstream tickling trout for his dinner. If you see a line of blue smoke wafting upwards, that'll be him. This parson goes his own gait and it's usually with a rod.' Isaac Cleghorn mopped his brow and sighed. 'I've dug in three of my parsons in this kirkyard but this one will happen put me away with all his scams.'

'He was ordained a fisher of men, not a fisher of trout!' snapped the teacher as she took the footpath towards Scarsbeck falls, along a primrose path edged with dog violets and garlicky ramsons with the last of the bluebells making a carpet under the trees which flanked the stream as it rose upwards through the ghyll to the cascading waterfall in the distance called Scarsbeck Force. Here kingfishers flashed past and dippers dived under the water, sandmartins swooped over her head; but Zillah was lost in her own troubled thoughts.

Enough was enough. I've been in the village for over a month and he's not looked at the road I'm on. Well, Parson Hardy, you are about to be told what I think of your chaplaincy so far!

Chapter Ten

Ralph Hardy stretched out his long limbs and sucked on the stem of his meerschaum pipe. This was the life, watching the telltale bubbles of air making smooth ripples on the surface of the pool. Tucked into a shady backwater, deep and cool where the trout sat out their afternoons undisturbed. He was lying on his stomach; with the grey-green of his tweed breeches, the buff leather waistcoat and white lawn shirt, he merged into the bank like any country poacher.

Bliss! This was why he stayed in Scarsdale, enjoying the scent of tobacco and bluebells, the drone of bees in the may blossom and the plop of a friendly dipper diving into the water from his perch on a boulder. Nothing in the world to disturb his slumbers.

As he peered into the stream, his reflection grinned back at him: the strong weather-beaten complexion of an outdoor man, a firm mouth with a full upper lip and a dark line of moustache, soft eyes, high brows, the right one of which seemed permanently to be arched in a questioning mode. His proud nose gave these strong features definition, or so his mother said. Liddy Braithwaite said it got in the way when she kissed him. He sighed, leaning over the water, but stiffened at the sound of rustling bracken as a shadow clouded his hiding place. He looked round and felt a twist in his back at the sudden jerkiness. 'Damnation!' He peered up at a neat pair of calfskin boots, yards of grey sprigged wool and a peculiar woman standing over him in a straw bonnet under which sat a white wimple sort of cap highlighting a heart-shaped face and a fierce disapproving stare.

'Is that you, Reverend Hardy?' said Zillah, in no mood to be ignored.

'Shush! Don't make another sound, you'll disturb my old trout. He's been dodging me for years.' He resumed his position on his back.

'I will not shush. I've been trying to arrange a meeting with you ever since I arrived,' she bellowed in his ear.

'I take it you're the Mission woman, come to save the dale? This is my day off and as you can see, this is no committee room. If you'd like to leave your card at the vicarage ...' Ralph was determined to ignore this intrusion but the air reeked with a pungent odour.

'I've left four cards on your silver tray and every day seems to be your day off. I need you to baptise one of my navvy children. Don't you ever tend your flock or do they have to be fish to get your attention?' Zillah settled herself down on the nearest rock, refusing to budge until she got some satisfaction for having the hem of her skirt covered in mud. She was going to have to do something about her hemline.

Ralph turned round with a twinging grimace. 'Look, Miss er . . .'

'Miss Herbert.' She held out her hand politely and he found himself staring into a pair of dark eyes, flashing like jet. A pair of pursed lips screwed up with disapproval and he burst out laughing at this fierce little woman who reeked of carbolic.

'I don't see that this is any laughing matter,' she snapped haughtily, her cheeks flushing at his perusal of her face and the intensity of his gaze.

'Please excuse me, Miss Herbert, you caught me unawares but I have no intention of baptising any navvy bastards who in turn have not the slightest intention of darkening the church doors again until someone carries them back in a box. They are obliging you only out of courtesy for the kindness you did for them. Oh yes, there's nowt happens in this dale that does not see the light of day, as Mr Cleghorn has no doubt told you. My sexton could have done your horse-doctoring effort blindfold in a tunnel, might I add. So no more on that subject, please.'

'How can you refuse an innocent child baptism? I have never heard such rudeness or discourtesy from a man of the cloth though having sat through four of your services . . .'

'Didn't you like my sermons then?'

'No I did not. Firstly you read them and secondly you read them out so badly no one could hear and thirdly, the bits I heard were not worth reading, nothing to get your teeth into, no gospel bite or amen moments. It was worth a hallelujah when it was over. You may fool your dozy flock but you don't fool me. It's a woolly lamb in the pulpit I see, not a roaring lion, and I have heard the soundest of preaching so I know the power of the spoken word to stir the soul and set the heart to quaking.' She paused to see the effect of her words. He was actually listening.

'I think you must dust down your shelves all of a rush on Saturday night and find some ancient homily to fill ten minutes on the Sunday morning.'

'However did you guess?' Ralph found himself smiling despite himself.

'Shame on you, Mr Hardy, to think so light of your calling to have backslidden into lazy ways and erroneous thinking. The Mission wrote to you asking you to give me support as my chaplain. You have not bothered once to step over the doorstep of the school to see how I teach my flock or offered to run a Sunday school in the camp. What on earth do you do all day, lie in bed and go fishing?' Zillah was so incensed she could feel her face blazing.

'How well your spies have informed you and it is none of your business how I conduct my parish affairs.' She had caught Ralph on the hop with her honesty and he was going to have to put this woman in her place, once and for all, before she made a nuisance of herself. 'We did not invite you to come to Scarsbeck, Miss Herbert; what you do for the Pastoral Aid Mission is your own affair. Don't interfere with the other missions at the camp either. The Nonconformists run the show and the Irish have their own priest. If any of these creatures do belong to the established church they are welcome to come to St Oswy's but I've not seen anyone so far. They've other things to do on a Sunday morning or have you not noticed that is when they sleep off their hangovers and wash their dogs, go poaching and shave their whiskers? We did not ask for a railway to spoil our peace but now it has I intend to ignore it. All things pass, young lady, and hopefully you will too. Is that honest enough for you?'

'I see. That is how it's going to be. No support from the church or in the schoolhouse either. It's not what I expected.' Zillah bent her head, trying not to look wounded.

'Blessed is the lady who expecteth nothing, ma'am, for she shall not be disappointed.' The vicar made light of the matter and noticed the water rippling. 'Shush, look, it's coming back . . .'

'Woe to the parson who neglects his flock! He shall also be disappointed.' Zillah picked up a large stone, dropping it with grim satisfaction into the beck, baptising the vicar with more than a sprinkling. Ralph spluttered in shock at the dousing.

'What was that for?' he shouted, shaking the drips off his clothing.

'I didn't come halfway across the country to the middle of nowhere to be thwarted in my endeavours. If you can't be bothered to get off your posterior to help the Mission then I must write a letter of complaint to the bishop. I'm sure he would love to hear about the welcome you've given me.' One look at her pink face told him this crazy lady would do just that and he was in no mood for more lectures.

'So just what have I to do, Miss Herbert, to make you go away and leave me alone?' replied Ralph as he stretched up and finally abandoned his expedition.

'You can change your hymn tunes, for a start,' Zillah said as she smiled.

'I can't do that, Ezra Bulstrode would have an apoplectic fit. He likes things as near to Rome as we can get away with. He calls me Father Hardy. Where else would I find such a good organist?' Ralph answered.

'I have witnessed glorious services with only a tambourine and cymbals for accompaniment. Where the spirit of the Lord is, there will be rejoicing and sweet music-making.' Zillah gestured wildly.

'This is the Yorkshire Dales and if you want that sort of thing you go to the chapel and the Methodists or the Baptist "dippers". We prefer a dignified service and no tub-thumping.'

'Write your own sermons, then. Visit Paradise camp for yourself. They won't send you to the lion's den just for being a parson.'

'I've told you that is not my patch. There are missioners from Batty Green paid to see to the men's souls. And don't look at me like that, all prissy missy,' he snapped, seeing those black eyes glinting.

'Why not? Are you a man or a milksop? What on earth are you doing in the Church if not to serve?' she snapped back.

'To be honest, I wonder myself.'

'What you need is a dose of salvation.'

'Oh, really! And what do you know about that, Miss Herbert?'

'Enough to know that there's only one true path in life. The road to heavenly bliss. All other paths lead to perdition and death. It is so simple. I can't see why everyone's so blind to the truth.' Ralph gulped in horror at her words.

'And you, I presume, are on the right path. How do you know?' She looked at him with amazement.

'Because it says so in the Bible,' she prompted.

'Which bit of the Bible?' he quizzed.

'All of it.'

'Scholarship tells us the Bible is a collection of historical books, written in different times by different people, so be specific, Miss Herbert.'

'It is the word of God, inspired by the Holy Ghost, and must therefore all be true. There is only one way.' The woman was tiring of this argument but Ralph persisted.

'So anyone of any other persuasion than your own is therefore doomed and lost?' he argued.

'Exactly, and that is why the missions go out into the world to rescue the misguided and convert the heathen and save souls. It is our duty,' she replied.

'Who says so?'

'The Mission says.'

'Why, Miss Herbert?' Ralph saw her confusion. 'Could it possibly be that the more they convert, the more heads they count, the more the pennies drop into their coffers? Surely you feel safer the more those around you think as you do, like sheep keeping in a tight bunch when there's danger. Now you are on your own here, don't you feel the slightest bit of doubt creeping in?' Ralph smiled patronisingly. The silly girl had not thought through her arguments.

'It says in Scripture: "All we like sheep have gone astray, everyone to his own way." Who are you to contradict holy writ?' answered the teacher.

'Have you ever read from cover to cover? Do you believe the world was made in seven days?' Ralph argued.

'Of course, and I read a portion every day.'

'What about Mr Charles Darwin?' Ralph saw her jump back.

'What about him? His views are known to be unscientific and against the teachings of Scripture. The Mission says . . .'

'There you go again, quoting other people. You've just accused me of not thinking for myself. I fear 'tis the kettle calling the pot black, Miss Herbert.' Ralph was beginning to enjoy their spat and saw confusion spreading across her cheeks, her eyes widening to show their pearly whites. She had the deepest, most soulful eyes he'd ever met.

'When I venture deep underground into the caverns and caves to explore, I find walls lined with fossils, frozen in time for thousands of years. I see man as only the tiniest drop in the oceans of time, a speck of dust in the universe. How dare we claim to have all the answers just because some men put their thoughts on paper?

'You should read your Bible with a critical eye or are you

one of those dippers who fling open a page at random, for the thought of the day, picking out verses out of context like a lucky dip?' He could see her wince at this challenge. He had her running now, running scared. 'Go away, young lady, and don't bother me until you've something useful for me to do. Get some Dales air on your cheeks, walk over these hills and build up your stamina, for believe me you will need it when winter comes.'

He watched her mouth open and shut like a fish gasping for air, a rosebud mouth of blush pink, juicy and moist. Underneath the plain clothing was a strikingly intense lady, a single woman of virtue looking to him for spiritual guidance indeed! If only she knew how expertly he could guide her in other matters. Enough, he was not going to break a habit of a lifetime and seduce a single woman. Ralph lay on his back with his straw hat tipped over his face, nonchalantly lifting his arms behind his head in the most arrogant of male postures. He sucked his pipe with satisfaction, seeing her discomfiture.

'It seems we have had our first chaplaincy meeting after all, Mr Hardy, and I suppose I must log it in my work journal as one of my spiritual conversations but not a very profitable one in my opinion. Good day . . .' Her words trailed away as she walked back down the path, her stupid skirts snagging on the blackberry twigs, and she stopped to yank them away without a backward glance.

Peace at last, he sighed, as he watched her disappear into the undergrowth, but strangely his triumph brought no comfort at all, only the aching of a stiff back.

Chapter Eleven

Fancy heard the thunder of wheels rumbling down the embankment. Instinctively he roared out 'Danger!' to his line of men and they jumped well clear, bodies diving out of the path of the runaway wagon in all directions as it careered down the gangway, slipping backwards laden with rubble. It happened so quickly; one minute they were clearing the gullet watching the spoil being dragged up the slope, the next it was running amok.

Now he watched the scene before him in slow motion as one of the grease boys tripped in its path, too small to avoid the wheels as they rattled down over his back; the piercing scream of agony echoed in their ears, as did the crash of the wagon as it toppled on its side hitting the incline on the other side. Then there was silence.

The other boys stood horror-stricken, frozen in shock at the remains of the child in front of them.

'Get the laddies away out of there,' he yelled to his gang,

taking off his jacket as he ran to see if the poor bairn was still alive.

He felt sick as he approached the track, knowing that no child could survive under that weight and dreading the thought of carrying the body back to some unsuspecting mother in the hutments. He could hardly bear to look at the mangled mess of flesh in front of him. As long as he lived he would never get used to the sight of bloody entrails scattered like a carcass on a butcher's slab. His worst fear was that it was Billy Flash underneath the sacking, unrecognisable, the wee boy whose dog he buried, but he remembered with relief that he had sent him off to the school cart with a clip round the ear for his cheekiness.

His men gathered like a shield around the body, quickly covering the sight from the other boys who hung back to see who the unlucky one was. Then Georgie Hunt was laid on a cart to be taken to the woodyard and sawmills where a line of coffins was stacked in the warehouse.

Fancy wanted to throw up his lunch. What a waste of a young life. This was no living for bairns, sprogging the wheels of loaded wagons with wooden sticks, at the mercy of heavy metal and faulty brakes. Fancy flung down his jacket in disgust and walked off the site. He had done his duty, followed procedures, informed the site engineer and the ambulance cart, seen to his gang and tea boys. Now he would see to himself and gather his thoughts.

How could the June sky be so blue and cloudless or the sun flash like a brass ball on emerald pastures? Skylarks trilled above him and peewits darted and dived around him in their summer dance. He just wanted to walk right off the earth, to get away by himself to make sense of such a happening. Fancy found himself taking the path down the moorside to the shade of the ghyll below, towards the coolness of the stream, to clear his head of the images which kept flashing before him in slow motion.

If only Georgie had noticed sooner, jumped faster, but he was a dull lumpen child. Guilt and relief that it was not Billy Flash did not make Fancy feel any better. Now you see me, now you don't! Thank God that toe rag was not yet a witness to that sort of death. There would always be danger on the track.

Life at the camp was settling down into a routine of sorts but the recent fine weather had made them work on late into the evening to clear out the first gullets and cuttings, transporting the spoils to bankings and preparing the land ahead for the viaduct scaffolding. They were making up for the lost time and for once the camp was full of fair-weather workmen.

Since the incident in the Fleece weeks ago, Fancy had not bothered to return to Scarsbeck but spent his knock-off time at the makeshift ale house or poaching trout out of the stream.

Now he made his way down to the ghyll opposite Middle Butts' lowest pasture land and noticed a lattice of wooden penfolds erected on the opposite bank where the grass dipped down to the water. Here the usual ripple of water over boulders was dammed into a large pool. A pile of rocks was stemming back the flow into a makeshift lake. The navvy smiled as he kicked off his boots and stockings, tore off his shirt and breeches and jumped into the stream with relief. The shock of the icy coldness and the jagged edges of the stream bed stung him for a second, making him gasp. For a few minutes he played like a bairn in a bathtub, splashing away the cares of the morning, the sadness which had driven him from his daily task. Then he saw a shocked face peering out at him from behind a tree on the other side of the beck.

It was the fair round face of the girl at the fight, the one who had tried to stick up for him, the girl who stood tall as a tree and watched him as he walked away. Now she was staring at him again, drinking in the view.

Fancy felt himself blushing at his nakedness. Had she been there all the time watching him strip and cavort about? He knew she had. And was she now going to embarrass him as he stood rooted to the spot, up to his neck in clear water? This was his den and he came whenever he could to bathe in secret. Now he was discovered and his hideaway exposed. This girl had no intention of moving from her hiding place so he brazened out his dilemma and waved to her breezily, trying to act as if he bathed before lassies all day long.

To his horror the girl stepped forward for a closer look and sat herself down on the bank with her chin resting on her hands.

'This is a washfold now, not a bathing pool. You'd better

get out quick or one of the shepherds will throw in his sheep and you'll get such a dipping! You shouldn't be down here.' She smiled.

'When did you make this pool, and by yerself?' he shouted back, refusing to budge.

'Aye, with a bit of help. Me dad showed me how. Now we dubs the sheep every year, get all the owd oil off their coats and the wool on their backs fair rises up afore clipping day. We get a better price for a fleece if it's clean. What are you on with coming here?' she asked, trying not to peer down at his nakedness.

'Sorry, I just come here for a wee bit of peace and quiet, away from the camp, to listen to the water and wait for the kelpies,' he teased, knowing she would be curious.

'Who are the kelpies?' came her query.

'That would be telling of the wee sprites. Have you never seen a will o' the wisp, they love to dance by the water . . .'

'And drown poor souls if they get the chance like the boggarts in the holes. I keep clear of suchlike and so should you, if you've got any sense,' she replied earnestly.

'My secret is out, Miss . . .?'

'Miss Birkett, Ellen Birkett, Mr . . .?'

'MacLachlan, Fancy Mac, Miss Birkett.' Now they were formally introduced but Fancy could not move, feeling the chill numbing up his legs. He was not going to retrieve his clothes in front of this lassie. She didna look the kind of lass who would be used to seeing men in their scuddies so he tried not to chitter and kept his hand splashing the water.

'Do you need a hand at the clipping?' he ventured.

'Nah, thanks. There'll be a gathering of sheep from down the dale and we all chip in and lend a hand, throw them in for a swim, dolly them top to tail and clip them next week if the weather holds. It's a right good time, a bit of a do, a dance and a singsong and lots to eat. It won't be the same this year since me dad went,' she sighed.

'He jacked in and sloped off, did he?' asked Fancy.

'Nothing like that, he had a bad turn and died on us last backend. Now nothing is the same.' Ellen sighed, spreading her smock over her knees coyly. 'Are you going to stay in there forever?'

'Only until you let me in peace to get out. I'll nay be shaming a lassie,' came his reply.

'You weren't so bothered when you jumped in? Mr MacLachlan, shame on you.'

'I didna ken I had a peep-show.'

'Don't be bashful. I know a tup from a ewe. I'm a farmer's lass. I know what's what.' Ellen laughed and her pink face gleamed from the reflection of light on the water. Still Fancy did not budge so she relented. 'If I go behind the tree again, will you get out and dress so we can continue our conversation, Mr MacLachlan?'

Fancy needed no second bidding and shot out of the water purple with cold, shivering. He darted behind a bush and dived into his breeks, wiping his body with his shirt. At last he was decent. He called out softly, 'Miss Birkett. You can come out now.' He turned but she was nowhere to be seen and instead he found himself facing the sour red face of the farmhand whose face he had rearranged at the Fleece.

'Get off this land. Get back to yer camp and don't bother my cousin again or I'll get the constable on you. I owe you one, Jock! Go on, bugger off!'

Fancy gestured to him defiantly and turned back up the path into the heat of the day. Nothing and no one would stop him seeing that bonny lass again.

Chapter Twelve

Ellie got an ear-bashing all the way home from her cousin; about the danger of consorting with a navvyman, the risk to her reputation, about ever talking unchaperoned to a stranger. Sunter seemed to think he had rescued her from a terrible fate, promising not to say a word to Widow Birkett as long as she would dance with him at the dubwash party. Ellie was fuming at being interrupted and stamped up the lane, her mind racing to remember every word they had exchanged. The vision of that handsome Fancy Mac in his naked splendour danced before her eyes, tantalising, out of reach now Sunter had spoiled the tryst. She wanted to race ahead and find a quiet shady corner to hug it all to herself.

Now she was being escorted back like a loose cow from the village street. Once indoors she would be caught up in the preparations for the dubwash. Mother was bashing on with the baking as if life and reputation depended on it, acres of pastry for gooseberry and raisin pies, curd cheese tarts, plum puddings to be boiled in cloths in the copper and of course her famous rabbit pies to get the feasting underway. This was to be flushed down with elderflower fizz which lay in deep bowls cooling in the larder on the slate slabs. The men would make alternative arrangements, bringing their own concoctions which even the Methodists among them found hard to resist.

For Ellie the afternoon would bring more stirring and mixing, slaving over the range, Mother barking orders like a flustered dog and all on a hot summer's day. It was much more fun at the dubwash, gathering up the hundreds of sheep, guiding them into the pens, putting on fleece body wraps to wade into the cool and pull the sheep through the dipping pool. There was so much joking and merriment.

Dad always had a little joke up his sleeve and sewed up a farmer's trousers here or an armhole there. The whisky bottle passed between them. Dad always let her guard the lambs to make sure they found the right mothers. She should be down with Beth Wildman and the other shepherds, not stuck in the kitchen with the women. Ellie felt her throat tighten at the thought of Dad not being there, leaning on the farm gate sucking his clay pipe. Their life had no order now, at the mercy of the Lunds' contrived concern and Sunter's fussiness. 'Oh Dad! You should be here and all would be well in our world and I would tell you about Fancy Mac and you would let him help on the farm and perhaps . . .'

'Ellen Mary Birkett, don't stand there like a month of Sundays! Get scrubbed up and give us a hand. We need to get a leg on!' came Mother's dulcet tones from the courtyard as she beat furiously on the best pegged rug, sending dust flying, puce-faced with the effort.

It was cool inside the stone house, dark and refreshing, until Ellie saw Mercy pulling faces at her. Girls of ten could be so silly and spiteful. Mercy was never the most appealing sister with her plain features; as wick as a weasel she might be but whingey with it. She would never speak about Dad. It was as if he had never existed and this made Ellie sad. Mother said it was better to let her get on with her lessons and forget him if it made her more biddable. Ellie was not so sure.

'We've had a visitor and you don't know who,' smirked Mercy. Ellie shrugged her shoulders. 'We'll have even more tomorrow so there!' This lack of interest made Mercy stick her tongue out. 'I'm not going to tell you then.'

'Don't bother yerself. I have my own secrets too.' That would take the shine off her apple, thought Ellie, walking away. Mercy skipped down the stone flags after her.

'Miss "Patabully" came a-calling all the way from the schoolhouse. I had to walk home with her and she made me stand up straight and stick me chest out like a lady, so there.' All this was delivered in one breath.

'So what was Miss Cora wanting out here? We are honoured. She never leaves the village unless it's to call at Scarsbeck Hall once a year to attend Miss Augusta's literary meeting.' Her mother was quick to enlighten her.

'She wants to find new lodgings for that 'ere Mission teacher on account of Mr Ezra's indisposition. You know, the young lady with the fancy bonnets what sits in their pew in church. I've never seen such expensive ribbons on such tall hats. When she walks down that aisle she looks like a chest o' drawers. Anyroad Miss Cora wondered if we, being an all-female household, might oblige. It being more proper for Miss Herbert, that's her name ...'

'Well, Mother, I hope you said yes?' Ellie liked the look of the young woman and an extra pair of hands as well as income would be welcome. 'She could have Mercy's room and Mercy can have the attic to herself.'

'That's not fair. It creaks up there. I shan't be able to hear anything. I'll be flayed of fright.' The girl sulked. 'I don't want no teacher in my house. She'll be on at me. She's a right tartar with the navvy class. Miss Patabully says we shouldn't mix 'cos they're dirty and Patabully says she's not a proper teacher, just a helper, so there.'

'Don't be disrespectful to your headmaster, Mercy Birkett. I've told you afore. I'm sure Miss Herbert will fit in a treat. Oh, was I glad that the old fusspot didn't catch me still in my washing gear with a dirty floor and messy tables. I took Miss Bulstrode straight into the parlour all beeswaxed and smelling like a posy, gleaming like a new penny it was. Her eyes raked all over it looking for a speck of dust, just like them farmers' wives will be doing tomorrow, sneaking up here for a quick pee and a sken, to see if I've bottomed it all out in their honour. Which I have. I don't want none of them clacking round the dale that Widow Birkett can't put on a good show.'

'Did she like the place then?' asked Ellie, seeing her mother flush with pride at being singled out by the fussiest woman in Scarsbeck.

'Aye, she did that, her eyes were on stalks at the size of the rooms and the polish on the oak and the French china plates what Amos Birkett brought back from Napoleon's war. I don't think she expected to see his portrait on the wall and that kist in the hall or yon silver plate but she said nowt. That's her way, but her eyes were greener than grass at the sight of it. Are you sure we do right to take in a stranger, Ellie? Whatever would your Dad think to be reduced to this?'

'You mustn't think like that, Mother. We can make use of the spare room, perhaps gain an extra pair of hands. Town-folk like to be around animals and when we get snowed in, Mercy will have her own teacher on tap. Who knows? She may even take a shine to Sunter and take him off our hands once and for all.'

'I hear she don't get on with the parson. Cleggy's missus told the baker and he told me, she called him a trout to his face, so it's said.'

'Well, she's not far off the mark then, is she, the time he spends at the beck. When will Miss Herbert be coming?' asked Ellie.

'Her trunk is on the cart even as we speak,' smiled her mother, 'so crack on, our Mercy, and clear out your room.'

Chapter Thirteen

The cart bobbed down the lane, a simple hearse pulled by a black Dales pony with a plume of dark feathers stuck in his harness. The coffin was laid on a bed of meadow flowers: buttercups and orange mountain poppies with branches of willow strewn at the sides. Behind the cortège came the family and friends and most of the camp women with black scarves tied around their sun bonnets, navvies in their Sunday best caps and officials in frock coats and stovepipe hats, to honour this first fatality at their works. The missioner from Batty Green in wideawake hat and a black suit carried his Bible, escorting the child down into Scarsbeck village.

It was not a day for blackness; the earth was burnt like toast and the bracken tinder-hot. The fierce sun glared down from a cloudless sky as they processed silently down the empty streets; St Oswy's bell tolled out the occasion and some of the villagers stood respectfully in their doorways, caps off, curtains closed. The silence was broken only by the bell and barking of dogs tethered in the shadows. There was no love lost for a navvy but nobody begrudged a child a place in their kirkyard. Cleggy made sure the grave was dug and the bell was tolling.

Miss Herbert ushered her class out of the temporary class-room into the sunlight which blinded them for a moment. Tizzy found herself at the back of the procession gathering in the straggling younger children who were excited to be let out of school to see Georgie Hunt's big day. They were lined up around the hole in the ground and the missioner, Mr Tiplady, who often wandered round the camp with his *British Workman* magazines and Bible pamphlets, read a lesson, said a prayer for George and looked solemn and important. Tizzy could see Mally and her neighbours trying to console the weeping mother whose small bemused children clung to her skirts. The gangmen looked uncomfortable at all the wailing going on.

Tizzy started counting, one, two, three alearie, five, six, seven alearie . . . she always did this when she was nervous, trying to keep her eyes from the hole, gulping hard not to cry. Boys never cried but she knew Georgie Hunt. He was one of her gang and she fingered his best marble in her pocket; the one she had bartered with him for one of her own bull's-eyes. She could beat him at football and he was going to be an engine driver. Now he was in pieces in a wooden box, going down into a dark hole, and he'd never see daylight again. Tizzy was shivering at the very thought. One, two, three . . .

Everyone told stories of gruesome accidents on camps far away or the other side of the one you were on. It didn't happen to you, though, or someone you knew. She was used to kiddies dying and going to heaven. They did that all the time, lying like waxen dollies wrapped in white cotton with lacy edges, and you went in and said goodbye before they put the lid on. Mally would not let her see George. None of the tea nippers had seen him. The lid was down and that was really scary. What did he look like under it? All mangled up and squashed, so the other lads whispered. Was he really put in a sack in little pieces and dumped on his mother's trestle table to put together again? She hoped not.

What if it had been her? Then they would discover her secret and Mally would be in trouble. Granda was so fuddle-brained he had never cottoned on Tizzy was missing and accepted her as dead Billy Boy. Then she remembered the pit and the burning of bodies done at the dead of night and she wanted to run far away from this kirkyard and the noisy wails and the preacher man droning on.

Tizzy felt faint in the heat. She and Mally were in too deep now to escape. One, two, three alearie . . . She was Miss Herbert's monitor, her and Poll Blewitt together made the little kids stab out their letters and she got them writing down numbers too. How could she own up to her cheating? If only Mally would jack it in and move away but she was off her meat for love of a brickie from Burnley they called Wobbly Bob, which Tizzy thought a daft nickname for a bricklayer. She wondered if all his bricks kept toppling off his walls but

Mally laughed and said it were summat to do with a Saturday night randy when he had had a skinful. Anyroad there would be no shifting Mally Widdup now. She had a good laundry round and helped out with cleaning in Upper Paradise in the better huts. The search for Ironfist was all but forgotten. Tizzy and Stumper the three-legged lurcher were left to their own devices most of the time.

Tizzy looked across at the line of gangmen to the tall figure of Fancy Mac, standing head bowed, clutching a real tam-o'-shanter beret, his bleached hair glinting like gold in the sunlight. One day she would grow up and marry him if he would wait for her. The signs were not good though. He was another off his meat, plastering down his hair, putting on his best shirt and tartan waistcoat to wander down to the village just in case, Mally laughed. She recognised the signs herself. 'He's going out trapping, Tizzy, and it's not foxes or rabbits he's after, that's for sure.'

Tizzy loved the way he took her aside and explained things, how to keep yerself safe, why she must go to school and how his forefathers in Scotland lost their land to sheep. Sometimes he showed her his leather book and read out strange poems in a foreign tongue. She knew they must be proper poetry for they made him go dew-eyed and pink. Oh, why couldn't he wait? But there again he thowt she were a lad, not a lass, and that was all her own doing.

There were no bullies in his gang or rough men who hit you and kicked yer backside if you were late with their hot water. Woe betide you if the tea weren't drummed up to their liking, then they would push you over into the mud or dunk yer head into a cesspit just for fun. Sometimes they teased and played cruel jokes. Teasing made her bottom lip tremble and tears fill her eyes for she could never tell if they were serious or not. But worst of all was when they wouldn't pay you at the end of the week and made you do rude things to get yer money. She hated that more than anything when they unbuttoned their flies and tried to get you to . . . She ran away then and refused to go back to that gang. She told Fancy scraps of this and he made sure that she worked only for his men. She could die herself for love of him after that.

Miss 'Sherbert' was fair, nagged a lot but did find a proper sum book for Tizz to get her teeth into. Pages and pages of problems and numbers to calculate. Better than Mally's gingerbread, having a puzzle to solve, calculate and a tick mark on yer slate. She had to slow down though to make them last out. This book was borrowed under sufferance from old Bulstrode. Miss Sherbert would sigh as she did the ticks. 'It's such a pity you can't be next door with the head-master,' she once whispered sadly. Tizzy had no desire to be in his class with the snotty-nosed village kids calling her names and holding their noses. Oh no! She was fine where she was; it was safer than poor Georgie's job. She was glad she had been at school the day he got hisself run over.

The missioner stepped back and the box was lowered into the ground. To her amazement Fancy stepped forward with a piece of paper to address the company. He looked so smart and clean-shaven even 'Sherbert' took a second glance as he proclaimed a few words in that strange gurgling language which sounded like music. Then he read some lines from a chap called Rabbie Burns, read it out proper in a deep voice and it got poor Sherbert dabbing in her pocket for a handkerchief.

> *'Accept the gift a friend sincere*
> *Wad on thy worth be pressin'*
> *Remembrance oft may start a tear*
> *But oh! That tenderness forbear*
> *Though 'twad my sorrows lessen.'*

It was a bit odd to see such a giant spouting forth and one or two looked a bit nonplussed but somehow it made Georgie's funeral special and dignified. Miss Herbert went to see if the parson were about but Cleggy the sexton said he weren't getting involved in this do and that got the teacher all fired up again. Tizzy was ushered back down the path to the cool of the classroom while the mourners took rest in the Fleece for the start of their wake and Cleggy's pony chomped away in his bag of oats, tied to the lych gate post in the shade.

Tizzy turned round again to watch the sexton digging the hole in with a mixture of curiosity and terror. Where was Georgie Hunt now? Did he feel it as the earth dropped on his head? One, two, three alearie. Tizzy decided in an instant that she was going to live forever; a hundred years if need be. No one was going to trap her underground in a box.

Chapter Fourteen

Zillah peered out of her bedroom window with excitement. At last a dry morning for the sheep clipping at Middle Butts Farm and a day free from sodden clothing steaming in the schoolroom. There was enough blue in the sky to make a sailor a pair of trousers and the mist had rolled off the fellsides leaving the grass sparkling and freshly rinsed, drifting off the tops like a gauzy veil. The roses by her casement window scratched on the tiny panes of glass, with dark leaves dripping glassy beads of rain droplets. Rain before seven o' clock, fine by eleven would be the order of the day.

Down in the walled kitchen patch, clouds of late apple blossom wafted a delicious scent upwards as she leant out further to welcome in the day. Blackbirds pinked and in the fields the cattle were heads down at their feasting. This really was God's own country, she smiled, so solid and sure of itself.

The Birkett women welcomed her not so much as a paying guest but as a friend. She loved the farmhouse with its airy rooms and cool stone floors and the bedroom was snug and comfortable with her own commode and washstand, a counterpane of quilted cotton pieces in a patchwork design and a small writing bureau where she must finish her latest epistle to Nottingham to thank Mama for the parcel of summer finery she had urgently requested to be sent to the farm.

You will perhaps wonder why I have suddenly decided to lighten my attire but as I told you, Mercy Birkett asked me outright why I always wore grey or black and who had died in my family. She is the sharp-faced, serious child with thick braids of corn-gold hair and freckles which she often tries to bleach off her cheeks much to everyone's alarm. Mercy frequently reminds me that she has given up her chamber for my comfort when we walk down to school together but these comments took me aback even though her mother scolded her child for being impolite.

Yet out of the mouths of babes and sucklings often comes a truth. If I am so full of the joy of the Lord why do I dress as if I am in mourning? I think at first I wanted to be taken seriously and would allow no frivolity in my attire except for my usual weakness when it comes to bonnets but even they are toned down somewhat.

You see it is all so different from my expectations. Daleswomen are a breed apart, very forthright in their opinion-giving. They wear sensible sturdy clothing suited for life amongst mud and mire and some knit even when they

*walk to the village. Everyone is so industrious. They are
never still for a minute, shaming me into appearing slothful.
I still find the farmyard smells hard to stomach but Ellen
Birkett assures me she doesn't smell anything!*

*Ellen Birkett takes upon herself the mantle of the man
of the house, eschewing farmhouse tasks in favour of a
farmer's day whenever she can. Sometimes she dons a
farmhand's smock and short skirts above her ankles and
men's clogs to scrape out the byres and sweep the yard, milk
the cows and tend to the flocks with her cousin's family.
She is very tall and statuesque, Papa would say, but of the
sweetest disposition. It displeases her mother that she is so
uninterested in household accomplishments and would rather
groom her tall carthorses than dust a room. The Birketts
are quite constrained by the lack of a father and keep to
a modest budget. They employ few servants and have no
live-in maid as is the norm in these parts. All the women
have to contribute to the task and I have made myself
useful picking gooseberries, topping and tailing them for
the sheep-shearing pies. Mistress Birkett allows me to skim
the cream and stir up the cheese curds for they produce the
most excellent creamy hard cheese and butter, the finest in
the dale so I am told by others. They are far too modest to
boast.*

*The rule here is that farm and stock come first and family
next alongside hired hands and self last. Caring for the
needs of others is like a daily sermon to my selfishness. Do
not be alarmed, I am still first and foremost committed to*

my Mission task, but after all those gloomy weeks at the schoolhouse where I was made to feel an intruder, it is such a relief to sleep in a soft bed with crisp linen sheets scenting of lavender. New beds are like strangers. It takes time to become first acquainted then hopefully comfortable old friends, and the bed at the Bulstrodes' would be rock-solid and starchy however long I lay there.

Sometimes at the end of the day Ellen and I walk the fields together to examine the stock and gather meadow herbs and flowers for her mother's remedies. We often share our views and find ourselves laughing together, not at each other but with each other. There is no side to Ellen, as they say in the dale. I have much to learn from her simple faith and honesty. She is much taken with one of the navvy workmen but it has to be a secret for her mother can see no good in any workman employed by the Midland Railway who robbed her of pasture land, giving but a poor rate of compensation, and whose noise and smoke is sooting up her washing line and puts cows off their milking. I think her mother wise to mistrust the average navvy but this handsome red-haired Scotsman is above the usual type, being educated enough to write his own verse in his native tongue, and commands much respect amongst the men.

You will be glad to know the monthly visitation by the Pastoral Aid Mission to inspect my journals and schoolwork went with only a minor hitch. I pointed out the discrepancy in the abilities of my scholars, especially Billy Widdup, whom I mentioned before. They were at a loss to advise how best to

*persuade Mr Bulstrode to accept him in his class. I have the
beginnings of a scheme in my head to achieve this and will
report further on this matter.*

*I have to say they were also disappointed in the response
from our lazy vicar, Ralph Hardy. Only a bolt of lightning
will shake his slumbers in this parish. He reported that I was
a regular attender at the services and seemed to be coping with
my tasks in the school. He accused me of meddling in parish
affairs and causing dissatisfaction amongst his congregation!
Nothing more would he offer to the visitors. I think he would
try the patience of a saint.*

*I then had to explain this criticism to their satisfaction
telling them how Mr Cleghorn, the sexton, would no longer
tolerate bait in the font and about the troublesome matter of
the amputated leg.*

*We have had another serious accident on site when one
of the workmen fell off the scaffolding which is being erected
over the village, much to everyone's consternation. His right
leg was badly smashed and bleeding and after a while became
black and swollen, requiring immediate amputation by the
medical officer who came up from Batty Green with his saw.
The poor man's screams could be heard over the dale, the
wind being in such a direction as to carry even a whisper
through the valley. The injured man was one of Mr Tiplady's
temperance converts and was concerned for his eternal
condition, worrying what would happen to his right leg on
Judgement Day if he was to rise up at the Last Trump.*

It seemed only natural to the missioner and myself that

this humble but not uncommon request for a leg burial on consecrated ground be achieved. Mr Cleghorn also felt that there would be no difficulty in propping up the said leg discreetly in St Oswy's kirkyard in a plot he reserved for other unfortunate appendages, should they ever occur. But would the vicar agree? He was adamant that this was not his business and refused to entertain the idea. So it was raised at the vestry meeting and passed narrowly by the committee, thinking no doubt that this might be a useful place to pop any other spare human bits out of the dale, as long as they were suitably labelled in boxes and the navvy bits were kept apart just in case any navvy wanted to collect his bits and pieces and cart them elsewhere when the railway was completed. The said limb was duly buried by Mr Tiplady and the vicar has not spoken to me in church since. His attitude is so petty but I will not be ignored.

Thank you again for the pink muslin, blue striped and the cream tussore silk, the lace shawl and cotton petticoats and summer straw bonnets with the silk flowers. I shall have to have their hems upturned if I am not to ruin them in one outing.

Yours joyfully in the Lord,
Your grateful daughter,
Zillah Jane

The letter was duly sealed and addressed. There would be so much to help with downstairs but Zillah leant out of the window just to make sure it had not started to bucket down again. How it could rain, soaking through her woollen jackets and skirts, but today the sky was forget-me-not blue and white may blossom dripped from the bending branches. By the big barn the shearers had set up their stalls in readiness as the sheep were gathered off the fells into separate bunches baahing and protesting, calling to their lambs and fussing at yet another disturbance of their daily routine.

Zillah looked up at the pink muslin dress with delicate cream flowers scattered over the full skirt. Thank goodness she had unpacked it earlier for it stank to high heaven of camphor candles to discourage the moths and was creased and limp like rags. She tried to flat-iron it herself but was defeated by the fullness of the skirt. Ellen came to the rescue and finished off the task. The dress was then hung up by the open window to loosen the stink and doused liberally with lavender water and a bag of last year's dried herb sachets which Ellen kindly donated to the cause.

Ellen herself was not bothered about the dressing up for she had a hundred jobs to tackle and as Fancy Mac would not be welcome at the feasting afterwards, any excitement she felt was limited. Zillah shook out her petticoats and dressed with care, her spirits rising at the sight of her pink cheeks and healthy glow. Where had that pale face and pallid complexion gone? Too many outdoor walks had put a blush on her skin and a sheen to her face. She was filling out and loosened her stays by two holes; all that open air and hearty food was sticking to her ribs. The Birketts didn't know about ladylike appetites and pecking at plates. They wolfed down

143

platefuls of meat and vegetables with relish, enjoying every mouthful, hungry, tired and sometimes burping at the table in satisfaction. Mama would be horrified to see how coarse and unrefined Yorkshire women were but somehow her opinion no longer mattered.

She brushed out her hair and let it hang for a few minutes, watching the way it swished and swirled as she pirouetted gaily. The sunshine streamed in through the window lightening her mood. She would never dare to go abroad like a wanton but as it was a harvest feast for a crop of fresh fleeces, Zillah would honour the occasion with a change of hairstyle. She tied ribbon at the bottom of her hair and rolled it upwards into a soft smooth effect, tying the ribbon round her head and fixing a silk flower onto her broad straw bonnet which had a pink ribbon trailing down from a bow.

Already the yard was full of farmers: the Braithwaite family with strapping sons, Warwick Lund and Sunter the cousin for whom Ellen had not one good word to say, and farming families from all over the dale. The Birkett farm was always a popular spot for the annual clipping in Scarsdale when the farmers' sons got a chance to compete with the hired shearers for the quickest shearings and most number of sheep shaved in a day.

Ellen was swathed in an old smock, guiding the flocks towards the shearing bay where the men sat on their stools, lifted up the ewes and began to clip with long pointed scissors from the neck down each side, all in a smooth swift pattern which made it look a simple task with wriggling sheep. The sheep was dabbed with dye and darted off. The fleece was thrown to someone who rolled it up tightly and then it was thrown onto a cart. It was a back-aching job, judging how some got up and stretched, supping their ale and pasties and catching up with how the others were doing in the competition. Zillah found a job for herself passing round refreshments and taking away the empty tankards to be washed at the pump.

As the heat rose during the morning so the scents blended into an oily, sweaty, pungent aroma of sheep oils and the sickly stench of the gowdings, the pile of dirty tail-ends of the sheep, unfit for a fleece, which had flies buzzing over them.

Zillah drifted into the kitchen where Annie and her friends were preparing a lunch of mutton pie and gooseberry and raisin tarts with bowls of cream, all to be washed down with freshly brewed elderflower cordial which was cooling in the still room with elderflowers floating like curds on top of the earthenware jugs.

No one would clip their flock until the elderflower clusters lay like snow on the branches and high summer was overhead. Zillah sniffed its rich perfume with pleasure. It was a relief to be inside out of the bustle in the cobbled yard and jovial banter in a broad Yorkshire dialect she would never understand as they greeted each other in thick accents, 'Nah then. How do, owt fresh?' and the reply came, 'Fair to middlin' but nowt fresh. See thee.' If she lived here for years she would never understand the language.

No sooner had the lunch been enjoyed than the women cleared away the trestle tables to prepare for the evening feasting and the merriment at the end of a long day. Back into the kitchen they went to bring out all their baskets of fancy food assembled earlier at home and brought together in one big meal which Ellen called a Jacob's Join.

Ellen changed out of her smelly clothes and put on a crisp blue shirt and a full skirt which looked as if it had been made out of old curtains of ancient brocade. 'We don't waste owt in this house. I think they must have come from the windows of Scarsbeck Hall, they're that heavy and holey, but Mother made a grand job, don't you think, and yer can't see the patches, can you? The rest of them hang over the parlour windows if you look careful.' Ellen laughed, seeing the look of astonishment on Zillah's face at their thrift. 'You look like a picture in that pink and quite different, Miss Herbert, more like a . . .' She hesitated, not wanting to offend. 'More like a lady if you don't mind me saying.'

'A little softer on the eye, perhaps?' Zillah answered as she smiled, glad she had honoured the occasion and it was appreciated. Mercy danced around her all afternoon fingering the lacy edges of her cuffs and looking longingly at the swish of her skirt. 'When I'm a teacher I shall wear a pink dress every day and a yellow one on Sundays, with sticky-out petticoats which rustle when I walk and everyone will turn round to look at me, so they will.'

Beth Wildman, the white-haired shepherd woman, stood by the farm door listening to the child prattle on, her dog at her heel. She smoked a long pipe like the men, she had on a waistcoat of lambskin over a man's shirt and a long skirt of an ancient plaid wool which was fading into a heathery berry colour. She lifted her skirt to curtsey to the child. 'My, aren't we going to be the grand one. What if I telt yer I sees you far away across the seas in a new land with a caravan of silks and satins at yer command? What would you say to that, my lady Merciful, would that be suiting you?' The child jumped up and down with excitement.

'When, when . . .?'

'That's for me to know and you to find out,' came the wise reply and Zillah, who disapproved of any fortune-telling as a rule, smiled and nodded.

'As for this young lady, she's already stirring up the dale, scattering dust in all directions for a right sweep clean afore you gets shut of the dirt but you'll be for losing yer own heart to the dale like little Bo Peep and not know where to find it for a while. But I'm a-speaking out of turn.' Her strange eyes flashed in mischief, seeing the teacher blush with annoyance at this unsolicited advice. 'Come on, Miss Merciful, you can show me round yer patch and we'll gather a few wild bits of herbs for yer mother. There's a doctor in every hedgerow if you know where to look.'

Stung by the wild woman's prophecies, Zillah scuttled back indoors out of the afternoon heat and busied herself dutifully around Annie Birkett's table.

'Where shall we put all these bowls of strawberries? The table is full,' she asked a distracted Ellen.

'Reserves go in the back pantry. Do you think we've enough?'

'Enough for Wellington's expeditionary force . . . a vat of steaming meat pie, bowls of peas and cabbage, jugs of gravy, hunks of crusty bread, a whole cheese wrapped in muslin, pickled eggs and piccalilli and that's just the first course. I spy a sea of puddings and an island of cakes and pastries, junkets and whipped cream concoctions with toasted almonds and nuts, bowls of red fruits glistening like jewels, cold custards garnished with petals and mountainous fruit jellies, finger biscuits and fancy breads, butter pats moulded and sculpted into pretty shapes. Praise the Lord for your Jacob's Join. Mistress Birkett's friends must have been baking for a week to put on this spread. Why so much?' queried Zillah, pinching a ripe strawberry and dipping it in the cream.

'The evening do is for everyone up the dale and they'll come down hungry and expecting a feast. Then the fiddler will strike up and we'll dance till we drop.' The teacher shook her head.

'I'm not sure it would be proper for me to take to the floor.'

'Why ever not? You can always dance the quadrilles with Mercy as your partner. Surely that would be teaching her how to dance? You have to have some time off from being a serious missionary, surely? Do tell me again about the man who read poetry at yon funeral. The one who stood head and shoulders above the rest and looked so winsome, you said?' pleaded Ellen once they were alone outside the farmhouse watching the guests arriving by horse and cart or on foot, strolling across to the shearing and chattering in groups as the sun glided westwards behind the hill.

'Oh, he was so handsome and spoke with such feeling,' Zillah replied coyly, watching Ellen blush into a beetroot smile.

'I know, I wish he were at the dancing tonight. It would fair cheer up my evening. Instead I'll be tripping over Sunter's feet again. He makes my flesh creep. Sometimes I think he's wrong in the head. He keeps saying he'll be leaving the dale and if I don't wed him that will be the end of High and Middle Butts. Good luck, he can go tomorrow as far as I care. I told him I'd drown mesen rather than wed him. I'll not be blamed for his doings.'

'Oh Ellen, you wouldn't drown yourself?'

'Not likely. He's not worth a splash of water and he knows my fancy is elsewhere now but please don't tell a soul I said so,' she whispered.

Zillah put her fingers to her lips, about to smile until she spotted the arrival of the Vicar of Scarsbeck parading his finery amongst his congregation; another silk shirt and fancy waistcoat and riding breeches which curved tightly across his buttocks without the decency of a long jacket to hide the rear view. Had the man no decency, dressed in such casual attire exposing his fleshly contours? He was teasing old Miss Wildman and slapping her on the back with his pipe. He waved to Cleggy and his wife who stood stiffly waiting for the last of the tables and chairs to be placed close by.

Everyone from the village seemed to be gathering here, watching the sun go down over the hill and bats darting from bushes in the still air. Perhaps they were all pretending that the countryside was still theirs alone, that the scaffolding was not criss-crossed over the bottom of the main street, that they were not tasting brickdust on their tongues or that the navvies were not ensconced on their favourite benches in the taproom of the Fleece.

Zillah wished she had brought down her fan for she felt a stifling flush on her face as the vicar caught her eye for a second and turned away and looked again as if taking in her pretty dress and loosening hair. It was such a pity they would never be allies for she could do with his help in getting Bulstrode to take on Billy Widdup.

Her first plan had been to get him into the church choir where he was bound to be noticed but the poor child sang so out of key there was no use even bothering Mr Bulstrode on that score.

She stood next to Blaize and Warwick Lund, tapping their feet as the dancing chords were struck, and witnessed Ralph Hardy march up to Mrs Braithwaite who looked like a fluffy sheepdog with lots of curling hair and a low-slung dress with barely a modesty fichu to hide her swollen breasts. The farmer's wife laughed at her partner and they chattered as they danced. Ralph Hardy smoothed back his hair and fiddled with the gold pin in his cravat. The man was positively preening himself and Zillah could not help noticing what a handsome couple they made as he swung the girl around the grass. His face had the intense animation that springs to life in a man who is conscious of an audience and is displaying his dancing skill with a pretty partner on his arm for all the other men to admire. His eyebrows arched up quizzically as if in surprise. He slid his tongue over his lips and gave the young woman a devastating smile like a hungry tiger on the prowl. Zillah was transfixed by their synchronised movements, how his hips swayed in the jaunty swinging steps, watching the farmer's wife smile back at him brazenly.

She had the wide-eyed, heavy-lidded glance of a vixen, shooting forth bold knowing stares straight into his eyes. A message was given and one was received. Zillah turned away, embarrassed at this display. Blaize Lund nudged her husband.

'Look at those two, bold as brass, the young hussy, at it again. I don't know how old Dicky Braithwaite puts up with all their goings-on. Parson's a bit free with his parish ladies, time he got himsen a wife and stopped his gallivanting even if Liddy Braithwaite was never nothing but a trollop for all her fancy ways . . .'

Zillah turned from the dancing as the music stopped but was stalked by the vicar who breathlessly caught her up. 'I saw you watching us, come and join us all . . . these country jigs get the blood beating faster.'

'No thank you,' she snapped as Mercy ran up and pleaded for a turn. She shook her head again, trying to look unflustered at this unwanted attention.

'Don't be so stuffy, Miss Herbert, a little levity might crack your enamel now you've decided to dress like a human being, not a plaster saint. I do apologise about the other business if that's what's bothering you. Let me escort you in the next dance to show we are friends again to the villagers.'

'We are always civil to one another, I hope, but my civility does not warrant any further contact. I am still disappointed by your lack of interest in my mission—'

'This is no night for sermons, please excuse me. Your preaching grates on my ear at every turn. I generally find those who take too hearty an interest in religion usually lack for satisfaction in other parts of their lives. It's not healthy in a woman so young.'

'Really, Mr Hardy. Could it be that I am at the receiving end of another of your boring homilies? Please do not tire yourself on my account . . . and yes, I will be doing the next dance but with Mercy Birkett at my side, not you.' She smiled impishly, flashing the merriest of eyes in triumph, knowing she looked twice as elegant and neat as that Braithwaite woman. Now it was his turn to stand at the edge as she swung past, her long dark hair unfurling down her back, leaping joyously into the affray with Mercy darting hither and thither to the thumpety-thump of the music. Hardy looked quite discomfited by their sparkling exuberance and that knowledge put springs on Zillah's heels for the rest of the evening.

Chapter Fifteen

'You'll be going to the Feast this afternoon, son?' asked Blaize Lund wearily as she watched Sunter slump over his lunch bowl in the dark kitchen of High Butts farmhouse.

'Nah, can't be arsed. If you've seen one fair you've seen the lot, St Oswy's Feast is allus the same. A few cages of manky animals, a juggler and magician, them fat ladies, dobbie horses and swings. Feasts is for babbies.'

'Eeh lad, I were only trying to cheer you up, you look as flat as a kippered haddock and no mistake with a mouth on yer like a cat's bum. Come on, buck yerself up, show a bit of gumption and you'll get more. Make summat of yerself like Grandpa Lawson tellt you. Do summat and have summat and then folks'll respect thee!

'Look, the jockey is set fair on the weather glass. 'Twill bring folks down the dale for a mixing at the fair. Yer cousins will be going too. Why don't you offer to cart them down and make theeself useful for a change? See that Ellie don't get up to any mischief while Auntie Annie is struck down with one of her heads. Annie's that worried she'll end up like one of them Ingomells girls from the estate lodge . . . got herself in trouble with a navvy and run off, so we are told. Her not sixteen. I bet Reg Ingomells is not so keen on railroads now!

'Come on, shake out of it and put yer best shirt on, plaster yer hair down neatly. It'll do yer good to mix in young company. They'll be selling ginger biscuits and you know how you like them crackly snaps. Remember when you were little how you used to follow that sweet man with his tray and shout, "Taste and try before you buy!" all over the green for him? You used to count the days to St Oswy's Feast and save yer farthings to spend on the coconut shies and rifle range.'

'I'm a big lad now, Mother, feasts is boring,' Sunter snapped.

'It's you that's boring, our Sunter. What's eating into you, are you still fretting about that do outside the Fleece with the Jock? Put that behind you, son. We had such hopes of you when you were a scholar and so did Mr Bulstrode. Then you just upped and left him in the lurch and let us down before the village. What went wrong with yer book learning?'

'I'm not going to go into all that again. Shut it, Mam. It's a closed book now. Bulstrode is not all he's cracked up to be, believe me. He let me down and all. It were him who withdrew my name from the scholarship exam. He makes me sick and he owes me. One of these days I'm going to pay them stuck-up Patabullys a visit. They can't just treat me like dirt . . .' Sunter jabbed his knife into the table.

'Stop that! I wish you would settle down to farming like all the other lads in the dale. Take an interest in all yer father's been building up, help him recover from all them dead sheep we lost last April.'

'I hate this bloody farm, I hate sheep even more and get off me back, yer bugging me. I want to leave this dale for good.'

'No one's stopping you, son, but it'll break us hearts if you do. It's not anyone's fault we had no more bairns after you. You know yer father caught summat at Hawes market which blew up his privates when you were a babby and ever since then I never could get caught. Don't let us down. There's plenty of other lassies to wed. Don't moon over cousin Ellie, she's that big she'll sit on you but don't say I told you. You know how yer father has plans for Middle Butts. I want you to be happy. Still, you could take yer old mam to the fair, give her a treat for once away out of these dark walls. Before we turn round it'll be backend and another winter'll be upon us again. I could do with an outing.' Blaize sighed softly and turned to her chores. Sunter rose reluctantly. 'Go on then, you've twisted my arm.'

The village was a mass of colourful tents and booths, awash with striped awnings lining each side of the beck in a walkway of coconut shies and market stalls, crammed with tables of fancy goods and trinkets to take home as a fairing. The fairground was parked up at the end of the street in a field and horses grazed on the common land while their painted wagon huts rested in the shade.

In the fierce heat of late July, the villagers were out in force in their Sunday finery parading down the main street, avoiding the cowpats and horse dung and the smell of the sad tigers which stared from their small cages with weary eyes, covered with flies, lazing in the heat, panting for water. There were navvy families too, dressed up in white moleskin breeches and clean shirts, carrying children on their shoulders for a better view.

St Oswy's annual Feast was held close to the patronal festival of St Oswald of Northumbria on the fifth of August. For as long as folk could remember there was a fair held in Scarsbeck to honour the saint after haytiming was finished. The travelling vans made a detour to set up their stalls in the hidden dale.

For a few weeks, haytiming drew all the local boys home to their separate dale farms and gangs of Irish hired workers from the camps downed their spades to earn extra spends while the sun shone. In three days fields were scythed, turned and spread to dry off, then the hay was forked onto sledges drawn by carthorses and dragged back to the barns to be stooked. Now the task was done on all but the laziest of farms, everyone was in holiday mood and the local brass band in military braid jackets blew gustily into their instruments to open the festivities.

As the sun beat down on the necks of visitors and villagers alike, some sought the shade of the trees edging the walled gardens of the finer residences, others sheltered under the scaffolding under the gantry boxes at the far end of the street where workmen, still on shift, waved and whistled at their audience. Others purchased flimsy paper parasols sold by one enterprising stallholder who quickly sold out.

Mercy Birkett was covered up in a wide sun bonnet and skipped among the stalls ahead of her sister. There was so much to inspect before she parted with a single penny. Which roundabout horse would she choose, what sweets and trinkets could she afford? Did she need to pay for the peepshow or the freak tent? The boxing ring at the end of the green was not going to get her custom as she peered up at the red face of the Birmingham Basher who stood like a colossus in embroidered green satin shorts and grubby white tights.

Ellie sifted through the trinket stalls with gaudy pottery statues of famous figures of history and paused over the figurine of Bonnie Prince Charlie on horseback. He looked just like Fancy Mac and she crossed her fingers, wishing him to be somewhere at the fair. Then she felt so guilty she bought a little jug for Mother and smiled to Miss Herbert who was talking earnestly to some of the navvy parents of her schoolchildren under the trees.

For one afternoon animosity between villagers and navvies was temporarily suspended as everyone enjoyed the fun of the fair. Outside the Fleece men spilled out onto the green with their tankards and ran the gauntlet of a pair of temperance workers with blue ribbons on their lapels, waving pamphlets at the men who snatched them up and chucked them down as soon as the Band of Hopers moved away.

Ellie laughed at the sight of old Cleggy the sexton in his uniform, blowing his cheeks into balloons as the brass section of the village band parted company with the conductor and the drummer. The conductor waved his baton furiously and fell off his box in the effort to reunite the music as it danced away across the crowd in opposite directions. Mercy put her hands over her ears to drown out the din.

It was getting hotter and stickier and Blaize sought relief in the chapel tearoom with other farmers' wives. Only the children darted in and out of the stalls, across the beck stones, racing each other tirelessly; babies wailed in their baskets on wheels and stallholders mopped their brows, shouting their wares to passers-by. The navvy families were the ones with the money and their children seemed to be indulged on every stall, babies carried in shawls around the women's backs. Ellie was quite shocked at the shortness of their skirts and the toughness of their black boots. Some wore twisted scarves around their hair like common gypsies, with tanned leathery complexions and faces old before their time. She was glad they were an unattractive bunch. Fancy would not be looking in that direction.

Further down the gangway Mally Widdup was treating Tizzy to a toffee apple and some spun-sugar candy and herself to a pretty cotton square for round her neck. The bustle was just like being back in Leeds on market days. Tizzy chased one of the schoolboys and bumped into Fancy Mac swinging his jacket over his shoulder. He cuffed her tousled curls teasingly. Since she cut off her braids to disguise herself the hair had grown back into tight wiry coils which were the bane of her life to flatten even with a cap on.

Suddenly Fancy stopped in his tracks and saw ahead the object of his desire: the tall fair farmer's daughter browsing at the ribbon stall, completely alone for once. He sprang over to her side in two strides. 'I'll be buying that for the lady . . .' He nodded in her direction, delighted to see her dart back with surprise and smile warmly.

'Thank you, Mr MacLachlan, but I can't accept your offer. It was for my mother, she's unwell.'

'Then we'll have two of them, one for you and one for her. Please, it's only a wee bauble.' Fancy winked.

'I shouldn't, not from a stranger. It's not proper.'

'How can I be a stranger when you've seen me naked as the day I was born!' Fancy laughed.

'Shush! Someone will hear you,' Ellie giggled, blushing, but wanting the moment to last forever. They locked eyes and lost themselves in the staring so much so that Fancy forgot to pick up his change and the stallholder coughed to bring them back from fairyland.

'Where can we talk?' whispered Fancy, touching her elbow, sending shock waves through to her stomach.

'Walk on ahead under the viaduct and follow the beck up to the foss through the glade.' Ellie wasted no time protesting. This was her chance and nobody was watching to spoil it. She had rehearsed this scenario many times as she lay abed making plans. 'You go first and I'll follow behind in ten minutes.' She pointed discreetly towards the viaduct. For once that dreadful edifice had its uses for it made a perfect screen to their tryst.

Fancy drifted off, his pirate's tail bobbing, glinting like burnished copper in the sunshine, swaggering past the boxing booth where the ringmaster called out, 'Come on, lad, try yer luck. Beat our champion for a prize.'

'Ach away!' he laughed, hoping for his own private wrestling match. He followed the beck into the shaded wooded glen where alder and willow arched over the limestone slabs of the river bed.

Ellie tried to look calm and casual as she ambled slowly in the same direction, hoping that no one would notice her absence. Just as she left the cover of the stalls, Mercy darted into view and tugged at her sleeve. 'Can we have our tea now, you promised! Where are you going to?'

'Just for a walk to cool off in the shade.'

'Can I come too?'

'NO!'

'Why not?'

'Am going me own gait, go and play on the swings.'

''Ave no pennies left. So I'm coming with you,' Mercy sulked.

'Here, have one of mine. Go on, shove off and spend it on what yer like.' Ellie tried not to sound desperate.

'Ta very much. Shall I come on after yer, then?'

'Please, Merciful, leave us alone for half an hour and I'll find you.'

'Who're you walking out with then? I won't tell, honest.' Mercy was dragging her heels.

'That's for me to know and you to find out, Miss Know-It-All. Hop it or I'll have that penny back off yer.' To her relief Mercy shot back to the funfair leaving Ellie marching briskly with a thumping heart.

Tizzy Widdup saw everything: the glow on Fancy Mac's face, the look of admiration in his eyes, and for a moment her spirit sank. Why wasn't she eighteen and pretty like the girl? Then he could look like that at her instead. As she followed him down the path she saw that same farmer, the poxy man who killed Tat, the fat lad, sneaking behind, cunning, glowering in the direction of the ghyll, and watched him from the shadows under the viaduct as he stalked the girl when she shook off a lass who skipped off towards the fair.

He was going to spoil Fancy's fun and spy on the lovers; perhaps the girl was going to get in bother from that horrible man. But Tizzy couldn't stop trouble. One, two, three, she counted to herself but he was a cursed man. She'd done it herself and he didn't realise who she was so perhaps there was summat she could try. She walked towards him as he passed the boxing booth.

'Here, mister,' she yelled and stuck her tongue out at him and made the rudest gesture she'd learnt from the navvies with her fingers. 'If you get any more spots, yer face'll explode! Spotty Dick!'

Sunter stared at the cheek of the lad. Something about the eyes reminded him of the navvy brat who caused all the fuss but she were a skinny lass, not a leggy lad. 'Bugger off, ragabash! Back to yer fleapit.'

'Bet yer can't beat that fist basher ... in that ring.' Tizzy seized the moment, pointing to the boxer waiting with arms crossed for his next opponent. 'Here, this is a tough one, good at killing things ... built like a stone wall an' all.' By this time a small group of village lads who were hovering for the next bout joined in the taunting.

'Get stuck in, Sunter, lad, show us yer muscles.' They surrounded him and pulled him further into the ring and the ringmaster stepped in quickly.

'Sixpence a go and a good prize if you win, yer money back if you stay six rounds. Come on, sir, wrestling or fisticuffs.'

Sunter was trapped in the circle and stripped off his jacket. The Basher circled him and made loud growling noises. Sunter felt like a trapped animal. His legs were trembling but he stood firm on sturdy thick thighs like tree trunks. He was well fed on beef, with round muscles in his arms from farm work.

He would be no match for a professional boxer but his rage was welling up, anger at being taunted by that slip of a kid into making a fool of himself before the village crowd, thwarted from following that Jock and his cousin. His muscles were pumped up with indignation and fury and he swung out wildly at the boxer to no avail. The boxer jabbed him, laughing with bleary drunken eyes as they circled defensively and the lads roared, 'Get on with it, Lund, see him off ...'

Sunter was feeling dizzier but madder, and holding on to that rage he stabbed again, thrashing out with his fists in a hopeless uncoordinated attack on the bored boxer.

The laughs of derision stabbed at his pride and he thought of all the humiliation he had suffered in Scarsbeck and most of all at the Bulstrodes'. Suddenly the face of the boxer disappeared to become the face of that stupid teacher and he stepped forward with a look of murder in his eye which made the boxer reel back in shock for a second. Then Sunter was on him like a tiger, screaming, kicking, beating his fists into his jaw, his cheek, knocking the man to the floor, kicking him in a frenzy of rage, his boots into his ribs, stomach, anything he could reach. The boxer curled up to defend his body but Sunter went on kicking, kicking, exhilarated by his success. Someone grabbed him and pulled him back but he went on kicking unawares.

'Here, here. Only a game, son, none of that!' yelled the ringmaster as his prize fighter lay wounded on the grass, gasping for breath. 'Take yer bloody prize and get out of here before I call the peeler.'

Tizzy crept out of sight in horror. She had seen that murderous look once before. One minute he was moonstruck and mad as a roaring tiger, the next he crumpled on the ground limp as a rag doll. 'Go on, son, out of here, you'll give us a bad name. 'Twas only a bit of fun, not a fight to the death,' yelled the ringmaster warily.

Sunter lay on the grass panting, sweating, his eyes focused on the dell beyond the viaduct where Ellie Birkett was canoodling up the foss with that Jock. If he told tales it would only be seen as his sour grapes. Now his head was clear again he had a much better plan to spoil their fun and staggered back to the chapel with a smirk on his face as the village lads stepped back in respect at his feat.

Chapter Sixteen

'I thowt you'd like a bit of a stretch, Mam, in the shade.'
Sunter gently edged his mother out of the tearoom towards
the foss path. 'It's lovely is this and I could do with a bit of
a sit down. And here, Mam, I got you a present.' Sunter
handed her the bright waxed flowers under the glass dome,
the prize from the boxing booth. His mother smiled, touched
by his thoughtfulness.

'I shall treasure this, lad. I don't know when I last had
summat given to me. Some iron pots at Christmas from yer
dad but this is just for my parlour. It's grand in here, peaceful
and cool as slate. Did you see Mercy making a nuisance of
herself as usual, pestering me for buns? I don't know where
Ellie was to let her go running wild.' Blaize peered at her son
in surprise at the shift in his mood from the morning. He
could change like a Yorkshire summer, fine at dawn, buck-
eting with rain by noon and a sunset fit for an oil painting.
'So you had a good time after all? Such a throng, nice to have

a bit of life in the place for a change. I've had a right good clack with half the dale.

'Poor Annie missed a treat but wise not to mix when yer down, you never know what you might pick up from them navvies. Still, we're safe enough in here in the shade. Why don't you dip yer toes in that beck? It looks ice cold.'

Sunter shook his head and turned to where a tinkle of girlish laughter echoed from further up the dell in the undergrowth, the raucous guffaws of a masculine response breaking the stillness.

'Sounds like someone's having a good time up there in them bushes,' said his mother, pricking up her ears.

'Still, what's a bit of wood for, when yer courting?' added Sunter slyly. 'I expect there's many a village bairn been tupped on these banks if the beck coughed up its secrets, eh, Mother?'

'Sunter Lawson Lund! Don't you talk smut with yer own mother,' she laughed but the smile was wiped off her face in an instant as she watched her own niece emerge, arm in arm with the big navvy, the very same who had brayed her son senseless outside the Fleece.

'What the blood and ... is that our Ellen I see coming out of them bushes like a trollop?' gasped Blaize, holding her bolstered chest in shock.

'Surely not, Mother?' replied Sunter, pretending not to notice.

'By heck! It is, the young hussy. Wait till I get back and tell our Annie what she's up to. It's a good job I saw it for meself or she'd never believe me. She dotes on that girl far too much. Come on, lad, I'm not standing here like an Aunt Sally.'

Blaize stormed forward, puffed up with indignation. 'Just one minute, madam, does yer mam know you're walking out of Scarsbeck Foss with a navvy on yer arm and bracken on yer skirts?' Ellie started at the sight of the Lunds and the smirky look of satisfaction on Sunter's greasy face.

'That's between me and my mother, Aunt Blaize. I don't tell you what Sunter gets up to when your back is turned,' came her defiant reply. She turned to Fancy for support.

'Miss Birkett and me were just enjoying some quiet moments away from the din out there.'

'Oh aye, we all know what you bogtrotters get up to in quiet dells. Shame on you, Ellen. You know what's become of Ginny Ingomells. Your mam will be heartbroken when I tell her. It was her very last word to me ... See our Ellie don't get up to owt at that fair. Sunter and I will escort you home and find Merciful who's no doubt tearing around the fair like wildfire. I'm surprised at you.'

'Thank you, Aunt Blaize, but we're quite capable of finding our own way home. Don't let us hold you up. I'm sure you'll be stopping off at Middle Butts to give yer sister the glad tidings,' snapped Ellie, looking daggers at Sunter, who shuffled off, defeated by her calmness.

'Indeed we will. Come on, Sunter, give me yer arm, I feel all of a do,' Blaize chuntered, storming off back towards the viaduct.

Tizzy Widdup had counted up to five hundred slowly, knowing it was all her fault. Now Fancy would really be in trouble and there was nothing she could do. Tizzy scampered down from the high banking, scratching her legs on the bramble shoots in a rush to catch them up.

'Fancy Mac! I'm sorry,' she called as she darted out onto the path. 'The dog man, the one that killed our Tat, he brought that owd biddy in a hat and they seed you. I tried to stop him afore but he's been following her all afternoon.' She stared coldly at Ellen, taking in every detail of her ruffled blouse and striped skirt and red cheeks.

'You did well, Billy Flash. It's nae your fault. Miss Ellen and me will be sorting it all out with her good folk when she goes home. I'll see she comes to no harm.'

'No, Mr MacLachlan,' said Ellie quickly. 'I think it better if I deal with the mess myself. If my cousin wants trouble, he shall be getting it from me. I want you to be welcome on our front doorstep properly, not shown the back entrance like a hawker.'

'Are you sure?'

'As sure as death and thank you, Billy, for guarding over us so faithfully. Am I right in thinking you are the famous Billy Widdup from Miss Herbert's class? I shall put in a good word about you.' Ellie shook her hand formally.

'Miss Sherbert's not bad for a teacher, strict but fair.' Tizzy preened with pride.

'As lads go, MacLachlan, this one is far too bonny for a boy, with all them curls,' laughed Ellie with dull eyes and a sinking heart. She must seek out Miss Herbert and prepare her for the coming storm over Middle Butts. There would be tears and tantrums, sulks and stubbornness, but Mother would have to understand that she wanted to walk out with Fancy openly, not all this hiding away. If that meant a miserable evening for herself, confined to her chamber with no supper while the St Oswy's Feast dancing echoed down the valley until dawn, then so be it. This was one battle she would not be losing.

Fancy watched the dancing with half an eye. He felt a terrible thirst in his throat, the first for weeks. Damn that Lund and his snooping, making trouble for Ellen. He was hot and irritable as he beat a path to the taproom, shoving his elbows into any ribs in his way, roaring his Highland war cry as a warning. Tonight he would be drowning his sorrows, forgetting the fair Ellen. His throat itched to slake his drooth, pint after glorious pint of nut-brown ale coursing into his veins, but still his thirst raged and burned within. How many more shillings must he spend to find relief?

He searched out the simpering spotty face of his rival in vain. One night he would corner him in a ginnel and beat him to a pulp. Some wag threw a piece of dynamite onto the coal fire as a joke, to liven up their evening. The explosion crashed around him, sending the taproom into a riot of yells as masonry flew across the room, smoke and coal dust gritted the teeth, plunging the room into darkness.

'Out, out! All of yer. Get out!' yelled Wally Stackhouse to his best customers, sensing mischief in the thick air. They made enough damage when they went on a randy. Tonight he was giving them no licence to wreck the Fleece. 'Be reasonable for owd Wally! Out onto the green with yer fun and games, leave the place standing, please!' He did his best to shoo them out of the door like troublesome wasps.

They were full of juice tonight and no mistake as he watched them gang up, link arms and rampage down the becksides into the dancing couples, knocking over the last of the stalls and trestle tables, spoiling the dancing in an orgy of silly cavortings, grabbing the women, swinging them in the air so their skirts flew high and the other lads cheered. Some dived down to the viaduct and started to climb up and swing dangerously from the scaffolding, balancing on the beams precariously, yelling out and singing their rough ditties to the audience agog below.

> *'We've met a lot of women and we loved 'em all a spell*
> *They can drive some men to drink and some to hell!*
> *But we've never met one yet, the woman cute who can*
> *Teach a trick to old Nick or this bold navvy man!'*

The young Dalesmen regrouped after the disruption of the dancing raised their own head of steam, charging into a pitched battle better than any wrestling bout at the boxing booth, piling all the men into a tangled heap of thrashing bodies.

'Send for the constable!' went out the alarm but Constable Firth was already grimly holding the man who had knocked off his stovepipe helmet and he marched this token triumph off to his lock-up cage to cool off. He picked up another drunken staggering lad and put them in together to finish off their fight. His key was missing so he tied them in with twine and returned to the fray blowing his whistle in a futile gesture.

The old guard of village worthies, thoroughly enjoying the night's free show, wagged their fingers and sighed for their lost youth. 'Leave'm be to cool off, let the fire burn itself out,' they shouted to the irate farmers who wanted to follow behind for another skirmish. The randy careered upwards towards Paradise camp, yelling, jumping over stone walls to catch sheep, but they were far too drunk to stand an earthly.

Back on the green, the youths returned to their dancing partners but most had been whisked out of reach by anxious parents fearing mischief for their girls. The farmers reclaimed the Fleece with relief and sat down with satisfaction. A randy at St Oswy's Feast was run o' the mill, just as it should be, and tonight they had quite a show. A lone navvy waved in vain for rescue, trapped on the top of the scaffolding. His audience waved back and went on their way. 'He can stay up there all night. That'll teach him to spoil our dancing!'

Once uphill, the cool air hit Fancy's legs and they buckled, staggering in any direction as if doped. He made for what he thought was his hut and collapsed in relief into his hard bunk, falling into a deep sleep with rasping snores while bemused cattle sniffed at him.

'Mam! Mam! There's a dead man in the trough. Come and see!' screamed Mercy Birkett from the farmyard, seeing a pair of stiff legs hanging over the side of the cattle trough as she pumped the water over the body.

Fancy was rudely woken by the splash of cold water on his face, soaked to the skin, his skull going round and round like a stairhead, a tongue like a bear's backside. His pockets were empty and his jacket gone. Fancy had not a clue where he was. Faces peered at him anxiously, a little face with pigtails and a familiar rosy fair face, then he was looking down the barrel of a shotgun as a weary woman with grey hair tied in rags shooed him up. 'Off my land! Off this farm. I know who you are. Keep away from my daughter or I'll pepper yer backside. Hop it, you drunken sot. And this is the swain she wants for herself?'

Fancy rose majestically, bowed courteously like a leaking galleon in full sail staggering from side to side, dripping, looking up at the window for sympathy. There was none.

'Serves you right to get a good soaking. Work like a horse and spend like an ass!' Ellie watched out of the window in fury. How dare that stupid Jock turn up blotto and spoil all her dreams? Mr MacLachlan could drown in the beck for all she cared. She slammed the window in disgust and burst into tears. Now she would have to eat humble pie.

She did not see her mother fall about laughing at the sight of the young navvy as he staggered disconsolately down the hill.

For three weeks more the heat haze shimmered, trapping in fumes of dust from the stone quarries in a cloudy plume until the sun burnt through the layers and a breeze scattered the waste further across the dale away from Paradise. Some families camped outside under the stars to stay cool at night, others erected tents over their livestock and the underground springs dried up into a muddy trickle.

The men worked on, backs tanned like leather hides, but Tizzy wore a thin shirt however hot and sticky she felt running errands, mashing tea, collecting tools to be sharpened and avoiding the school cart whenever she could. She did not want to be moved up, as Sherbert threatened. She would stay only until the long school break for the summer.

Granda Fettle and the night soil men struggled to dig in the waste in the hard ground. The middens were stinking with rotten food and faeces and were a breeding ground for rats: large brown beasts with beady eyes and ropey tails which leapt out of the soakways and poultry runs when Tizzy scuttled home to the van at dusk. The rats scavenged over the hut roofs like an army on the rampage, terrifying the womenfolk and the navvies, whose shotguns blasted at them. Afterwards the navvies strung up their bodies on ropes like washing.

Tizzy lay awake each night terrified in case they were lodging rats under their boards. She always inspected under the truckle bed, in the flour bin, behind the closed window nets just in case a beast was lurking to bite her. She would rather stew in the heat than share a van with vermin. Stumper did his best but with three legs his chasing days were over. How she longed to have Tat to guard her now. He would have seen them off.

The camp stank and Mally complained as she stripped off to her bare skin to cool off in the darkness; the sweat of her canteen clothes reeking of vegetables and greasy dripping made Tizzy dive under the cover to draw breath. There was no water to wash in, unless she trekked down with a bucket to the beck in the morning. 'Me head aches with this heat, Mally,' she whinged.

'I hope yer not sickening for summat, I hear there's a bad sickness down at Batty Green with a pox hospital for the worst cases, with fever beds where you're not allowed out once yer in. Someone at the canteen said it were smallpox again. Mary Ann said her huts had leaflets telling them to whitewash their huts and drink strong tea. She said some trampers were turned away at the contractor's hut. They were in a bad way. I think we should have a good clear-out and beat our blankets just in case.'

This made Tizzy's forehead burn even more. Surely smallpox would not come to this faraway camp? What if it were here already, caught at the fair in the mix-up of folk that gathered last Saturday in Scarsbeck? What if death was creeping up the valley, over the hill, sticking to the stick bundles of bogtrotters or fair folk, stalking through Paradise in the dead of night, uncaring like the angel of death in the Sunday school leaflets in the reading hut, marking out the first-born . . . not Mally though, she wasn't a son. What if her headache was just the beginning and she woke up covered in blistering pox? Tizzy felt panic rising. 'Not us again, Lord, one, two, three, four . . .'

Chapter Seventeen

Cora Bulstrode sat at the high desk overlooking the rows of forms in the temporary classroom, watching the fingers of the wall clock creep slowly towards breaktime. She handed round the box of knitting for spare moments. The only sound came from the click-click of needles and her efforts to untangle the bodged stitches of the infant boys who were a ham-fisted lot compared with the girls.

The seams of her own Monday morning had fallen apart when a child banged on the schoolhouse door to tell her that Miss Herbert had collapsed in her classroom and needed attention. Susan was at the dolly tub and the copper was boiling for the next wash but she must inform poor Ezra of this rude disruption to his routine. His class were demolishing that great epic 'The Wreck of the Hesperus', struggling to parse each verse, but he dutifully rose to the occasion, admonishing the pupils on pain of death not to move a muscle until his return. She watched through the door as he escorted the white-faced teacher out into the fresh air.

Cora could admit it was as hot as an oven in the classroom but to collapse in a heap was so undignified and quite unnecessary. She had a sneaking feeling that perhaps the minx had feigned the whole episode just to get herself alone with her brother. She trusted no woman around him and this one especially with her refined accent and dainty ways. Her enthusiasm for classwork was far too energetic to be healthy. Miss Herbert was little more than a Sunday school teacher but behaved as if she was fully trained like Ezra.

As if her pupils mattered. Here today, gone tomorrow, most of them. Already her class had halved in size what with children absconding to make hay on the farms or families disappearing overnight without so much as a by your leave.

Now poor Ezra decided to combine the two classes briefly while she was left to hold the fort with the younger children. She did not agree with his decision but knew better than to argue. He knew best, after all. Ezra was head of the household like their father before him and Father's word had been law. He was such a dutiful master and even now would be trying to stuff some rudiments into these poor lumpen scholars.

It really was inconvenient to be stuck here while Miss Herbert reclined on their sofa in the cool, drinking camomile tea prepared by Susan, eating their fancies and making crumbs, leaving the wash boiler to go cold.

*

Tizzy Widdup watched the headmaster warily as he scanned over their efforts with a sneer on his face. He kept mopping his brow and looking at his silver watch and chain which bobbed over his round belly. She had been scared when Sherbert just dropped to the floor. She never thought her teacher could be so frail and human. Sherbert was always bouncing in with some grand scheme, never looked defeated by how thick some of her mates were when it came to reading and writing. Having tried herself to bang in letters, Tizzy knew it wasn't as easy being a teacher as she first thought.

'You, you. You and you ... Rise. Turn. March into my classroom and the rest of you, not a peep until Miss Bulstrode comes to instruct you,' barked the headmaster to the subdued class who sat stunned at the change of batting orders. Tizzy was one of the chosen and shuffled obediently into the next classroom. They were never allowed in this hallowed room, not even for assembly. If they were required for anything they had to stand in the tiny corridor between the old school and the extension and wait to be questioned, caned, admonished or whatever with beating heart and trembling legs.

The classroom held fifty pupils all sitting in neat rows on benches with desks attached, inkwells and proper pens. The ceiling was arched with treacle-brown beams like an upturned boat and the long thin windows were high up the walls letting the sunshine rays beam down like a torch shining on the speckles of chalky dust. On a raised platform was the high desk and behind on the wall in golden scroll was painted a text, 'Thou, O God, seeth all'. There were two blackboards and maps suspended from the arches, brown cupboards and shelves of tattered books. Tizzy spotted a specimen case of old stones and shells. It made Sherbert's classroom seem very bare.

As they stood awkwardly at the back of the room, the other pupils kept turning slyly to stare at them. Tizzy felt like a specimen herself and slouched against the wall hoping she could melt out of view. 'Shuffle up, rows nine and ten, and make space for them,' came the order, reluctantly obeyed.

Mr Bulstrode looked jolly enough with a round face and a sort of grimace which you could pass off as a smile but he had no lips so his mouth was always a hard line. 'Let us show our new pupils what is expected in this class, starting with the six times table.' The class dutifully chanted the multiplication table in a singsong meaningless way.

Tizzy was not impressed for she knew her tables backwards, sideways and inside out. They were good to play with when she was nervous. Suddenly she felt a jerk on her sleeve from a fierce girl with long yellow pigtails who then kicked her shin with a heavy clog. Tizzy kicked her straight back sharp and hard. The girl squealed. 'Please, sir, he's kickin' me.'

'Merciful Birkett, are you telling tales again? Fetch the card for her neck, monitor.'

'No, sir, honest. He's just kicked me.' She raised her clog to show the red mark.

'She kicked me first, sir.' Tizzy lifted her shin to show a weal of broken skin.

'He's lying, sir.'

'Out here! Both of you together. How dare you waste our time with such idle concerns. Wait until breaktime and kick each other to pieces if you must but I will not have this bickering. Merciful Birkett, hold out your hand.' The girl gulped and unfurled her fist to receive two hard raps on her palm from a thick stick. 'Go to your seat and be silent, stupid girl.'

Tizzy stood in front of the silent class awaiting the same fate, trying not to shake. The teacher rose to his medium height, towering over the child, and shouted, 'I'm sorry you find our learning so boring that you create other entertainments. No doubt you can rattle off your tables in your sleep. Let's see how much Miss Herbert has managed to drum into your thick skull. Entertain us then with your nine times table.' Ezra Bulstrode stood back expecting silence. Tizzy rattled off the table at breakneck speed.

'I see I must congratulate Miss Herbert on her diligence but can you apply these numbers? What is the sum of nineteen by six and eleven by forty-one?'

'Five hundred and sixty-five, sir,' came Tizzy's prompt reply. The headmaster had to jot down his calculations.

'Correct. Do you read as well as you number? Read this aloud.' He shoved a book of poetry into Tizzy's hand. 'Read.'

Tizzy barked out every word without meaning or emphasis but pronounced every syllable.

'Who taught you before you came to Scarsbeck?'

'No one, sir. I allus could count. I like numbers. I do them for fun in my head.' Tizzy was feeling dizzy with all the attention, fifty pairs of eyes boring into her body.

'Your name, boy?' said the master, peering at her intently.

'Widdup, sir, Billy Widdup.'

'Ah, Master Widdup! The famous prodigy. Miss Herbert has already been your champion. Now I see why. Sit down, Widdup. I'll deal with you later.' Tizzy staggered back triumphantly. No beating. As the lesson droned on, Tizzy felt the headmaster staring at her with a bemused shaking of the head. She would be glad when it was time to go into the yard and get out of this inspection. The other teacher from the schoolhouse came in and she watched Bulstrode point again in her direction. Miss Bulstrode, who looked like a string bean, screwed up her eyes to inspect her. Tizzy was beginning to feel like the freak at the peepshow last Saturday.

The rest of the class was dismissed and Tizzy was summoned to stay behind. 'I shall be transferring you from Miss Herbert's room. She has indicated before that she thought you more suitable material for my instruction. It seems she's a good judge of potential. I want to study you closely and see what metal you're made of, not dross or base metal I trust but one hundred per cent pure gold. You will stay behind tonight for another interview and all of us will put our heads together to see if further study might make a scholar of you.'

'But, sir, I'm a part-timer at the camp. I work with a gang.'

'Not a word, boy, this is a golden opportunity for you to better yourself under my tutelage. Miss Herbert can arrange minor details. Who are your kin? They must be made to understand the importance of your talent and release you from other obligations.'

'But, sir.' Ezra Bulstrode waved his hand to waft away any protest. His eyes were cloudy and moist as he patted the boy on the head. 'Good lad, off you go. Stay in this playground and come at my bell. What do you say then?' Bulstrode held onto the lapels of his dusty black jacket, waiting for bursts of gratitude.

Tizzy darted out into the sunshine with only a breezy, 'Ta-ra for now.'

Once out into the yard she stood blinded by the brightness. This game was getting out of hand; Mr Bulstrode was taking her seriously. What if he found out she were a lass? Mally was right, this was going too far. Miss Herbert would be disgraced and they would be chucked off the camp and Mally would lose Wobbly Bob and her job. Fancy Mac would disown his tea masher. They would have to tramp on and Granda was too old. Ironfist did not care. It was up to her to carry on the fooling of everybody but she felt a stab of fear in her belly. Would she be brave enough to brazen out her disguise?

Her arrival stopped the skipping, the game of tag, the marbles competition and the handstands. Mercy Birkett, whose hand was still stinging from her caning, marched up to Tizzy sticking out her tongue. 'You smell.'

'No I don't . . .'

'Yes you do, bowdykite, bogtrotter. All navvies smell, my mam says. 'Snot fair, I got the cane and you didn't. That's Mr Patabully, carrots for the lads, nowt but sticks for the lasses.'

'It weren't my fault. I just did what he asked.'

'Show off! 'Snot fair. All navvies are bastards, my cousin says. Are you one as well?'

'I have a mam and a dad but they live away.'

'Where do they live then?'

'I dunno.'

'My dad's gone to heaven, so there.'

'So's my gran and me big brother, Bi ...' Tizzy stopped in time.

'You smell and you're not sitting next to me. I'll get fleas, my mam says.'

'No you won't. My sister works in the laundry house and these are my best clothes, so there.' Tizzy felt tears welling up but boys didn't cry so she turned away from her tormentor. After a moment she continued, 'Well, I can do sums better'n you and that got me off the stick.'

Mercy Birkett was put out at the truth of this. 'I hate Patabully.'

'So do I,' said Tizzy, glad to be agreeing on something at last. 'He seems keen to keep me face in a sum book. Why?'

'Teacher wants you for the Fawcett,' sang Mercy to the familiar hymn tune of 'Jesus wants me for a Sunbeam'. 'To shine for him each day. You'll have to stay behind and go to his schoolhouse, do sums and writing. Take an eggsand-wichstation. 'Snot fair, only boys do the Fawcett. I'm top of the class for writing. Girls should be allowed too,' explained Mercy as she cartwheeled across the yard.

'Suppose so.' Tizzy was in no mood to argue on that score. How on earth had she managed to land a Fawcett, whatever that was? It sounded like hard work and more school. If only Miss Herbert had not passed out none of this would have happened. Tizzy watched the boys kneeling over their marbles and she sauntered across, fingering poor Georgie's best bull's-eye. He was best off up in the sky playing his own game of taws. Soon she was in the thick of the game as the other lads eyed her bull's-eye enviously. Tizzy was bursting to go to the lavvy but crossed her legs, trying to forget the urge.

The bell rang and everyone shot to their feet for the line-up. Tizzy was paired alongside the Birkett girl again who sniffed and turned away. They spent the afternoon doing handwriting with quills and ink. Mercy laughed at Tizzy's feeble efforts and splotched lines. When they came to stand for the evening prayer she whispered through her hands, 'I'll wait for you s'after ... I can show you the beck and a kingfisher what fishes from my branch, if you like.'

'Ah don't know how long this palaver goes on for,' whispered Tizzy to the sound of: 'Hands together, softly so, Little hands shut tight, Father just before we go, Hear our prayer tonight.'

'I don't mind,' smiled Mercy, looking human at last. 'You can tell me what you do there.'

'Are we friends now?' answered Tizzy.

'Aye, I suppose so, but don't tell anybody. It'll be our secret.'

'I've got a secret,' blurted Tizzy, but drew it back quickly.

'Tell, tell or go to hell!' laughed Mercy.

'No, it would only get us into trouble.' Tizzy flashed her eyes.

'Honest, Billy?'

'Honest injun,' replied Tizzy, relieved not to have spilled the beans. If she didn't find a bush soon she would wet her breeks.

'Let's swear on a gravestone then,' was Mercy's bright idea until she caught sight of her cousin on horseback riding up the street.

Tizzy stared at him. 'I hate him. He killed my dog and got my friend into trouble. He's dead meat.'

Mercy nodded. 'That's my horrible cousin, he kicks cows into the barn and swings chickens round by the neck till they're dead.'

'Shall we play a trick on him, then?' asked Tizzy.

'How? When? He's bigger than us,' Mercy cautioned.

'I don't care. I'll think of something,' said Tizzy. 'Have to go back now and face the Patabully parade. Wish me luck, Mercy. See thee later.' Tizzy dashed for the empty privvy in the schoolyard, spat on her hands and gave her face a cat's lick, pulled up her scratchy socks, straightened her shirt into her trousers and dawdled nervously up to the schoolhouse gate. She was for it now.

After Billy's interview was over, they sat sedately in the back room. Miss Herbert seemed remarkably recovered, sipping tea and smiling. Ezra was full of excitement at his discovery.

'You were right, Miss Herbert, to bring his talents to my attention. Master Widdup is an exceptional child, such a pleasant appearance, courteous and with a head for numbers. What a gift in one of such lowly class. We shall have to tailor his instruction carefully to fulfil the requirements of the Fawcett but in six months we shall surely see our hard work come to fruition. I am not a gambling man, of course, but I'd like to lay odds on him achieving our goal, dear sister. Isn't it fortuitous that Miss Herbert being indisposed allowed me to step in to see this uncut diamond for myself? Lots of polish, eh!' Ezra laughed at his little joke.

'Yes, dear, most fortunate for all concerned.' Cora had never seen her brother so excited, not since the last scholar, Alec Braithwaite, who fell by the wayside after only a few weeks and never returned to thank his tutor. Not one word of appreciation. He was such a saint to labour in such harsh conditions. She often wondered what drove him to such sterling efforts. Perhaps it was the way Papa had tutored him privately, given him the opportunity to go to the university. Only Father's untimely death robbed him of the chance of carrying through his studies to a degree. Now he dedicated his life to poor students.

Miss Herbert was looking so pleased at the outcome, positively preening. For one moment Cora wondered if the woman had set up the whole encounter but no, surely a missionary would not stoop to such duplicity?

'I will visit the camp and speak to Billy's kin on camp. I foresee no problems from them. I know Billy's shillings do help the family purse, the shillings he earns as a runner for the gang,' offered Zillah Herbert as she gathered up her schoolcase and gloves.

'What if they decide to move up the line? These families are so unreliable. I hope you will not waste your efforts on an untrustworthy scholar, Ezra dear.' Cora was not happy with this decision.

'I'm sure there are no worries on that score, Miss Bulstrode. I have always found Billy to be reliable as a monitor,' defended Miss Herbert promptly, jabbing a pin into her ridiculous boater trimmed with striped ribbon to match her silk school shirt. Such extravagant clothing on a teaching assistant.

'Master Widdup seems an amiable child, small for his age, a bit on the thin side. I hope he will not be a sickly child. I need robust scholars. Perhaps you would make a note to see that he gets a full glass of milk and some fruit after school with a few tasty sandwiches. Build him up a bit so that his concentration is fully occupied in his head, not his belly. Lads of that age are all stomach gurglings. Oh this is an important day! I take back everything I said about your Mission school, Miss Herbert. Are you settled in your new lodgings?'

'Perfectly, Mr Bulstrode. The Birketts are a charming family. I am most contented to be there.' She smiled sweetly at Cora who remained tight-lipped, watching the woman glide out of the door like a siren.

Now Ezra was giving orders again. She had some of her own making. No navvy child, scholar or not, would be crossing the portals of his precious study until she personally saw to it that his face and hands were scrubbed raw, nails cut, hair inspected for fleas and his breath smelt for the faintest whiff of alcohol. Master Widdup would get a dose of purging oil and a spoonful of poppy juice if he showed the slightest sign of sickness in her house.

Chapter Eighteen

Zillah struggled up the hill to Paradise in the dusty heat, her cottons sticking to her skin, trickles of sweat dampening her forehead, making the straw boater itch at the band and the veil of netting smother her nostrils. She sniffed her handkerchief for a whiff of lavender water to cool her senses. The track was unusually quiet for a weekday afternoon, no packmen bending to their burden, no carthorses plodding with their load. A strange unfamiliar stillness hung in the air, broken only by the sound of a dizzy skylark warbling high above the heat haze.

The gangs were down by the ravine laying wooden planks across the prepared soil, no doubt welcoming the shade of the tall ash trees. Now that the cuttings and embankments were carved out of the landscape, temporary tracks would bring the hoot of small locomotives carrying supplies of iron tracks to lay the line. The men whistled rudely as she passed a gang and her blushes were hidden under veiling. They knew who she was, shouting, 'Give us a hymn, miss. Can we come to yer class? Let me turn yer pages, miss?' The shouting had worsened since she abandoned her black clothes in favour of summer cottons.

The teacher checked her basket. There were eggs for Mary Ann and a rattle bought at the Feast for Janey, a bag of wool rovings for Mally Widdup to card and spin up into yarn and some blush cherries from the tall tree in the kitchen patch.

At last she came in sight of the contractor's caravan on wheels where she was stopped by a clerk. 'No one in the camp, miss, not with the sickness. Go back to Scarsbeck and keep yer veil down. Beg pardon but it is terrible sickness,' said the man with a stern anxious look on his leathery face.

'I have visits to make: I'm from the Pastoral Aid. Let me pass, please, I'm on the Lord's work, young man.'

'Not even the Angel Gabriel himself would want to wander round this camp without a mask and a pomander, miss. They've isolated the fever huts all at the far end. The doctor calls in from Batty Green, it's carrying them off like flies down there, so it's better to be safe than sorry, miss. Go back. There's ten huts down with it here and four dead already.' The man tried to wave her back with his hands but Zillah stood firm.

'Thank you for your concern but as I said, I am on the Lord's work and I take the risk. Stand back and let me through.' Zillah carried on walking into the camp.

The clerk shook his head wearily. 'Be it on yer own head. I have my orders too, you know.'

The teacher sensed fear stalking Paradise as she walked purposefully along the rows of huts. Women were indoors and there were no children romping noisily around the buildings chasing dogs and poultry. Goats were tethered in the shade nibbling the dried-out plants of withered vegetables. Each hut was now painted white to reflect away the sun's rays and through the open doors she smelt a mixture of limewash and carbolic; bedding was strung out on ropes to air in the light. Women sat in doorways smoking their dreadful clay pipes, inspecting the missionary with suspicion as she marched past on her way to Mary Ann's hut to inspect Janey's progress.

They were used to her weekly visits and she wondered sometimes what they made of her trailing skirts. Mary Ann would put on the water to boil in a pan and bring out her one china cup which was cracked and stained brown in the bottom. It was hard to swallow the strong tea but Zillah never flinched.

Her admiration was growing for the way these young women struggled to feed, clothe and care for their families in such cramped conditions, sharing their huts with rough lodgers, preparing gallons of stew and pies to feed muscles with beef.

She was ashamed that her own curiosity had never crossed the baize door into the servants' quarter at home. It was an unknown, unseen world. No one had ever thought to prepare her for this harsh existence. It would have been unthinkable to mix two such different worlds, like mixing ale with wine.

Now she was bringing some good news, the promise at last of a baptism service for Janey alongside a group of other navvy children from the school whose parents she had badgered for weeks to get their offspring christened together. This was an important victory in her campaign against the 'late' Reverend Hardy. It would give him something to think about.

The white gravel chippings on the path to Lower Paradise scuffed up a chalky dust into a cloud; as she approached Mary Ann's hut, she smelt smoke. A group of women were standing round a bonfire of clothing and furniture shaking their heads. They looked up at her arrival and scattered suddenly, leaving the teacher to knock on the hut door. There was no answer.

'No point in going in there. It's empty, been fumigated. If yer wanting Mary, you'll have to go down to the fever hut . . . Poor do for her man when he comes home. No babby, no dinner, no hut. She's badly, is Mary.' The woman in the doorway kept her distance as she shook her head. 'Down yonder is the fever hut on its own. They've brought a nurse up from Batty Green but there's nowt much to be done, is there?'

Zillah felt her stomach churn as she hurried down the makeshift path noticing other rings of stone with smouldering bundles dotted round the perimeter of the camp. The sickness was everywhere. The fever hut stood on its own; a bleak outpost of sanitation and safety, she hoped, for Mary Ann and Janey. As she approached she noticed a tall familiar figure shutting the door behind him. What was he doing in the camp?

Ralph Hardy looked up in surprise at Zillah's arrival and shooed her back with his hands. 'Don't go inside, Miss Herbert. I'm sorry. She's gone now.'

'Gone where?' she asked innocently.

He raised his eyes heavenward. 'To the saints in glory, let us hope.'

'Oh no! Who? Only last week at the fair Janey cut her first tooth. She was so hot and crotchety then. Oh dear, I must see them and pay my respects at once. Poor Mary Ann and her husband too?'

'Her man is not here. She was minding the hut until he returned from Batty Green on a temporary job. He must have brought the fever with him. Please don't go inside, remember them as they were. I don't advise it.' The vicar blocked her path.

'Let me pass, Mr Hardy. I brought that child into the world and you wouldn't baptise her. Surely I have the right to bid her farewell? It's too cruel. How can God allow such a thing?'

'It's our carelessness which makes this sickness spread, Miss Herbert. Not the Almighty. The conditions here are hardly hygienic and this is the price they pay. I've registered ten bodies in this camp this morning. A sad day for Paradise.' The man sighed.

'Some Paradise, Mr Hardy, Janey never got her baptism. I just hope you can live with that!'

'For goodness' sake, woman, do you think that God would bar a baby from His presence? They have their needful place.'

'I just wish he wouldn't take so many of them,' said Zillah, thinking of her own little sister who never survived infancy. 'So this ill wind brings you to Paradise at last. I must admit I'm surprised to see you wandering in such a cesspit. I thought you said it was not your concern.'

'I am so sorry to disillusion you but as one of the few people in the dale to have the cowpox scratch I have my uses. We'll have to organise a special burial for these victims in a communal grave, I'm afraid, to protect the rest.'

'The church couldn't be bothered to come when they were alive but now they are dead they get your undivided attention.' Zillah marched past the man, not looking into his face for a response. The man, ruffled by her rudeness, stuck his hat on his head, raised it briefly and strode away to another hut.

Zillah opened the door into the bare hut. No one could hide the sickly smell of death in the room however many coats of limewash were plastered on the walls. There was a line of beds down each side of the wall. All the furnishings had been stripped, from the stove to the tommy cupboards where usually the men kept personal belongings hung on the wall. A woman in a starched pinafore was sitting on a scrubbed chair and she rose quickly to shoo her out. Zillah took a deep breath, sick at the thought of the mother and child isolated in this hut to face death. It was so unfair. 'I've come to see Mary Ann.' The nurse gestured to a bed and sat down again.

'Oh Mary!' The girl was hunched on her bed, stuffing a cloth in her mouth to control her sobs. Janey lay in her arms as if asleep, wrapped in a shawl. Zillah looked at both of them, unable to speak. She drew back the shawl and recoiled in horror at the disfigurement of the baby's pitted swollen face pockmarked beyond recognition; a mass of raw pustules like flesh peeled back from its skin. Surely this was not little Janey, plump and rosy-cheeked? How she must have suffered. Janey had known so little life and comfort since her crude entrance into the world. Now she no longer looked human.

Zillah dropped back the blanket in disgust, tears of rage and sadness all mixed up. She wanted to vomit. Why? Why? Yet she felt ashamed at this primitive reaction to the horror of the scene, ashamed of her weakness in doubting God's goodness. Where was the good in this suffering?

She gathered the girl into her arms instinctively and they rocked together, trying to erase the horror of it all. There were no words for those minutes, only the sound of hinges squeaking as they rocked back and forth.

How could the likes of Mary Ann, the Widdups or the others she was beginning to know and respect fight against such a killer? How could she bear to live disfigured, pockmarked as Mary now was? It was then that fear flooded over her; fear of the same mutilation. What if this visit would pass the disease on to her? Would she be brave enough to bear the disfigurement, the looks of pity as people averted their eyes from her pockmarked face? How could she put the Birketts at risk, she reasoned to herself as she turned and fled out of the camp, hardly stopping to draw breath until she was safely over the beck and up the slopes of Middle Butts Farm.

Zillah tore off her outer clothing, tore them into pieces and pushed them bit by bit onto the range fire. Only then did she weep with shame as she finished her latest epistle to Nottingham.

Dear Aunt Jane,

Sadness sits upon my soul today. I have seen suffering I will never forget and we have lost our little namesake to a terrible plague in these beautiful hills. They are so green and yet so treacherous, harbouring disease in the camps, carrying pestilence over green fields in the wind from shantytown to shanty camp.

It has erased any pleasure I might have had in telling you of some success. You see I have to confess to contriving to ensure my brightest pupil, the boy Widdup, has at last been noted, tested and transferred through to Mr Bulstrode's excellent tutelage. Through a shameful indulgence of overacting, I convinced him of my indisposition, requiring him to take over my class for the afternoon. All other devices having failed, desperation made a cheat of me. It has been a hollow victory, however, for since this ruse the children have not been allowed to attend school owing to an outbreak of smallpox in the sadly named Paradise.

Fields are all given peculiar names in these parts and the railway huts find themselves in Paradise field. Anywhere less like Paradise I would be hard placed to envisage.

Miss Bulstrode has forbidden her brother to allow any contact with children from the camp until further notice. She is the sour-faced host who made life at Scarsbeck so uncomfortable; like a watchdog guarding her den, baring teeth at all but her brother. So I have no pupils and take the infant children for walks in the sunshine while the headmaster instructs his older pupils. I fear most of my class will have disappeared by the autumn.

The fear of this terrible fever and the chance of casual work tempt families out into the field gangs. Some choose to disappear during the night away from the camp sickness, no doubt to spread it further up the line. Sadly it is the babies and the old who are the most vulnerable. Her mother will recover but is so disfigured. I cannot shake off a feeling of heaviness in my limbs at such a waste of life. I see her face before me wherever I go.

Have no fear for my safety; there have been no outbreaks in the village and farms, I think due to the airy coolness of stone walls and slate floors which are well scrubbed. These Dalesfolk are keen on cleanliness if not godliness, washing, scrubbing and suchlike with rough hands to prove it, but their health is good and appetites sturdy.

I have this foolish thought that this plague is a punishment for my duplicity. Could I be to blame? I cannot summon up any enthusiasm for my usual tasks here. The Birketts must despair of my lazy ways.

I know I have forced the issue of Billy's education with his kinfolk. His sister and grandfather are simple folk, eager to please. *They promise to make Billy attend his extra coaching lessons. I know this will cost them dear. You can be sure I will do what I can discreetly to alleviate the shortfall in their purse with small gifts of food and clothing.*

Papa will no doubt say I'm interfering again, getting overinvolved in a cause, as usual. Surely I should champion rare ability when I am privileged to discover it? There are few enough lights smothered under bushels in my classroom.

As there is much sadness to attend to, I cannot desert my post as you all would wish for the annual trek to Scotland and the glorious twelfth of August. I know this will disappoint your plans but when there is so much fear and suffering in the camp, this is no time for me to indulge myself with a holiday.

Yours sadly,
Zillah Jane

Chapter Nineteen

'When will it rain again, Beth? Come on, you're my weather glass. How long do we have to wait? The fields are tinder-dry. It's not natural for us to fry in August. Sir Edward says his grouse will be poor this year.' Ralph Hardy mopped his brow as he sat by the shepherd woman's fireside blowing pipe smoke out of the open door.

'Nothing's gone right since yon railway cut through us like a knife, slicing up the fellside, disturbing the spirits, the boggarts and pixie folk are breeding mischief. It'll rain soon enough when I'm in the ground. I wish I *could* help them folks with the fever but there's little yer can do if it takes hold, just cooling and soothing and a strong body to fight. I've heard you've been visiting and doing what yer can.'

'Not much, Beth, just registering the poor souls for burial and visiting the families. They're a tough lot up there and keep to themselves but they're glad enough of a bit of con-cern from the village.' He was not going to tell her that he could not sleep at night, his dreams disturbed by the haunting faces of the dead.

'You make sure you don't touch owt, if in doubt, burn it. Keep yerself fresh . . .' said Beth, and seeing him smile, 'No I don't mean "market fresh" drunk like the farmers after a trip to Hawes. Wash yer hands, dab on them herb oils I give yer.' Beth lay back tired and frustrated, her leg bound tight and lifted up on a buffet. 'And here's me laid up after nobbut a fall, jiggered by just a knock on a rock. Still, a few days'll see me right.' Lad the sheepdog nuzzled into her lap and she stretched to stroke him. 'You should be outdoors, not getting fat by the hearth, dog. I don't know what's come over me.'

Ralph knew it was more than a fall. She blacked out somewhere on the fellside. Lad had whined and drawn the attention of a passing drover who found her confused, unable to speak and only aware of the gash on her best leg.

It was as if all her strength had seeped away into the moss, leaving her pale and listless, her speech slurred and laboured where once she was wick to answer back. A tongue-lashing from Beth was Ralph's tonic. Suddenly his white witch was mortal, frail and in need of care herself.

'Come back with me, let us look after you at the vicarage for a spell. I promise I will wait on you hand and foot.'

She cackled feebly. 'Away with you, vicar! What will the village think, settling yer fancy piece up in the holy house? And that schoolmarm will create a stink. She's a sight to behold and not above giving you the bright eye! Quite a lady by all accounts and kindly enough . . . you could do far worse.'

'Never, never, never will I consider that opinionated, interfering, over-righteous schoolmarm! She may have the merriest eyes in Scarsbeck and a pert little body but if I have to live in hell, I'll wait till I'm dead.'

'My, my, she has got up yer nose. Watch out, vicar, there's arrows flying overhead, wear a breastplate or you'll get struck. I'll not be here to see the fun but I'll be watching just the same. Don't look like that. I'm not budging from my own hearthside till I can stride over Scarsdale tops with Lad and me sheep. If me time's coming, so what, I've had a good enough turn, seen a few seasons. So no moping about owd Beth Wildman, the Crow Woman. Bury me at midnight out by Scarsbeck stone cross, high enough for a good view and deep enough not to have scavengers picking over me bones. These owd bones can feed the cloudberries on the fell, bring out a bit of colour. I want no fuss and no fancy words. If yer put me in the kirkyard, I'll haunt yer every night till you do as yer bid. Think on.'

Ralph looked sternly at her. He had never heard her talking in such a way before. 'Stop being morbid, Bethany Wildman, you'll be seeing a fair few sheep clippings yet. Where's your spirit – in your boots?'

'Can't you get into yer thick skull, young man, there comes a time when a body's had enough of cold winters and aching skiatics, when thee's seen enough of what's a-coming to know you don't want to be round to see it? Railway tracks and steam engines bringing town folk tramping over dale as have no right to be there, clodhopping, breaking walls down, scaring sheep, knocking the bogs into marshland. I see nowt to stay around for. If me time's up I'll snuff it but I don't want Lad to pine. Find him a good home and I'll leave yer in peace.' Beth spat into the fire defiantly.

'What's got into you today? Here I came to cheer you up and now I'm crying in my tea,' answered Ralph.

'Yer a good lad, vicar, for all yer wicked ways. I've said me piece to you and only you. If it jumps in yer chest, obey it and you'll be a good shepherd to yer flock after all. I keeps on at yer but you will shy off. What are you afeared of?'

'I don't know. Who am I to show anyone the way to guide a flock along a track?'

'Tracks is for drovers to drive them from one sale to the next. That's not shepherding. A shepherd lets his flock roam free in the right places, lets them free from a distance like, a shepherd knows each of his flock not as a bunch but one by one. Only then will they trust you and come when you call.

'As I recall, I once lost one of me sheep at a sale in a mix-up; a good ewe that sometimes gave twins regular, so I scoured each pen till I found her mixed with someone else's lot. I could tell her by her crooked teeth. All crossed over they were. So I tellt some gaffer what I was looking for and he checked the pen for me. I was right, it was my sheep and I got her back. T'other farmer had no idea it wasn't one of his. Just shows it pays to know yer own.

'Watch over folk, listen and keep yer distance. Come closer when they wander off. Leave 'em alone and they'll come home, wagging their bloody tails behind them.' Beth laughed at the nursery rhyme. 'Leave 'em alone and they wander off some cliff like the stupid sheep they are, daft and canny at the same time. Need a lot of looking after do sheep.' She lifted her hand as he stood to leave. 'If I do get badly, come and sit with me awhile until I'm safely away . . .'

'There you go again getting maudlin. I shall go straight home and get Cleggy to bring you a bottle of my best brandy. He can sit while you down the whole lot in one go. That'll put a smile on your face, a flush on those yellow cheeks, the lash back in that tongue of yours and fire in your belly.' Ralph bent over, grabbed her hand and kissed it. It was as cold as ice.

Tizzy and Mercy met secretly by the beck during the school holidays to plan their surprise for Sunter Lund. Mercy told her new friend about the stones hanging in the cowshed, stones with holes in the centre to ward off the evil eye. Sunter was careful never to move the stones tied with twine to the stalls. Tizzy told how she had scared him with her curses and together the idea of scaring him witless was born.

Now they were waiting at dusk in the shadows on the track past Middle Butts near the copse of high trees which whooshed and crackled as the evening breeze rustled through the glade. Already the dry leaves were curling up. They had blackened their faces with grate polish and then painted whitewash in stripes to look like bones on the sacks hung over their heads and bodies with a hole for a face. Mercy had made crepe poky bonnets with straw sticking out for hair. The final touch was candle lanterns floating in oil in case they blew out. They were hiding, listening for the clop of the cart as he staggered back from market, 'fresh' with ale from his stop at the Fleece.

At the sound of hooves they crossed over into the straw field and climbed onto the stone wall just enough to swing the lanterns eerily and wail in high-pitched voices. 'Coming to get you, Lundy Butts ... boggarts of the potholes is coming for you soo–oon, Lundy Butts.' They crept along the wall keeping pace with him but crouching down out of view.

Then Tizzy sprang up and screamed like a banshee. The horse reared up at the noise. Sunter struggled for the rein and stopped it dead. There was silence, only the arching flickering shadows reflected on the trees.

'Who's that? I'll bloody get you for that, Jock! Bugger off!' He could make out figures, leaping and waving.

'Murderer ... your time is nigh.'

'If that's you, Jock, I'm coming to have you, once and for all!' With one leap he scaled the stone wall, cursing as he stubbed his shin. He could see fleeing figures in the distance, running from the gate back to the wood. 'Come back here, cowards. I'll find you!' As Mercy fled from her cousin she dropped the lantern. There was no time to dart back for it. To her horror the hot oil and candle flame spilled out onto the dry straw igniting the ground at once in a line of fire; fire onto ground as hot as oven plates; tinder, kindling twigs, dry leaves fuelling the flames into a blazing wall. Soon the whole field was alight; the crackling fire had Sunter galloping towards Middle Butts. 'It's afire!'

The children stood back in horror at the accident. 'Look what we've done!' yelled Mercy, frozen with fear.

'You go back and I'll run to the camp for help too,' shouted Tizzy, her feet scorching in the smouldering grass. 'Run, run, Mercy. No one will see you in the dark!'

The heavy clouds of choking smoke brought men down from the camp to lend weight to the fire-beating, throwing soaked sacks around the barns and buildings to steer the fire out from the farm up onto the moor. Whipped by the wind the torch of fire spread across bracken and heather. Sparks flew like fireworks and through the night Lunds, Birketts, navvies, farmers, struggled to control its wayward path.

A chain of women carried buckets from the trickling beck. Annie Birkett and Zillah took turns to pull on the well-rope, hauling up water to douse the firebreak while Ellie led horses and cattle to safety near the beck.

The black silhouettes of men fought tirelessly to and fro, choking from smoke and dust. Mercy dashed around in a frenzy of remorse unable to do anything but get under feet.

As dawn broke the farm stood safe, blackened by smoke, the garden a trampled mess, while the bracken and moorland smouldered under the first downpour of autumn.

The navvies under Ben Robson, the resident engineer on duty, brought a stirrup pump but the stream was almost dry. The beck was a good firebreak though and there was no danger to the camp on the other side. The railway track through Middle Butts pasture lay in ruins; the sleepers had burned to dust and iron rails buckled in the heat. Half a mile of useless embankment charred and all the equipment left overnight destroyed.

Fancy Mac and his gang helped to clear up the mess around Middle Butts, silently lifting cartwheels, checking for any sparks and dampening the hay with wet sheets.

'Yer could have lost all yer fodder. A rum do.'

'How did it start?'

'A spark of lightning?' The men sipped tea with parched throats as the questions came thick and fast.

'He started it!' Sunter accused, his clothes splattered with scorches, pointing his stubby finger at the gangmaster. 'You, Jock, were behind that wall with a torch trying to make a fool o' me. I saw yer. He chucked down his torch and fled. I saw it. He's yer man!'

Fancy stepped forward, towering over the man, pointing his own finger angrily. 'Yer out of order, sonny. Ach away with yerself . . . There's a dozeny men here who was drinking in ma hut when Mr Paisley shouted us to help out doon here. He can telt ye the truth of it, so he can. I wouldnae put it past yon fool to have started it hissel.' Sunter rushed at him but Warwick held his shirt.

'Come away, son, it's no use a-blaming. A spark could kindle a flame in this drought. It's just one of those things and land is better for a bit of burning.'

'But I'm telling you. It were him or one of his. I seed it

with me own eyes, calling out names. You should send for the constable,' pleaded Sunter to an audience which shrugged shoulders and turned backs wearily. Sunter was a fool to himself to spoil for a fight after these lads had worked all night to put out the blaze.

Annie Birkett shook the manager's hand, saying thank you for their efforts. She stopped short, looking up at the sooty face of Fancy Mac. 'Our last meeting was a cold one, Mr MacLachlan. This one a mite too warm though it don't change owt.'

She smiled as he bowed courteously with a flourish. 'I'm after catching yer drift, mistress, and I'll do ma best to resist temptation but I'm no promising, mind.' Fancy searched out the smiling eyes of his fair Ellie, sensing with relief that all between them was forgiven at last.

High up on Paradise field, Tizzy watched the fires blaze, shaking at the terrible consequences of their stupid plan, hugging Stumper for comfort. As the crowds gathered to watch the fire rampage, she crept back to the wagon and dived under the cover to hide her tears. Was it true about the boggarts? Were they teasing her like the gangmen who hid their mugs and claimed she'd lost them? When she let loose her cursings on Lund had she set off another fire in the hills which no one would control? Her secret was running amok. Like Georgie Hunt she was trapped before rolling stock waiting to be crushed and buried. Was there no way out of this pickle but to confess her guilt?

*

Zillah was bone-weary from the night's drama. Now she must face the morning's funerals for the smallpox victims taking place in the burial field by the side of the kirkyard in land donated by the Dacre family, hastily consecrated for this purpose. The navvies were to be cordoned off in death as they had been segregated in life.

Zillah was sick of funerals, wreaths, bidding cards, funeral biscuits and wearing heavy black garb on another August morning with an ink-blue sky. She was sick of sad faces and the stench of burnt turf, the roasting flesh of the few beasts caught by the firestorm.

Smoke seeped into the farmhouse covering walls and surfaces. There was black dust everywhere. Annie was crotchety. Mercy was sickening for something, pale, wan, off her porridge and very tearful. Ellen was frantically trying to clear up the mess, relieved that no further damage was done and that the overnight rain, thank heavens, had cooled down the smoulderings.

What a summer! This northern high ground was as harsh and unforgiving as it was beautiful. She felt so powerless against such strong forceful elements, so small, so vulnerable. For once in her life she felt out of control.

The vision of Janey and Mary Ann kept disturbing her concentration; Janey was birthed with such optimism and such naivety. Nothing was turning out as she hoped. It was changing her in ways she didn't like, making her question why she had come in the first place. Who was she to think she could change anything in this strange hidden world?

For the first time since her arrival, the teacher yearned for city streets and civilised society, lofty drawing rooms and crisp clothing, dainty food, polite manners and refined society. Suddenly everything about her old life seemed so appealing, so normal. Then the tune of the chorus came into her head: 'Yield not to temptation, for yielding is sin. Each little victory, some other will win.' How could she think of deserting her post in the hour of need? A good night's rest, a few of King David's psalms to read and a mug of Annie's blackcurrant cordial would make a new woman of her.

She made her way up Church Brow to St Oswy's lych gate where a long queue of funeral carts stood nose to tail right down the street.

The sexton was waiting with a line of resident engineers, gangmen and families. Isaac Cleghorn lifted his stovepipe hat and scratched his head, flummoxed by the absence of clergy to officiate at the burial. 'Parson knows about the sidings. It's not like him to be late for a big do.'

'Is it not?' snapped Zillah Herbert. 'This is the giddy limit. I'll be writing to the bishop and my Mission. How dare he insult the families with his lackadaisical attitudes? Perhaps he's gone fishing again. Shall we send out a search party?' Zillah stamped her boots, embarrassed by this disarray.

'Don't fret, Miss Herbert, the hole is dug and bell tolled, the people are present,' answered Joseph Hirst, the subcontractor, calmly. 'All it needs is for someone to say suitable words. Fetch the books and pass them round and we'll say them together ourselves.'

'Is that sound? Will it count like with the Almighty?' queried Cleggy as he shuffled lopsidedly to collect the hymn books from the back of the small church. They were passed along the men and the few visitors from the village who dared risk attending.

Zillah could not concentrate on the singing but a burning frustration at this insult choked in her throat like acid. How dare this man call himself a priest. She would have him publicly defrocked!

Beth Wildman tossed restlessly on the bed, hair ruffled up like cotton fluff, her face a sickly gold in the firelight. Ralph sat patiently by her side as he promised. He had been called in the night and rode up at first light, telling no one of this errand.

I will miss this old witch more than she will ever know, his only friend in this godforsaken dale. He could feel his back twingeing as he stretched out to feel those hands which nevermore would soothe away the pain. How quickly her hands had aged; knuckles gnarled with wrinkled tissuey skin like chicken bones.

There would be no reason now to ride out onto the moor, watching her limp over the moss, her crook raised like a staff. He would miss her cantankerous cursings, her shepherd's wisdom and her foresight.

It was Beth who prophesied the doom and gloom, the April blizzard and the sickness. He could see her marching down the aisle at that useless meeting, putting the fear of

God into those gullible faces, those black feathers on her crow bonnet dangling as she warned of death filling up the churchyard ... Oh God! The service for the burial of the camp victims. He stared in disbelief at his gold watch. The funerals were two hours ago. He should have been down there but time always stood still in Beth's domain.

Now, in keeping this promise, he had broken faith with his own promise to others. No one knew where he was. They would presume the worst. He put his head in his hands; there was nothing to be done now but apologise on his return. He was not leaving Beth alone. Damn it! The one time he tried to be a good shepherd he ended up losing his entire flock. It's no good, Beth Wildman, you'll just have to pull through and get me out of this bog. He smiled and turned hopefully towards the bed. One look at the still frame told him he was now on his own.

Tupping Time

Backend 1871

When apples be ripe
And nuts be brown
Petticoats up,
Trousers down.

Anon

Chapter Twenty

He was there again, half-hidden in the shadows watching the schoolhouse, using twilight for cover, staring into the open window as Susan lit the lamps. For three nights now he had just paced up and down with his hands in his jacket pockets. What did that greasy lump of lard want from them now? There was nothing Ezra could do for that stupid boy. Cora drew the curtains quickly to blot out his view.

He was the poorest of their scholars; why ever did Ezra take him on in the first place? Sunter Lund always smelt of the farmyard, resisting all her attempts to scrub him up to standard; a sulky boy, ungrateful. He failed Ezra's special tests and Cora was glad to be shot of him.

Why Blaize Lund had kicked up a fuss she could not understand. The woman was nothing but a plumped-up farm servant; a live-in who wooed and wed the farmer's son one summer and bore him an heir only months later. How could they expect to make a thoroughbred out of a carthorse?

Sometimes Ezra's enthusiasm and philanthropy were hard to puzzle out.

Cora crept up to the landing window in the darkness. The figure had gone. The street was empty once more but this vigil unnerved her, setting her teeth on edge with the sour knowledge that he would return.

'Can I borrow a needle?' whispered Zillah with some urgency as she watched Ellie stirring the pan of bubbling damsons on the oven range in the kitchen of Middle Butts.

'Are you taking up knitting then?' said the other girl, lifting out the stones one by one as they surfaced, bobbing in the scummy froth.

'Not exactly . . . if I don't poke something down my stays this minute, I'll scream. I'm being bitten alive with lumps and bumps everywhere . . . in the most awkward of places,' confessed Zillah as she squirmed, trying hard not to scratch at the very thought of the beasts lurking under her corsets.

Ellie laughed as she arranged purple stones into a neat pattern on a large white plate. 'Them's just thunder bugs! Do you no harm, they're that tiny you can't see them but you keep up that scratting and they'll swell up. So no touching or yer'll get a scar.'

'How can I stop? They're everywhere.'

'Go to the apothecary and get some flowers of sulphur, his green powder should calm them down a bit, and pray for rain to douse them away. We allus gets them in dry weather off the fields, Miss Herbert.'

'I wish you would call me Zillah.'

'No, that wouldn't be right, you being Merciful's teacher.' Ellie turned back to her stoning. The smell of the damsons bubbling had both of them sniffing into the pan. 'I have to get out all the stones or Mother will be on at me again. She wants to win a prize at Scarsdale Show with her damson cheese and our butter and our cheese too.' Ellie had refused to enter for the sponge cake competition after each of her efforts collapsed and had to be crumbed up into a trifle base. Surely she could not ruin the jam if she hugged the pan. Then she would count up all the stones to see if Fancy Mac was still her sweetheart. Miss Herbert was hopping from one leg to the other as she pointed her in the direction of the dresser and a bag of spun wool by the wheel to ferret for a needle. 'Loosen your stays, miss, or would you like me to poke it down yer back?' Zillah was already sighing with relief as she directed the sharp point to hit the spot.

'If my mama in Nottingham could see me now, she would disown me. In four months I've lost all my decency and you tell me to loosen my corsets! Why, Ellen, what with short-ened skirts, thick boots and a tight cap to keep away the nasties no one would recognise me any more. I'm such a plain Jane. Still, I suppose there's little vanity in country living, none of your frills and furbelows, just sensible garments.'

'I think you're beginning to pick up our accent as well. I've never liked to ask what really brought you from all them comforts to this bleak hole,' ventured Ellie.

'I have quite forgotten myself if I'm honest. I suppose the

Mission work came just at a time when I needed to escape. You can stay too long in comfort, it makes you lazy and unquestioning of how other people live. So I came with my baskets full of schemes and dreams, thinking I had all the answers and the Lord in my pocket. I thought I was being obedient to some heavenly vision. I think I got carried away by the idea of mission work, being an instrument for good and all that. Sometimes I wonder now if I've done anything useful at all, or just interfered and meddled a bit, I'm not so sure as I was. I often get a terrible feeling that I've brought trouble on you all.'

'How can you be blamed for the smallpox or our fire or for poor Janey's death? Don't be so hard on yourself. Look at the miracles you've managed at school with young Billy Widdup . . .'

'He's more absent than he's present this term and Mr Bulstrode is making me responsible for getting him back to school again. I fear all I do is keep the children quiet and contained for a few hours and I came with such plans for their instruction.'

'You can't be held responsible for the Bulstrodes' idea of doing things; a couple of queer ones who never mix with dalesfolk. I think he's kept right under her thumb, poor man.'

'Then there's the parson. I just can't stomach him.'

'But he apologised about the funeral mix-up and he was seeing owd Beth on her way to rest. He and her were good mates. Can't imagine Scarsbeck without her. Still she got her way in the end, got hersen buried up Scarsdale Cross end; but

I'll not be going in that direction until her spirit settles down in the sod.' Ellie sat down at the table to join her lodger.

'I just don't understand how he gives in to such strange requests. It's so confusing, don't you think? I can't find anything in Scripture to support this.'

'We do things our way here. Offcomers, with respect to you, must find us an unholy lot but what's done is meant kindly.'

'That's what's so hard to swallow. I read my rule books and there's nothing in them to cover all these happenings. I know Miss Wildman was a good shepherd woman even though she never darkened a church door but my Good Book says she's unredeemed.'

'She did many a favour, did Beth. I don't know about rule books but doesn't it say "by their deeds they are known" or summat like that?'

'Yes, yes. It doesn't tally, does it? I feel as if I'm in a foreign country with a strange language I'll never fathom out. I met Cleggy Cleghorn this afternoon digging round his dahlias at Church Cottage. "Not bad for the backend show," he smiles to me. "Backend of what?" says I, turning round to look. "Just the time of year, miss, backend of summer, leaves turning, wind freshening up, sun slipping, nights drawing in," says he. "You mean autumn," says I. "Aye, backend," says he. I think he must think me a dimwit.'

Ellie was distracted by the caramel smell, a burning smell of sugar, and dashed over to the pan. The jam was blackening. 'Oh no! We've let it burn. What shall I do? Mam'll leather my backside if I've wasted her precious fruit. How can we save it?' panicked Ellie, lifting it from the heat.

Zillah examined the sticky black mess, praying it was redeemable. 'If we grease a copper mould, skim off the worst bits and hide the jelly pan, perhaps she won't notice. I'm sorry, it's all my fault for distracting you from your task. Come on, it's worth a try.' Seeing tears fill Ellie's blue eyes she asked, 'How is that young Scotsman ... or should I not enquire?'

'I still walk out with him behind me mam's back. What she don't see won't hurt her, will it? I wish she could take it into her head that he's a grand chap, is Fancy Mac. His grandad kept cattle but were driven off his land by sheep. He's of farm stock. She's so hard about him, so I must lie. He's a gentle giant, one I can look up to for a change. I'm that churned up inside I can't do right for doing wrong. Is there owt in yer rule books about that?'

'Having a sweetheart suits you, your eyes are so bright they must glow in the dark!' whispered Zillah as she sieved out the jam carefully into the mould with shaking hands. The bottom of the pan was caked in black crust.

'Have you ever felt like I do, Miss Zillah?' Ellie opened a tin of soda and sprinkled it over the pan.

'No, I can't say that I have. There was a young man in Nottingham whom Papa thought suitable but I didn't ... a bit of a limp lettuce. He did nothing for my tastebuds but his prospects were good. So I made a scene, stamped my foot and behaved rather badly. I'm past all that sort of nonsense now. I can't see any man changing my mind.'

'Not even our vicar?' Ellie watched the teacher blush.

'Least of all the vicar.'

'But he's so handsome and learned ... a real gent.' She prodded the sensitive spot.

'Handsome is as handsome does, Ellen, and I fear no gentleman, if rumours are to be believed. He's never done anything to alter my first impression of him.'

'Shame, I thowt he'd sharpened up in the pulpit. He don't read so much, don't mumble and bumble so much and we all think it's your doing. He's not been near Liddy Braithwaite's on market day for weeks and she's that sourfaced she'd turn milk.' Ellie soaked the brass pan and carried it out to the yard to hide behind the water butt. Zillah followed her, bristling under this scrutiny, feeling hot and flustered by the turn in their conversation.

'So she should, a married woman. It's disgraceful!' sniffed Zillah, ready to mount her high horse of indignation.

'I was wondering if he had other fish to fry nowadays,' chirruped Ellie with a look of mischief in her eye, watching the blush creep up from Zillah's red neck.

'I don't know what you mean ... and if I do then you're greatly mistaken. We have not exchanged one civil word since the vestry meeting and the funerals. I may have to join the chapel if things continue.'

'You can't do that, miss, never. Once you're church you stay church, no swapping coats. Make up your differences. It's lonely in winter up here. You need friends and company to warm yer heart when the house freezes over and water comes in ice blocks. He's not a bad parson for all we go on about him.'

'He's far too worldly-wise for my taste. We have nothing of common interest, nothing to draw us together, Ellen. I think we should clear up this mess and put the damson cheese to chill in the cold room out of sight. I'm beginning to itch again . . .'

Zillah was finding the idea of winter depressing; the thought of long nights and cold classrooms, muddy treks back to the farmhouse and Mercy's incessant chatter. Whatever was she doing here, itching herself to bits, isolated in a lonely farmhouse, a crosspatch with everyone? If only she could escape her duties and sneak off for a break from this Spartan regime.

Chapter Twenty-One

The tall navvy with muddy moleskin trousers tied under the knee with thongs inspected his new watch and chain as his team of gangers were clearing debris from the track. He paused to admire the way the line curved gently as it hugged the contours of the slope, tucked in against the worst of the wind, banked up neatly with bare earth. Soon the autumn seedlings would burrow into the soil for spring's green sprouting of shrubs and wild flowers, hiding their handiwork from view. In the distance the line levelled out across the fields to the scaffolding at Scarsbeck.

Fancy lifted his cap in respect at the sheer madness of building a fast track under and over mountains and gullies. Only the finest engineers, latest equipment and navvy nous could achieve such a feat. He felt for once a tingle of pride in the steady rhythmic progress of his own team. No one could say his gang was not on top of the job. His reverie was disturbed by the sight of a carriage and four horses trotting sedately alongside the track with faces peering out of the windows.

Pity it was still the open season for tourists, visitors from Scarsbeck Hall up from the city for the grouse-shooting, tramping through the camp in heathery tweed suits and deerstalker trilbies, enjoying a day away from their guns at this local menagerie, casting snooty eyes over the menials at work as if they were exotic animals.

How Fancy hated those imperious English accents with their superior manners! It was such land-hungry Sassenachs who robbed his grandfather of his living and reduced many of his race to penury and exile. Now a bunch of gentry were alighting from their carriages waiting to be escorted by that servile Scot, Henry Paisley, on a conducted tour of the construction site with a ride down to Blea Moor tunnel works. Fancy stood back to let them pass, resisting the urge to spit on the floor after them.

'Mind yourselves, ladies, please,' ordered the resident engineer as three ladies descended carefully onto the roughly scattered gravel track. Fancy noted their unsuitable clothing and feathery bonnets held tightly against the biting wind. It tore at their ringlets and ribbons, raising their flimsy skirts, much to their discomfort and much to the amusement of the gangmen who smiled impishly at each other.

The group trooped past the workmen like schoolchildren on an outing behind the waiting engineer. The man paused to acknowledge Fancy and ordered him to tag along to instruct the party. They all walked silently towards the viaduct, the wind ripping at skirts and sending hats whirling and rolling down the soil embankments. Then they halted by the huge viaduct, looking up to see cranes swinging back and forth.

Henry Paisley pointed to the rescue hut built onto the wooden frame where workmen sheltered in bad weather. Huge posts were set deep in concrete, dwarfing the low-slung cottages at the end of the street. Fancy felt sorry for the poor sods who now had to live with a giant straddling over them. Who could stop the Midland Railway or protest at its progress? Nothing now would halt the track-laying. Fancy knew that the weather would have the final say.

Everyone now bent forward into the gusting wind as they watched stonemasons and bricklayers at work under the arches, filling in its curves. Wobbly Bob waved to Fancy from his precarious platform. Fancy was glad that the Widdups now lodged in his hut, out of that dreadful wagon on wheels where the old man snoozed not knowing night from day and fettled up tools, hammering late in the moonlight.

The visitors huddled together for shelter, not impressed by the rough conditions or the sight before them. One man condescended to offer his opinion to the workmen, shouting loudly, 'Hold on tight, chaps, another blast on its way.'

'This is nae a wind, man, but a wee puff of smoke. You wait for the Helm wind to rattle down this valley from the north. Watch for the mist to cap yon hill like a nightcap and then take cover, tie yersel in against a hurricane or the Helm'll blow a body off yon scaffold like a leaf off a tree . . .'

Another man in a black bowler hat drew closer and brought out a notepad, introducing himself as a reporter from the *Lancaster Guardian*. They were ushered into a waiting open wagon on wheels attached to the end of a line of empty goods wagons, drawn by a twelve horsepower locomotive for the trip southwards on the tramway down to Blea Moor tunnel shafts.

The ladies shivered in their finery, hair and hats dishevelled, faces already covered in a film of dust, and turned to each other loudly. 'How can anyone bear to work among savages and dreary hills? It's so depressing, so cold and dismal. Are we safe to go further?' They eyed Fancy with suspicion, lingering over his dirty clothing. He was in no mood to humour the silly bitches and snapped back, 'You can stomach anything, lady, if the pay's good enough and yer bed is waiting warm and dry in a wee bitty hut, so you can.' Ignoring his quip, they turned to Henry Paisley for support and Fancy saw a flicker of a twitch at the greying edges of his moustache.

'As you see, ladies, the men are far too busy to bother you but just in case, Mr MacLachlan here will escort you and ensure your every comfort. Hop in, Fancy, and mind these lassies. Tell this reporter anything except that we are running behind schedule. I'll take the gentlemen in the next wagon and pray it dissna rain.'

They rode up the incline in silence, surveying each side of the temporary tramway, smoke from the little engine blinding eyes and choking throats with coal dust. Leaving the hidden valley behind they passed stone quarries and marble works, crossing over the bleak fell track where isolated huts pointed the way to Blea Moor tunnel.

'This is the worst jobbie, ladies. Not a drop of rock comes oot this tunnel without gunpowder and I'm told it's like a roasting oven in there,' offered Fancy to his pupils.

As if on cue, a man crawled out of the tunnel on all fours and rolled over to gasp for fresh air. He was caked in black dust, coughing and choking, spitting black phlegm in spurts onto the turf.

The overseer, a walking gangmaster in brown corduroy jacket and trousers, pulled the man up roughly and yelled, 'Five minutes, Taff, spit it out and get back in!'

'Thanks, Ironfist, I'm coming.' The miner looked up and grinned at the ladies from two white slits in a boot-polished face. He staggered to his feet, straightened his limbs and rolled towards the hole. The ganger turned to his audience, raised his cap and grinned but his eyes were hard as granite. Checking his watch he, too, sauntered towards the tunnel.

'Sturdy men, your average navvy, eh?' said the reporter. 'Fine figures, thick calves, real backbone of the construction industry. 'Tis pity they are so wild and lawless.'

Fancy turned quickly. 'Don't believe all you read about us. We like a dram or two, our sturdy hurdies come from backbreaking work and so does a thirst. As you've seen there are all types and tripes needed to build this railway, but you call us all navvies. I wonder why that is?'

The reporter nodded as he wrote, looking up at Fancy's

question to say, 'But our readers like to hear stories of the wild goings-on . . .'

'Sorry, canna help youse. As I said afore, we drink to slake our drooth in this furnace.'

The reporter winked. 'Come on, young man, yer not telling me there's never any trouble here. Why, the papers are full of magistrates' tales and the house of correction at Wakefield could be a navvy camp.'

'Aye, there's trouble. I mind a few weeks back a poor laddie who had to be strapped down on his bed with leather belts. He was shaking like a man who had seen the fires of hell! No bairn should have tae hear his pa screaming like that for the want of a dram. It went on all night but being the strong ox, like you was saying, he burst those straps and smashed a pane of window glass, grabbed a jaggy piece and tore at his throat from end to end. We reckon it took him all morning to choke to his death. They called oot the minister of the kirk from his bed in Scarsbeck to sit with him and calm his woman and bairns. Is that the sort of trouble yer readers are after hearing?' asked Fancy, watching the ladies holding handkerchiefs over their mouths in disgust. Ironfist . . . Ironfist, why did the nickname ring bells in his head? The reporter was still scribbling onto his pad, oblivious to the scenes around him.

The party was marched across the turf to view the shaft headings where the airholes were sunk deep to relieve the tunnel atmosphere. A steam engine was hoisting up spoil out of the shafts, tipping the containers onto a huge pile of rubble.

Huts were dotted here and there, high and unprotected by the shelter of hill or tree. Fancy knew these were the roughest huts where men lived like animals in cages, one on top of the other.

The rain began to spit and spot upon the bored contingent of visitors who looked anxiously for the return of their wagon to Scarsbeck dale and afternoon tea with Sir Edward Dacre's shooting party back at the Hall.

Fancy watched them scurry towards their transport. He was going to walk back alone over the moorland track towards the valley opening out before him. His jacket was warm enough and his boots worn in and watertight. His chest was snugly fitted with Ellie's knitted waistcoat.

The navvy stopped to watch the last of the summer curlews, buzzed and threatened by a hawk. They soared high, circling around, wailing and screeching at this attack. The hawk lost interest and flew off. He was getting to know these fells. They were not the hills of home, majestic and mysterious, rising from the foot of deep blue lochs, but they were Ellie's hills. In her presence he was knowing a peace for the first time in his life, a warmth which soothed his anger. He could settle here on high ground. When he was with Ellie he had no urge to tramp off.

Fancy was beginning to recognise local birds. His favourites were the hawks and merlins, peregrines and harriers. Ellie was afraid of them, fearing for the small creatures which were scooped up in claws high in the air. For a farmer's lass she had the tenderest of hearts. Now he recognised the lark's song and the peewit's chatter, the bobbity wagtail, flycatchers and swallows from swifts. Why had he never noticed before what a mixture of creatures there were living on a bare hillside? Whenever they walked out together, she would stop and point him towards some moss or lichen, bird or wild flower, pansies, blue harebells, the smell of the clovers. He could smell the hills of home there. How he looked forward to their secret meetings, out of sight of prying village eyes. She was so honest and feared this deception but risked her mother's wrath nonetheless.

No woman had ever turned his heart before or broken the barriers of his nonchalance with such freshness. Fancy knew he was loving her for her enthusiasm, her sense of the wonder of things. He sat down where he stood to pour out his emotion into his verse book. It was torn and tattered, his most precious possession, and now it was filled with lines about Ellie. She was opening his eyes to the magic of these hills, to the wonders of nature, to the joy of pure loving and it terrified him. The pain came again; the knowledge that he was trapped by silken threads invisible to the eye of any man, the two of them bound together by a thousand tiny threads twisting over their hearts, drawing each into one heart. The muse was coming so fast he could not feel the torrent raging above his head until the paper began to crumple and stain with the rain.

He needed no party of toffs from their distant world to remind him of his menial station in life as he strode down towards Paradise camp with his cap brim dripping raindrops.

Fancy struggled with the knowledge that he too was a stranger here. What could he offer Ellie but a wandering life amongst other strangers? It was no life for a creature who loved the land and growing things. A workman's hut was no place for her to live. For the first time in his life he felt shame that he had not made the best of his education or tried to better himself with the railway. And then there was Ironfist. Why did that name keep dancing into his head?

Chapter Twenty-Two

Tizzy could hear voices raised behind the study door, one loud and foul-mouthed, the other calmer, trying to reason. She stared down at the hall tiles with their criss-cross pattern of black and brick-red star shapes to avert her eyes from Miss Bulstrode who was eavesdropping, straining to get the gist of the argument, her keys dangling from her belt as she plucked at her lace-edged apron.

'Come back into the kitchen, boy, let Susan inspect your hands. I'm sure the headmaster's uninvited visitor will be leaving soon. You should not have let him in, Susan, barging in here without a by your leave, stupid girl.'

'Yes, ma'am,' bobbed Susan Hindle and scurried past, white-faced. Once out of view she stuck out her tongue and smiled at the poor pupil, shrugging her shoulders defiantly, raising her eyebrows under the floppy mobcap worn ever since the unfortunate incident of the lice.

'Sit down, boy, until you are called. You can have another

glass of buttermilk but don't expect such an extravagance every time you come. This is an exception and we must all be patient while poor Mr Bulstrode bears the burdens of his office.'

Tizzy was bearing her own burden of deception, here under sufferance chewing a ship's biscuit which nearly broke her front teeth, trying not to make a moustache of milk over her lips. At least milk was better than the usual tea treats of manky cake crumbs from the tin which were furry with green mould. Susan sometimes exchanged the crumbs for an apple or a lozenge from Mr Bulstrode's special jar. His sweet tooth was the only luxury in his saintly life, lectured his sister once with a sigh. She seemed to live on air and leftovers like a sparrow darting for sandwich droppings.

Every visit got harder to stomach. Why on earth had she ever allowed her disguise to get this far? What a fuss about a stupid examination she would never attend. Sherbert got so steamed up about this coaching. She called at their hut, throwing Mally into a fit of clearing up and stowing ale bottles out of view, trying to make the lodgings look less like a dosshouse, pretending she slept with her little brother as the hutkeeper and not with Wobbly Bob as his common-law wife. Missionaries seemed to take that sort of custom badly and would want to see marriage lines.

In the event Sherbert brought yet another bag of hedgerow rovings: wool Mally could spin up into scratchy socks or spencers and a jar of purple jam that was so solid it stood upright on yer spoon and tasted of burnt treacle toffee. Mally sat there all prim and red-faced as Sherbert went on about the Fawcett giving Billy a step up the ladder of life.

She herself got badgered by Bulstrode at every turn in the classroom. He picked her out and made a fuss of her arithmetic, showing her work as an example to the rest of the buggers who sat there stony-faced and gave her hell in the playground afterwards. Mercy Birkett, her only friend, blew hot and cold according to how well she had beaten her in English grammar. Tizzy had tried to get extra shifts as an errand boy for the tommy shop, delivering groceries to the far-flung huts, but her arms couldn't carry the weight of tins and bags. The older lads resented her efforts, tripping her up, and she was soon replaced. They were getting stricter about the under-twelves going off site to school and checked on the half-timers. There was even talk of evening classes. Paradise was getting respectable.

To be fair, Bulstrode was kind enough; he never rapped her knuckles if she got a sum wrong. He was a soft squashy sort of man like the pictures of Father Christmas she once saw on a picture card. His cheeks were red and fiery, his bushy beard a sandy white, his belly was plump and round like a horse's backside. And he peered over half-moon spectacles with funny eyes which stuck out of their sockets. He liked patting her head when she did well, fingering her tight curls which would never grow straight, and now she knew why he was nicknamed Patabully.

It was the study she hated, all closed in, dark and smelly. The walls were cluttered with books, large leathery tomes standing like sentries over the lesson. There was a smell of stale baccy and something she had never smelt before, sweaty, musty, sickly to swallow. The fire was always banked up high, the curtains half-closed. For that hour Tizzy could never breathe.

Patabully sat so close she could taste his breath. He would lean in to point out each task of algebra, geometry, calculus. They made up problems to solve, drew graphs and looked at map references. The tasks were interesting and absorbing but always Patabully intruded heavy on her shoulders, stroking her head.

He said there were special herbs to rinse into your hair which made it shine golden and he showed her wonderful pictures of ancient history and foreign costumes and strange battles where men with bare bodies were fighting all tangled up like knots, one on top of another. He liked those pictures best of all and would get all excited as he turned the pages, mumbling so fast she could not understand a word he said but nodded politely, watching the clock on the mantelpiece creep slowly, twenty to, quarter to, around to five o'clock. They always seemed to end with those pictures whatever the subject of the lesson.

As soon as Miss Cora knocked on the door the book was slammed shut and put up on the top shelf before the door was unlocked. Why did he have to lock the door? No one ever intruded uninvited. They were never disturbed but Patabully had his own peculiar routine for each lesson and Tizzy as a fraudster was in no position to complain.

Once out into the fresh air she would see if Mercy was waiting to hear all about the lesson and walk her back to the fork in the track. By the time she ran back to Paradise Tizzy was ravenous, raiding any tuck box left unlocked by the lodgers in Wobbly's hut. On good days, Mally left a pan of stew on the boil in the copper and she wolfed it down straight from the pan. Studying was definitely hungry work.

As she waited for her lesson in the kitchen, listening to the row down the corridor with Susan polishing the brasses with flapping ears, they heard a door slam and Tizzy jumped up to see Miss Bulstrode dart away from her listening post to hover in the hallway. Tizzy saw the familiar bulky shape of Sunter Lund striding out, brushing past the woman roughly. She hoped Mr Bulstrode had given him the hard word. That made her feel better as she gathered up her exercise book and pencil, making for the study whose door was ajar.

The sister nipped swiftly inside to quiz her brother and it was Tizzy's turn to eavesdrop. She could hear them arguing.

'What did he say, Ezra?'

'Nothing to worry you with, dear,' came the reply.

'What does he want with us? I told you he's been stalking this house for weeks.'

'Whatever he demands, he'll not be getting from me.'

'Are you sure? He is so angry, Ezra, why?'

'Not another word, Cora, come on, it's time for Master Widdup. We don't want to send the child back in the dark.'

'Oh Ezra, how can you be so calm about all this? He has violated our house. Shall I speak to his mother?'

'Do not fret on this matter or concern others in our affairs. It only raises curiosity and speculation … most unwise, dear.'

'But you look so troubled.'

'Nothing I can't control myself. Bring the boy to me. Work is the best antidote to worry. Find yourself a task.'

Tizzy drew back from the door. This strange drama had shaken the calm of the household. Why should that stupid cowman threaten the Bulstrodes?

'Come in, Widdup, sit down. As you gather we have had a most unfortunate incident this teatime. Nothing that concerns you, boy, but it's delayed our studies. Don't hover, child. You heard nothing of his words, did you?'

'No, sir, but that's the geezer who killed my dog, sir, and I hate his guts.'

'Language, boy, language. I would like to take the roughness out of that tongue of yours. Let it be a lesson to you. There are none so bitter as those who fail my test, who are not worthy of the honours, attention and time so generously bestowed upon them by the Fawcett. It is in my power to withhold and withdraw as befits the suitability of my students. The higher the fewer and you, Widdup, are chosen for the honour. Mr Lund was not. I'm sure, child, you would not be so foolish as to let me down when your time of trial comes.'

'No, sir,' gulped Tizzy, pink with shame.

'Righty ho. Pull up a chair and let's make the most of the time that is left to us. Open your textbook and …' There was a crash of broken glass as an object hurled through the window landed on the desk, scattering papers and books and broken shards of glass everywhere. The room was sprayed with splinters as the panel of the window collapsed inwards. The draught from the hole made the fire flare up into a blaze. 'What the . . .'

The two women rushed into the room for it was not yet locked. Ezra Bulstrode brushed the glass from his jacket. His broadcloth had taken the brunt of the blast but the thickness of its textile kept him unscathed from the attack. They stood shaken, trying to compose themselves, while Cora fussed around screaming.

'You could have been killed, Ezra.'

'Calm yourself. It was just an accident . . .'

'That was no accident. Look! A brick on the floor, a brick thrown through the window deliberately. Call the constable. We must report Sunter Lund. How dare he come in here and—'

'That's enough! There are ears present, sister. We'll not demean ourselves before the village. Just a silly incident, best forgotten. I'll have the window repaired tomorrow and we can board up the hole until then. Our lesson, young man, is postponed until Thursday when I'm sure we will be undisturbed. Perhaps it is best not to broadcast this episode abroad. Petty minds, Master Widdup, petty minds and we must rise above such petty minds,' urged the teacher with hands held to his side as if strapped on and a look of fury in his red face. The effort to look composed and untroubled was spoiled by the hard thin line of his mouth. Miss Cora was shrieking and flapping like a blackbird whose nest was threatened by a tomcat. Tizzy hurried out of the dreary room into the kitchen to find her cap, letting herself out by the back door into the school yard, relieved to breathe the cool dusk air.

Tonight there was no Mercy Birkett hanging about under the shelter, kicking leaves in all directions. There was no one in the village street to witness the commotion. Only the flickering shadows of trees waving across the stone walls, the flutter of leaves falling. Somewhere out there was a madman, a killer of dogs with angry eyes and a petty mind. That was no comfort to Tizzy as she raced back towards Paradise, her lungs bursting with the effort to run uphill against the wind, heart pounding for fear of who might be stalking this path. She crossed over to the railway track where the last of the day shift were preparing to knock off. She made to carry a bag of empty flasks and snapboxes, tagging behind the weary navvies as they tramped back to camp. This was not a night for walking alone.

Chapter Twenty-Three

The screams of children pierced his sleep and the terrible vision of the dying navvy with his stare, eyes glazed like a dead fish on a slab. The dream awoke the restless parson with a start. He jerked upright and felt his back stabbing at the sudden movement. Damn, damn, damn. The wailing still echoed around the fields outside the vicarage garden. It was the time when the sheep were separated from their ewes for the September fatstock sales. The night was riven by the bleating; mothers crying for their lost children on the moors.

The harvest moon shone through a gap in the curtains, streaking onto the walls, the dropped clothing, the bare floorboards. This noise would deafen anyone but sleep was already elusive. Ralph's bed was crumpled into a heap of boulders, crumpled under him. How he longed for a decent night of uninterrupted slumber and now he would have to get up and find his pot to relieve himself.

He drew back the curtains, stretched his aching limbs and arms, cursing the stupid sheep as they called to one another in the moonlight. Since Beth Wildman left him to fend for himself he too was feeling like a motherless lamb. There was no one to hear his troubles, all he had experienced at the camp over the past weeks. The way that navvy destroyed himself, bled to death, choking on his blood, and all he could do was sit mouthing platitudes, meaningless words. What a waste of life, what a disgusting end for a human being, a violent unnecessary death. It made no sense. Damn, damn, damn.

Ralph could no longer pretend that Paradise camp was no concern of his parochial duties or that he had no responsibility to relieve conditions there. They had most outward comforts, more than many of his parishioners: warmth, food and dry beds, but little to relieve nights of boredom but a cask of ale or bottles of coarse spirits. He was shamed by the efforts of the Quaker women from Dent village who visited each week to teach knitting and reading. Missioner Tiplady from Batty Green braved the bleak moorland to deliver magazines and newspapers to the reading room and even the Mission teacher visited families with comforts bought from her own meagre wage, so the Birketts had informed him. What had he done to alleviate their boredom? Nothing, damn it! Nothing but a few perfunctory visits to the small-pox victims and then only because he knew it was safe for him to touch them, having once had the protective pox scratch on his arm many years ago.

He spent August shooting grouse, catching fish in the beck, pretending it was none of his business, but only guilt was his companion. Why did they have to build this railway slap through his parish, disturbing his slumber? Now he saw the faces of scarred children down the sights of his shotgun, heard the sad tales of suffering in his ear as he galloped away across the fells. There was no escaping this burden.

As he surveyed the moonlight torching the first autumn frosts in his garden the landscape shimmered like a silvery lake; the spider's web across the window ledge glistened like a crystal lace net. All things bright and beautiful indeed. All things cold and troublesome more like. There was only a gaping hole in the pit of his stomach to comfort him. I'm a useless apology for a priest; a sham and a faker. There is no good in me, nothing of worth. Thus he would have wallowed all night if the voice of the Crow Woman had not whispered in his ear, 'Stop all that drooling. Yer no worse than many others. Get off yer backside, stir yer loins and do something useful for a change, parson.'

Ralph smiled to himself. Trust her to have the last word. Perhaps she was right. This was no job for an idle bachelor. The vicarage bed was cold, in need of a woman's warmth, the house austere without a feminine touch of softness in the furnishings. The upper floors should be ringing with the laughter of children in the nursery. The noisy bustle of family life would support his more depressing work in the parish. How on earth would he find himself a decent filly in this godforsaken part of the Dales?

Sir Edward's society girls would not wish to moulder in this backwater. And that left only one other female of quality, the dreaded Miss Herbert, she of the missionary zeal and fervent hymns who sang off-key and interfered at every turn. Never, never, never. There must be a better helpmeet than she in the dale. But he was damned if he could think of one at four o'clock in the morning. She would definitely be last reserve.

For the moment he must think up some scheme to lift the spirits of the camp and the village before the onslaught of winter; some competition or game perhaps, a cricket team or football match. Scarsdale against Paradise. Now that would cheer the troops.

With that thought he straightened his crumpled bed, poured himself a large whisky and jumped back under the cold covers. Soon he was dreaming of bowling down the aisle of St Oswy's with the Herbert woman guarding her wicket with a large black Bible, batting sixes in all directions until she was clean bowled by his overarm swing and he took her there and then on the chancel steps.

Chapter Twenty-Four

'You can't buy that ram, ye don't know owt about it,' yelled Sunter across the pen full of tup hogs gathered in the street for a final inspection before the annual tup sales.

'Shush! I don't want all of Hawes knowing our business,' snapped Ellie, turning to see if they were being overheard. Secrecy and silence, casual glances were all part of the performance at an auction sale. Never show interest in the object of your desire in case you gave another buyer a notion for your fancy. Dad's advice was etched in her brain. How she wished he was here by her side instead of Uncle Warwick and Sunter who was as helpful as a teacloth mopping up a flood. She felt the coat of the young beast; it was tight and in good condition.

'Father, tell her not to be so stupid. Yon's a right craggy fell sheep off Tan Hill way. It won't be any use on our fellsides. We need a good-looker like them Wensingdales over there, long coats and fat lambs, fine wool. Stick to what you know.' Sunter was shaking his head at her choice.

'Happen Ellie knows her sheep, son, if she's Jim's daughter. He could allus spot a bargain but why the stranger in the pen, lass?' said Warwick Lund, examining the ram himself, feeling down its back carefully to size up the flesh.

'I just like the look of him, the gleam in his eye ... he'll know what's what when tupping time comes, he'll serve our ewes right and the cross should toughen up our stock for the future. I've heard that sheep out of Swaledale do well in heather and stick out the winter better than most. I've seen a few crosses down in the far pens getting a lot of interest. That puts them out of our price range. I reckon this one will slip by cheap, the odd one in the pen.' The street was packed with wooden pens and farmers leaning over, viewing.

'But his wool is rough. Go for summat tried and tested, not from away.' Sunter sniffed at her choice and walked off, embarrassed to be seen with one of the few women at the sale. Auctions were men's work; from the drovers who brought in their flocks for the preview to the landlords who served ale and pasties for farmers who whispered advice to each other into their glasses and set up auction prices between themselves. It was all a big show: beasts washed and combed out, prettified for the ring, bad points disguised like painted women, good features exaggerated for their brief moment of glory. Ellie would shame them with her ignorance and make them the laughing stock of the dale for introducing strange breeds into their flocks. Trust her to pick a black face and grey muzzle, a right scruffy creature in his eyes, just like yon Jock, oversized and cocky with it.

'I do like this one, Uncle Warwick, his horns are strong and his coat tight, he stands square on. He's my choice. I know he'll serve us well and added to our other rams we can try him out and test him against the rest.'

'She's off her head, spending good brass on rubbish. I'm having nowt to do with the job.' Sunter stormed off again.

'Don't mind him, he got out of bed wrong end this morning. He's that prickly these days, you should wed him and be done wi' it,' sighed Warwick, hoping she would take his cue.

'Do you really think so?' Ellie laughed and he had to smile. She was far too canny to be caught by this question.

'Well, you watch out in the ring, not a place for a greenhorn lass. One look at your bonny face and the buggers will line up to catch you out.'

'That's where I was hoping you and Sunter would come in handy. I'm not paying a guinea above my price for yon tup but I've got a feeling about this one. What do you think?' She pleaded with her blue eyes to great effect.

'Go on then, you've twisted me arm, good and proper.' They sauntered over to the temperance tearoom and Ellie ordered a plate of stew sitting amongst the other farm families trying to catch their conversations in case she was missing something. They then took their place in the auction ring and she surveyed the tiers of dalesmen, hunched over their sticks, taking stock of the exhibits as they were led around the sawdust ring, waiting for the bidding to commence.

It was Beth Wildman who had taken her aside at the

June clipping and advised her to invest in new blood. For all she was a humble shepherd woman she knew sheep like she knew the village. 'Yer father would say the same, if he'd been spared, but it's in yer eye too, so no worries, lass. Go for what hits yer in the belly even if it makes no sense to others. Go for it and you'll not go far wrong.' Now there was no one to advise. Dad always said he felt safer buying fifty sheep than five rams. It was best to get a young ram from a reputable sheep breeder and she knew Dad thought highly of the Tan Hill stockmen who were getting noticed around the North Riding dales. Never listen to gossip until after the sale, when the auctioneers and farmers were tanked up with ale; that's when the true nature of what you'd bought would come to light and she remembered his shame on buying poor stock at one sheep fair. Stick to what you can afford, don't lose yer head and get carried away with the excitement. She could hear his words ringing in her heart as it pounded in her chest.

Her tup was paraded round the ring and she sat back trying to look bored and uninterested in the proceedings, hardly daring to move. Surely it was only a middling sort of sheep, nowt to get worked up about. The bidding opened and soon it was between Warwick and a farmer from Dentdale. So someone else saw its potential. This was the nasty bit, to stay the ground bidding up cautiously and firmly, wearing out the opposition with the possibility of upping the price and then dipping out of the sale leaving the opposition stranded with an overpriced tup.

Uncle Warwick stayed firm and the farmer, assuming the price would go on rising, dropped out. There was a second of silence and no other bids. The gavel banged down and Ellie jumped up.

'Sold to . . .'

'Birkett, Miss Ellen Birkett.' She smiled proudly as the farmers turned round in surprise at a female voice.

'I still think yer daft in yer head!' sulked Sunter on the way home in the cart.

'You always did, cousin, and that's why it would be dreadful if we wed. Imagine the offshoots of two mad beasts. Wait while spring and see my new crop of lambs.' Sunter stared ahead sternly. He would be long gone by then.

Chapter Twenty-Five

The lovers lay tucked for shelter under a mossy boulder on a limestone ridge overlooking Scarsdale, sitting on Fancy's jacket hiding from the rain as it blew like smoke across the valley. They lay together, limbs entwined, oblivious to their soaking. Fancy's dark eyes smiled as Ellie stirred beneath him; her left leg had gone to sleep and she shifted to shake some life back into the limb. Neither minded the wind or the rain, it kept their trysting safe from prying eyes on this deserted spot. For once the building works were silent and the Sunday knock-off obeyed rather than ignored. Ellie sat up and pulled her skirt back over her legs. She ought to be getting back to the farm with Mother in one of her moods. Sabbath or not, she would be in the kitchen, hard at the bottling and preserving, waiting for company to call to try out her elderberry cordial and seedcake.

Ellie felt guilty for skiving off secretly, pretending she was checking on her new tup in the field. She had been tupping all right! But that was nobody else's business but her own. She was fed up laying down eggs in buckets, vegetables in sand, airing the window blankets to keep out draughts, sorting out ewes to be starved and then flushed in rich pasture before the tups were allowed to run with the flock. These were not the autumn tasks she relished. She sighed loudly and said, 'I do love the backend of the year, Fancy, trees aflame with colour, seeing all our cattle in the fields, hay stacked high in the barn and the way the shaved fields are mixed up golden and bronze, all them shades of grey and green like a crazy quilt spread over the valley. Show me them poems again . . .' Ellie stretched over his legs to root in his pocket.

Fancy caught her hand and pulled it away teasing, 'Ach, no, it needs more work on it afore I read it . . .'

'It's fine as it is. Read it to me again, Fancy.'

'Give me a kiss first!' The girl flung her arms round his neck and pecked him on the cheek.

'Not like that . . . you can do better.' Fancy held her tightly into himself and they rolled together down the slope, laughing as they landed in a heap of sheep droppings, kissing tenderly, fiercely as if sucking the juices out of each other's mouths. Ellie lay back, feeling the rain on her brow. If Mother could see the state she was in now, defiant and unrepentant. As she gazed up at the clouds of slate, she could hear Mother ranting to Miss Herbert as they all left for church that morning.

'Can you put this nonsense out of her head? She won't

listen to a word I say. He's not good enough for her, nobbut a drunken sot, a bogtrotting Scotchman. She's bringing shame on our good name consorting with navvies. I'll not have one sitting at my fireside in Jim's chair. I told her right at the start if she should look in that direction ...' Mother ignored her daughter, speaking to the blushing Miss Herbert who shifted awkwardly, not knowing where to look at this onslaught, while Mercy, mouth agog, listened in the doorway. Ellie had turned to the teacher, arguing back.

'And I'm telling her that me and Fancy is walking out and that's the end of it. She should not be bothering you, miss, it's nowt to do with anyone else what I do. Mr MacLachlan would be willing to help on the farm. Together we could do the hard work, the cowing and bulling and raise enough sons to keep up Dad's herd. It makes sense, Mother.' Annie Birkett had shaken her fist.

'I won't hear another word from her, Miss Herbert. You carry on with him, milady, and you can walk out that door as you stand. That's my last word on the job. Sunter and Warwick can take over the farm tomorrow and you can wander round every blasted railway line in the land with that ragabash to yer heart's ruination. I'm sick of that railway, the noise and stench of it. I'm sick of seeing drunken navvies peeing in my hedgerows, rolling down to Scarsbeck as if they owned the place. They can flash their money all they please but it don't make them respectable and yon Fancy pants is no different than the rest. He'll get his way with you and dump you for some flighty piece. They're all the same, scattering their seeds to the four winds ... nobbut rubbish. Navvies know nowt but work and wickedness. You'd think she'd think better of herself, Miss Herbert, than to throw herself away to a navvy?'

Ellie turned to look at the cause of all this bother. He was her shining man, tender and loving, and now she was his woman. There was no way she would give him up just to please Mam. Everything about him glowed. His fiery hair, boot-polished eyes, his firm strong body freckled and tanned by the sun. As he curled over to scribble in his notebook she raised herself on one elbow to snatch the paper from him. 'I love that bit about navvy time:

> 'This is navvy time, the time of the wildmen,
> Who struggle over bog and moor,
> Tramp from sea to river to beck,
> Our tracks cut into dale and over
> The hills, scattering sheep and cattle
> In the low pastures.
> We dam up waters, turn the millwheel
> Make engines steam, we cut out an iron way
> Blast out the mountains to leave our
> Rough mark forever
> In the spirit of the place.'

'It's no finished, I canna make it rhyme like it should but that's how the words fall.' Fancy was embarrassed by her reading it aloud.

Ellie sat rigid, upright, afraid. 'You won't just jack it in and leave now, will you . . . now we lay together? Mother says that's all a navvy wants from a girl.'

'Hey! Who said anything about leaving? Ellie Birkett, how could you be thinking such a thing with the job only just begun and me with my hut furnished with newspapers lining the walls and a line of lockers on the walls and the prettiest girl in the dale on my arm? Shame on you. If ever I came to leave, I hope I would not be going alone . . .'

'Is that so?'

'Aye, I would be hoping that a certain lassie would away north with me.'

'I have a farm to keep. How would Mother manage on her own? The vultures from High Butts would soon be scavenging.'

'Then we can stay and I'll help you all I can.'

'But Mother is feared that you carry my heart in your knapsack already. She will not stomach our meetings.'

'She's off her head to fear I would harm you. Why should she think I would shame you?'

'She says there are no wedded women in your camp,' Ellie whispered, blushing at her boldness, feeling crumpled and dishevelled. Fancy burst out laughing.

'Is that all that bothers the wifie? It's no true . . . we have a few with brass rings on their fingers. Let me take you down to Scarsbeck right this minute and get it seen to by the minister of the kirk. And if she canna hold with such a public display, then I ken a place over the border at Gretna Green village where the blacksmith will wed us over his anvil, the old way. No one will stop us there.'

'Oh, Fancy, would you do that for me?'

'Name yer day and we'll get on with it. Over the hills to Kendal up Shap Fell to Carlisle on the fast train and then you can return with a husband on yer arm, how about that pleasing your mammy? The choice is yours.' He hugged her with wet arms.

'Never mind her, I'm choosing what I want. How romantic to steal away in the night and come back wed with no fuss and no palaver. Yes, please, Fancy.' Ellie sighed deeply as the rain dripped down her nose.

'Name the day, why wait? It's our wee secret. We could be there and back in a few days.'

'As long as we're back for tupping. I shall be needed then to check out my new ram. Won't it be exciting to sneak off by moonlight, but can we really make it happen for us?'

'Whisht! Our minds are made up and no one can stop our plans if they dinna ken what we're up to. We can meet by the track at Scarsbeck Cross and tramp over to Dentdale up the west line. Are you sure that's what you are wanting?'

'Sure as death, Fancy. Once it's done then there'll be peace and no one can gainsay the deed. Mother'll have to make a place for you at the table or bite on her own sour grapes.'

'I widna be so sure about that, lass. She seems awful stubborny to me,' said Fancy as he shook out his jacket and brushed down her skirt, his heart beating at the rashness of the promises so glibly made. How would he survive on a daleside tending stupid sheep?

Chapter Twenty-Six

Saint Luke's late sunshine warmed bowls of fruit on the stone window ledges of St Oswy's church. The scents of the harvest table wafted over the congregation: apples, medlars, pears, late peaches from the orangery at Scarsbeck Hall, filberts and sacks of oatmeal, speckled eggs carefully selected for colour and texture and a display of vegetables from the produce show giving a flourish to the display.

The pews were jam-packed with the great and good of the dale jostling for seats at this annual gathering and the bun fight in the parish room which passed for a harvest supper when all the best of the produce would be auctioned off and the rest distributed to the poor and needy in baskets. Arguments would rage for weeks down the ginnels in the cottages as to whose basket was bigger and better than the one they got from the chapel harvest.

All was safely gathered in barns and hay lofts: oats for the havercakes, nets of onions, potatoes and carrots, parsnips and beetroot, fruit stored in cool lofts, lines of apples shining like amber, rubies, emeralds and topaz. The pitted windfalls were left in the orchards for pigs to forage and fatten before their slaughter in late November. Ewes were heads down in the lower pastures ready to be salved with tar and butter oil and tup rams bought at the tup sales soon to be let loose on them so the next harvest of lambs could begin again.

None of the altar fixtures and fittings had missed a share of the decoration; trailing ivy wreathing the altar rail wended its way across the lectern and up the three-tier pulpit; bunches of Michaelmas daisies and the few chrysanthemums which had survived the early frosts stood dotted at random, their very sparsity catching the eye in an effective manner. There were vases of stiff gladioli standing like spears and branches of copper beech poking round the pillars. The candle rails were garnished with yet more ivy to highlight bunches of grapes donated by the Hall but there were only stalks left on; the culprits in the choir stalls spitting pips at each other during Bulstrode's painful hour when the village growlers massacred yet another of S.S. Wesley's anthems for small choirs.

Ralph Hardy surveyed his congregation with satisfaction. It was a good turnout under the circumstances with the usual descending orders of the dale firmly in their stalls waiting for a lecture, a pat on the back and a chance to doze or check who had put on the best show: the landowners and yeoman farmers to the fore in their boxed pews, tenant farmers in the middle and the smallholders and cottagers at the rear. In each pew families sat like organ pipes in order of size. Farmer red-faced in tweeds and muffler, wife in poky bonnet and firm stays upright with her best Paisley shawl on display for those of lesser means to envy. Then the children, descending in height, fidgeted in stiff collars and boned bodices, kicking the pew backs with boots or clogs according to means. Rows of offspring ensured many another harvest in years to come.

The parson did a quick tally; all present and correct from each of the Anglican farmsteads. The villagers were augmented by Wally Stackhouse and his brood from the Fleece who always managed high days and holidays and a free feast, the Bulstrode woman and shopkeepers who had organised the harvest display. The church smelt like a fruit market at noon and Ralph's stomach began to gurgle at the prospect of the goose pie supper to follow. He was hoping for a good auction to raise funds for new lead flashing for the church roof seeing as how the stuff that had lasted two hundred years disappeared overnight a few weeks ago. The constable needed to look no further than Paradise camp for his villains but no one there could help them as the suspects had jacked in and sloped off with half St Oswy's roof on their handcart. They had last been seen at the Hill Inn at Chapel le Dale refuelling themselves on their way to Ingleton. Mr Hurst could only shrug his shoulders and offer a donation to start the fund.

It was unfortunate that they did not wait until after the September flash floods which soaked the valley, flooded the beck, leaving pools of water on the pews and hassocks soaked through. Someone had turned the tap on upstairs and no mistake and his congregation huddled for cover under umbrellas. Thank providence that this afternoon was warm and the heavens above cloudless, a typical Luke's little summer in mid-October; the lull before the onslaught of winter.

Ralph had his eye on a jar of Lund's heather honey stuck among tasteless marrows the size of Wellington boots, and pumpkins like lanterns ready for the Halloween capers. The tomatoes he viewed with suspicion, knowing full well that many were fertilised with manure straight from the communal privies and pig pens in the back yards of Scarsbeck alongside other overstuffed dubious offerings up for auction. Dalesfolk wasted nothing.

Cora Bulstrode had done her best to raise the sheep exhibits into some artistic shape; sheep fleeces and carded wool lay draped around the spinning wheel and carding brushes. Then there was the Mission teacher's effort to display butter tubs and pats with golden squares stamped with traditional leaf patterns. There was a whole cheese in muslin cloth and bottles of Annie Birkett's prize-winning primmyrose wine. One bottle of that had him on his knees pleading for mercy. What a cornucopia of God's gracious goodness in keeping with his own efforts to redeem his priestly function. They were going to get a first-class lecture in line with recent events in the parish and his new-found enthusiasm to put fire back into his sermons.

As he peered through the undergrowth on the lectern to find his reading he remembered the notices in his pockets to read out at the intimations. The notices would provide a break in the hymn-prayer-hymn sandwich; a breather for the audience to cough, slip in a lozenge, stretch and stare around. He had to admit the church looked a picture thanks to all the brass-polishing, pew-dusting, hassock-beating bevy of ladies who kept the ancient church as spick and span as their own neat front parlours. He never saw any other part of their homes when he visited. Only the welcome hearth of Beth Wildman. He wondered if she was watching over his efforts.

Then he saw Liddy Braithwaite sitting with her lips pursed tightly, arms folded menacingly across her ample bosom which for once was covered up. Her husband sat by her side, his tanned pate shining as smooth as a russet apple. Ralph thought himself mad to even contemplate he could carry on with their joyful trysting. Sacrifices had to be made, he sighed, and turned to his task. 'My text today is from St Matthew's Gospel, chapter six, verse nineteen: Lay not up for yourselves treasures upon earth . . .'

Isaac Cleghorn sat hunched up in his black verger's robe, his eyes cast down by the vicar's text. Surely the parson had not got wind of his good fortune on Friday night during the storm?

Just minding his own business returning from Batty Green along the tramway track, Nippa plodding uphill against the wind. Then there was this almighty crash and wallop as forked lightning speared the ground and the horse shied up. Steady on, son, as the rain poured on us heads. We're a good half mile from any shelter. Still Nippa stayed calm and Cleggy sang out the old hymn, 'The God Who rules on high can thunder where He please.'

It was pitch-black and the track turned into a quagmire when he heard voices calling out, shouting from one of the gulleys down below. So he had to stop like the Good Samaritan. Not one to miss owt fresh to spice up his tales around Scarsbeck, he got himself close to the edge and shouted back. There was a goods wagon on its side, deep in the mud, plunged straight off the track, and he could make out the outline of three navvies scratching their heads, looking gormless. 'What's up?' he yelled.

'Wagon were struck by lightning, jumped clean of the track into this hole; full of stuff for the tommy store from Burgoine and Cock's warehouse at Batty Green, vittels, tins, bottles all sinking into this shaft if we don't crack on and get it sorted out. What a terrible thing to be happening on a dark night,' said the tempter's voice from the shadows.

'Give us a hand to get it upright,' yelled a nameless, faceless navvy from the hole.

'Not so hasty,' Cleggy argued. 'It'll take more than me and the horse to shift that heavy thing. Shall I tote mesen back to the camp and fetch help?'

'Aye, happen you do right.' Temptation's voice again.

'But it's off my own way to go up there. I might be persuaded by some reward for my trouble and in such bad weather.'

The men whispered. 'If we were to lighten the wagon of

its load and add some extra boxes to your cart would that be suiting you?'

Cleggy needed little persuasion to fill up his empty cart with as many boxes of tins and comestibles as Nippa could carry. He lifted his cap and trundled to Paradise, leaving some vague message at the camp gate about a derailment somewhere in the neighbourhood which might only be lightning.

Even now this hoard was sitting under these stone flags; all was safely gathered in awaiting a second dispersal, buried in the House of God in the sexton's cellar at the back of the church with the key chained to his waistcoat. Surely the Almighty would not begrudge him a reward for initiative and enterprise? He was in the process of spreading his bounty over hill and dale and bought Nippa a new blanket at Hawes market for keeping his secret safe . . .

'Lay not up for yourselves treasures upon earth . . . where thieves break through and steal . . .' Cora sat bolt upright as the vicar expounded the virtues of honesty in all things. She watched Ezra slumped on the pipe organ bench turning over his music restlessly while waiting for his choir to do their turn in the harvest show. He was always the same when the Fawcett exam was looming uppermost in his mind, agitated and withdrawn, tirelessly shifting papers in his study, his appetite poor, picking at his food without interest. Surely she was right to tempt his palate with that piece of fresh salmon simmered in gooseberry wine and fennel with a butter and herb sauce. He had eaten the steak with relish. It was good to see him relaxed. That incident with Sunter Lund and the broken window had unsettled them both. He sat back and asked how she came by such a fresh cut when the Ashman's cart had not called for days.

The salmon was tenderly and truly poached to perfection, he complimented her, and she had blushed in the knowledge it was well and truly poached all right, from under the nose of the gamekeeper at Scarsbeck Hall, right out of Sir Edward's salmon stretch of the Ribble, delivered to her back door by the skivvy sister of the Widdup brat, wrapped in newspaper as a thank-you for Billy's extra lessons.

At first she had been tempted to chuck it straight onto the rubbish dump but it would attract vermin and cats. You never knew where these navvy creatures had been but one look at its prime pink flesh and bloom convinced her it would be a sin to waste such bounty. Ezra needed nourishment in his thankless task of pumping knowledge and standards into that cheeky child. Surely there was no harm in using what had already been blasted out of the water, sliced up and scattered to the four corners of the dale long before she got wind of it. She was just making sure the unlawful deed was redeemed by her best recipe and Ezra's satisfaction.

'Lay not up for yourselves treasures upon earth ... where moth and rust doth corrupt ... This reminds me that Mr Hurst from Paradise would like it to be known that a wagon was derailed and its contents, mainly tins and groceries, mysteriously disappeared into the mud. Should you be offered any suspect cans, be assured that you may be handling stolen contraband of dubious origin. Not that I think any of this God-fearing congregation would stoop to such calumny. If any one has any information concerning the events of last Friday, you are to declare it to the contractor's office at once and there will be a small reward, I am told.'

Was it Ralph's imagination or did a wave of shuffling and head-lowering ripple through his flock?

Annie Birkett sneaked a glance through the corner of her black bonnet at Blaize Lund who was dabbing her cheeks with her handkerchief, trying not to look guilty. Annie stared ahead defiantly. *Just wait till I get home, I'll have the labels off them tins of peaches and shove them in the back pantry on the top shelf out of sight. Wait till I get hold of Cleghorn . . . spicing up my groceries with temptation by selling surplus railway stores at reduced prices indeed!* She and Blaize had been delighted to stock up their larders with tins. You got sick of yer own stuff in a long winter. Peaches and cream for Christmas tea perhaps? By then no one would be asking where they came from.

They had shared a caseful and all in innocence but she was not giving a single one back, oh no! Surely they were entitled to a few treats after all that storing and bottling, hands soaked in pickled onions and gooseberry relish, beetroot chutney, bramble jam, raspberry jam, rowan jelly, rosehip cordial, raspberry vinegar and elderberry syrup, herb jellies and apples, apples, apples. She was sick of stirring and setting, peeling, mixing, sewing and mending winter woollies and flannel petticoats, darning stockings and not much help from Ellen who still spent her time outdoors like a farm boy. There was no talking sense into that one.

Short cuts were a godsend for a farmer's wife. Perhaps one day women would have cupboards full of tins to see them through the worst of winter. Those tins would be staying put, her own buried treasure which she prayed wouldn't rust as the parson warned. No, it was dry as toast in that back pantry. Her jewels would be safe there.

Mercy Birkett sensed her mother's discomfort. She had seen the tins but her lips were sealed. The only person looking eagerly up at the parson now was Miss Herbert in a ravishing bonnet of golden straw lined with stripped blue silk and a bandeau of ruched ribbon circling the base. She knew all of Miss Herbert's wardrobe for she sneaked in sometimes when she was out on her Mission work and tried on everything in her trunk. One day she would trail dresses behind her with a handsome prince to call for her in a carriage and four. She would be the envy of Scarsbeck for her finery.

She had no treasure to hoard for moths to get at but she hated moths flickering around her candle, fluttering across her face in the dark, making her scream to be rescued by Ellie who brought a cloth and flung the creatures out of the window. Did God really see what they got up to? How many eyes must He have to watch everyone at the same time? Surely He missed a bit here and there?

If there was big stealing going on He were not going to get steamed up about a few cake crumbs, nicked from the testing plates at the produce show. She and Billy had crept under the table and watched the feet of the judges going round the sponge cakes and biscuits and bread buns, oatcakes and tea-breads. She had smuggled Billy in with her and he'd stuffed himself silly so he was sick on the way home. He was such a sissy. She stood a foot above him already. The other lads thought him soppy and left him alone. He was too pretty for a lad, she heard Miss Herbert clacking to Ellie. She was just as brainy as him any day. It was not fair that he got all the fuss so she popped some beetles in the school kettle which Miss Herbert asked her to fill up from the beck to heat on the stove for her luncheon. She liked Sherbert really but she had stolen her bedroom and was always sitting sewing with Ellie while she stood awkward like a pig in a parlour, waiting to be noticed.

One day they would all realise that she really was a lost princess waiting for the king and queen to rescue her and take her back to their royal palace. Mother would stay on as her grateful maid and Ellie would brush her hair and dress her in silks and satin dresses covered with pink rosebuds. Then they will all notice me ... She sighed as she sniffed the fruity smells. I wish the vicar would shut up and we could all get on with the feasting. She turned to look up at her sister but she had that faraway dreamy look in her eye which sent Mother into a fit of grumps and sighs. Middle Butts was no fun any more.

'For where your heart is, so shall your treasure be also ...' Ellie watched the dust speckling in an arch of sunlight onto a child's head bobbing two pews ahead. My heart is with Fancy Mac, so shall our treasure be in our sons, golden-haired William, Kester and James. They will sit in this pew as jewels in the crown of our marriage, the stars in our firmament. Mother will smile at us proudly and memories will fade of elopement and scandal, suspicion of a navvy offcomer marrying with a born and bred like the Swaledale tup they had purchased to perk up the flock and add strength to their stock.

As it was with sheep so could it be in the village with blood strengthened by new sires. She had chosen him and he, her. In their hands and loins lay the future of the dale. One look at Mother's scowling face doused her dreams in cold water. She would never forgive a shaming, going behind her back to marry out. Ellie would be disowned and her destiny would be to tramp the land as a navvy wife. I will have my Fancy, she vowed silently. In a few weeks she would run away then return to face the furies. She hugged her plans to her chest, made notes in her head preparing for her absence. She was going in search of her treasure and no one would stop her.

'I hope to get up a football team from the best of our village to play a select eleven from Paradise whom Mr Paisley assures me will not disgrace themselves on our village green, Saturday week. I'm looking to all you young men here to defend the honour of Scarsbeck and Mr Stackhouse has kindly offered refreshments to the teams after the match.'

Wally Stackhouse sat in the back row glumly. The vicar

had just thrown cold water on his own scheme to earn a few pounds from the navvies, not give them away. Too many workmen now drank from their own ale casks, supplied by brewery carthorses straight to the camp stores and then secreted at dead of night in huts and bothies for all-night sessions. He had a licence to pay for and taxes to account for. Surely a late-night cock fight behind the far barns out of earshot of the squeamish would offend no one? He would place a guinea on Trojan Red, his own fighting cock, to claw his opponent from the camp to shreds. With a few barrels wheeled up for customers he could count on a good night's takings. A football match was a bit tame, not the same draw for folk, but he couldn't give the parson back word. Lay up for yourselves treasures ... He was all for putting a bit by for old age and sickness or both. He would put his trust any day in gold to see you through to the end. When push came to shove, a gold piece would butter more parsnips than a sermon.

Sunter leant forward with interest for once at the talk of a contest with the camp. His team would show them. He had a reputation as a fighting man to uphold now. He could put off his escape from the dale for a few more weeks until they thrashed them navvies, rubbed their faces in the mud and kicked 'em to kingdom come. It would give him more time to soften up old Bulstrode and extract some juice as his dues, put the fear of God into that cow, Cora, and talk some sense into his stupid cousin. He knew she was sneaking off in the bushes with that Jock. If she didn't see sense then she must be punished. This Lund was cock of the midden now.

Chapter Twenty-Seven

The firelight flickered in the grate. Only the oil lamp by her bedside was lit. Zillah stirred, smelling the mustard poultice around her chest. The tight pain had gone and the hammer was no longer ringing in her head. She lifted her head from the pillow and the room did not spin. I'll live, she smiled to herself with relief for the first time in days. What day was it? She should be at school . . . how were they managing without her? Miss Bulstrode would be furious at her absence and the headmaster drained by his sister's twittering.

Whatever sickness had hit her and laid her so low was passing over at last, leaving her battered and exhausted but glad to be alive. The room was dark but it was not evening. It was that gloomy time of year, almost November, and she could not adjust to the loss of daylight on days like this when the mist lay thick as a blanket over the valley. Soon there would be even less light and she could hear the patter of rain on her window, battering the last leaves from ash trees.

Zillah was tempted to snuggle down under the goose-feather quilt and go back to her dreams. She sat up slowly. Away with sloth! Duty made her pile up the pillows behind her into cushions against the hard oak headboard. She stretched over to ferret for a pencil and her writing case. Poor Mama and Aunt Jane would think her dead, for she had sent no letters for weeks.

It was difficult to focus her eyes on the blank page; her hand was trembling and her handwriting as spidery as an old woman's. Her nose was dripping dewdrops and she smelt like a navvy, her nightdress whiffing of fevered unwashed sweat. Zillah gulped another spoonful of the soothing poppy juice from the apothecary's bottle to clear her head and caught sight of herself in the washstand mirror. What a sight! Wild eyes glowing like burning coals, a white face flushed of cheek, hair in rat's tails poking out of her lace nightcap like Lady Macbeth fleeing the hounds of hell.

It was hard to concentrate on her task with a full bladder so she struggled to get her limbs out of the bed to search for the pot. As she sat on her tiny throne the room loomed above her like the room in *Alice in Wonderland*. She felt as tired as if she had journeyed into some far country without a guide. Now she was oddly disconnected from the real world outside her sick room. How had she come to be in this state? Zillah struggled back up to the mountain of bedclothes and settled back to write her letter, again remembering it all.

Dearest Mama and Aunt Jane,

You must fear your errant daughter to be a stranger as it is so long since we all met face to face. I fully intended to return to see you last month but have been so severely indisposed as to make all travel impossible. I have been confined to bed for some time but now am recovering sufficiently to put pen to paper.

Thank you for the trunk of winter clothing which Maria packed so neatly and cautiously. Had it sunk by accident into Semerwater Lake, all my garments would have lain dry and safe like buried treasure. Twelve flannel chemises, six flannel petticoats, six pairs of flannel drawers, six alpaca underskirts, six wool house dresses, two morning dresses, a morning robe and two housecoats, two dressing jackets, my half-cloak and four pairs of boots. All present and correct.

Having sampled a Yorkshire spring I am sure all my winter clothing will be layered one on top of the other. Warm as the welcome is here, the farmhouse is draughty and doors rattle when the wind comes in a certain direction. I am getting acquainted with a needle and cotton to shorten some of my hemlines from the mud. The Birkett women are kind but very busy and I cannot expect them to mend my clothes. You offered to send Maria as my maid but I do not think that will be appropriate and Maria would find conditions here very uncomfortable. There are plenty of women who will do alterations in the village.

Thank you for thinking about me. You worry that I am bereft of decent company. In fact I find the company here most congenial and sincere, unfettered by society manners. There is a freshness in conversation which allows people to say exactly what they mean without lacing everything round the edges like table doilies.

The severe cold which has confined me indoors is due entirely to my own curious fault. It will teach me not to expose myself so thinly shod to the rigours of the village green on a wet Saturday afternoon in order to watch some strange ritual sport which only an uncouth savage would consider enjoyable. I blame the violent game of football entirely for my undoing. How can I describe this activity which almost caused a riot in Scarsbeck?

Our village green, which stretches in a thin line through the main street, widens at one point into a large rectangle opposite the school where the children let off steam at playtime. Here two large net bags were erected upright at either end like snoods. Then two teams of about ten men assembled with a leather ball about the size of an atlas. Apparently the aim of the above game is to kick the said ball from end to end in order to get the ball in the net which is guarded by the only man who is allowed to handle the ball. It was explained to me several times that there are strict rules but I was not able to fathom why everyone was getting so excited when Mr Lund kicked the ball into one net to great applause and then when it slipped off his feet into the other net the village turned on him in derision and the poor lad was booed and spat on for the rest of the game. The whole afternoon was taken up with men kicking the ball at the same time and kicking shins and legs even when there was no ball. The entertainment seemed to provide an excuse for much screaming and shouting from the boundary line by crowds of spectators waving rattles.

On Paradise side was Mr Paisley and his navvy team in knee-breeches and thick boots who brought gangs of workmen and women to cheer them on. The village team was headed by Mr Stackhouse from the Fleece hostelry and seemed to be full of farmers' sons from all over the dale. So it was like two opposing armies on the touchline who jeered at each other and threatened to flood the field and join in. There were people viewing from the viaduct scaffolding and one of my pupils fell off halfway through but was unharmed. A locomotive sat on the top of the viaduct track hooting on the engine every time Paradise looked likely to score.

The battle was overseen by our bold vicar in short cotton pants to the knee and thick striped stockings. I could see him dashing from one end to the other, running through the teams blowing his whistle at any infringements and trying to control the passions of the spectators as they roared abuse at him from both teams.

Once this game got underway only a thunderbolt from the Almighty would have stopped them in their tracks, such was the intensity of play. It was a revelation to me how grown men and some women could be so partisan in their support and get so hot under the collar by the mere kicking of a ball into a net bag, calling their opinions to the umpire in terms no lady would like to overhear.

*Resolving to make these observations part of my local
education as to customs and traditions, I stood faithfully
at my own vantage post feeling the dampness creep up my
stockings and into my skirts as the mizzle soaked my hat and
veil and outer jacket. My umbrella was frequently challenged
for holding up someone's view so I kept it folded and the rain
dripped upon us relentlessly.*

*In fact the mist got so thick that we could no longer see
how things proceeded at either end of the pitch but it did not
deter the battle. As they seemed to change ends after a short
interval, I was thoroughly confused but stayed fast.*

*Apparently there was some incident which required
one village man to kick the ball straight into the bag with
one navvy standing firm against him, like David against
Goliath, to win the game. David was no match for the tall
Mr MacLachlan who towered over his posts and saved the
penalty kick, much to the relief of Paradise and calls of foul
play from Scarsbeck.*

*Mr Sunter Lund took up the ball and ran with it in a
sulk, chased by the umpire and the Scotsman, and the teams
collided into a pile of bodies kicking and fighting, throwing
the ball to each other across the field. Now that was more
exciting as a game and then the crowd seemed to want to
join in. I saw Miss Ellen getting upset at the fate of her
navvy friend and the poor parson was nowhere to be seen.
There was no point calling in the constable as Mr Firth
was stuck with the village team somewhere under the pile.
Reverend Hardy scrambled out with a bloodied nose and blew*

his whistle to no avail but one by one the teams untangled themselves, leaving only the Scotsman and Mr Lund battling on.

The fight turned ugly with the redhead navvy screaming, 'I'll see you in hell afore long!' which had Miss Ellen in tears. I don't think any of this was in Mr Hardy's rule book but the mist was so thick that the match was abandoned and the teams, mud-splattered, bruised and battered, staggered into the Fleece to quench their thirsts. I beat a hasty retreat to the schoolhouse to beg a cup of tea from the Bulstrodes before my sodden trek back to the farm. Cora admitted me only when I stripped off my wet outer garments so I shivered by her meagre fire. I am sure she was watching from behind the safety of her net curtains, Mr Bulstrode having retreated to the church to play the organ. Miss Cora explained that any physical displays give him a headache.

I enquired about my star pupil only to be told that he was making satisfactory progress towards the December examination. Walking back to Middle Butts we were overtaken by the vicar in his horse and trap and he offered us a welcome lift back home. We were in no position to refuse this kindness and we all chatted amiably along the stone track completely surrounded by swirling mist and mizzle. Ellen was upset about the public fighting. Our vicar was disappointed that the match had not had the reconciling effect he planned. He says he will persevere with other activities over the winter and perhaps organise a Christmas show which he hopes will involve both camp and village in the season of goodwill. I said I hoped this activity would be more peaceful than the rehearsal for Armageddon I'd witnessed on the village green and everyone laughed.

I was feeling quite exhausted by the afternoon's end and Mistress Annie took one look at me, insisting I steam my head over a bowl of balsam oil to clear it. She reprimanded me severely for standing on wet grass and poured a glass of elderberry syrup down my throat to cure all or kill me, she laughed. I was sat down before a huge plate on which was the largest Yorkshire pudding, the size of a dessert plate, golden, crisp and light, into which she poured a jug of hot thick gravy full of goodness and bits and stood over me until my plate was emptied.

They set great store by producing these puddings made of batter, oven-roasted but light to the touch. Poor Ellen cannot get hers to rise at all and they collapse on the plate like soggy dishcloths. Within a few days I felt so feverish I could not stand upright and was shoved into bed and dosed with all sorts of herbs and potions. I think I had a sick visit from the vicar, chaperoned by Merciful. He seemed concerned about the deterioration of my health. I took one look at him standing there in his black cassock, not the cheeriest of sights is the woozy sight of a cassock and prayer book. I think I thought he was preparing me for Kingdom Come and went all weepy, so Mercy informed me later. He held my hand and said I would soon be on the mend but I have no recall of this event. I must have looked a fright with my red nose streaming and my hair all a mess. If I am not careful I shall have to reconsider my opinion of the ever-late Mr Hardy. He is trying to get more involved in his parish at last. I am told he is quite well-connected in the district, being a distant cousin of Sir Edward Dacre, a Hardy from Pickering, and his sister, Dorothy, is married to Lord Howard's nephew. I am still not sure of his spiritual condition but it seems to have taken a turn for the better since that shameful episode of forgetting the burials.

Poor Mary Ann has left Paradise and gone to Batty Green. I will always put flowers by the smallpox plot to remember Janey. I am rambling on incoherently as if there is a lot to straighten in my own mind. I think I have been guilty of taking so firm a stance on things religious as to quite put people off my views. Perhaps our established church is no worse than most and has bumbled along for centuries so who am I to be so severe a critic of clergy and congregation alike?

That verse: 'In my father's house are many mansions' troubles me. Does it mean that Heaven is full of different rooms? When I joined the Pastoral Aid Mission I was assured that there was only one room and everyone must be squashed in tight. Now I am thinking it means that there are lots of rooms for different points of view. When my turn comes I'd like to be in the same room as the Birketts and the Pringles and Mr Cleghorn and all the other kindly people I have met here. I feel as if I have lived here for months with a veil over my face and that somehow now the veil is lifted and I can see clearer. Does this make any sense?

On a fine day this dale is as close as you can get to paradise; but a sort of paradise flawed. In contrast Paradise *camp is a festering sore, an ugly boil of a place. Mr Tiplady and his Bradford mission do their best to provide comforts but their efforts are as plain as their mission hut, which is serviceable, bare, cold and Spartan. I thought I could abandon all my old practices and join wholeheartedly with them. Yet I yearn for the prayer book and quiet peace of St Oswy's. I like the seasons of our church's year, Easter, Whitsun, Harvest and Christmas each rolling round as the year turns. Now it is almost All Hallows' Eve and we remember saints past and present united over the ages. Do they too have their own mansions, customs and opinions which might be strange today? Then there are the future saints yet to be born. So you see I am questioning everything.*

It will be hard to leave Scarsbeck when my term finishes. Once the families move on up the line I will be expected to go with them to help set up more schoolrooms. I am assured there will be many years of work here on the line but am no longer sure if Zillah Herbert will be the right person to continue the task. My Mission journal lies neglected and I have logged only two sick visits; both have been to me. This letter will have to be logged in as a spiritual conversation. They are very concerned to inspect my outreach work.

I find it so hard to work alongside Ezra Bulstrode. He is the most distracting little man, nervous and twitchy, and his sister startles at the slightest noise. He places so much store on the scholastic achievement of a few to the detriment of all, I fear. It seems to be affecting his health. I trust it was God's will for me to coerce young Billy to compete in their arena?

Bulstrode is a man driven by demons and subjected to a sister who displays such malice of the soul as that ancient mystic once said. I do not like to malign my own sex but her malice is so biting in its effect and so much worse in a woman. Had I stayed at the schoolhouse I would long ago have returned to your fireside.

It is hard to recall that it is only six months since I made my snowy entrance into this dale with a trunk full of dreams and schemes. Now I cannot foresee my being able to return to Nottingham until the festive season.

Papa will have gone to sleep in reading this long epistle but the fog in my head is clearing and my stomach gurgles with hunger once more. No doubt Nanny would consider that a good sign. I do not wish to be a burden to my hosts and will drag myself up ere long. Mercy checks on my progress, peeping round the door to see if I have passed over and she can whip away all my bonnets and shawls for her dressing-up box. The minx thinks I have no idea that she creeps into my closet and rummages through my clothing. I have a good mind to take some clothes and dunk them in butcher's blood and hide them with a dagger to teach her a lesson!

I shall write to you with another chapter of my adventures in 'Paradise flawed' as soon as possible.

Yours penitentially,

Zillah Jane

P.S. Mercy Birkett whispers I am called 'Sherbert' by my pupils. I hope that is because I fizz sweetly in water and not because I am acid and sharp!

Chapter Twenty-Eight

Mally Widdup peered into the boiling copper boiler in the Paradise communal bakehouse, her red face scalding from the steam. All the cloth puddings tied with string were bubbling away except one which bounced on the surface stubbornly. That one blessed pudding bobbed up and down and every attempt to drown it failed. Something must be wrong. Stay down, yer bugger, you've got two pounds of best beef and a thick coat of suet dumpling inside, what's wrong with yer?

Tizzy and her mates stood around looking puzzled. 'We're starving . . . when's tea?' Tizzy whined.

'I don't know, do I, not with this here playing me up. I hope it hasn't gone funny. I paid good money out to that butcher from Scarsbeck for this cut, if he's diddled me with rubbish I'll send Wobbly Bob and his gang to sort him out. As if I haven't enough to do but stand over a stupid pudding all night. Here, pull out the string and I'll have a sken.' Mally yanked on the string tie to draw out the dumpling onto the table. Then she saw Tizzy and the nippers sniggering, and she peered more closely at her catch. 'What the blood and stomach pills!' As she picked at the scalding muslin cloth, a firm leathery football was revealed underneath. 'You little divils! No wonder I'll never get that to sink down. Who did this?' She tried to hide the laughter in her voice.

'Gotcha! It's Mischief Night. Remember, remember the fourth of November,' Tizzy teased triumphantly.

'Tizzy Widdup. How am I to get my work done when I get mithered by a bunch of nippers?'

'Who calls you Tizzy?' said one of her gang.

'Only Mally, a nickname 'cos I gets her in a tizz,' answered Tizzy quick as a flash, glaring at her sister for almost blowing away her secret. Not that she didn't wish the game was over and done all together but Tizzy was sunk in too deep to bob out like their Mischief pudding. It was her idea to beg the football from Fancy Mac as a memento of his heroic deed. Saving a penalty from that horrible Lund tyke had given her something to gloat on. Yet all too often, a fed-up-of-being-a-lad mood came over her. She hated getting up at dawn for the early shift, shivering in the wet dewy grass and mud, collecting, delivering, running at the gang's beck and call like a skivvy maid. She might as well join Mally doing washing and cleaning. Then she was expected to clean up for the school cart and start her lessons and then some more. Standing for inspection at the schoolhouse door while Miss High and Mighty Patabully fussed. She had to sit all proper at the kitchen table and learn manners, but whatever they were she didn't have them. Elbows off the table, sit up straight, spoon to the mouth, chew twenty times on crumbs and fiddly bits. Sometimes Susan gave her titbits and she felt as grateful as Stumper who nosed around the navvy hut sniffing up the droppings.

Sometimes Tizzy was so tired during lessons that she felt like nodding off but the eggsandwichstation was only a few weeks away and she was stuck watching the mantelpiece clock as Bulstrode placed timed problems and sums in front of her as a practice run.

'If a train a hundred yards long travelling at sixty miles an hour passes another train, one hundred and fifty yards long, travelling at the same speed, how long would it take for them to pass each other?'

'Easy, peasy!' Her arithmetic was on target for the Fawcett but what then? Trains would never go that fast.

Tonight she would not be thinking about any of that. It was Mischief Night and every Yorkshire lad would be out on the streets heaving gates off posts, playing tricks with shaving soap and tar and feathers; a chance to pay back old scores. A gang of nippers would be roaming over the camp and if there was time, they would sneak down to Scarsbeck to do over the village school. Tizzy planned to keep out of that one if she could. Still, there was no harm in egging them on.

Two days ago Miss Herbert had donated a pile of soul cakes to pass round the class when she talked in the Scripture lesson about holy saints in glory to the whole school. She had made them up in the farmhouse under Mercy's mother's instructions and they tasted like little gingernuts full of treacle and oatmeal like Mally's chewy parkin. Sherbert's efforts were thicker and gooey and stuck to the roof of yer mouth. Mercy Birkett was that puffed up Tizzy had to trip her up in the play yard and she ran crying to the headmaster who gave them both the stick across their palms. So now she hoped the schoolhouse would get well and truly plastered with tar and feathers tonight.

They were going to have a busy evening emptying rubbish, fetching all the tools and wheelbarrows on site into a pile or decorating bushes with hammers and brushes, cans and buckets. Under cover of a starlit November sky they crept around unguarded huts with Stumper hopping behind them, setting other dogs barking, geese hissing and poultry pens squawking. 'Gertcha!' yelled the workmen who had long ago forgotten what it was to go Mischief hunting.

'Away or we'll tan yer backsides,' said Granda Widdup as he and his cronies pushed the night soil cart from midden to midden on their rounds, unaware that his grandchild was in the thick of it.

No one took any persuading to take the track down to the village, to give the local kids a run for their money. Tizzy scampered ahead, glad of a night away from studies in the noisy hut with navvies arguing or snoring around her. This was going to be the best of Mischief Nights.

At Middle Butts Farm, Mercy was screaming in a paddy of rage at not being allowed to join in the fun and tricks down in the village among the scholars. "Snot fair! I can never do anything stuck up here. Why can't I take the lantern and the dog and go off? Ellie can call for me later in the cart. She won't mind,' she ordered.

'You, madam, have mending to darn, a Scripture verse to learn for your confirmation class and bed to go to soon enough. If I hear no more, you can help me bake some more oatcakes and throw them over the pulley like stockings. You like doing that.' Mother was trying to distract the child from her tantrum but Mercy was not so easily smoothed these days. Since Jim died there was always a sullen edge to her tongue.

'I'm not a babby. I want to go outside and do Mischief. 'Snot fair! Ellie can come then.' She looked to her sister for support but Ellie shook her head vehemently.

'I am not harnessing the horse up just to please you.'

'Why not? You're a pig and go with navvies. Everyone says that, snotface.'

'One more word out of you, Merciful, and you go straight upstairs with no candle. I never heard such talkback from a girl of ten.'

'Eleven next month.' Mercy was unrepentant.

'That's as may be but no daughter of mine wanders out in the dead of night unescorted. Not with a heathen camp on our doorstep and thieves abroad, stealing sheep and beef cattle. There's plenty to occupy you here. So there's an end on it,' snapped Annie Birkett as she sifted the oatmeal in the bowl.

Ellie watched the brass hand of the grandmother clock creep like a snail towards the appointed hour. She was trying to stay casual and not tremble. Upstairs lay a small wicker valise containing a few toiletries, her Bible, a change of smalls and her best blouse.

Soon she would creep upstairs to change into her Sunday skirt and jacket under her workaday cloak and her best blue bonnet.

Ellie composed a letter of explanation and assurance which would be left on her bed. Mother would have to understand that love cannot wait for permission. Not when it was as strong as Ellie's. At nineteen, nearly, she was old enough to know her own mind. The first cut would be the deepest for Mother. Then she would realise that they were doing her a favour running away. It would mean no wedding feast and fancy clothes, no expenses on all the fuss of a wedding party. She rehearsed her exit carefully. Just by going to check the yard and retire early she could slip her bag into the shippon. Then she would sneak out the front of the house down the wide staircase, change once more and make her way on foot to Scarsbeck Cross for nine o'clock. The stone stood at the crossroads of all the trackways on the moor. A safe place to meet. By this time tomorrow or the day after, at the latest, she would be a happily married woman.

Cora Bulstrode stood sentinel behind the hall curtains watching shadows dart hither and thither across the green. She knew what they were up to, the evil ones planning to destroy the school and all Ezra's work. Since that letter arrived on the mat the house was filled with gloom leaving Cora sleepless, pacing around her bedposts each night. Now there was more mischief abroad and the village was conspiring against them. How could the stars shine so brightly, Orion torching in the sky?

Surely theirs would be the triumph? This must be Ezra's finest hour. This child was their best pupil despite his shabby and lowly station. Why was her brother now sitting in his study locked in despair? We will not be defeated by the powers of darkness and ignorance. We have not worked for twenty years to be defeated by greed and threats. Cora felt the flush of fear flood over her like a wave. Let the dark powers come. They would stand firm. She summoned Susan to make Ezra a warm drink and ordered her to retire out of sight. Cora would stand guard a little while longer to thwart any unwelcome visitors to their school.

Sunter Lund stared into his frothing pint, his third mug. Since his shaming at the football match he could feel the jibes and nudges behind his back as he sat hunched in a corner in the Fleece taproom. He was sick of this hole, the same stupid faces slavering onto their frothy chins, the smell of sawdust and smoke, stinking cats mewing around his ankles. Same owd faces chinwagging about nothing. If he lived here another twelvemonth he would grow owd and dull before his time like most of his schoolmates. Now he was full of plans and expectations not to leave this dale empty-handed.

Mother said, 'Have summat and you'll be summat.' He was only following her advice and it were paying off. There would be those in Scarsbeck surprised at his enterprising ways. Tomorrow he would be seeking his fortune out of this bloody place in pastures new.

For the first time in his life he could feel a surge of excitement in his belly. He was in control of his life. He would leave this rotten pigsty without a backward glance. Life was going to be grand for Sunter Lawson Lund from this hour forth. He swallowed the dregs of his pint and strode out of the room, remembering to duck under the lintel.

He paused in the doorway and headed towards the green. It was a grand sky full of stars stretched over his head. From east to west was a broad belt of flame, the strangest sight he'd ever noticed in a night sky, and he stood transfixed at the sight of such a grand omen for his future.

The Paradise gang was on the rampage but there was little left to tackle. The village had been seen to by their rivals, forks and spades, bins and buckets hanging on the trees like decorations, shaving soap over the school windows, gates removed, milk churns on barn roofs, nothing out of the ordinary. Now the streets were deserted and strangely silent. Tomorrow the village would gather at the annual bonfire on the green to light up a few fireworks and burn their flourbag-faced, straw-stuffed Guy Fawkes. There was a pile of offcuts from the sawmill, some tree prunings and some bits of rubbish piled into a pyre ready for the show.

All the lads stood silently looking at the bonfire, each having the same mischievous thought. 'Shall we?' said one.

'Why not?' said another.

'Nah!'

'Go on ... 'Tis against our faith to burn Guy Fawkes, we don't hold with Proddy dogs. Best mischief of all to burn their bonfire afore the day,' laughed one of the many Catholic boys in their gang.

'How do we light it then?' asked Tizzy, not so keen on firelighting since the escapade in the summer at Mercy's farm. The ground was damp, the wood wet and soggy.

'We'll soon get a spark up. Give us yer rags.' Each of them pulled out an oily rag from their pockets or up their sleeves, the rags they used around the track for wiping and polishing. They smelled of oil and were body-warm. They huddled together out of the wind to strike a flint into some life. Some rags smouldered and others ignited brightly. These were stuffed under the wood into the drier holes. They crackled and smoked and fuelled by dry cloths flared up into life, setting the whole bonfire ablaze.

'Find the Guy and put him on so they can't burn him!' shouted Tizzy, watching the sparks flicker and spit, smoke stinging her eyes. What a grand do! Tomorrow the village would wake up to their trick and a pile of ashes. The schoolchildren would be blamed.

'There's a Guy over there!' Tizzy yelled as she noticed the outline of the effigy slumped against a small wall. 'Come on, drag it on the fire and see how long it lasts.'

As they drew closer, admiring village handiwork, the group circled around the Guy. 'Give us that jacket, it's too good for burning.' The smoke swirled over them as they tugged at the jacket. The Guy was stuffed hard and refused to budge. 'Turn it over and drag it in flat ...' Tizzy bent closer and started back with a scream. The face was white like a flour bag but the staring eyes looked up as if asking a question. The back of the head was sticky with dark blood like thick jam on thick black hair. 'It's a man ... a dead man ... and I know him. The dog killer. Run! Scatter before we're blamed. He's dead. I cursed him. Run!' Tizzy could hardly drag her feet from the body. Her limbs were as heavy as stone, her heart pounding. She could hear an owl screeching and a clock chiming so loudly it crashed in her ear. Lund was dead, dead as Tat, and she should be glad but it was all her fault and she would be hanged as the murderer if she was caught.

Tizzy ran and the gang fled in all directions at the grim discovery. This was mischief beyond their knowing, mischief beyond navvy kids. Instinctively she took the quickest route back to camp by the Birketts' farm, the pathway which Mercy showed her as a secret route. It was all going wrong again. She kept seeing Lund's staring eyes looking up at her. Who had bashed his head in? They had seen no one in the street, a few shadows perhaps ... Tizzy scrambled down the bank across the Birkett pastures fenced off from the railway line. Then she saw a shadow moving down opposite her. Fear gripped her belly and her legs. The murderer was abroad, stalking through the copse, stalking through Scarsbeck like a devouring dragon in the night. She would be the next victim. Hide! Hide! Find somewhere to crawl in. Her legs would not move and she heard the scream choke in her mouth like a nightmare when the sound will not come out. Tizzy sank to the ground hoping it would swallow her up but it stayed firm. There was only one thing to do ... two, four, six, eight ...

Ellie waited by the stone cross which stood like a huge finger pointing up to the firmament of stars. As she waited a shooting star flashed overhead and vanished: a star to wish them well.

Down in the valley she could hear the clock of St Oswy's chime nine strokes, then the quarter past and the half past and finally a quarter to ten. Ellie stamped her frozen feet, listening for the welcome scuffle of chippings on the track which would herald Fancy's arrival. Only the screech of owls calling across the treetops in Scarsbeck Foss disturbed the air. Paradise was sleeping, the village was abed and she the only creature alive. Wrapping the cloak around her body layered with extra clothing she became alert and nervous at this uncanny silence. No sheep were bleating or dogs barking. Then she heard the ten o'clock chime like a tolling bell putting paid to her dreams.

The thought that Fancy MacLachlan was not coming slowly crept upon her like a dull toothache. This was no place to be standing, alone by the very grave of Beth Wildman who lay under the peat in her coffin with a bunch of lambswool in her hand to show her trade at the last trump. No doubt she was lying there laughing at this silly girl, saying, 'Yer not the first and yer won't be the last to be told a load of lies by a fella as he lifts yer petticoats and pulls down his breeks.'

'But Fancy's not like the others, not one of Mother's navvies who wants only work and wickedness . . . not my Fancy,' she argued to herself to keep up her flagging spirits. She was glad there was no one to witness her fears or her shaming. Picking up the valise she turned towards the farm track, stopping once more just in case, willing her lover to loom out of the shadows to blot out her doublings and her anger with smothering kisses.

Her eyes were drawn to the flames on the green and to torches and lanterns making strange patterns; there were voices shouting carried upwards like smoke in the still air.

Why so much noise of a night? Something was happening down there which would be carried like fire over the dale quicker than the newfangled telegraph wires which now were strung along the track like washing lines. There was only one place to go now, she whimpered to herself as she trundled sadly and reluctantly back to the safety of home. You've been made a fool of and so much the worse for being a first time by any man. No one would ever do that to her again. It was not too late to hide her shaming if she quickened her pace.

As she reached the gate of the farm she could see lights beaming out in the front parlour like beacons. Her flight had been discovered. Ellie had no energy left to deny the charge. She would be the fool of Scarsbeck for weeks like Reg Ingomells' daughter who had fled the dale and returned with a sickly bairn, confined indoors as a warning to foolish girls everywhere. There was time to hide her valise and finery in the barn and brazen out her absence if she was calm.

Everyone was assembled solemnly in the kitchen with Aunt Blaize and Uncle Warwick sat by the fireside like a party expecting company. Not a word was spoken as she entered until Mother looked up and snapped, 'And where have you been till this hour? I came to waken you but your bed was empty . . .'

'I couldn't sleep for worrying about that new tup and the flock by the track. I went to check that no one had stolen them. I told you navvies have been butchering sheep by the roadside, selling to strangers out of the dale. Nowt up with any of them.'

Ellie could see Aunt Blaize look up, her face drained of colour as if someone had painted it with flour. She suddenly looked old. Miss Herbert was holding a teapot, usually Mother's job, shaking her head, wearing a thick shawl over her nightdress, rag curlers poking out of her nightcap. Ellie stared at each in turn. 'What's up?'

'Sit down, Ellen, sit down and prepare yourself for a shock.' Annie Birkett stood stirring a bowl of batter in slow rhythmic circles.

'Oh, no! Not Fancy,' she nearly blurted out but only her lips moved. 'Has there been an accident?'

'Nay, no accident, child, but the Devil abroad tonight seeking whom he could devour. Our poor lad, our bonny lad, cut down in his prime ...' Aunt Blaize burst into wails and Uncle Warwick patted her shoulder, the best he could manage to comfort her.

'Please, I don't understand, which bonny lad?'

'Yer cousin, Sunter, of course, he's been found outside the Fleece with his head stove in. Even now your poor uncle must go down and identify his corpse.' Annie sat down, still stirring the batter.

'It can't be. Not Sunter. How can anyone ... who would want to harm him?'

'Calm yerself, there's worse shame to follow. The whole village knows who threatened him not a week ago. I'll see you in hell afore I go! Remember, Ellie, before the whole assembly at the football? They've gone to Paradise to get that fancy man of yours. The murder will be laid squarely at his door. I hope you are satisfied. I told you there would be trouble from that quarter. Now shame is brought on this house—'

'No, no, I don't believe you. Not one word of it. Fancy is not like that. He would not kill anyone, and not tonight.' Ellie fled the room, racing upstairs, stumbling in the darkness, flinging herself on her iron bedstead, rocking back and forth, back and forth as the rusty hinges groaned with her weight. Her cheeks felt the smooth edge of an envelope. She crumpled it in her hands and flung it across the room. 'No, no, no, this can't be true. This will not be true!'

The Scattering

Winter 1871

The Lord is my Shepherd:
I shall not want . . .
Yea, though I walk through the valley
of the shadow of death,
I will fear no evil . . .

Psalm 23

Chapter Twenty-Nine

He woke with a start. His arms were stiff and his head ached as he lifted a stubbly chin and peered into the gloom. For a moment Fancy thought he was lying in his bunk bed but there was only a turf roof above his head, the smell of peat up his nostrils. Where the hell was he . . . inside a beer cask? Why was he kipping in a sod hut with bare stone walls alongside empty jugs and tankards and not a soul to keep him company? His brains were as shrivelled as prunes and the tongue in his mouth was as rough as a scrubbing brush. Fancy tried to raise himself to scrabble inside his head for scraps of memory. What in the name of blazes was he doing in a soddy? Moments rattled and flashed past him like an express train. He tried to reach and grab them but caught nothing. He was well and truly betwaddled but half recalled a steep tramp uphill under bright stars. The rest was a fug of half-dreamt pictures.

He was sure he saw Billy, the nipper, cowering on the ground greetin', sobbing like a bairn, 'Don't hit me! Don't kill me. I saw nowt, honest ...' He remembered that he shook the kid to make him see sense, telling him that it was only Fancy, his gangmaster, not some villain. The pictures blurred again. He was heading in the wrong direction downhill and Billy pushed him back crying, 'Go back! Run, mister, run, they'll be after you! He's dead!'

Who was dead? That bit he couldn't be sure of. Someone was killed down there and now he was getting out of Paradise. But he was going anyway, jacking in the job for a few days with his knapsack. Why? Why was he leaving? Wake up, can't you? Fancy hit his head with a fist to knock some feeling into it. Yes, yes, the nipper had stopped him crossing the beck to the track at Middle Butts, stopped him on his way to Ellie. Now he remembered. The two of them should be halfway to Kendal and Gretna Green. There was no soddy hut at the crossroads and no Ellie. Scarsdale was temperance-mad; a dry dale except for the Fleece so why did Billy warn him that someone was dead and he would be blamed for it, if he didn't scarper? Fancy could see the white-faced child shaking with fright but pushing at his own jacket. 'Go back!'

'It wasny me as killed abody, Billy, why should I run?'

'Navvies is allus blamed first. You brayed him outside the public house, you knocked him down over Tat. He killed Tat, he deserves to be dead and I cursed him with a spelling.'

None of this jabbering made sense, the child was off his head. 'I'm away the now ... to see Miss Birkett.'

'Don't go that way, you head back and she can follow you later.'

'I canna leave her in the lurch out on the moor.'

'Leave it to me, mister. I'll tell her the story.'

'Then give her this book as a token, I'll write her a message on the front page.' He had pulled out his pocket book and scribbled words in it quickly, shoving it into the boy's frozen hand. 'Be not concerned, I will return for you.' That was what he wrote. He had given Billy a silver bob for his errand and pushed him in the direction of the cross track. 'Give it to the woman standing by the cross, don't let me down. Explain to her . . .'

Fancy could remember the starry sky and chilled air as he tramped back up the side of the Whernside track out of Scarsdale towards Blea Moor and the tunnel huts. The rest was a blur. It was freezing cold and his throat was dry. He must have called in for some juice like old times on a tramp. What was his next plan? To hide in Batty Green amongst hundreds of other navvymen or to make for Ingleton and the railway south? His head was thumping, too many whiskies again, that first drink gave a lift to his spirit, I'm no to blame for this; the second tot tweaked his fighting fists, I'll take care of myself. On then to sup the hard stuff; ready to jump over the wall and roar like an engine to defend his name but he must have knocked back the strongest brand liquor and that must have flattened him for hours. Now he felt as dry and salty as a smoked fluchtie.

Poor Ellie would be left waiting and wondering again but not for long. Billy was a trusty nipper. He would see that she got his message. It was better to retreat to fight again than to be locked up for a crime he had never committed. With his record there would be only one verdict and one rope to string him high.

It was almost light and the noise of the first shifts on the tunnel shafts blasted in his ears. He could still creep under cover towards the bustle of Batty Green or kip down again and sleep off his hangover. He was sure he had not been alone. There had been a huddle of miners slurping on the benches. He could see one of them, a thick-set man with dust rims under his eyelids, muddy hair and breath like a sulphur works on a bad day; a maudlin man spitting on the floor.

'A rum do is this life and who be you, stranger? On a tramp, are you? North or south?' Fancy rehearsed their conversation in his head.

'I'm getting oot of this place and fast.' The man nodded.

'Me too, going to take the first packet from Liverpool to sign on with the Union Pacific Railway and see the world. Where are you heading, Jock?'

'Dinna ken, dinna care, just oot.'

'Sounds like woman trouble, lads . . . another flea bitten hard.'

'Ach, no, it's no like that. I'm gettin' oot afore I'm blamed for something I didna do,' replied the stranger.

'Up the spout is the lass?' the miner laughed. Fancy grabbed him by the lapels.

'Say that again aboot my lassie and yer dead meat, sonny.'

The miner changed his tone. 'Hold yer sweat, meant no harm but women is allus trouble in my book. Take my own dearie, ups and leaves me with three brats, slopes off. Don't bother with them. Nowt but trouble and strife.'

'Where's yer bairns now then?' asked Fancy.

'How should I know? I've not seen them for over a year. Back in Leeds or thereabouts with their granny, I hope.'

'Don't you send them money or a letter?'

'None of your business, matey, lettering were never a strong point of mine but putting a stick of dynamite in a hole underground then I'm yer man,' the miner laughed.

'Aye, Ironfist is good at sticking his rod in a hole, hey?' There was a crowd on the bench guffawing. 'For one as never sees his bairns he's allus on about them but we never seen them.'

'I told you, I have three, Martha and Billy and little Matilda. If I were a writing man I would sit down now and send them a line but there's no paper and no penny post here.'

'Give me their address and I'll drop them a note. It's awful unfair for these weans not tae know where you are.' Fancy thought sadly of his own childhood.

'Send it to Widdup then, Manny Widdup, my old dad, Quarry Huts . . . that's all I can recall.'

'Widdup? Billy Widdup? Are you Billy's dad? He said you were a tunnel tiger. Good God!'

'That I am and Martha and little Tizzy. He knows 'em. Fetch him a pint of the best.'

'I know no Martha but little Billy is one of my nippers, a grand chap. It was him that saved my skin. Ironfist. I ken that name once at the tunnel huts, it struck me then as I knew the handle.'

'Aye, that's me, and where's me laddo then?'

'He tramped with his sister to find you. They dock at Paradise not three miles from this very spot. A bright spark is Billy. Wait till he knows you're here.'

'Have another drink, fancy me own kids docked on me doorstep under me nose and me not knowing. I owes you for that. Wait till I gets across there. At Paradise, you say? To whom do I owe this bit of a turn?'

'Just call me Fancy, no more on that matter. You never saw me. I canna stop. I must tramp on. The little question of the law on my tail. If they ask tell them you saw me heading west.'

Ironfist put his finger in the rough direction of his lips and smiled. 'Our eyes are blind, our ears deaf and our gobs is shut, mate. Yer a gent for a Jock and if we see anyone sniffing too close we'll head them off in the direction of the nearest blind shaft where they'll soon be acquainted with the vicinity of its bottom.' They all shook his hand and crushed his fingers with such bone-cracking strength it made his arms ache.

Fancy jerked back his head again, feeling a jab of pain behind his eyes. He had nodded off again among empty benches and tankards. It was all a silly dream. He picked up his knapsack. Nothing was missing, no letters to post either. He felt in his pocket for the poesy book. His pocket was flat. That bit had been true at least. Ellie would know he had not deserted her.

*

They were at Ingleton Station, lurking in the shadows, watching the passengers who entered the platform, waiting for a sighting of a tall red-haired Scot. By courtesy of the new telegraph poles installed along the line, news of the murder was relayed across the West Riding. It took three of them to hold him down, pin him to the floor and handcuff him. He was dragged to the lock-up behind the courthouse and left to sober up. Next morning Lachlan MacLachlan, alias Fancy Mac, was charged with the unlawful killing of Sunter Lawson Lund on the night of the fourth of November 1871 by the magistrate at Ingleton and ordered to be detained until he appeared at Sedburgh Assizes. Fancy was returned to his cell, his protestations of innocence bouncing off the stone walls. He asked for paper and they laughed that a navvy could read and write. He was told to make his last will and testament. He begged for a visit from the missionary but was told he was needed elsewhere. In desperation Fancy scribbled a note to the Reverend Ralph Hardy, shepherd of the Scarsbeck flock, asking him to rescue this sheep lost between a rock and a hard place.

Rumours were rife in the camp about the disappearance and arrest of Fancy Mac for the murder of Sunter Lund. It had taken hundreds of policemen to surround him and he fought like a Highland chieftain. He would be executed without trial even before the coroner's inquest to be held in the schoolroom at Scarsbeck.

Tizzy hugged the events of Mischief Night to herself. She was glad she had driven him out of the camp giving him hours to escape but was puzzled that he had been captured so easily.

Billy Two Hats had taken over the gang but he was not strong and fair like Fancy and their work rate had gone down already.

Mally said Fancy would get a fair trial if they could find anyone to witness that he was nowhere near the green at the time of the murder. Their gang could testify that no one was on the green. Tizzy had seen only shadows and that proved nothing. Her meeting with Fancy was her own secret; she ran to the beck to a secret hidey-hole and pulled out his poetry book, fingering his verses reverently. He would understand that she was the guardian of his book, not Mercy's big sister. Tizzy did not want Mercy poring over the pages and laughing at his spelling mistakes.

How could he expect her to run to the crossroads in the dead of night with a murderer on the loose? His poetry book would be safe with her. The less people knew that Fancy was abroad that night the better. She was his faithful sheepdog, protecting him from harm and his strange verses from curious eyes. Ellen Birkett could jump off Scarsbeck Foss for all she cared. The Birketts had caused enough trouble already and Sunter Lund was Mercy's cousin.

Whatever those two had planned together for Mischief Night was finished with. Miss Birkett probably now thought Fancy false to his promises. Tizzy was glad about that. Now Fancy would have to wait for her to marry him, wait for her to put skirts back on and grow a bosom.

Chapter Thirty

The wind blew from the north-west at Martinmas, a chill moist wind, harbinger of a severe winter to come. Zillah was glad of her trunk full of clothes which she layered one on top of the other to keep out the draughts. The house was in mourning, black drapes over mirrors and ornaments; a huge wreath of evergreens interwoven with purple ribbon hung at the oak door and everyone went tiptoeing around the farmhouse in black weeds. Visitors came and went quietly offering condolences and biscuits, tokens which were passed up to High Butts where Blaize Lund hid from her friends and neighbours, shamed and grief-stricken.

Ellen tried to make funeral biscuits but her mind was never on the task and the biscuits were shrivelled and black. Mercy for once was silenced by the solemnity of mourning and hardly uttered a word on their walks down to Scarsbeck school. She seemed to relish all the fuss bestowed on her in the school yard by the other scholars.

How quickly Sunter Lund was translated from sinner to saint! No one could speak ill of the dead and especially one that had been brutally murdered. Thinking about the football match and the fact that he scored an own goal, Zillah remembered many shouts of murderous intent from the touchline on that occasion.

A murder in the village was a once in a lifetime event, every gory detail to be savoured and relished, burnished and embellished for a more dramatic effect. At every turn in the street groups of village women gathered and clacked to each other about any new turn of events, pausing briefly to stare at her as she passed. Zillah's very presence at Middle Butts, her championing of the navvy cause, made her worthy of a second viewing as if in some way she was an accomplice to the dreadful act itself. She scurried past the spot where the bloodstains were still evident on the limestone wall.

Someone had placed branches of rowan tree criss-crossed around the site as if to cleanse the green of this evil. To hear the grocer, draper, seamstress and apothecary going on about the poor boy, it was hard to recognise this was Sunter Lund who was now bedecked with glowing virtues never seen in his lifetime, by all previous accounts. 'Still, they've got the blighter what did it so praise be! We can all rest easy in our beds.'

The schoolroom had been packed for the coroner's inquest. All the details were taken and a verdict of unlawful killing was recorded. A post-mortem by the police surgeon had revealed that one blow had crushed a weak point in his skull; a blow delivered with little force by a blunt heavy object was all it had taken to send the poor man to his day of judgement.

Poor Blaize had been carried out in a faint at this point and Ellen and Zillah rushed out to comfort her. The children from the camp who found the body were summoned and questioned. Zillah had felt it was important to attend to give them support. Mr Paisley represented the company but there was a hiss of protest when some of the parents from Paradise tried to get in as well. There were boos and hisses from the villagers and they were removed from the room. Zillah watched Billy Widdup tremble as he gave his evidence in a soft girlish voice no one could hear. When he got to the sighting of what they thought was the Guy Fawkes there was an uproar of protest that these ruffians had torched their bonfire and the coroner once more had to threaten the court.

As Zillah looked around the tall classroom, the grim disclosures seemed so in contrast with the innocent setting. Miss Bulstrode sat white-faced throughout the proceedings, hanging limply on to her brother's arm. Both gave evidence as to being called from their fireside to summon help but had seen nothing untoward on the evening in question.

Mr Walter Stackhouse, licensee publican of the Fleece, gave evidence that he had seen Lund leave his premises at half past eight and that the lad had not banged his head on the door lintel, indicating him to be sober at the time.

As news spread up the dale, by virtue of reports in the weekly *Scarsdale Chronicle and Gazette* published for the benefit of farmers and tradesfolk in the wider area, a stream of visitors were spotted like migrating birds descending for a brief stopover, walking around the green, pausing at the grim place of death to savour the wickedness of folk.

Wally Stackhouse, not one to miss an opportunity, placed an extra bench and table outside the ale house where visitors could chat to local residents about this terrible tragedy and sup a pint or two in the process.

Suddenly Scarsbeck was invaded by sensation-seekers, peering in windows, poking about the village, trampling over newly dug front gardens, strolling up to the viaduct construction to ogle the navvies at work, purchasing mementoes from the marble works and patronising any shops willing to supply extra information on the event.

As the news spread far afield reporters from the *Lancaster Guardian*, *Leeds Mercury*, *Police News* and *Daily News* travelled up to the shantytown and through Batty Green to interview anyone who would give comment on this sad case.

Eventually Sunter's body was released for burial and the family plot was dug out by the sexton who cursed the hard frozen ground and jiggered his back. A new headstone of shiny Dent marble was erected in his memory, his name etched in gold lettering. This too became a magnet for the morbid on account of the words, especially composed by the Lunds, being widely quoted by the newspapers.

Here lies our dear son, Sunter Lawson Lund
Snatched from the bosom of his family on
November 4th 1871
When I was in the prime of life,
A fatal blow cost me my life,
No man in this world can boast of his might
When alive of a morning, dead at night.

In all of this Zillah could not fault the Reverend Hardy who much to her surprise made frequent visits to High Butts to console the mother in her sad loss. He seemed to time his visits with a second call to Middle Butts farmhouse when the kettle was on the boil for afternoon tea with oatcakes and cheese and a slice of boiled fruitcake, the recipe for which was one of the family's secrets for five generations and kept under lock and key. Along with a bowl of fruit pie and cream and a plate of ham sandwiches, she began to wonder if this little detour had something to do with not having to prepare himself an evening meal.

The kitchen was usually full of women and she herself was often back from school trying to lend a hand now that Ellen was fully occupied on the farm. Zillah was worried at the strain of the past weeks on the girl, who had lost all her sparkle; her eyes were dull and sad, her hair unkempt and her tongue brutish and scolding to Mercy. It was as if Sunter's death had hit her harder than anyone, quite out of proportion to her general indifference to her cousin.

Zillah was slightly unnerved to be sitting in the company

of the vicar and not arguing with him. He sat in the visitor's seat, not in the parlour which was chill and stiff but slouched by the fireside, his long legs stretching out to warm his boots, his eyes deep in thought. Here was a man carrying the worries of the world on his shoulders with a furrow over his brow which tightened his features, a strained puzzled expression on his face as if a clammed-up question were on the tip of his tongue.

'More tea, vicar?' Annie Birkett jumped into the silence. Zillah felt him wince and draw back. She could wait no longer in suspense.

'What troubles you, Mr Hardy? You look like Atlas carrying the world.' He looked towards her warmly.

'I fear a miscarriage of justice, Miss Herbert. I have cause to visit a certain prisoner in jail who is accused of a terrible act but who proclaims his innocence with every ounce of his breath and I am inclined to believe him,' said the vicar, looking around the room at anything and nothing.

'Does he, indeed?' sniffed Annie, sensing the direction of his drift. 'And would I be right in thinking this villain lived not a mile from where I'm standing?'

'Yes, I'm afraid you are, Mistress Birkett,' answered Ralph tentatively.

'How could you even dare to sit at my fireside and not think that such a man is nothing but a liar and a cheat as well as a murderer? Were you not there after the meeting yon first night when he bashed our Sunter to the floor? You saw for yourself.'

'Yes, I admit I was present as you recall but there was provocation and the killing of a child's dog to avenge, as there was the night of the fire when the deceased accused the man of setting the fields ablaze. Don't count the fight at the football match, that was just high spirits . . . as on other countless occasions in this village when lads drink and fight. It strikes me as just too convenient to lay the blame on him alone. Mr MacLachlan is a fair man—'

'Don't you even mention his name in this house. He has brought shame on us by his pestering of Ellie. Now she's brought low with sadness on two accounts. I want no more talk of this matter. The sooner they pack up Paradise camp and send them on their way the better. There can be no more doings with them after this.'

'Not all workmen can be branded murderers and thieves. I have seen many civil and courteous craftsmen at work on the site. There's still much to be completed, years of work ahead of them in this dale.'

'You've changed your tune, Mr Hardy. Time was when you couldn't abide any of them.' Annie Birkett stood firm.

'But I can't stand by and watch a man hang for a crime he may not have committed. I see I'm distressing you but there are facts to be accounted for. What does Miss Herbert have to say, sitting so quietly?' Ralph Hardy was looking to Zillah for support, his grave grey eyes blinking nervously.

'I can have no view on any of this as a guest in this house. I've seen the sorrow all this has brought to this family. I would not wish to offend. But I have to say that there is much distress in the camp. Children are stoned on their way to school and spat on by the other scholars. They are afraid to come down into Scarsbeck and my classes have halved, putting the future of the Mission effort into jeopardy. Miss Bulstrode will not condone any navvy children in the playground and wants them out of sight. How can I teach children under those conditions?

'I'm torn in two by loyalty to both village and camp. Perhaps it would be better to remove the pupils back to the reading room at Paradise and teach them there. The children have a right to be taught whatever their circumstances. How can I take sides in all of this? My best pupil was about to take an important examination. I have to confess that my dealings with the Scotsman have been civil and courteous and law-abiding so I've no reason to speak ill of him. He's young with a fiery spirit to match his hair. Surely you don't hang a man for that? He was well-matched by young Mr Lund who was by all accounts rough-natured, hard on his animals and uncouth at times.

'What I do notice is that suddenly he's been canonised by his murder as if his true character has to be bleached by death.'

'Oh, Miss Herbert, that's unkind and unfair! How could you?' snapped the older woman, sinking back into her chair.

'Because I'm not family . . . you're all so close to this tragedy, you see it only as a mother and aunt. I see only what I observed in the past. I've no reason to blanch away stains of character as if they never existed. As for you, Mr Hardy, you must do as your conscience dictates. Never disobey an impulse of the heart, my nanny once said. The truth will out. If the truth we hear is false then we must make sure that justice is done for all and the real villain is punished. If there is anything I can do to further the campaign for truth then please, both of you, make it known.' Zillah found she was weeping and fumbled for her lace hanky in embarrassment.

'We agree at last, Miss Herbert.' There was no sarcasm in his voice and she looked up in surprise at his gentleness. Their eyes locked for a second and Zillah dropped her glance quickly, heated by the intensity of their meeting of minds, anxious that Mrs Birkett should not be excluded from their new alliance.

'You must do as you think fit, vicar. Far be it from me to stop you tending to yer flock, black sheep and all. I only know that Paradise will get no more milk, eggs, cream or cheese from me or mine in this dale. They'll have to look for provisions to Burgoine and Cock's delivery cart. We may only be plain country folk but when we make a stand we can turn stubborn as donkeys when it suits us. We never asked for a railway up our backside, pardon my bluntness, but that's what we feel. Bethany Wildman knew a thing or two when she cursed the meeting. She saw trouble in the wind and no mistake. What a canny old bird, every word of hers coming true. There's been more burials in a six-month than in two hundred years round these dales. She's best out of all this trouble, bless her, and laughing at our foolishness, no doubt.' Annie folded her arms on her chest waiting for a reply.

'I'm sorry to bring hard words and little comfort but I do need to talk with Ellen. She may clarify the situation slightly,' said Ralph as he stood up to take his leave.

'What's she got to do with any of this?' Annie was on the defensive again.

'Just a few questions to further my enquiries.'

'You sound more like a constable than a minister. Please yourself, she'll be milking in the shed. I can't think she can add legs to yer snake . . . so if you'll excuse me I have stock to see to and pigs to fatten for the kill.'

'You sound just like Beth . . . adding legs to yer snake. She used to say that.' Ralph tried to soften the parting. Annie ignored his comment and Zillah led him to the door.

'Thank you,' he said.

'Whatever for?' asked Zillah.

'For not jumping down my throat at every turn.' They both smiled awkwardly.

'Am I really so sharp?' asked Zillah.

'Like a diamond on glass, Miss Herbert, like a diamond on glass.'

Zillah stood puzzled as he walked towards the milking shed. Could that have been a compliment or a complaint? She did not know which.

Nobody was in the mood to celebrate the annual pig-killing. Ellie noticed the arrival of helpers and bakers was a muted affair. Usually they gathered for a good supper and company, sitting down at the old spinet in the parlour to twang a jig on the strings. Last year after Dad passed away Mother scarce had the energy to bother and it was Aunt Blaize who had chivvied them up. Now it was their turn to return the unwelcome favour.

Mercy had hidden up in her attic away from the squealings of the trapped pigs, stuck through the throat to bleed into the bucket, their thick dark blood poured out for black puddings. Now Ellie could see only the colour of blood in Sunter's dark hair. She would never fry a slice of black pudding again.

The Lunds had no heart for the annual task of laying down hams and bacon for the winter months, for all the sawing and slicing, soaking, scalding and scrubbing. It was left to her to scald one carcass and scrub off the bristles. They wasted nothing from toenails to snout. Soon there would be a line of carcasses hanging from the flitch hooks in the back larder.

In the past she would stand in there with satisfaction knowing Christmas was on the way and they could withstand the worst of winter. Now she thought only of Fancy dangling at the end of a rope but blocked the thought out quickly.

Mother was in the kitchen with the other women stirring herbs into the innards for brawn and sausages and preparing the fat to be rendered down into lard.

Miss Herbert fled to the camp to take a reading class for the older boys, escorted by Cleggy on his cart to Mr Hardy's rehearsal for the Christmas show. The teacher had no desire to sample the slaughtering and since the anger of the village had turned on the navvy families, she avoided the Birketts' farming friends.

Ellie could understand all this but she felt nothing on the matter any more, only a chill numbing indifference, an uncaring matter-of-fact busyness. That was what got her out of bed of a morning in the dark cold air of this November frost. There was ice on the jug on the washstand and smoke on the breath. There were so many tasks to do on this farm and she cursed the days she had complained about her poor cousin. How she missed his bulk, his strength with machinery and harnessing up the carthorses. He had shielded her from the brunt of the heavy work and now she was dependent on hired hands and her uncle who was having his own problems.

There was no possibility of hiring extra men. The dreadful prospect of selling stock and tackle to keep a roof over their heads clawed at her stomach. They must manage to pull in their horns. Thank heaven, Miss Herbert's lodging money was regular. If she chose to find a room at the camp then they would be in trouble.

The parson's questioning still troubled her. He had come into the cowshed as she was milking, her cheeks pressed against the warm flank of the beast. He had pried about her dealings with Fancy. She did not want to think about him ever again.

'Fancy is as Fancy does!' she quipped lightly and said that they were walking out at the time of the murder but that was all over now.

'He says he was on his way to meet you that night when

one of his boys jumped out and told him of the murder, begging him to leave the camp. Had you planned to meet him?'

'I dunno, do I? I've not seen hide nor hair of him, have I? How do I know what his plans were?' she snapped.

'So you had no plans to elope together?' came his next heart-stopping question in her ear.

'Whoever told you that was a liar. How dare he besmirch my name? What if my mother should catch wind of such a rumour?'

'You know your confidences would be safe with me, Ellen. But if, say, he was on his way to meet you then him being down at the green at the same time would be well nigh impossible, would it not?'

'I dunno, do I? I never seen no one that night,' Ellie replied cautiously.

'So you say, so you say. But it troubles him greatly in his cell to think that he let you down by running away. Only the knowledge that he sent you a message consoles him. He wanted to warn you.' Ralph waited for this to sink in.

'Well then, there you have it, he must be lying. I never got no message. I was in the field minding my tups, checking the stock as I told my mam. I know nothing of no message. It just shows how a man will holler lies when caught in a gin trap.' Her mind was racing with this new information but she was not going to admit to standing like a frozen statue half the night praying he would turn up and not show her up. There had been no message. 'What time was all this then?' Ellie asked casually, but her cheeks were aflame.

'He told me he arranged to meet you at the standing cross at nine o'clock and that he met the nipper at half past eight, the lad who had witnessed the finding of the body. The boy warned him and pressed him back in the opposite direction. He says he gave the lad a silver shilling for his trouble, to give you the message.'

'I saw no child or any shilling message. I know nowt of what you say.' Ellie kept her eyes averted. She could not lie to the vicar's face but the young man did not push his argument further. He withdrew from the cow byre, mounting his horse. She heard the clatter of hooves on the cobblestones.

She sat on the milking stool pulling the teats like an automaton, yank, yank, until the cow protested and the warm milk squirted out of the bucket onto the floor. She sniffed the warm hide and the fresh smell of dung and fodder. Enclosed by the slate boskins with only a cow for company, only then did the tears flow like milk down her cheeks. He's made his bed, he must lie on it. I don't care. None of it was my doing. Fancy made a fool of me. He should have come for me and together we could have faced danger but not a word, the lying sod! He's lying to save his neck. It's nowt to do with me what happens to him now. Her words were hollow, rattling in her head, jumping like balls in a fairground bagatelle; one by one each thought dropped into her stomach to dance and churn her guts into a flutter. Who are you fooling, you daft cow? She did care but terror consumed her as she thought of her recent denial and like St Peter she waited for the cock to crow thrice.

Chapter Thirty-One

'Why should that bloody railway company ride over us like a steam engine? There's been nowt but trouble since they camped in this dale. I'm sick of them thieving sheep and my churns of milk. I lay them down on the slate slab at the farm gate and before I've reached the end of the track, damn things have disappeared. They poach our best spots, shoot at anything that moves . . .' Dicky Braithwaite sat on his usual bench smoking a clay pipe and spitting out his views while his companions nudged and winked; knowing full well that his wife, Liddy, was poaching one of the resident engineers who lodged in their farm cottage for herself.

Each nodded in sympathy with his words while Wally the landlord kept their jugs topped up from his bucket under the bar counter. He was missing the navvy custom since they were barred from the Fleece on account of the murder. This gaggle of farmers was not the prettiest sight in the dale, sitting all night and blethering till closing time on one pot of ale if he were not vigilant.

The voluntary ban on supplying Paradise was proving a painful sacrifice to most of the Scarsbeck traders. The cobbler and bootmaker had piles of handmade workboots with metal tips lying uncollected on shelves, the baker's bags of extra flour would soon be full of mealy bugs, the butcher's horse stood idle in the yard and even the haberdasher's doorbell fell silent now that the constant stream of navvy customers no longer called in for extra buttons and darning thread.

The principle was sound enough but livings must be made. There were rumours that the railway company was fixing up a temporary track all the way to Batty Green, organising a special transport wagon for the Saturday market to stalls with cheaper prices. It made Wally weep to think he was refusing good brass and custom in supporting this protest.

He counted the heads in his bar, just the usual disgruntled farmers and their sons who drank in their own corner, all nodding like sheep and troughing into their pots. His football team, defeated and disheartened by the sheer strength and numbers of the invading army, had lost heart in any further contest. 'We should be taking every last penny off them, not skulking in a sulk, I reckon. Make 'em pay for being here ... skim the coffers of the Midland Railway Company a bit more.' Wally tried to chivvy them up.

'How come, Wally? Farmers can't stand against their landlords, against the likes of Dacre, Earl Bective and such,' argued Dicky, seeking home truths in the bottom of his tankard.

'Come on, me laddo, there's more than one way to skin a rabbit. We have to get back at them in their pockets where it hurts, be awkward and cussed as only we Dalesfolk know how.'

'Yer talking riddles, Wally.' Isaac Cleghorn shifted his stool, ears flapping like an elephant, to join in this conversation.

'If I were you, Warwick Lund, I'd not be sitting on my arse letting my loss go uncompensated. I'd be up there demanding cash for the loss of my son and heir or I'll be putting a stick or two of dynamite up their backsides so to speak.' Warwick looked up in surprise at his words.

'Go on, then . . .' The room fell silent.

'Listen, you lot, what's the one thing of theirs that most gets up us noses, eh?' Wally leant over Warwick's shoulder.

'I dunno,' said Dicky, shouting across the room to his son. 'Can you think of owt, our Tudge?'

'Nah,' answered his lumpen son.

'Think about it, what did we have the meeting about in the chapel? What sticks out like a boil on a pretty lass's nose?' They all looked blankly at each other. Wally persisted. 'The viaduct, of course, at the bottom of our main street. Ten bloody posts sunk in fifty foot of concrete, a scaffold full of timber, ten arches about to be faced with thick black limestone. Well, lads? Think about it then!'

'You mean . . .'

'I mean . . .'

'Nah!'

'Why not? If them nippers from Paradise can torch our bonfire, we must have our own little fireworks party. Give 'em summat to think about on a cold night. Show 'em when Dalesfolk is displeased we have our own ways to hit back.'

'But, Wally, we can't just burn it down; six months it's taken just to set in them posts and six months more to link up the arches, or six years maybe?' whispered Dicky, turning for support.

'So set them back a few more months and we screw more pennies off them for lodgings, vittels, ale. Make hay while the sun shines or should I say ... while the hay burns.' Wally laughed and Cleggy choked on his ale at their plotting. As clerk to the vestry meeting and the parson's assistant, as worthy of this parish, he should not be listening to all this but he drew in his chair just the same.

Cora Bulstrode huddled over her sewing machine, jerking the handle with fingers as tight as coiled springs. The tension in the stitches was dragging the fabric; she flung the blouse on the floor in disgust and paced the room. Why could she not even sit down for five minutes? Sewing once was her joy, now it was her pain. Cora could not concentrate on the simplest task, the easiest pattern. What was wrong with her? Their troubles were over now that nuisance, the Lund simpleton, had gone for good. Now all they had to focus on was the Fawcett, getting the child through the examination and out of Ezra's study back to the camp. Perhaps then the two of them could settle back once more into a comfortable routine and find some peace.

But first she must tackle the Herbert woman, who much to her surprise had stayed the course and found favour in the village despite her unfortunate connections. There was a crop of Dales children who needed that extra classroom. The shrinking navvy Mission class could disappear up the track to Paradise as soon as the Widdup child finished the test, leaving them free from any more interference from the missionary's enthusiasms getting in their hair like nits.

How she kept pleading with Ezra to insist that Mission classes were better conducted in the reading room on site. It made sense in bad weather not to have to dry their mufflers and smelly clothes over the stovepipes but Ezra was in one of his excitable moods again and would not listen to a word she said.

Cora was sick of the Fawcett, sick of the strain it put upon them. She might as well live like a spinster for all the time her brother allotted to her company. When he was not coaching the brat, he was playing the piano loudly until it drove her to distraction or he would be rehearsing his singers, playing the organ for hours in the cold church. Now he was involved in some glee club men's choir at the camp with Father Hardy, of all people, preparing music for a Christmas concert; of all the stupid things to be doing with his time.

She had actually heard him say that Father Hardy was right to encourage some cultural activities up in the camp. If they were all now confined to barracks on account of Sunter's death and the coming trial, then he too would be adding his support. Will he never rest still? Will he never take me away from this place?

Since Sunter Lund's untimely demise he seemed to be taking on a new lease of life, relieved there would be no more broken windows and disturbances from that quarter. His passing was a blessing to the village and a blessing for Ezra. No more begging letters to cause them anguish. What was in them she was forbidden to see. Ezra had thrown them on the study fire in disgust. When she pleaded with him to tell her why he was so torn apart he just broke down and wept like a child in her arms. She had cradled him softly and told him not to worry. Cora would take care of everything as she always did when Father had chastised him for poor studies and low marks and he emerged from the study beaten and cowed.

Cora would always kneel on the hearth rug and hold him tight to take away his fears. Now he came to her again as she knew he must. Oh how strong she felt, omnipotent, full of grace and calm. No one could take that feeling from her, not now, not ever. In all things she alone was powerful.

There was only one more stile to mount, to get that Widdup brat up and away and tonight he would come for the final preparations for the December timed examination in the schoolroom. How quickly weeks had passed since their summer discovery to the final testing. How hard Ezra had worked to bring the child up to the mark. What sacrifices they had made to give one boy a chance of a lifetime. One more name etched in gold on the polished oak list of Fawcett scholars. The price of this passing was costly for all of them, so Widdup must pass.

*

'The vicar wants to see you, Billy, after school, he is making more enquiries about Mischief Night. Mr MacLachlan says that he gave you a note on the footpath and asked you to take a message, is that true?' Zillah Herbert caught the pupil before he darted off towards the schoolhouse for his coaching lesson.

'I have to go next door for me test, miss. I'll be late.'

'A few minutes won't make any difference now. I know you want to help your friend as much as you can. If you're telling lies, young man, it can only harm his cause. I wish you could remember what you all saw that night. You must have seen the killer.'

'We saw nowt, I told them, and I never saw Fancy, only on the footpath down by Middle Butts. That's when I stopped him.'

'Why was he going in that direction?'

'I dunno.'

'I think you do, boy. You know he's been seeing Miss Birkett against her mother's wishes. She told me you intervened once before to warn them at the summer Feast. You've always been their ally. Did he ask you to give her a message?' the teacher insisted, touching the child's arm, but Tizzy shrugged it off.

'What if he did?' said Tizzy, turning away.

'Did he write it down? Please, child, try to think what you did with the message. Miss Birkett says she received no message. I think you owe all of us an explanation.'

'I meant no harm but it was just the book. It were spelt all wrong and you know how Mr Bulstrode and you go on about spellings. We gets the cane if we gets our spelling tests wrong. I didn't want anyone to laugh at his spellings. Lines of funny verse, all them sloppy words. He can't have written stuff like that to her. Look.' Tizzy reluctantly pulled out the battered leather-bound notebook and shoved it into the teacher's hand in disgust.

'So he gave you this book to give to Miss Birkett, am I right? And you didn't take it for fear of him being scorned for his letters?' Tizzy nodded, her eyes watering like pebbles under the beck. The teacher thumbed through the pages. 'Where's the message?'

'On the front inside, see.' Tizzy pointed to the scribbled note. 'I never spent the shilling, here, it's still in my bag with my marbles. I could have spent it but I didn't.'

'You could have saved a lot of heartache, child. By your stubbornness we are all embarrassed. I'll have to give this to the vicar and show it to Miss Birkett. It was her book to keep, not yours. I'm so disappointed in you, Billy. I really thought you had more about you. Your friend's life hangs in the balance and you withhold vital evidence, evidence which might just point to his innocence.'

'I never, miss, I never meant no harm. I never thought.'

'You children seldom do think before you act. But all's not lost. We must go and see the vicar after your lesson. Perhaps it's not too late to save your friend.' Miss Herbert scurried back inside her classroom leaving Tizzy shaking with shame. Now she had to go and do that stupid test and tell more lies. She was not in the mood for sums.

*

The fire blazed brightly in the grate, the room was hot and smelly as ever, the curtains drawn, a smell of stale baccy and the greasy smell of hair oil lingered, the stuff Granda used to plaster on his whiskers in the happier days when they were a family with Mother and Ironfist; the days before the tramping began.

Tizzy couldn't concentrate; she could hear the clock, tick-tocking on the mantelpiece, one, two . . . one, two. The light was dim and she caught sight of the flushed cheeks of Patabully as he sat drinking in the sight of his pupil trying to complete the paper on time. She squirmed impatiently. All she could see on the page was Fancy alone in his prison cell, waiting for her to release him, and she'd let him down. She was going to let everyone down.

'Well, well, let's see your offerings. Time is up, pencil down.' Bulstrode sprang to his feet excitedly and snatched away the paper. He was not going to be pleased. How could she bother with a stupid sum when her friend was arrested and she'd cursed a man to death? All these questions and his pryings, the stone-throwings and fights in the school yard. Stuff the bloody Fawcett. It was over.

'I'm sorry . . . it's not finished, it's just—'

'No excuses, boy, I can see for myself that this is a dismal attempt. You have the gift and you are throwing it away in my face.' He tore through each page, pausing to shake his head. 'Oh dear, oh dearie me, has it come to this, Master Widdup? I see I will have to give you one more lesson. What must follow is a test in itself; a lesson in submission to a higher authority. Oh yes, failure must be punished. Superior knowledge is gained at great cost. You have been my scholar for six months and we have not needed to apply the test.

'Now the time of trial is upon you. I don't grant favours to riff-raff and dullards with no hope of scholastic learning. I choose only the brightest candidates, those who are capable of bettering their chances. I coach you for months and if this is to be my reward you will have to be instructed and sub-dued. Is the door shut?'

Tizzy turned to look. She was hot, tired and uninterested in any more lessons. 'Shut the door and lock it firmly. We must not be disturbed in our task.' Tizzy obeyed wearily, watching the strange smile on the master's face, puzzled. 'Kneel down, boy. You have earned my special blessing.'

Tizzy knelt on the rug, her eyes downcast now she was going to get the slipper. Or perhaps he would pray over her like they did at Georgie's funeral. She heard him breathing, rasping as he fumbled with his clothes, rising from his arm-chair, towering over her.

'Hold out your hand and take my blessing. Don't look. Hold what you are given.' She raised her head as if in a trance and felt a stiff rod of warm flesh, pulsing. 'Into your mouth and feed on my flesh, "Oh taste and see how gracious the Lord is."'

Tizzy drew back in shock but he yanked her head down by the tufts of hair. 'Put my blessing in your mouth, suck out my joy, my seed; suck and receive my strength for your studies, for your success. Do not fail me as others before have failed and lived to regret their failure; petty minds, child, only petty minds like Sunter Lund balk at my orders.' His words were tumbling fast. Tizzy turned away in disgust, her heart thumping with fear. This was not right, he was rude like the rough navvies at the camp. 'I can't, no!' He pushed her forward onto the floor.

'Then take my punishment, be chastised and trained into obedience.' There was no stopping this madness.

'Mr Bulstrode, please, no, I don't want . . . please listen.'

She twisted and jerked away, crawling out of his grasp. He was on all fours like an animal; a man possessed by demons with a mask on his face, a blue-red-purple face. He was deaf to her pleas, lunging at her body, at her clothing, but he was weak and flabby in the exertion and his panting became loud. 'I waited for this test and you'll not oppose my will. Fathers have will over their sons forever.' His voice was a faraway voice in a different tone as if he was someone else.

'Please, sir, I've learnt my lesson. Stop this. I'll scream.' Her throat was dry, not a sound could she utter. She felt his hands running down her breeches, searching out between her legs.

'You will obey me, son, do as I say. You are mine to do with as I wish.' He was pumping against her body, crying out, moaning.

With the last ounce of her strength she shook him off shouting, 'I'm not your sodding child, I'm not your son. Do you hear? I'm a bleeding girl, a girl in disguise. I'm Matilda Widdup and I've fooled you all so don't you touch me, sir.'

The man looked up and froze for a second, clutching at his chest, the colour draining away from his face, and he gasped for breath. He was sinking on his knees and his swollen organ collapsed as he sank backwards, choking for breath. He curled on the floor gasping and Tizzy sprang up to unlock the door. She fell into the open arms of Miss Bulstrode who was listening outside.

'Help! Please, Miss Bulstrode! He's gone daft in the head ... he tried to ... Get me out of here! He went for me like an animal.' Tizzy was clutching at the woman, sniffing her lace apron, burrowing her head into the woman who drew back at first and then relaxed, holding her fast with bony arms.

'Calm yourself, I'm sure there's been some misunderstanding. He's very overwrought. Let's go and see.'

'Not back in there, miss, please. I'm not a boy, I'm a girl. I tried to tell him but he fell down ...'

'Shush, child, it's all a bad dream.' Cora stared at the crumpled figure of her brother. He lay on his side staring up helplessly, unable to talk as only his lips moved to mouth, 'Cora ... the Fawcett ... we're lost. No more ...' The woman knelt down and held him briefly, turning to the stricken child who clung to the door.

'Fetch Susan, tell her to run to the apothecary, and quick. Mr Bulstrode is unwell.' She then spoke to her brother. 'Calm yourself, dear, you were provoked, first Lund and now Widdup. I told you another one would kill you.' She stroked his hand and his forehead.

Tizzy raced into the kitchen to find Susan. 'Put yer cloak on and run. This is a madhouse, I hope he's dead, but get help. I'm getting out of here and you, too, if you've any sense ... a couple of loonies.' Tizzy turned back into the hall but Miss Bulstrode barred the way, catching hold of her jacket.

'It's all been a terrible mistake, child. We must find you a safe place.'

Tizzy saw her fierce eyes glinting with fire and drew back. 'I'll be right when I get some air. I can manage, I'm used to running back in the dark, honest.' She turned to go but this time Miss Bulstrode clawed into her elbow.

'No, child, it's not right for you to be alone in the dark. I will escort you back safely. We don't want you to come to any harm. We'll leave the headmaster for the doctor to find. He has been so overworked his brain is tired and disturbed. He would not want you to be left alone tonight.'

'I have to see the vicar after school. I promised Miss Herbert,' said Tizzy, pointing to the kirk lane.

'I'm sure you did, child, but I know a quiet path where we can be alone and you can tell me all that has happened. We will not be disturbed. There is so much to discuss, don't you think? You have given us all a big surprise.' She smiled so sweetly, gripping her wrist so tight, that Tizzy could not struggle.

They turned up by the viaduct and she thought she saw lanterns flickering in the dark but the six o'clock shift had knocked off and the wind was howling.

'This is not the way, Miss Bulstrode, the track goes up there, see.'

'I told you, I know a place where we can have some peace and quiet.' Tizzy did not like the sound of that at all.

Chapter Thirty-Two

The schoolroom was dark and Zillah felt her stomach rumbling with hunger. It was almost seven o'clock. Where on earth had that child got to? If he was still doing the test then his chances were slim. Now she would have to hire the sexton to come and collect her, for the drizzle had turned into buckets of rain tipping over her head. It really was too much if the child had scampered home without reporting back to her.

The cupboards had been tidied and her desk neatened and sorted out, the room swept and dusted and the stove banked up with slack. She was hovering anxiously to hear the results of this rehearsal.

Zillah tied her bonnet, wrapped around her cloak and decided to slip across to the schoolhouse to check that the boy had gone. He was usually reliable but the killing and the aftermath had certainly shaken the child. Now there was all the responsibility of upholding Bulstrode's expectations. Perhaps they were wrong to push the child so hard.

The door of the schoolhouse was ajar and Zillah rang the bell. She stepped inside out of the torrential rain. 'Anybody at home?' Susan jumped at the sight of her.

'Thank God! Come in. I thowt it were Dr Fielding. It's Mr Bulstrode, taken right badly. See . . .'

'Where's your mistress?' asked Zillah, reluctant to intrude.

'Gone out with the kid, dragged him off home. She was looking funny herself. Hardly looked at her brother. I'm reet scared. He looks far gone to me, can't move a muscle.' The two women hurried down the hallway to the study door. Susan had lit candles and banked the fire, covered the man with a blanket, doing her best to take the gloom out of the room. The walls glowered down, ceiling-high with books, enclosing Ezra in a tomb of learning.

Zillah bent down to the man with compassion. He looked so pitiable, prostrate, speechless, motionless like a crumpled rag doll. 'Has there been a fight in here?' she asked, looking around at the disarray of books and papers, overturned chairs and general scattering of his belongings.

'I'm not rightly sure what's been going on. The kid comes out like it's seen a ghost yelling some nonsense. I think he took a turn and scared the mite. Who'd want to be locked in with him? Her ladyship hovering by the door as usual. She don't half give him some stick and he orders her about; a right pair they are, deserve each other. I tell you I shall be glad to be out of this gloomy hole and no mistake. He don't look too good, does he? I wish he'd stop staring at me, do you think he can hear us?'

Zillah gazed around the room with interest; the locked door had always been a mystery to her. And now all was revealed; a shabby little study with walls of books. So many books. Shelves full of weighty tomes; an Aladdin's cave of knowledge. She picked up some of the fallen books.

'I wouldn't look in that one, miss. You'll get an education. I don't know what to make of them pictures. See that one, open at this page. I've never seen the like. Sodom and Gomorrah! Makes yer want to wash yer hands and eyes after a peep on them pages, miss.'

Zillah stood in a daze as she turned page after page of pictures, strange prints of naked bodies and parts of bodies all twisted up with each other, men and animals, men and children, men and men in unnatural acts. She could see no education in any of them but the sight of the writhing figures made her feel sick and she slammed the book quickly shut. Who would want to look at such things? Only someone sick and feeble-brained.

Bulstrode's eyes followed her as she moved and she stared hard at him. 'Where've they gone?' His eyes turned away. He was imprisoned in his own body, helpless and afraid. That satisfied her yet made her ashamed at the same time. They had stumbled on some terrible secret and she wished she was a hundred miles away from this stinking place. She looked again at her headmaster, hardly believing he could feed himself on such filth.

'Where would Miss Cora go with the boy?' asked Zillah of the maid.

'Dunno, miss. She wouldn't let the kid out of her sight, which wasn't like her. She can't stand Billy Widdup, can't say as I took to him much either, cheeky brat. It's not right to take a scruff out of his station and give him big ideas, my mam says it's against nature. I bet she's blaming him for making the master ill like she blamed Sunter Lund for pestering them and sending letters and breaking the front window.'

'When was all this, Susan? What had they to do with the Lunds' boy?'

'Well, he were a Fawcett once but he's been coming back at the master, storming in and threatening him. The mistress kept earwigging behind the door. Worried stiff, she were. They were both glad when he were killed. I could see they were relieved. She said little bits whispering that Lund had it coming to him.'

'Well, thank you, Susan, but let's deal with the present. I think we need some help. Call in a neighbour woman to sit with you. The others may come back so I'll go up to Paradise. I'm sure that's where I'll find that rascal tucked up in his hut.'

Tizzy was pushed up the footpath by Miss Bulstrode from behind. The track was slippery and muddy, caking the soles of her clogs, making them smooth with no grip. Her legs ached and she was starving but every time she stopped a finger was poked into her back. 'Where're we going? This isn't the quick road to camp, is it? This is going up to

Scarsbeck Force. I can't see, it's too dark, miss. You come in front.'

'Keep going, I want to show you a lovely spot. One of the beauties of the district, don't you think? A trickling beck straight off the moor, crashing sixty feet down into a deep black pool, a spectacular waterfall tumbling twice over rocks. Can't you hear the rush of the water as it falls? It's in full spate, listen to the beck as it floods over those rocky boulders,' shouted the woman, pushing forward.

'But it's dark, miss, we can't see owt. Why do we have to come up here? I want to go home for me tea. You should be seeing to Mr Bulstrode. They'll be wondering where we are ...'

'Shut your voice, Billy Widdup, there's no one to hear us.'

'I'm not Billy Widdup, he's dead a long time ago. I'm Tizzy, his sister, Matilda Widdup. I never were a boy. It were all a trick but it went wrong. I tried to tell the teacher.'

'Do you expect me to believe such silly lies? You have turned poor Ezra upside down with your lies and wickedness, worn him out. Now you try your tales on me. Enough of this nonsense. Whoever heard of a girl as a Fawcett scholar?'

'Why not? Mercy Birkett could do it blindfold. She's much better with her composition than me. She wants to be a Fawcett. I don't, not any more,' yelled Tizzy as she clung on to the branches of willows by the edge of the water.

'Shut up! Keep going. You should be praying that Bulstrode recovers for if he dies ... "The Lord is my Shepherd, I shall not want, He leadeth me beside the still waters ..."' The woman was singing wildly.

'This isn't still water, miss, it's a roaring torrent. I don't like it here. Let's go back now. What if we slip?' The finger in her back dug through the wet jacket like a knife.

'I said keep going. There'll be peace in the valley, peace in the valley, peace in the valley, ere long.'

Tizzy shivered. This was no peaceful valley, more like the valley of the shadow of death, but she knew exactly where they were. Mercy had brought her many times to play by the pools and search for sticklebacks and frogs. It was always a dark and shady place, a gorge of black walls towering above your head. Once twilight slid down the rocks they used to scamper back into the sunshine. Now in the darkness Tizzy felt there was no guiding shepherd in this place to lead her to safety, only an evil presence creeping out of the dampness, slithering out of the crevices, stalking behind her footsteps, making her cry.

Zillah pulled the bell rope at the vicarage, dripping puddles of rainwater on the step. Dogs barked and bounded around her as the studded oak door creaked open and the surprised face of the clergyman smiled at the sight of this drowned rat.

'We have to find the child.'

'Come inside, Miss Herbert. What is it that drags you out on such a wild night? Come in.'

'I'm sorry to trouble you but I fear trouble. Something happened at the schoolhouse tonight. Ezra Bulstrode has been struck by some paralysis and lies near to death but his sister has vanished with my pupil. Their maid is afraid they will come to harm in the storm and so am I. What shall I do? I must go.' Zillah turned but Ralph Hardy caught her arm gently.

'First you come inside and have a drink, dry your clothes and sit by the fire to collect your thoughts. Tell me what you know and together we'll work out some course of action. Is anyone with Ezra?'

She nodded wearily. He guided her to his study where a fire burned brightly and the candles flickered. Zillah suddenly flopped uninvited into a large fireside chair with a sigh.

'If I sit down, I'm not sure I'll get up again.' She looked around the room. For a bachelor it was well-appointed with faded Chinese rugs scattered around the oak floor. The walls were littered with animal heads, stags with antlers, a glass case of silvery trout, stuffed heads and hunting prints. Tucked by the fireside were a line of delightful miniature paintings in gilt frames. She felt herself relaxing in the warmth.

Judging by the length of time it took for Mr Hardy to return with a pot of tea and a pile of muffins, Zillah assumed they were alone in the house and his cook had gone back to the village. He proceeded to toast them with a brass fork in front of the fire, kneeling down, looking quite boyish and human.

'We should be on our way, Mr Hardy. I didn't come for tea. You are kind but . . .'

'Sit still for two minutes and dry yourself. If we are to be soaked to our skins in a chase then warmth inside your stomach will prevent a chill.' His voice was firm and his smile disarming. For once Zillah decided to let the man have the last word. 'You were right to call here first. I can harness up the trap. Poor Ezra. Should I go there first?'

'They're waiting for Dr Fielding to call. He can't be moved but he's safe with Susan and her mother. Something is terribly wrong. I can feel it in my chest, Mr Hardy. I thought at first that young Billy had run away from his meeting here with you. He did get that message from the navvy in prison. He refused to give it to Miss Ellen. The navvy gave him his poetry book to pass on to his friend but the silly child kept it for himself. There's just so much to relate I don't know where to start but we must be on our way ...' Zillah stood up and wrung out her top skirt, watching the steam rise off the garment. 'Thank you for your hospitality, but I must go.'

'So you keep saying, but where exactly do you intend to go?' asked Ralph.

'To Paradise first to check if Billy has returned to the hut. I fear all of this is my doing. I pushed him so hard to become a scholar.'

'Yes, yes ... but explanations come later. We must put the tackle on the horses. You can ride?' said the vicar impatiently.

'Only side-saddle, I'm afraid, but I can drive a trap. I'm not exactly useless,' Zillah snapped back as they made their way to the courtyard and the stable. Taking orders from this man as he flung over tackle, belted up, shouted to her to hold steady, made Zillah wish she had not bothered him. Yet she swallowed back her remarks in gratitude that someone else was taking control and she was no longer alone with these strange findings.

As they rode back down the brow and into the main street, she could see the doctor's cab outside the schoolhouse. Then they turned to the track beside the viaduct, surprised to see men gathered with lanterns in the shadows who stood back sheepishly at the sight of the vicar and the schoolmarm. Ralph halted to shout over to the party, 'Have you seen Miss Bulstrode and a boy on this track?'

Wally Stackhouse stepped out of the shadows. 'We've seen nowt but rain, Mr Hardy. What's to do?'

'There's been an accident at the schoolhouse. Miss Cora is upset and we fear she may come to harm on such a night. There's a child missing too.'

'Who's that then?' All the men came forward to hear the news, Dicky Braithwaite and Tudge and Warwick Lund. He looked surprised to see the teacher out in the dark. 'Are you all right, miss? Shall I take her back to the Birketts'?'

'No, Mr Lund. Thank you but I prefer to be out looking for my pupil. We need help to search for them. This is no night to be out on these moors, is it?' said Zillah firmly.

'Is this one of your navvy nippers, Miss Herbert?'

'Yes but a lost sheep is lost whether it's black or white, Mr Stackhouse.'

'Aye, yer right enough there. We've no quarrel with a kiddie.' There was a general shaking of heads and promises of

336

help. The vicar suggested they searched through the village and back lanes up onto the high road while the two of them would take the Paradise track. 'If we can borrow a few flares from the camp then that can be a signal if the pair of them are found. There's still a good chance that they're safe in the camp anyway.'

'Right enough, vicar, you can rely on us.' Wally waved them on their way with a wink and Zillah blushed at their obvious amusement to see this couple out riding under cover of darkness. It would be clacked all around Scarsbeck in the morning that the vicar and schoolmarm were hitching up to the same wagon.

'And what do you think they were all up to gathered under the viaduct together on such a dark night?' laughed the vicar.

'Up to no good, I fear, but this little drama has salved their consciences and redeemed their purpose there, I hope. Damaging railway property would carry a stiff sentence should they be caught, don't you think?'

The rain beat on their faces and Zillah worried at the state of mind of Cora Bulstrode to be out in the storm with a child. As they approached the camp she tried to locate the exact hut where Billy and his sister were lodging. There were lines of huts dotted on the slopes of the field, dark and indistinguishable. Then she saw Stumper, the dog, tied to a post. There was only one three-legged hound, surely? His noisy welcome brought Mally to the door. She peered out seeing the horse and trap, relieved at the wanderer's return. 'Is that you, Tizzy? Oh, Miss Herbert, I didn't recognise you, have you brought our Billy?'

'No, Mally, we were hoping he was here. There's been some trouble . . .'

'What's the toe rag been and done now?' sighed his sister.

'Nothing like that, may we step inside and explain?' The room was filled with a trestle table and men lined up on either side tucking into tin plates of stew and dumplings and black peas. At the far end of the room was a line of bunk beds and mattresses, at the other a stove over which hung a rope pulley of steaming socks and shirts. The room stank of bodies, damp socks and boiled meat. Mally had papered the walls with magazine pictures and cuttings in a collage effect which brightened the inside but some of the pictures were peeling off in the dampness.

Everyone in the room fell silent at the entrance of the two strangers. Then they were recognised and urged to sit down for a mug of ale. Zillah stood by the door and softly told their news. 'We think Billy has been abducted. There's been some dreadful misunderstanding, no doubt. The lady has disappeared, very distraught thinking her brother, the head-master, to be dead. She may be blaming young Billy in some way. We just don't know. I'm sorry, Mally, but I thought you ought to know. The vicar has already organised local men in the village to start a search.'

'I'll come with you and fetch Granda . . .'

'You stay here just in case they come back,' ordered Wobbly Bob who went to the rack on the wall and lifted out a shotgun. 'I'll gather a few lads and we'll go hunting if you can tell us where to start.'

'We're not sure but they can't get far in these conditions. Comb down from the camp towards the beckside. I'll get the others to come down the other side and together we may be able to flush them out of their hiding place. I think she's hiding somewhere. Don't worry, Mally. We'll find them.' Ralph was trying to sound confident but Zillah could tell it was an act of bravura.

'Oh, Miss Herbert ... what if she's harmed?'

'Miss Cora? Her mood was strange but I'm sure she wouldn't harm herself.' Zillah was surprised at this concern for the woman.

'Not her, she can go to hell ... our Tizzy. She's only eleven.'

'Tizzy, Tizzy who? I don't understand.' Zillah looked at the girl, whose cheeks were flushing as she beckoned the teacher towards the bedroom door.

'I'm sorry, Miss Herbert, but there's something you and the vicar should know. Something we ought to have told you a long time ago.'

Chapter Thirty-Three

Tizzy listened to her teeth chittering; she was so cold it was hard to grasp why she was stuck on an overhanging ledge of rock with water cascading down Scarsbeck Force in front of her, the roaring flooding torrent drowning out any sounds. 'I can't see anything, Miss Bulstrode, can we go now?'

'Stop snivelling. How can we go home with you? Can't you see, boy? You must cast yourself upon the waters. I can't have you telling more tales, more wicked lies to all and sundry. All those wasted years, all that work has worn out his brains and you, stupid child, come along and ruin everything just like Sunter Lund haunting us with threats.'

'I hated Lund. He deserved to die. I told you afore. I cursed him so I'm not one of him.' The woman was not listening but rolling her eyes so high to calculate her next move Tizzy could see the whites gleaming.

'He wanted to leave ... Lund wanted money from us. Shouting at Ezra, 'Give me fifty pounds and I'll disappear.

Give me my due and I'll never tell about our little secret, all the filth you made me swallow. You said I failed the test, you made a fool of me. Give it here or I'll make a fool of you ...'

Doors have ears, how could all the village not hear his threats? Ezra was upright and said no. He broke the window in his rage and sent him letters. Ezra was strong and burnt all of them, all but the one he never saw. I had to know. How pure and white lies a letter on a mat but inside it was black as dirt filthy with lies. He was a menace. Menaces must be destroyed so I gave him what he deserved. I waited for him to call, waited until he was safe in the Fleece. It had to be so. Poor Ezra needed me to see to things as I've always seen to things. For I am the strong one and sometimes he is weak ... Do you think I don't know that he's different from most men, with special requirements to comfort him? He's his father's son, trained from a child to be an obedient scholar. No one will tell lies about my brother and live, do you hear, child? Not you, not anyone.' Tizzy felt fear stabbing into her stomach like hunger pangs.

'What happened then, Miss Bulstrode, did your brother hit him hard?'

'What's my brother got to do with this? He was too weak to stand up for himself like he was against his father. It's I who take care of things as I always have. I left the house and crept through the school yard, waited behind the wall and walked to the viaduct. There were stones of all shapes and sizes, stones waiting for masons to dress for the arches, piles of heavy stones, piles of chippings sharp like flint, stones dressed and shaped to size. So many stones to choose from. And there it was: sharp and solid, black as death. How easy it is to crush a skull! You hide and wait until the man comes out unaware. A man pausing to look at the stars, looking up heavenwards as I bashed his head and watched him fall, crumpled up for a second blow. It had to be so and now you go and spoil it with your lies, Billy Widdup. You see how it must be. You see what Miss Bulstrode must do?' She was coming forward, smiling oddly.

'I told you, I'm not Billy Widdup. He's dead. I'm Tizzy, just another bleeding lass.'

'Girls can't be Fawcetts. Ezra would never choose a girl. Girls have no brains, no hopes, girls must be obedient to fathers and brothers whatever they demand. We are pitiable creatures, weak flesh. Girls are nothing . . .' said Cora, spitting into the child's face.

'NO! No. You're wrong. I thowt that at first when Lund killed me dog. I were that mad I snipped off me braids and put on breeches just to show them all that girls have brains, a girl can be strong as a lad. I did a tea boy's job and no one ever guessed. I can get the scholarship. I see girls grow babbies in their tums and they can't be weak to do that. It's a lie, Miss Bulstrode, honest. You must be strong to kill a man. I won't jump. Never, not down into that hole. You can jump if you like, I won't stop yer, but I'll not go with yer.' The woman stepped back from the edge as if in deep conflict. 'Look, it weren't your fault Lund got done in. He were cursed from the start for killing Tat. If anyone killed him it were me ... not you. You just finished off the job for me like. I'm not sorry he's a goner. If we tell the truth of it, it's me they'll blame, not you.' Tizzy was thinking fast on her feet, arguing for her life. 'Take me back and you'll see. I'm only little. They can't hang me, can they? But they'll hang Fancy for what he never done. You'll be safe to look after Mr Bulstrode but we have to go back first, please? It's getting so cold here. Aren't you frozen? Feel me hand, it's like an icicle.' Tizzy shoved her hand onto Cora's cheek.

'Yes, yes, it's cold, so cold and wet.' For a moment the crazed woman weakened, her eyes half closed with resignation. She sprang back to life like a startled cat with tiger eyes, wary, watchful and glinting like sharpened steel. 'You're trying to trick me, Billy Widdup, pretending to be a girl indeed, too sharp for your own good. You don't fool me. No use prolonging the agony, child. Come here! Jump or I'll push you in ... why struggle?' She lunged forward to grab Tizzy but the girl edged out of arm's reach, sweating, sliding sideways inch by inch back down the side of the cold rock.

'If I have to go, you'll be coming with me and who'll look after the headmaster then?'

This is a useless exercise, thought Ralph to himself; a wild goose chase down the stony track to Scarsbeck. There was no certainty of finding the woman and her charge. Why should she want to drag that child along unless she knew also what Mally had confessed to them, unless she too knew that Billy was no lad? Was this the shock which made her brother

343

collapse? They had all been duped by the child, made fools of, especially the missionary woman who had relapsed into stunned silence as she trudged on behind the search party. Where would they be hiding on this wet night? Not on the open moor if they wanted to survive. Perhaps they would be found frozen with cold in the morning. Sheer wetness might make them take refuge in some barn but which one? There were hundreds of stone shippons, pinfolds and shelters to keep out of sight.

Ralph tossed each suggestion like a ball around his head. Oh Bethany Wildman, where are you when I need you? You would know where to look; you would get one of your feelings and turns and see them in the dark. Everyone was now looking to him for a lead; village and camp, looking to him to salvage the rescue, support the weary and coordinate the search. Look at me, damn you, am I being a good enough shepherd for my flock? You said you would haunt me if I didn't buck up so where are you when I need you? Come on, where the hell do I look?

They combed the beckside watching the water frothing like brown ale over the boulders; a little stream transformed into a river, swirling away anything that stood in its path. If lost sheep fell into the swollen water their bodies would have been carried away long ago. Damn the woman, damn the stupid brat! He was stumped ... stumped, why that word? 'Stump!' he said aloud and the three-legged wonder wrapped itself obediently around his ankles. Stumper, of course! Thanks, Beth, he smiled to the skies. That dog was not as

stupid as it looked. He had often seen it trailing round the
camp after the Widdup child, hopping on three short legs;
perhaps there was just a chance? 'Stumper, go, boy. Where's
Tizzy?' What a silly name for a girl. 'Yes, you find her. Go
on!' The dog pricked up its ears at the familiar name. 'Go
find her, boy. Everyone shout her name. There's just a chance
she may hear us.' For the first time in his life the vicar was
praying for a miracle but he didn't hold out much hope.

Tizzy managed to edge the woman away from the pinnacle.
'Mind you don't slip, Miss Bulstrode, one slip and you're
into the deep. It'll be cold down there and they'll never
bury you. Can't you feel the icy spray? The cold is coil-
ing over us like a snake, squeezing us to suck out the hot
juices.' Mercy would be proud of her poetic effort. 'Here
we are lost in the dark with no one to hear us if we call
out . . . in the valley of the shadow of death. What was it
you sang? "The Lord is my Shepherd." I wish I could sing
like you but the sound comes out all wonky, Miss Herbert
says. Sing it with me and happen I'll get it right. You have
a nice voice, miss.' They sang the hymn to Brother James's
air. 'He leadeth me, He leadeth me the quiet waters by. Yea
though I walk through death's dark vale, yet will I feel no
ill . . .' 'That's us, in't it?' Tizzy was trying to sound brave
and sure but she was so tired and slow, it took every ounce
of strength to push each slippy clog in front of the other.
Her trousers were soaked through and the skin on her
thighs chapped with the rough wet cloth. She was not going

to give in, hoping that someone had missed them by now. The rain was easing off. 'If we get down off this rocky bit we'll soon find the path and get back home. You can see to Mr Bulstrode.'

'You've killed him,' said Cora, stopping to rummage in her head as to why they were climbing back down again.

'No, I haven't, honest. Susan was looking after him till the doctor come. She sent word for him, remember, miss? Secrets are safe with me. I've got a few of me own to sort out. We've all got secrets in this dale. Let's sing our hymn again to cheer us up. "The Lord is my Shepherd, I shall not want . . ."' Tizzy growled without conviction. To her relief her companion looked up, smiled her thin-lipped twisted smile and joined in.

The sound was faint, echoing above the roar, bouncing off the echo chamber of the walls of the stone gorge. The search party was following the path upstream to Scarsbeck Force. Stumper stopped, his stubby ears pricked and his tail wagged. Ralph silenced the searchers with his hand. Zillah darted forward.

'What is it?'

'Shush, a sound, the dog is listening too. They must be near the Force. Good God! Whatever are they doing up there?' As they drew closer they could hear the faint tinkly sound of singing. Ralph was calculating how long it would take for him to scramble up the bank to come at them from behind, to escort them down to safety.

'Let me go ahead, now,' ordered Zillah calmly.

'Don't be so stupid, it's a man's job,' whispered Ralph.

'She's my pupil and Cora knows me. A man will only blunder in and startle them. I can coax them back,' replied the teacher.

'I forbid you to go . . .'

'You can't stop me.'

'As your chaplain . . .'

'Hah! When have you ever been that?' Zillah snapped.

'As chairman of the school managers, it's my responsibility to oversee—'

'I'm not answerable to your school board.'

'It's not safe for you to go alone, Miss Herbert.'

'The Lord will guide my path with the light of His truth.'

'Don't be so pompous. One slip and you'll be at the pearly gates.'

'I must go, it's all my fault.'

'I won't argue with that, woman, but if you go up the path, give me time to skirt round the top, higher up the bank.'

'It's dangerous, you'll fall, the lichen and moss are like ice,' pleaded Zillah, alarmed at his plan. 'Why must we always argue?'

'Because you're the most pig-headed woman I've ever met.'

'And you're the most stubborn man . . .' They both burst out laughing as the search party shuffled up awkwardly behind them, wondering what the hold-up was. 'If we stand here arguing all night, a vicar, a woman and a three-legged dog, what will this parish think of us?'

'When has that ever stopped either of us?' laughed Zillah as she stepped forward into the darkness.

'Will you stop that terrible noise, child. You may be a quick thinker but you're no singer. Give me a hand, my legs are stiff.' Cora Bulstrode was back to being a sour apple but Tizzy, not sure if this was another trick, turned only slightly. She felt herself sliding on the mud of her clogs, bumping down.

'I can't stop. Help me!' She panicked as the momentum pulled her downwards, grabbing out for the sharp thorny blackthorn branch which caught her fall. As she stood up slowly she noticed, far down in the valley gorge, the flicker of lanterns. Could it be? She shouted, 'Here! Over here!' But no one responded. Then came a bark and the warmth of a dog's body, the familiar smell of Stumper. 'It's me dog, miss, he's come to fetch us. Look.'

'Keep him away from me, he's got fleas. Stay back. I'm not going back.'

'Is that you, Tizzy? Is that Miss Bulstrode I hear? Praise the Lord! You are found. We were so worried about you, Cora dear. It's only Miss Herbert who's lost her way as usual. It's so late. I've come to take the child home, Miss Bulstrode. The headmaster sent me to fetch you both. He's so anxious for you. The child won't be ready for the examination tomorrow or is it today? I've no idea of the time, dear me! All that work for us to do, Miss Bulstrode, seeing to the school while the headmaster recovers. I'm sure he would want you to carry on his good work in his absence. Your nursing will soon have him on his feet.'

'He's dead! He's dead. All of them are dead. What's the point of all that work? I tried to warn him that the Lund boy was a danger. He wouldn't listen. I tried to persuade him to give him money but he wouldn't listen.'

'You had to kill him, didn't you?' Tizzy said, her voice suddenly faint. 'You killed Mr Lund.'

'No, it was you, Widdup, you cursed him and he had to go.'

'Now how could I bash his head in when I were out playing Mischief? You told me you waited behind the wall and what did you do with the stone?'

'He shouldn't have been looking at the stars, Miss Herbert. No, they were my stars, he'd no right to be stealing my stars. Now his blood is fixed into the stones of the viaduct. I put the stone back where I found it . . .'

'I'm sure you did, Miss Bulstrode, but it's all over now. Come down and have a warm cup of tea. I'll put the kettle on myself and we'll tell poor Ezra all about your little adventure.'

'Do you think he'll understand that they were my stars?'

'Come down and tell him yourself. Here's Father Hardy come to escort us safely back. Isn't that kind of him, late as usual but I think he heard enough of your story to know what to do next. It's time we all went home.'

Sandwiched between Ralph and Zillah the sad little party wound its weary way back to the waiting group of navvies, back to the warmth of Scarsbeck where the navvies were thanked with ale and buns at the Fleece, back to Dr Fielding who gave Cora Bulstrode a sleeping draught and examined the child for exposure, declaring Billy Widdup to be unscathed but very definitely female.

Chapter Thirty-Four

Zillah sat at the high desk overseeing an empty classroom; only the ripe scent of fifty bodies stuck on wooden benches mixed with chalk dust, coal fumes and stale air lingering around the room remained. She bent over her quill pen, scratching a letter long overdue.

Dearest Aunt Jane,

Please forgive the delay in replying to your epistle. Please reassure Mama that I was never in any mortal danger during the search for Miss Bulstrode on the moor. I promise to dose myself regularly with 'Dr Wakelin's chillproof powders' but I have received so much fuss and attention from my dear hosts, especially Miss Ellen who is overjoyed at the outcome, that I am in grave danger of being suffocated by kindness.

It is hard to believe that it is only a week since poor Cora Bulstrode was escorted by cab to the Asylum at Lancaster, there to await trial for murder. She is so totally disoriented

*and disturbed in mind as to be unfit to plead to any charge, I
fear. Her brother is a pitiable sight, being unable to move or
speak, and has been removed to a sanatorium near Harrogate
with little hope of recovery; condemned to a living death. He
was a good teacher in his way, a conscientious choirmaster and
organist but distant and unpopular by all accounts and with
most peculiar tastes in literature. Sadly neither of them will be
missed in the village.*

*It was the unanimous decision of the board of school
managers to appoint me temporarily to the post of acting
headmistress, staying in the schoolhouse until such time as a
suitable replacement can be found. I fear Mr Hardy has had
a hand in this for he now takes his position far more seriously
than of late and calls to give the children their lessons in
Scripture every day. (I do not think he trusts my grasp of
theology to be sufficient to cope with the task.)*

*I really must try to be more charitable towards his motives.
He lingers overlong and stares so hard when I reply that I
am most confused and find myself stammering and blushing.
I shall have to discourage these visitations as it puts me quite
off my concentration.*

*You will be pleased to know that I am to be resident in the
schoolhouse. To this end and with much help from Susan,
Blaize Lund, the Birketts and Mrs Cleghorn I have cleared
out all that remains of the Bulstrode regime, burnt much stuff
and packed away their personal clothing in boxes which now
are stored in the loft of the vicar's stables. I am sure no one
will ever come to reclaim these goods and they will be sold*

*for charity. Thus are the gloomy couple disposed of. What a
task we have had, opening windows, banishing darkness and
clutter, whitewashing and painting, stencilling pretty patterns
on plain walls, polishing and reclaiming each room. The
transformation is delightful and I look forward to collecting
some furniture of my own to brighten the effect further.*

*Much as I have loved my stay at Middle Butts, the
convenience of being across the yard and no more weary walks
with Mercy Birkett will make a harsh winter bearable. The
Birketts are distressed at my leaving but they have reason to
look forward to a future now that Ellen's young suitor has
been released from prison.*

*Winter is gripping us tightly, its icy fingers squeezing our
breath. The trees and rooftops glisten with hoar frost, a silvery
coating of powder which changes from grey to blue to pinky
purple as the low sun crosses over the valley.*

*So much has changed since we last exchanged letters.
Tizzy Widdup, as we must now call her, although I much
prefer Matilda to Tizzy, was allowed to sit the Fawcett out
of respect for Mr Bulstrode's application on her behalf. She
had no difficulty in achieving a satisfactory mark but of course
there is no question of her taking up a place in a boys' school.
The nearest establishment for girls, near Kirby Lonsdale,
would not consider taking on a child from such a background.
If she were a city child then perhaps a place would be made
for her as a pupil teacher and a respectable way forward for
her prodigious talent could be found. But this is 1871 and a
land of few opportunities for women without means. I was*

very interested to hear that you attended a lecture on the emancipation of women by Miss Lydia Becker and that there is a growing movement in favour of further education for older women. I fear it will take centuries for any such ideas to reach Scarsdale.

What is worrying me is that Tizzy and her family, such as they are, are like rudderless boats bobbing on the ocean tossed any which way by the tide of necessity and circumstance. There is no firm hand at the tiller guiding them forward. If only the father could be found to take on the responsibility, he might be an influence for good. So I have taken upon myself to inform the contractor and request that he telegraph up the line and down to see if Mr Ironfist can be found.

I have also been thinking for some time about a way to communicate to navvies across the country; something which might make the workmen pause to think about their wretched condition; a newsletter to give addresses and news of relatives and friends on the line. Something which could be passed from camp to camp. Ending up no doubt as wallpaper decoration on some hut. Would it not be wonderful to imagine Mr Emmanuel Widdup, alias Ironfist, sitting by a wall plastered with paper and suddenly out of the print he sees his name and is reunited with his family? I shall remember them in my prayers daily.

You may be aware of the work of Henrietta Cresswell and I've heard there is a lady in the north, Elizabeth Garnett, who is already attempting to produce a pamphlet. The

Pastoral Aid seem to be eager to develop this idea. Who knows what these seeds may produce as a harvest?

My days are filled with school duties and preparations for our Christmas service and performance. My evenings are taken up with rehearsals for the navvy entertainment in Paradise reading hut which will be followed by a country dance and feast. Now that the atmosphere is less strained between camp and village and the murder has been solved, there is a degree of cooperation again. It is not exactly jovial or even cordial but certainly less frostbitten than of late. The village supply wagons are back in the camp much to everyone's satisfaction and benefit. Mr Hardy is hoping his entertainment might just help heal the mutual suspicion.

If you could see the state of the construction works and the village street, mud and mess everywhere. We skate on ice or mud. I cannot foresee the camp being disbanded. Paradise will be above us for many years. There is talk of building a brewery. Over my dead body!

I am strangely reluctant to contemplate a life outside this dale. I talk of us and we when I should be saying they and them. That old shepherd woman was right when she said that this valley would wind itself around my heart. My Paradise flawed, I wrote once to you. How can a life on this earth be anything but flawed? But there is something unique about this hidden dale.

Once the new master is arrived I suppose the Mission will want me to move onwards and upwards. I am not eager to anticipate that moment of departure.

It is sufficient joy for me to be returning home at long last to the bosom of my family. I am glad that Mama and Papa have recovered from my spiritual elopement and have accepted the decision that their marriage plans were never mine. I see the possibilities in such an estate eventually but until now there has been no one on the horizon of sufficient interest to make me examine the prospect further. I will say no more on that score for fear of ever raising their hopes in that direction again.

Marriage to a spiritual cause is satisfying but it can be lonely of an evening with no one to share all your disasters and triumphs. On the other hand the single life has much to recommend it when the time comes to choose what you do and when, do you not think?

I have a pass for the train from Ingleton to Leeds and from thence to Nottingham. I am to be conveyed down the temporary track on a wagon to Batty Green, as a special dispensation from the Midland Railway for my efforts on their behalf. By the time I arrive at Batty Green I shall no doubt look like a chimney sweep.

Do not expect to see the same Zillah who fled from you all only nine months ago, who braved a blizzard for fear of being sheltered in an ale house, putting the lives of all fellow travellers at risk for her principles. My rigid views were like spikes in the ground as barriers and spears. So much has happened here to challenge my thoughts and humble my opinions.

Now I will examine the size of a snowflake, the direction

*of the wind and take advice before putting one foot out of
doors. Your niece is learning sense at last.*

*Soon the farmhouse will be reeking of spices, Christmas
pies and a dish called frumenty which I am assured is all
part of the traditional feasting. My ribs are bursting with
farmhouse fare and I am in danger of rivalling a plum
pudding, such is my girth. My waist, I am ashamed to say,
has expanded a full two inches at least. It is with great joy
that I look forward to our reunion.*

Yours in anticipation,
Zillah Jane

Fancy stood on the platform with his bundle, the gates of
the House of Correction in Wakefield firmly closed behind
him. Free at last but he felt nothing, neither the usual raging
thirst nor the anger burning his throat; just an empty cold
pit in his guts. What should he do next, where was there to
go? Who cared?

All those weeks in the jail planning where he would roam
if justice prevailed and now opportunities were endless. Only
the vicar had bothered to write and explain the circumstances of his release. He was assured of his old job on site if
he chose to return to Paradise.

What was the point? Someone else would be giving orders
to his gang. What was the point of freedom if there was no
one to share the journey? The silence from Ellie Birkett was
deafening. Not a word from the minx. She no longer cared
but why should she? He had fled from her to save his skin.

His pride would not let him beg pardon. Who would want a jailbird navvy with shaven head and no whiskers? He could feel the wind on his neck at the place where his long pirate's tail warmed him like a scarf. Hair will grow but no one could redeem the time lost. The other convicts on the station would no doubt be going back to some warm fireside.

He watched the waves of families step forward as the engine chugged into the station, surging into the third-class carriages at the back, women with shawls full of infants and baskets full of food; children carrying cages of squawking chickens. He might as well join the crowd for the ride.

In the corner of his carriage sat a woman in a battered straw bonnet and shabby skirt, a tired, crumpled face, an ordinary woman with her bairns by her side; a boy with ginger hair tufted like a helmet and a snivelling baby on her knee with a face round as a ball, his mouth plugged by his thumb as he stared anxiously at the stranger before him. People might think they were all one family off on a tramp somewhere. The woman looked suspiciously at his clean-shaven face, bunching up her children more closely as if he might harm them. It made him want to cry.

Fancy turned away to hide his grief, staring out of the window, soot-stained, staring at lines of grey buildings and factories with chimneys belching black smoke; Leeds spread in front of him, mile upon mile of grime and grimness in the dark December afternoon. Then he noticed they were following a river and the landscape widened into a valley and the houses were lighter and sparsely spread. He could see the outlines of hills topped with snow. The sky was bluer and brighter; his spirits were lifting at the sight of hills.

The train was heading north. Fancy had not cared which train he was boarding but now he was glad. There were worse places to be than Yorkshire and he knew that the hills would shout louder to him as they puffed up the gradient. Go back, don't run away. All his life had been one long journey to find somewhere to belong. If he did not go back he would never know. Like the invisible face in his dreams which haunted him for years until he met Ellie. All those months loving Ellie and the dream had been absent. She was the sun who burnt away the gloomy mist on a summer morning. That was a good line to hold in his head until he found some paper and a pencil. The words were coming back too.

Go back, go back over the track, quickity quick, he could feel the rhythm of the wheels on the track, lickity split ... Go back and face the demons, that stern grey face of Annie Birkett and the sad blue eyes of her daughter. Only when he saw her eyes would he know.

'Hurry up, we're packing, Tizzy, shift yourself. It's time we were on our way. I'll be glad to see the back of this place; folk gawping at us as if we're out of a peep show. I know when I'm not wanted. That Wobbly Bob has done nothing but complain about me mutton stew and the way I flat-iron his shirts. He can sort out his own washing from now on. I know when I'm not wanted so we're off to pastures new to try our luck elsewhere,' said Mally as she whisked the bundles onto the handcart.

'Where the heck are we off to now? It's too cold to be tramping,' muttered her sister as she tied a piece of string around the dog.

'Only down to Batty Green. There's more life there and they've opened a bakery, a brickworks and lots of shops. Plenty of women's work. I had a look last Saturday, we'll soon get fixed up. There's even a school and all ... you needn't look like that. I can't wait to be rid of this place. I never did like Paradise, it's far too quiet.'

'I'm bringing Stumper,' answered Tizzy.

'You can take what you can carry, I've told Granda to collect his stuff and meet us by the Blea Moor track. He can please himself otherwise.'

'You're a top and a whip, a hard woman, Mally Widdup. Can't I stay for the school concert? I might get a part.'

'Well no one will give you a solo, that's for sure, not with that squeaky voice of yours. If we get there quick you can join the other school and perhaps they'll be dishing out a party or two. Sunday schools is allus good for bun fights. No one'll know us down there, we can have a fresh start.'

'I suppose so. Do you think we might find owt about Dad?'

'What do you think? We can manage on us own without any fellas. I fancy a job in the bakery, think on, lots of buns and fancies for tea. Stop dawdling, I've made me mind up.'

'I'll have to say ta-ra to Mercy. She's that gobsmacked at

me being a lass, her mouth keeps opening and shutting like a fish. She's not kicked me for a week and mithers me to death about the Fawcett. She's on at Sherbert to change the rules and give her a go. I don't hold out much hope. I never want to hear about any of that again and I won't do any more cursing either.'

'You never said what happened, what he did to you.'

'I've done with all that too.' The events of the past weeks were already being shoved into a back cupboard in her mind. Tizzy would not be sorry to leave Paradise camp and all those pictures of Patabully which were giving her nightmares.

'Never you mind . . . least said soonest mended. It's all over now. I take it you won't be putting on any more breeches.' Mally smiled as she started to shove the cart out of the mud.

'Why not? There's not much going for me in a skirt, is there? So why not stick it for a few more years? No one'll know us down there,' answered Tizzy, guiding the wheels out of the ruts with a push. 'How else will I get a wage?'

'Oh no! Not all that rigmarole again,' sighed Mally with another heave to. 'Granda will be that confused again. Promise me you'll jack it in when your jugs start sprouting out of your shirt but until then your secret will be safe with me . . . as long as you behave.'

Tizzy Widdup beamed up at her big sister with relief. 'Hang on a second, then, while I get changed behind a wall. I never did throw out them clothes. Come on, Stumper. Let's see what Batty Green'll make of us lot.'

Chapter Thirty-Five

'Come on in, Ellie, Mam's starting the Yuletide puddings, stir and make a wish!' shouted Mercy from the doorway into the yard. Ellie lifted her head briefly, shrugged her shoulders and carried on with her task. Why should she get excited about stupid cloth puddings with so many jobs to do and so few hands to do them? Upstairs Miss Herbert would be packing her stuff to take down to Scarsbeck before her journey to Nottingham. What a hike just to see yer relatives at Christmas. Humbug! She was getting just like Mr Scrooge in the magazine story. What did she want to make wishes for?

Truth was she was going to miss the teacher summat rotten. She was kind and ladylike for all her funny ideas. Miss Zillah had been loaned to them, got them out of a pickle with her rent. How on earth would they manage now with just the three of them?

Uncle Warwick was losing heart, all the stuffing knocked out of him. They were talking of taking a cottage in the village and cutting the losses. Sunter might not have been the best son in the world but he had given them all hope for the future. Mother and her might as well pack it in themselves in that case, for on her own Ellie was no Jim Birkett. Last year it had been Father missing from the feast; now there was another empty chair. They were all punished by this murder.

There was a terrible heaviness around her heart which slowed her down. If things had only gone to plan then perhaps this would have been her first married Christmas. She would feel like making an effort if she had someone to bake and scrub for. She might even bother to watch what her mam did rather than ignore her cookery lessons. How she would have dangled him proudly on her arm among visiting company as they gathered in the polished parlour to light this year's fire from last year's yule log. Candles would burn around the punch bowl and they would sing:

> '*We wish you a merry Kersmass and a happy new year,*
> *A pocketful of money and a cellar full of beer,*
> *A good fat pig and a new calving too,*
> *Good master and mistress, how do you do . . .*'

They would sit by the fireside admiring the greenery decorating the mantelpiece, sniff the spices of the Christmas loaf while sharing a bowl of hot frumenty together. Now she could summon up no enthusiasm for the usual round of callers, the circles of knitters clacking as fast as their needles, rolling out balls of spun gossip from lap to lap.

It did not help that Mercy was stuffed full of excitement and wanted to do everything to the book, perform all the traditions, singing carols at the spinet and inviting the mummers' play into their parlour. She was still a child and thought that Christmas was a magical time of surprises and feasts. Mercy was going to have to learn that there would be no money for extras this year. Christmas was just another day with stock to feed, jobs to be done. *I'm just a wet blanket dampening any spark of festive spirit*, Ellie chided herself.

If only she didn't feel so guilty. She had meant to write to Fancy and explain how that wretched Widdup brat refused to hand over his book to her, leaving her thinking the worst of him. The vicar had brought the book and she had slept with it under her pillow ever since. At first she had taken heart from his words on the front page: *Be not concerned, I will return for you.* It was over a week since his release and there was not a sight or sound of him in Paradise. Why should there be? What had she done to encourage him? So she must just keep busy and put her head down.

Her legs and hands felt as if they were tied to lead weights dragging her feet; shame, guilt, weariness and anger, if she were honest, those were the weights. The anger was the worst of all, anger at being alone, stuck out in the wilds without support, anger at Mother for being so stubborn and Mercy for being so cheerful and bumptious all the time. Little sisters were such a trial. She was angry with Fancy for sloping off to save his own neck. Anger at that child for interrupting their escape so effectively. But most of all she was angry with herself for being too proud to write to a prison, for not giving the vicar some sign of hope on his prison visit. I could kick myself for being that stupid. Here I work all day like a carthorse and waste my time like an ass, moping about what I can't change now. No use crying over spilt milk, Mother says ...

Ellie looked up in surprise to see Mother standing in the doorway with a strange look on her face.

'We've got company just arrived ... wanting to know if we need a pair of extra hands round the place. I said I'd have to discuss it with me daughter.'

'Oh not now, Mother, I'm busy. You see to it, but I thought we agreed we'd manage without extras?'

'Aye, but this one's different. I reckon we owe this one a chance to prove himself. He's tramped a long way by the looks of him, tired out and a bit downhearted. Come and see what you think. See if he'll be suitable. Won't take a minute.'

Ellie slammed down her pail and chuntered as she crossed the icy yard. Inside her eyes were dazzled by the lamplight. Then she saw the tall shadow of a man on the flagged floor and looked up.

'Look who it is!' Mercy was jumping up and down but Annie caught hold of her arm and pulled her towards the door. 'Come on, Merciful, I think Ellie might be wanting to deal with this on her own.'

'But, Mam ...' The child was yanked firmly out of earshot and the door slammed shut. Only the ticking clock broke the silence between them.

'You've come back. Oh Fancy, you came back!'

'Aye, lassie, the rover's returned and if you'll have me back I'll no be stepping a foot oot this farmyard without you on my arm . . .'

Later they sat stiffly by the kitchen range while Mercy banged down the pewter plates onto the table giving the lovers a fierce searching stare of curiosity.

'Have you told him about what happened here while he were gone?'

'Not now, Mercy, Mr MacLachlan doesn't want to hear all the gory details with his supper.' Ellie shooed her sister from the table but Mercy was determined to have her moment of glory.

'I bet he doesn't know about Billy Widdup being a lass not a lad . . . How Patabully got him alone in his room and . . .'

'That's enough, Merciful.' Widow Birkett clipped the child on her bottom. 'I don't know where you hear such tales.'

'It's true. Susan Hindle told me herself. She says they've all sloped off now from Paradise. She never even come to say ta-ra. Her name's Tizzy Widdup. What a daft name for a girl is that. No wonder she got mixed up.' Mercy nodded with satisfaction to her audience.

Fancy sat back on his chair scratching his head smiling. 'There was always something a wee bitty strange about that wean and yon lassie owes me an explanation why she didna give you ma message. Tomorrow, I'll get myself down the track and catch up with the Widdups. I've got some news of me own for them. I met up with the faither of the crew on me jaunts. Mr Ironfist Widdup, the tunnel tiger, just as Billy always said. I think it's about time those two caught up with each other, don't you?'

Ralph Hardy gathered his revellers and surveyed the motley bunch of choristers, handbell-ringers and performers, all gathered by the lych gate in Scarsbeck waiting for Cleggy's wagons to convey them up to Paradise. A harmonium, extra chairs, barrels of sandwiches and buns, teacups and saucers were all carefully loaded onto a second wagon and three village wags had jumped aboard to hold the furniture steady on the bumpy ride up the track.

The mist curled over the fells, hiding the stars; with each jolt the travellers jostled and cheered, waving to each other in party mood. Ralph could see fires like beacons scattered around the camp, sparks darting into the darkness like fireworks. It was cold but dry and the track for once was nailed down with frost.

On arrival there were plenty of willing hands to unload the cargo, swinging storm lanterns to guide the party to the reading room–cum–Mission hut which was serving as a temporary classroom and was now decorated festively with paper chains. Some of the managers' wives busied themselves with the tea urn and added their own baking to the feast laid at the back of the room. Once the doors were open children started to slide across the room, but were cleared away quickly to sit on makeshift wooden benches. Dressed in their warmest cleanest shirts and skirts they filled the rows up fast.

Ralph scanned the open door waiting for the rest of the

contingent to arrive from various collecting posts along the village. If he was honest he was looking for only one face, one pair of bright eyes. He kept glancing around just in case he had missed her entrance. Damn it! Where was she? She had promised to accompany their duet. How could she be late? He saw the Birketts striding through the door and Ellie's beau waving to his gang, looking already like a farmer, not a hired hand, in Jim Birkett's tweed jacket and corduroy breeches, with shoes polished to glass and his hair a mass of tight red curls. No wonder the poor man wore a tail to drag out the kink of it.

Ellie had a grin on her face from ear to ear. They would be good for one another, those two, hope for the future in that alliance of fresh blood, strong arms to clear up land and set the farm back on track. Once poor Annie got over the embarrassment of having a navvy for a son-in-law, she would crow like the rest of the village roosters at their wedding. Whether they liked it or not the railway was bringing change to the dale. As fresh water needs a current running through it so a stagnant pool grows brackish and stale with the lack of a flow. Things have to grow, move, change if they are to stay alive. People have to change and shift too and that idea would make a good sermon for Sunday, he thought. A new year coming, a fresh start for all but progress was often painful, full of traps and difficulties like the problems besetting the contractors in building this railway line. But like Christian in *Pilgrim's Progress* . . . Not bad to have his sermon plan ready on a Thursday night.

Where had she got to now? The whirlwind in the valley who had stirred up the mud? Then with relief he saw a flash of bright green tartan, her dark ringlets bobbing as she turned to talk to pupils and families. Hadn't she noticed he was looking at her, damn it!

He wished he had a thick length of rope to bind her to him loosely so that when he pulled she would be jerked back to his side obediently like a dog to heel. As long as he lived he would never be able to reel in that crazy little woman. She was always ahead with some scheme or other. Now she was hoping to set up some navvy Mission newspaper and was planning to meet others in the Midlands when she returned to Nottingham. He would have to get himself involved if he was to keep up with her.

For the first time in his life Ralph was terrified that this crazy woman would slip away from him and disappear. She can't do that to me! A man who has resisted all ties now trying to lasso a steer. How could he presume she would even contemplate his suit? They were never alone, chaperoned by children and friends and committees. It had never been a problem in the past to isolate a girl and steal her away but this one was different. It never seemed to bother her and that worried him most of all. Surely he was not going to get himself rejected? That was not in his plan. It was not looking good.

'Is it time to start, vicar?' said Cleggy as he clung on to his bell-ringing group. Ralph nodded. The contractor's assistant welcomed the visitors warmly and the proceedings began.

Ralph was pleased that he had bothered to set up the concert. It had diverted them all away from the terrible events in the village. All the years he had harboured such a pervert. He had seen the books and tales were beginning to creep out of the woodwork of his unnatural way with choirboys and scholars. Poor man, tormented no doubt by fear of failure and his sister's pride. Ralph could not gloat over their sad fate, only mourn the waste of such talents. Somehow there was always someone at his vicarage door wanting to talk it all over. Once that would have bored him but now something was shifting within him and he was quite enjoying the novelty of being needed.

Now, as he watched the performance, the simple acts on the makeshift stage, he felt like a proud father watching all his children perform. Soon it would be his turn to face the candles. Where was that wretched woman?

Mr Tiplady, the missioner, sang his favourites: 'My Mother's Bible' and 'After The Battle' in a fine tenor voice. The choir sang some carols and the bell-chimers joined in but managed to be one line behind them. Everyone clapped anyway. He stood with Henry Paisley and they recited the ballad of Batty Green, the dramatic but true tale of the loss of a horse and goods down a ravine, composed by Mr Burgoine the warehouse owner. It obviously came from the heart. How many sitting there had sampled the free bounty of plundered goods under cover of darkness? Then it was the turn of Mr Bulstrode's glee club to sing in harmony, navvies alongside a few farmers, an unlikely combination. Ralph could see Miss Herbert nodding her head to give them the beat as she played their accompaniment without a fault. For one night at least harmony reigned in Paradise and he could glow in the pretence that all was well and all would be well. Tomorrow would be another story.

All too soon their concert was over and he stood at the front to receive the formal vote of thanks. Everyone was encouraged to contribute to the collecting plate in aid of a man who had fallen off the viaduct and who having lost half a cup of brains was now blinded but miraculously still alive; he needed treatment in Leeds Infirmary.

The supper was a great success. The visitors spread themselves around the room clutching plates, chattering, basking in the warmth of the welcome and congratulations on their efforts. Soon it would be time to leave but Henry Paisley insisted that they must all stay on for the second part of the evening. 'Right, lads, shift the chairs back and clear the floor. Nothing like a bit of singing and music to get us all on our feet, warm us up on a cold night, what? Let's have the jolly-up man.'

From the back of the hall a young navvy in white moleskins and shirt with a tartan waistcoat jumped onto the platform with his accordion and started to get everyone's toes tapping and stamping. The floorboards were bouncing to the crack of boots and clogs.

'How did that yen get ahold of my waistcoat?' yelled Fancy pointing his finger mockingly. He shook his head and smiled at the vicar. 'I must have been skint at the time but I canna mind a thing about it.'